SpaizZzer

Tree of Aeons

book two

aethonbooks.com

TREE OF AEONS 2
©2023 SPAIZZZER

This book is protected under the copyright laws of the United States of America. No part of this publication may be reproduced, stored in a retrieval system, or transmitted, in any form or by any means, without the prior permission in writing of the publisher, nor be otherwise circulated in any form of binding or cover other than that in which it is published and without a similar condition including this condition being imposed on the subsequent purchaser. Any reproduction or unauthorized use of the material or artwork contained herein is prohibited without the express written permission of the authors.

Aethon Books supports the right to free expression and the value of copyright. The purpose of copyright is to encourage writers and artists to produce the creative works that enrich our culture.

The scanning, uploading, and distribution of this book without permission is a theft of the author's intellectual property. If you would like to use material from the book (other than for review purposes), please contact editor@aethonbooks.com. Thank you for your support of the author's rights.

Aethon Books
www.aethonbooks.com

Print and eBook formatting by Josh Hayes. Artwork provided by Fernando Granea.

Published by Aethon Books LLC.

Aethon Books is not responsible for websites (or their content) that are not owned by the publisher.

This book is a work of fiction. Names, characters, places, and incidents are the product of the author's imagination or are used fictitiously. Any resemblance to actual events, locales, or persons, living or dead is coincidental.

All rights reserved.

ALSO IN SERIES

Book 1

Book 2

Book 3

YEAR 78, MONTH 1

An eruption.

A fine way to start the new year.

The damned volcano erupted and destroyed every single thing near it. About half of my beetles failed to escape, so they died, all buried under debris, dust, lava, rocks, and all the other things volcanoes spit out.

I figured volcanoes, especially those that still pumped out lava, would be somewhat dangerous, but I forgot about the risk as I didn't see any major eruption. I was lulled into complacency and thought it was one of those 'stable' volcanoes.

That said, I wondered why my roots didn't sense the seismic movements. I recalled back on Earth, volcanoes generated tremors or minor quakes before they eventually erupted. Did the magic in this world mess with such processes?

Oh, well. This was just a minor setback, a bit of delay to my volcano expansion plans. If life went too easy, I'd probably think something bad was going to happen. That probably pushed my plans back by a couple of months to let the volcano's environment settle—also for me to rebuild my forces before attempting another assault on the magma golems that spawned closer to the now partly exposed caldera.

I was eager to test out the new large beetles in combat since these creatures were larger, with bigger legs and horns. I really wanted to see how they performed against those golems.

But I had to wait.

So I turned my attention to the next few things I had in mind.

In New Freeka, we had a massive hall with a few external biolabs, and Jura helped to guide the Valtrian soldiers. The hall itself was filled with animals and plants gathered from the region over the last month.

The men were mostly idle, so we sent them out on gathering missions to collect different kinds of plants and animals, as many as they could find, whatever they'd not seen before or whatever they noticed that was different from New Freeka, then bring it back. With this small bounty, I went through all the plants and animals they'd brought back. The soldiers, with Jura's supervision, loaded the biolabs, five of them located side by side, with specimens.

After the biological analysis, some soldiers were tasked with moving our collection to designated patches of unused lands where another group with [Farming] or [Planting] skills would attempt to replant these specimens.

My intention was simple. There was a lack of plant diversity in the valley, and that needed to be addressed. I hoped to somehow unlock more [unique trees], like the [ginseng trees], so that I could produce new items. By expanding and discovering new species of crops, it would improve the variety of my [subsidiary tree – crops].

The first step of analyzing the plants took five days and the animals another four days. The reason I asked for the animals was to throw off whoever was observing us on the goal of getting more plant varieties, but it was a waste not to analyze the animals since they were already collected. After the animals were 'scanned' by the biolabs, they were placed in an area that was meant to be a menagerie.

*[**New crop species unlocked** - Wheat, Jackfruit, Light Corn, Black-potato, Rye, Red hops, Blueberry, Fireberry.]*

*[**New Tree type unlocked**: Common herbal bushes. Bushes containing a wide variety of herbs. Herb varieties appear at random.]*

"How's the register coming along?"

"It'll take some time, Counsel," a young junior [Herbalist] responded while he and his assistants bowed.

"Understood, but this is something the Tree Spirit wants completed as soon as possible."

They nodded. Trevor and Dimitree had separately built a compilation of the plants of the valley and their characteristics, which they could identify using the data from the biolabs. But I had Jura hire an herbalist to start work on a physical copy of a register, just to compare the kind of information an herbalist would normally take down and one prepared by my tree-minds.

The herbalist, together with the gardeners and other farmhands, would later be assigned as the ones tasked with management of the 'gardens' within the wider compound of the Valtrian Order. It was one of those odd jobs in an organization growing larger.

I'd left the animals gathered through this collection exercise in the care of the [Rangers] and others like them. From the refugees, there were some with the right skillset. [Rangers], [Flock Tenders], and [Herders] also possessed some skills with animals, so they were best suited for the task of caring for the collection of animals.

It wasn't a perfect match in terms of skill and job class, but oh well. Maybe they'd gain a better version of the class someday.

YEAR 78, MONTH 2

The Valtrian Order had a separation exercise. The military force we observed was a little too large for my liking, and from what I could see, their competencies were lacking. So, like what companies did when their staff size was not optimal or when their payroll costs were too high, we had—

Re*tree*nchments!

I briefly imagined myself as that dude from TV, walking up to guys who didn't make the cut, saying, "You're fired!"

But that's not exactly a nice way to do things.

Jura and the captains identified those who were not so good at their jobs based on their performance during the collection exercise, and then they spoke to those non-performing soldiers whether they had other secondary talents they didn't reveal to us. We offered them an opportunity to take part in the other roles happening in the Order if they had some interest or relevant skillsets. If they didn't, we gave them a small payout and sent them on their way.

I wanted to hire herbalists and all those other 'specialists.' To do so, I needed money, and money sadly didn't grow on trees, so I had to streamline the payroll and prioritize areas where I wanted skills and people.

One must cut away the rotting branch for a new one to grow, eliminate the 'deadwood' or 'non-productive' parts. Even though we tried to be diplomatic about it, there was still plenty of crying, anger, and cussing.

I feared retaliation.

"Ivy."

"Yes, Master."

"Monitor those we have fired. See whether they do anything unusual. Let me know if there is any attempted retaliation, but do not interfere unless I instruct you to do so."

"As you command."

Ivy was my new tree-mind assistant, and her assigned task was monitoring the Valtrian Order and its interaction with the citizens, reporting any unusual matters. I also tasked her to observe all financial and trade transactions within New Freeka.

Monitoring the activities of about three to four thousand employees of the Valtrian Order was a laborious affair, even with my trees everywhere, and Ivy pretty much had little capacity to do anything else.

A part of me felt like I had become that which I hated in my past life, the 'big brother' that intruded on everyone's privacy or that overly micromanaging boss who looked through everything I did with a fine-toothed comb.

Despite that, this was a magical world, and I had to pick the bigger baddie here. I acknowledged my faults in doing so, but curbing corruption and finding traitors took priority. Survival trumped privacy.

For now.

Even in their somewhat perilous situation, people would find ways to cheat or steal, to take a little more for themselves. So I thought I would be ready since I knew about it and knew it existed.

I knew nobody was innocent. But Ivy's report still stunned me.

The extent of misconduct was massive.

Almost all of the employees engaged in at least one minor misconduct with surprising regularity.

It was usually relatively small, like a coin or two per transaction, or a little slip of coin to move up the queue in the burial services. Some soldiers would steal utensils from the mess hall and bring them home for their families. Or they intentionally tore or stole a piece of uniform so they could use the cloth for something else. Administrative staff stole paper or writing equipment.

When Ivy first reported the extent of such things, I just felt mad. I almost wanted to lash out in anger and kill all these people.

"Were you expecting saints from these former refugees? The fact that they adapted to a new way of life so quickly is admirable." Meela sometimes dispensed a bit of wisdom.

Well, true. This world didn't possess a properly regimented education system to teach a sense of morals, and parents trying to survive probably had a different set of morals than me. Even if there were some attempts to create a good education system, there wasn't enough time or stability for its effects to really sink in since the world got hammered by the demon king with great regularity.

If there was anywhere with a proper education system, it was probably in those fantasy places, the mountaintop cloud cities, the moving giant islands, or the walking towers of the great deserts. If such places existed.

I also wondered how many years of formal education the citizens of New Freeka had.

Ultimately, after some thinking, I decided to just have the worst offenders retrenched and just put up with the minor infractions among the rest. Perhaps someday I would have a group of morally upright employees, but for now, these were the cards I had, and unlike a game of cards, I couldn't redraw.

"Should I continue monitoring them, Master?" Ivy was not fond of the task, but she still obeyed.

"Well...yes."

"It's taking up most of my processing ability. Filtering through all the language and small talk was really challenging."

"Ah, well...*fine*. Will it help if you restrict the scope to within our compounds and just the area around them?"

"A lesser area would mean less to monitor, so yes, it will help a bit. But I estimate it'll still use up seventy percent of my available processing power."

"Unfortunately, I'll need someone to watch these guys. Please, bear with it. Maybe it'll get easier once you gain some levels."

"As you command."

YEAR 78, MONTH 2 (CONTINUED)

The first large beetles emerged from their pods. The volcano started to stabilize, so I sent the large volcano-adapted beetles on their first missions. That was why they were created, after all. Their initial combat performance was encouraging, as they easily defeated the lesser monsters, but their first encounter with the massive magma golems was disappointing.

Though they now had the size, they still lacked the necessary firepower to take out the golems. At least they could take three punches from the golems before dying, unlike regular beetles, who just got squashed underfoot.

According to Jura and the data gathered from the adventurers' guild in New Freeka, magma golems were considered monsters for adventurers around the level fifty to sixty with suitable gear. A person with suitable skills could possibly take one out at level forty.

Given that my regular beetles were a match of soldiers around level twenty to thirty, I guessed the large beetles still needed a lot more upgrades to give those magma golems a good fight.

Ah. Back to the research queue.

*[**Eye-Tree Stage I research option unlocked** - 13 months remaining.]*
*[**Beetle** - anti-magma armors stage 2 - 4 months remaining.]*
*[**Tree** - volcanic adaptation stage 3 - 13 months remaining.]*
*[**Roots** - Volcanic mineral harvesting - stage 1 - 3 months remaining.]*

Following the acquisition of the various new plant species, I had both Dimitree and Trevor attempt to use their abilities to improve the plant diversity in the valley. To some extent, the valley on both sides was largely dominated by my type of tree, though at least the ThreeTree of mana granted some visual varieties.

I needed to look up some pollens and bees, and flowering plants as well.

Oh, well.

At least with the improved inflow of gems and rare crystals, I'd managed to upgrade the rootnet to support a larger capacity of tree-energy. The upgraded rootnet would take up to one hundred thousand normal trees, which also meant more artificial souls. I'd probably make some more tree-minds to take some load off Ivy, since the task of monitoring so many people was monumental.

"TreeTree. I've got a proposal."

Huh. A proposal from Alexis. "Well, let's hear it."

"I've been talking to Meela, and I'm thinking of using the biolab to make a body. Not a full flesh-and-blood kind of body since it's clearly not at that level, but I'm thinking of experimenting with treefolk corpses as a transition between regular sentient species and...well, trees."

Huh.

"Well, my theory was that treefolk exist as some kind of magical evolutionary in between a tree and regular humans. So looking at treefolk was a good starting point to figure out what the magical mechanics within their body are that allows them to do what they do."

"So you're asking for my permission to do this experiment?"

"Yes. The goal was to be able to create flexible wooden...uhm... armor as a vessel for souls." *I think she means robots.* She wanted to create a body for herself. Well, there was still that dryad body formed from her corpse. Maybe she'd forgotten about that already?

"I am rather fond of the treefolk. They give me no trouble, have shown willingness to defend the valley when instructed, and have been polite and respectful whenever contacted."

"Ah...so that's a no?"

"I will ask the treefolk for their permission. Conducting autopsies on the dead should be approved by their kin."

"That makes sense." Well, Alexis seemed to understand that, at least. "Ah, there was also one other thing..."

"Huh?"

"I am thinking of expanding. I'll need space...and materials... and some of your beetles."

"What do you mean?"

"Ah, I reached level thirty, and I have this new skill called [Locational Survey Tools]. It allows me to take control of a few beetles and place research equipment on them, and this will speed up research on environment resistances. Kind of making a...a research-oriented scout out of the beetle. I can operate two at any one time."

Hmm. Actually, I thought that sounded a bit like the Moon Buggy, but an actual bug! Or perhaps the Mars Rover. Fascinating. She went into the whole science route, which made sense as a spirit haunting a massive research biolab. Would a flying bug with this be essentially a flying science vessel?

"Fine, you get two beetles. Let me know what materials you need."

Alexis clapped her ghostly hands in joy. "Thank you."

The treefolk chiefs visited a few days later, three of them: the one from before and two I hadn't met. It seemed their number had increased over the years as immigration brought more and more treefolk to the valley.

"It was an honor to be summoned by the Tree Spirit..." The three treefolk prostrated themselves before me. I had forgotten they revered tree spirits. "Your presence bathes the entire valley in a warm energy that fuels our health and gives us strength."

Wait, did my powers work on treefolk? Why did he talk like he did?

Holy cow, if it did, that opened up a big—no, *giant*—can of worms I needed to explore.

"You feel my presence?"

The oldest of the treefolk, the one I'd met before, still prostrating on the floor, was the one to speak. "We always have. The energy and radiance through the roots, each step we take, we feel your growing dominion. Even in the depths of winter, we feel and share in the warmth through our rooted feet."

Wait, is he trying to just suck up to me? Hmm... Anyway, let's get down to it.

"Ah...the reason I wish to speak to you is to talk about the dead and the deceased. I'd like to first understand about cultural norms, where the body of the deceased treefolk is normally split into many parts, some as tools, fertilizer, and some as ornaments... Is this an unbreakable rule, and is there any taboo around giving them to me for my...studies?"

The treefolk chieftains all shared a glance, and then the same elder treefolk raised his head to respond. "It's a cultural practice. Most families will want to keep their deceased family members' bodies to assimilate into their own. If you want a body...we would have to provide one without any family members, as I doubt any of ours would part with it. Every bit of a treefolk should be recycled."

I see. Interesting. "Very well, then. That will have to do. And you can stand up now. You've prostrated long enough."

"I'm not sure whether Vice Counsel Laufen has relayed our message previously..." one of the other treefolk chiefs said.

"Oh, what was this about?"

"It's regarding the recent gifts to the children. While the rest of the population benefit from it, we, the treefolk, do not."

"Ah." So was this a complaint?

"We're wondering whether we...we can get something more suited for our young saplings."

Oh. Customer feedback. Now why didn't Laufen tell me about it? "When was this message delivered to Vice Counsel Laufen?"

The three chieftains looked at each other. "Uh...last week, perhaps? When she came to deliver a gift for our newest sapling."

Speaking of treefolk mating and childbirth, they were actually really interesting and different from the rest of the humanoid races, although they also had humanoid-like appearances. There were actually a few ways treefolk mated, and it depended on the male, female, or whether the treefolk was a hermaphrodite, containing the mating organs of both. In short, treefolk retained their own plant-like mating systems yet also incorporated the mating systems of humanoids.

Their available ways of mating included actually having intercourse, a form of pollen-fertilization where the female organs opened up for the male organs to fertilize. Or, oddly, and perhaps unique to treefolk, via third parties, usually an insect or a 'carrier,' like a bee or a butterfly that carried the fertilized pollens from the male organs to the female, who then, if he/she judged the pollens to be suitable, allowed it to fertilize him/her. Apparently, it was taboo for a treefolk to self-fertilize, for the hermaphrodites, but in times of great disaster, it was permitted to keep up the treefolk numbers.

There was also another external variant of mating, in which the female organ produced 'empty seeds,' something like an unfertilized egg, which she could leave in a specified location for any interested male treefolk to leave their seed. Most sub-species of treefolk were able to produce large quantities of such unfertilized eggs. The decision to either go for an external or internal mating variant was a choice of the treefolk, whether the female wanted quantity or quality because internally carried treefolk would emerge much stronger, bigger, and longer lived. If the male or female was strongly magically attuned, internal mating and carrying the baby within the female also had a higher likelihood of passing off the magical talent to the child.

The only plant-like reproduction system not retained by the treefolk was the grafting or cutting methods since the soul couldn't be severed in two. Only one part of the body would retain the soul, and the part without the soul would wither away without the sustenance of the soul's presence.

So, given the huge variety of ways in which a baby was carried, or the condition of which a new 'sapling' was created, I could see why the humanoid 'childcare' center was not suitable.

I mean, I would have to figure out how to adapt—

Ding.

[**New subsidiary tree type unlocked**: *Treefolk Incubation Pods. A subsidiary tree filled with multiple pods, used to incubate and nourish fertilized and germinating external seeds.*]

[**New subsidiary tree type unlocked**: *Treefolk Nursery. Makes sapling-friendly nutrient-rich foods. Can also make special sap for pregnant treefolk mothers or females to boost quality and health of their fetus or eggs.*]

Uh. Dammit.

I kept forgetting how much the system liked this kind of stuff. I was even betting there were extra points because they were treefolk. Maybe I'd also get new equipment when I put the treefolk under the biolab.

At least I had something. "Chieftains, I'll have something for you soon."

YEAR 78, MONTH 3

"This volcano thing was going to take a lot longer if you don't find some other kind of powerup."

"Huh."

Alexis's modified drone-beetle made the journey to the volcano. Her research tree had a root that transformed into some kind of garage-like structure where the beetles were stored and modified. So that was the first of many bombshells.

"Although your large beetles can take a few punches, the magma golems are way stronger than your large beetles. I estimate you need at least ten upgrades before you get anywhere near defeating them with three large golems. The gap was just too large. If I estimate the golems as level-sixty threats, your large beetles right now are about level thirty-five, and if each research upgrade gives two levels' worth of strength, you will easily need ten to fifteen upgrades just to be at equal rank, not considering elemental and type weaknesses."

I was sad. A tree conquering a volcano. *Say it again. A tree conquers a volcano. Man, that just sounds absurd.*

"I recommend finding alternatives. Something to breach the weaknesses. Find an elemental type that allows a good counter. Water or cold type? Or even wind."

I totally didn't hear that. I was just too wrapped up in sadness. Maybe my approach was wrong.

What if I was not looking to conquer the volcano, but...absorb it?

Could I terraform the volcano? Alter the surroundings?

"So, as I was saying, magic would help. Think about it, magic-casting beetles."

"Huh." Oh, wait, Alexis was talking. "Sorry, could you repeat? I wasn't paying attention."

She sighed. "I mean, you need magic. Or water. Acid's not going to work on the magma golems. It's...it's just, uh...you know, science? Water. Spells."

Okaaaaay. But damn, there must be other ways about it. Or would it be better to just focus on one area of the volcano, like a 'safe zone?' "Ah. Any other observations from your probe?" The information I had was from what I could see via my subsidiary trees, but maybe she saw something else.

"Uh...the mana density is quite high, but I can't seem to figure out what's wrong with it. It's not a pleasant kind of mana..." Ah, yes, mana. The weird thing that everyone's soul produced, also produced by things like leylines and certain objects. From the bodies I had examined, there were certain 'colors' to each mana, and it seemed mine was primarily blue, which was why it was the first color I unlocked.

The colors, type of mana, and the quality of it had tremendous influence on the way it felt and behaved. In a way, the description by most common mages was that mana was like air. There was stale air, good air, bad air, smelly air, dry air, wet air...

I wondered whether mana took the form of some kind of special atom. What was mana at its smallest unit? And why did the soul produce it? Did the soul maintain some kind of law of energy conservation?

"Hey, hey, if you want to have theoretical discussions, you can do it with me," Alexis vented. "I like those kinds of topics, too. And seriously, do you have a problem staying focused on any particular topic? Stop hopping to other trains of thought all the time."

But did they all deserve to grow? Those thoughts were worth exploring. So I did.

"Focus. Back to the volcano. You need magic and the right elements. Do you have anything? The spiders and the beetles were not ideal, obviously, since they were weak to fire."

Well, other than myself, I couldn't think of any.

"So, magic! Doesn't have to be pure magic but imagine beetles with magical cannons that shoot water. Or spiders that create a freezing field. Flying beetles that release water like fire rescue planes. Oh, wait. You might not know what that is. But you get the picture?"

"Hmmm…"

"Oh, come on, you want this volcano or not? You do it your way, it's gonna take a lot longer."

Ah. Alexis pushed her magic agenda again. "Let me think about it."

YEAR 78, MONTH 4

The treefolk-specific saps and nutrient foods were super popular, augmenting some of the key challenges treefolk faced during pregnancy. The main thing was, as the pregnancy matured, ideally, they should stay put, their feet firmly rooted to the earth. This allowed them to draw nutrients and mana from the earth to feed the growing fetus within their wooden bodies.

But being stationary for months was not feasible in an environment where non-humans were consistently hunted by others. So, to be safe, they had to constantly migrate and move around to evade their hunters. This led to a nutrient shortage, their bodies compensating through consuming the parent's nutrients to feed the fetus and so weakening the parent.

Their children were generally weaker, though the most recent children were in much better shape. No longer having to run and having a relatively stable valley to stay in helped a lot with the quality and overall health of the children. Perhaps more than any other race, they needed stability and a familiar environment to mature properly.

"The treefolk's loyalty was probably the highest amongst all the nonhuman races, followed by the centaurs. If we were to admit members into the Valtrian Order, we can create a special group for them."

"Isn't that species-ism? That is the root of future discord. The other races will dislike their special privileges."

"Is it not a waste to make the most of their abilities?"

"If we go down the path of making the races compete with each other, that will not go well. Right now, New Freeka is dominated by elves, followed by the centaurs. If they start competing, that will further entrench the existing rifts among the races."

"Why do you care, Master? They were disposable, were they not?" Ivy retorted, and I wondered where she got that angry persona from. Was it from observing people for too long? "All of them are slimy. At least the treefolk aren't so slimy because their material demands are different." Ivy hit level ten a few days ago, and amusingly, her skill was [Citizen File], using her constant monitoring of the citizens to build a dossier on the people. It took effort, and a few months to do it, but Ivy had the time.

I'd gulp if I could. Ivy was right. They were disposable. In the larger scheme of things, loyal servants were more valuable anyway. *I should get more loyal servants.* Better a loyal servant than one hundred fighters who would stab me in the back.

The Valtrian Order stabilized as the processes around the birth and death and the quasi-military force regained some semblance of structure after my earlier retrenchment exercise.

The new leadership team met in Jura's new office in the center courtyard of the Valtrian Order HQ. All rooms were covered with vines and trees, such that I could always monitor them, even the toilets.

The group consisted of Jura, Laufen, Madeus, three captains, two herbalists, two administrators, and a master of ceremonies.

The three captains of the Order, the military arm shrunk to only nine hundred strong, were each leaders of a group of three hundred. The two herbalists led about one hundred workers to cultivate and maintain the various herbal gardens and farms around the Valtrian Order and produce herbal medicines and ointments. The two administrators were responsible for treasury and purchases, funds, and payment of salaries, managing an administrative staff of fifty.

The master of ceremonies was a position I'd wanted to give Wesley, but he declined, claiming he wasn't interested in paperwork. So, instead, another priest was roped in to take the role. Somebody had to sort out the planning of the deaths and all the paperwork around them. Almost all of them, except one administrator, were elves, though I had hoped for a bit more variety in the Valtrian leadership.

This was a weekly meeting for everyone to get updates on the plans and matters and was where everyone spoke to me.

"The councilors were not too happy with the retrenchment exercise, Tree Spirit. Many of them complained to the councilors and demanded their positions be reinstated."

"Tell them they are free to let Jura know they can challenge a beetle to a fight. If they prove themselves more useful in battle than any of my beetles, I will give them their position back, *and* a small reward."

The three captains glanced at each other awkwardly.

"In fact, please put up a notice. Let this be known."

The captain who'd brought it up shrugged and nodded. I felt he regretted it. "Ah..."

"The acquisition of more herbs and plant varieties is ongoing, and the peace accords with Salah were recently finalized. That means we will see more movement of noncombatants, especially from the various magic councils of Salah."

"Watch them carefully. They will be spies. Salah will take this 'peace' to gather information on our true depth." Well, the truth was I would probably get Ivy to watch them, too. She was getting better at spying on people throughout New Freeka.

"Would it not be New Freeka's military to do so? They might think we were taking unnecessary action that might provoke Salah."

"New Freeka's unreliable, and the leaders are...compromised. And if getting caught spying would provoke Salah, I prefer to think of it as a warning."

"Compromised? Really? Who?" one of the captains asked.

Jura jumped in, "Secret. But the logic is simple enough. Once the leaders saw the beetles, Salah attacked..."

"Ah..." Separately, I turned to Ivy. "Do you have a file on the captains? I feel they were suspicious as well."

"Yes. I already have some observations. They've not done anything big so far, but there is some...suspicious activity. One of them, from conversations gathered, have human relatives in Salah, and all three wrote letters, delivered via the merchants to other countries."

One drawback, the written word was a bit harder to spy on as our visual quality was a bit low-resolution. One of the reasons I wanted the Tree-Eye ability. "Can we get a copy of the letters?"

"Difficult. We'll need Jura to do so, but we don't have trusted agents in the merchant group, so it will be rather tough to do so discreetly." Ah, that was something we needed to fix, and the fact that Ivy existed as a tree-mind meant she was my eyes and ears but not my hands and legs.

Meanwhile, the leadership continued with their discussion. Typical leadership mumbo jumbo. Funny how people in positions of power always ended up having discussions about structure and plans.

"Okay, updates." Jura steered the conversation back to regular matters like finances, hiring, what the plan was for the next week, and updates from the New Freeka High Council (NFHC).

"There is a traveling group of druids. They seek permission to go through our lands. The NFHC has agreed to grant them the right of passage and go about their restoration work."

"Huh, didn't those nomads come here before?"

"A different group. Just keep a lookout for them."

"Traveling to barren lands and returning greenery, surely there were better uses of their talents," one of the captains joked, though the mood was a bit more cordial. The earlier banter between the leaders was getting better. Jura's [Diplomat] class really helped put others at ease.

"All you think about is fighting. Everything else is pointless to you. Maybe it's part of their class requirement. Some jobs have certain accomplishment barriers. Perhaps druids were like that." Another captain poked his colleague.

"Do mages have accomplishment quests, Madeus?"

"My mage class doesn't. Or, perhaps, not yet."

Jura looked at the few pieces of paper before him. "Ah, I think we were straying off the agenda again. Anything else?"

"We have some responses to our request to hire adventurers to bring back exotic plants from the faraway continents. The message we got was that they will arrive in a month, and they demand their payment be ready."

"Yay." I liked that.

The captains frowned. "Is this the best use of money?"

Jura grinned. "Fun fact, the Tree Spirit gets more powerful with every new type of plant he encounters. So it's worth it."

"Anything else?"

The master of ceremonies raised his hand and nodded. "I have a proposal. The Tree Spirit should have a divine title."

"A divine title?" almost everyone asked in unison.

"Ah, in various sects and religions, there were often special titles to refer to the minor deities and heroes, something that cemented that person as a divine being. Currently, referring to the Tree Spirit as the Tree Spirit is…clunky and awkward and makes the prayers and ceremonies a bit less…proper as religions tend to be. A divine title was a gesture to recognize Tree Spirit's special position in our society. Like how some refer to God as God, capital G."

Jura scratched his chin. "Are you asking the Tree Spirit for a name or title?"

"Ah, I am thinking…of having the senior leaders group together and do a study on the proper ways to venerate the Tree Spirit. A few of the faithful shared their troubles that the Tree Spirit, as the Tree Spirit, does not differentiate it from the many other tree spirits in the world. The masses, those who pray, must know and be assured their prayers were going to the correct and true Tree Spirit."

"Ah…that's the kind of thing only a priest will think about."

"So, perhaps we can spend some time to think of a name—"

"Aeon."

The master of ceremonies immediately knelt before the small tree in the center of the room.

"Ah, truly the Tree Spirit is divine for the Tree Spirit already has a divine name. Kneel before Aeon, everyone, for we were the first to be graced with his divine title."

The rest of them looked at each other, probably wondering what the hell this guy was trying to do, but decided to go with the flow that the master of ceremonies created, and so they knelt. Even Jura and Laufen joined in.

"Oh, to the great and mighty protector and watcher of the valley, we offer our prayers and thanks to thee, O mighty and powerful Aeon."

If I could have rubbed my head, I would have. But I really liked the name Aeon. I think it was a name deserving to be much more than just the name of a chain of supermarkets.

One of the captains rubbed his head. "Is it pronounced like… Aye-on? Or Aye-yon?"

"I accept both pronunciations."

[Hidden Conditions checks met.]

*[**Special skill obtained** - Possession of the devoted.]*
   [A special familiar contract with a chosen devoted believer. Limited to five at any time.]

YEAR 78, MONTH 5

Things were rather quiet in New Freeka and the valley, and I thought that was a good thing.

I needed a different approach if I wanted to hold the volcano. The inner volcano was filled with giant golems, who were clearly still leagues ahead of the large beetles. If the location was bad, the golems could easily hold off my beetle horde like a wall made of lava. So, while the various research continued, I thought of other methods. Alexis was right. Beetles were a bad matchup, even if it would annoy Horns.

Anyway, let's talk about New Freeka. This month, I received a magical cactus, some kind of coconut variant, and a gourd-shaped fruit, which was often used to store foods due to its magical preservation qualities, so that went into the biolab.

> [Skills acquired.]
> [Cactus defense system.]
> [New crop type acquired.]
> [Milk coconut and brownwood gourds.]
> [Subsidiary tree limit increased.]

Other than that, for the Valtrian Order, things were pretty

much the same. Training, scouting, purchasing, and trading, and the birth and death rituals continued. The populace of New Freeka adapted to the new routine, and a new set of uniformed group, the Valtrian Order, in town. Jura and the team decided on a dark brown color, like tree barks, as the Valtrian Order's color. New Freeka used blue.

The druids came. They didn't seem too interested in the valley, and it seemed they had some kind of messiah complex that drove them to seek out sick trees and damaged environments, so their stop in New Freeka was a brief one, just to resupply.

It was peaceful. I even managed to successfully protect my ginseng tree and make it last past their first year. And that was nice for a change.

YEAR 78, MONTH 7

"Practice," Lausanne grumbled. As Jura now had responsibilities in the Valtrian Order, the time he had for Lausanne was significantly reduced. She often sought him out for practice sessions, even in the quarters.

In his place, the captains and men of the Valtrian Order often became Lausanne's sparring partners, and in a way, it was good for her.

Lausanne, now level twenty-five, was actually better at the sword than a regular soldier, who was usually only about level twenty to thirty but had their levels dispersed over various skills.

"For a nine-year-old, she's pretty much a genius." The captains lavished their praise on Lausanne, though she just shrugged. Of course, the captains didn't know I'd easily used four to five hundred essences collected throughout the years to build up her combat sense through [Dream Tutor], [Power-leveling], [Learning Aura], and most recently, [training room].

"Perhaps that's the other thing you should be doing." Alexis was really bored these days. When she wasn't using her two probe-beetles, she tried to make conversation with me or everyone else. "Maybe you can train an army of super-warriors."

"Heh. It's too early to tell how far Lausanne will go. She's currently my test subject to see how effective the abilities are. But if it works, I'll consider it."

"You should train more than just Lausanne. You can then compare the differences, perhaps each of the different individuals as your test subjects. Vary them a bit, then you can see what influences their growth and whether there was an actual...limit."

"You've been thinking about this kind of thing, haven't you?"

"I'm a research spirit floating around, stuck to my tree. What's there to do other than tinker with my lab equipment and think about such things? Was it wrong?"

"Ah...no, that's not what I meant."

"Then what do you mean?"

"You know what? I think you have a point. I agree I should have a few test subjects to see how the training thing works and fully explore the limits of these people."

Of course, that meant I'd need to find ways to consolidate and upgrade all my training-related skills, such that I could distribute the resources to more people other than Lausanne alone. Part of the reason why I focused only on Lausanne was because I had no idea how effective my abilities were and how they actually affected Lausanne's growth, so I just went all in. The problem with [Dream Tutor] and [Learning Aura] was that the effects were small, but they accumulated over a long period of time. It wasn't as if Lausanne became super amazing the next day, and I'd been using [Dream Tutor] on her since she was...five? Maybe four. I forgot.

"Since she's got that special skill, well, use your seeds as well. I'm really eager to know what they do."

"Huh, I'm confused now. Should I focus on Lausanne or train more people?"

"Both! You can focus on Lausanne since she's got that unique skill, but you do need other people as a 'base case.' It's really basic. You can't draw conclusions on a sample of one. More samples, more robust conclusions! So diversify! Expand your sample size!"

"You know, the validity of your methods was distorted by 'skills' and 'abilities.'"

"Those were outliers and variables we can adjust for. That's normal!" I thought Alexis spoke a lot like a scientist, and I thought it was part of the job.

"Meela, do you think she's talking like a scientist?"

"She talks like that all the time. It's normal."

"Hey!"

"But I'm not disputing the essence of your argument, and I agree with the idea of having more...test subjects. Well, it's time for me to get Laufen to work on the orphanage."

"Wait. You're experimenting with orphans?" Alexis clearly didn't like that.

"Who else do I experiment on? Do you see any other young children I can run some tests on? You think the rest of the New Freekans are willing to give me young children to test on?"

"I'd like to say it's ethically wrong to use your abilities on young children who were unable to decide and give consent. You know what? Testing on young children now feels eerily similar to trying to train orphans into war machines, so I take back my earlier statement. Please, don't test on young children."

"This was a magical world, and frankly, I am not doing them any harm. When you feed a child a supplement, you want them to grow strong, but did the child give consent? When you forced him to eat his bitter medicine, did he give consent? So long as your intent was to help them, I think it's fine. And with orphans, as the Valtrian Order as the caretaker and guardian, we were empowered to make decisions on their behalf."

Meela tried to break up the argument by butting in, "Alex, think positively! Maybe TreeTree can make Batman! That'd be cool. I think a lot of superheroes were orphans or lost their parents. Superman, too! So I think it's a good idea. You won't abuse them, right? Right?"

Alexis facepalmed. "I don't think TreeTree knows who Batman is."

Uh, I did, but I kept my mouth shut. "Well, no permanent pain, I suppose..." Frankly, I didn't know. There was no progress without pain.

"Hmm..."

YEAR 78, MONTH 8

The Valtrian Order's Orphanage for young children was up and running. All we needed was a building where we could build rooms and then employ people to take care of the kids. As a rule, I insisted the children we took in were less than twelve years old. Those older were able to find work and could live on their own in this world. For humans, thirteen was quite a normal age to start holding some kind of semi-permanent job, either as an apprentice or some kind of live-in worker, and this was also seen in the other non-humans.

In New Freeka, connected to the orphanage's large building were a few subsidiary trees, two of which were [training rooms] for teaching and sparring. There would be quite a lot of young orphans in this world, after all. With so much war and slaughter going on, it was common that families were broken. Anyway, my intention was to train these orphans, those willing, into warriors for the Valtrian Order, so the remaining Order soldiers regularly came to give the young kids simple lessons. In a way, it acted as a 'feeder' into the future Valtrian Order guards.

For monitoring and tracking, one of the subsidiary trees was a biolab with multiple pods. The decor was intentionally bare, and I had the herbalist use it as a 'medicinal' room to mask the true intent of the pods, which was to take magical snapshots of these orphans' progress over the years.

Feedback in terms of the orphanage was mixed, even from the orphans themselves. Many of them were living in empty, abandoned homes, some taken in by the people of New Freeka. Some orphans resisted the structure and rules that an orphanage had and preferred to continue living on their own.

Well, my order to Laufen was: *Don't force the kids*. If they wanted to live on their own and thought they knew better, then go ahead. Either the world would teach them a lesson or they would truly show their mettle.

Out of the town's population of fifty thousand or so elves, dwarves, and centaurs, about five hundred to a thousand were young orphan children, but not all wanted to stay in this new set of quarters, so it was often the really young ones. There were also families who couldn't, or were unable to, raise their children, so they surrendered them to the orphanage.

Oh, well. I wasn't going to be the morality police, so whatever men and women chose to do with their lives, that was their problem. I'd take the kids, and I'd use them.

The good thing was it put some jobs on the table as the orphanage hired a lot of workers to cook, to care for the orphans, and to teach, and some retired elderly men also helped out as trainers.

The thing about old people in a world with great and frequent destruction was often that they were quite high leveled. Being on the run for decades must have given them a lot of survival-related skills and actual [skills]. Either they were good at fighting, good at running and hiding, or good at improvising and making the most of what little they had.

Ah, well, I guessed there had to be some truth to the old people being awesome trope after all.

———

"Eat this." Lausanne stared at the green fruit right in front of her. She picked it up with her tiny hands and shook it.

"It doesn't look ripe."

"It's not meant to be ripe. Eat it." It was a green fruit, made out of the passive seed [spark of brilliance]. Small, the size of a grape, it was lime green, and from my point of view, it had a faint emerald glow to it. It was my first time creating a fruit out of the seeds.

"Uh...okay." She started to chew on the small fruit.

She walked a few steps, chewing.

"Okay, I ate it. It tastes sour, but it's not horrible. Was this some kind of new fruit you want us to sell, TreeTree?"

"No. It's a special fruit. Just for you."

"Huh. If it's a special fruit, shouldn't it be sweet and really yummy? It's quite sour, and I can still taste the bitterness on my tongue." Lausanne downed a cup of water, probably hoping to wash away the taste.

"Not all things in life were meant to be sweet, my dear Lausanne."

"Is that some kind of word of wisdom I should remember?"

"Perhaps."

"Is this why you called me here, TreeTree?"

"Not just this..." If I could smile, I would have. "Lausanne, would you like a special familiar contract?"

Lausanne immediately nodded. "Yeah, sure. Special in a good way, right?"

"Yes."

[Lausanne has accepted the special familiar contract. 50 star mana consumed. 1 star mana will be consumed per month.]

Star mana. I had three hundred at the moment. That was the maximum number of star mana storage organs I had, and with the current maximum number of star leaves, I produced thirty star mana a month.

"Oh, wow. Was this like Uncle Jura's Bamboo?" She activated

the familiar, and then two large twisting roots emerged from her body. They transformed into a wooden sword and shield, Lausanne's current favorite fighting combination. "Whoa, it responded to me! Can you hear it, TreeTree?"

"I can't." Well, the familiar didn't have an artificial soul, but it probably had a kind of 'programming' to it, like an…animal?

"Well, it just says sword and shield mode." Lausanne grinned. "But it's cool. I can tell it things in my head!" The wooden sword transformed into a whip.

Huh. That was pretty cool.

"And it can change shape!" Lausanne tried out the whip, and it worked like a rope, allowing her to pull herself forward. "I can use this to swing from branch to branch, too! Like the monkeys!"

"Don't let your mom see that." The idea of a young girl swinging around like Tarzan was probably going to make Laufen have a headache.

"Ah, yes. Ah, yes. Sorry, I got excited." The two roots could transform into various shapes, but there were certain limits to the size and length. "It's kinda cool that they don't drain my mana as much as the normal familiar, too!"

Ah, I supposed that was the benefit: stronger, more flexible, but costing less. I guessed the star mana I gave it supported it.

"Thank you, TreeTree. This was nice."

"Good. Let me know if you get any skill notifications tomorrow."

"Okay!" Well, the next day. "Erm…I didn't get a new skill, but one of my skills transformed."

"Oh, which one?"

"It's the [Blessed by a soul tree]. It's now [Blessed by a soul tree – advanced]."

"Huh…" Well, that was amusing. Now, she was even more compatible with my abilities. I hoped she didn't eventually transform into a tree.

"The cool thing is the roots were a bit longer and bigger now. I think it makes my familiar stronger!" *I see, so the special familiar's effects are going to be less impressive on the other guys.* Now I wanted to know whether I could fuse this special familiar with an artificial soul.

Lausanne showed off her slightly bigger sword and shield.

"I'm gonna go practice. Don't tell Mom I'm in the forest."

Lausanne tried to be a monkey, and she used two roots like vines to swing from tree to tree, but only with the bigger trees since the smaller ones didn't have enough clearance.

Oh, dear, what have I done?

YEAR 78, MONTH 10

Demon king preparation status check.

The demon king appeared Year 70, Month 4.

The demon king died about five years ago, around Year 73, Month 3, Week 2.

Going by the ten-year gap between demon kings, that meant I should have had at least five years left. Five years was a good amount of time, but halfway there, it was time to discuss the matter again.

"The next demon king should be about five years away. Though we won't know for certain, that's the approximate time range. What should we do?" The audience was me, my tree-minds, Horns, Alexis, and Meela. I'd have another discussion with the Valtrian peeps next time.

"It depends on the type of power the demon king has." Alexis thought about my question.

"We won't know until he appears, and we'll be running out of time if that's the case. What are the normal, common powers a demon king would have?" I asked.

"Extensive destruction abilities and demonic hordes?" she responded.

"So, okay, how do we prepare for that?"

"Hide? There is really no way we can fight back unless we have the powers of the heroes, and running isn't an option," Meela wondered aloud.

"Agree, hide. So that means we need to figure out a way to make use of the tunnels and the abandoned dungeon as some kind of shelter and build barricades and strong gates," I said.

"Uh, I think that's missing the point, TreeTree. You're massive. You can't hide," Alexis said.

"That's fine, but it's more for everyone else around me. I think I can take whatever the demon king's horde can throw at me… except the demon king himself," I answered.

"So what were you going to do if the demon king comes for you?" the girls asked.

"We'll think about it, then. For now, let's work on the plan to hide."

"How about the [ThreeTree of Mana]? We can't hide that." It was Dimitree who brought up his part of the world. "If necessary, we need to build a massive wall around it, one that even the demon king can't destroy."

"That's impossible. If there is one thing the demon king doesn't lack, it's destructive firepower."

"The elves say there were other trees who've managed to somehow make their forests disappear. How do we do that?"

"That's hiding. And, well, that's a good point. If there was an ability to temporarily warp the valley into pocketspace, that'll help."

I had no skills anywhere near that level, though I supposed [secret hideout] was like a slow step on that path? Perhaps someday, I'd get the ability to create a massive secret hideout that included myself in it. Though that was probably going to make my mind melt because the secret hideout was inside me, but I was inside the secret hideout. So, what was inside what?

"Can't the demon king detect such abilities? Seems kinda odd that an incredibly powerful monster like itself would allow such things to happen..." I also wondered, which led to the next question. "Are demon kings...sentient?"

"I have no idea. They have a certain kind of intelligence, but sentient? No one has ever communicated with it," the two former heroes answered.

YEAR 78, MONTH 12

Winter.

With the volcano project hitting a slow spot, I decided to try other projects.

As I tapped the Valtrian Order's growing network of contacts, I was aware of three faraway sites I wanted to explore.

Farther north, movements of the ground revealed a previously covered massive hole that went really, really deep. It was as if somebody dug a hole vertically. It was currently spitting out many different kinds of snake monsters and snake-like creatures, which was why I suspected it likely contained some kind of magical source. That said, my data was quite lacking. It was currently being extensively attacked by adventurers, as the snake hide seemed to fetch good money, so there were plenty of adventurers trying to make their way down. Travel time by beetle was three days.

The second was one of the regions near the Nung-Salah border. There were a few dungeon-like areas. There was no detected leyline, but there were still a lot of monsters appearing in that area. As it was rather sparsely populated and heavily damaged from all the battles, there wasn't much adventurer attention compared to the snake-hole, but the presence of multiple dungeon entrances and unusual monster hinted at a dungeon. If so, I wanted the core. Travel time by beetles was three days.

The third site was deep into one of the nearby kingdom's territories: a lake that seemed to be inhabited by magical beasts and strange, unusual plants. Rumored magical. Five days away.

My first choice was the one with the potential leyline, but that meant I had to deal with the adventurers. Still, a leyline was too good to miss out, so I was going to start my subsidiary tree expansion at that location.

The dungeon-like areas, if I decided to attempt those, would be for the cores. It was a good reward financially, and I'd like to study cores in much more detail. Perhaps there were variations of cores between dungeons. If a core was sentient, or had the potential to be, I would like to attempt using an artificial soul on one. My suspicions were that they would work similar to a root-brain complex, and that would be something fun to test out.

The drawback was the active war zone. Salah and New Freeka were at 'peace,' but the Nung-Takde and Salah War was still ongoing, with the situation at a stalemate. It seemed they were periodically fighting battles on a few fronts, though both sides weren't trying anything bold to end the war. It was an odd state, skirmishes here and there even though trade routes had been strangely re-opened. I wanted to scout out the location, so I planned to have beetles in the location, just to find out where the 'dungeons' were.

As for the lake, it didn't seem to be that much of a problem, just far away. New types of plants were always welcome—magical and potentially rare plants even more so—and this seemed more appropriate for a small strike force. Send the guys in, get the strange plants, and get out. Simple, suitable for a covert strike team of beetles.

"I want to go."

"Huh?"

"Take my probe-etle there."

"Is that a name you came up with?" It sounded like something you stuck up an arse. *What do they call that again? Is it an endoscopy? Oh, wait. It sounds like probiotics! The kind of weird bacteria shit those multi-level marketers try to sell!*

"It sounds better than scout beetle, doesn't it?"

"Which one?"

"I have two probe-etles. I want to see the lake and the giant hole in the ground."

"Fine."

"Yay. Meela, do you wanna go? You should totally consider fusing with one of the beetles, then we both can still go travel. You can be my probe's bodyguard!"

"Wait, you can see through the probes?"

"Uh, yeah. It's called a probe, right? Of course I can see through the probe."

"I don't want to be a beetle. That's disgusting." Meela frowned. "I'd rather be a tree."

"I take offense to that statement," Horns chimed in.

"Aww, come on. We finally get to do some traveling!"

"I rather like the relative peace and safety here," Meela said. "I might get attacked as a beetle, and people will hate me. I can't cope with that!"

"Meela, that's a lie and you know it."

The two girls argued, but it was a rather friendly spat, so I ignored them.

———

One of the merchants brought garlic and ginger today. They were apparently really popular with nobility for cooking.

> *[**Crop variety** - Garlic added. You can now produce essences of garlic and garlic-flavored woods, fruits, and saps.]*
> *[**Crop variety** - Ginger added. You can now produce essences of ginger and ginger-flavored woods, fruits, and saps.]*

Ooh, that was gonna make some people stink. I wondered whether they had stinky fruits in this world like durians. They should, right?

But you know, this recent interest in garlic and ginger gave me an idea. I had the ability to produce fruits, vegetables, and herbs. What if I were to set up a market and sell my produce? Or, even better, set up a restaurant? I wasn't sure how many restaurants they had in New Freeka, but certainly, if I had the ability to procure and produce unique types of vegetables and fruits, that would give me a unique selling point!

I could make special ginger-ginseng soup. Or fried potatoes with garlic, herbs, and spices.

"A restaurant? You need cooks, though. A chef!" Meela asked.

"But it could work!" I repeated. "You girls know any recipes from where you were from?" All I knew was how to cook instant noodles with eggs.

"Uh...I might. But honestly..." Meela said.

"If I get an ability to create a [Tree-kitchen] or [Res-Treerant], I'll fuse you to it."

"Does that mean I'll be stuck in a cooking game forever?" Meela seemed frightened by the prospect. Oh, wait. Did they not know I could reassign them because their souls were stronger than the artificial souls?

"I think a beetle is still better."

"But a cooking tree sounds like an appealing idea at least. It could even end up a case where I could be the spirit that runs a hotel and restaurant. It's like those cooking simulator games!" Meela laughed.

Alexis looked a bit concerned. "Meela, were you sure you want to be a..." Her dreams of traveling with a beetle bodyguard was clearly fading away...

"A hotelier! Master chef!"

"Wait. You're not serious." Alexis facepalmed, only she was a spirit, so all she could do was soundlessly smack herself with her ethereal hands.

"Maybe one of your [subsidiary trees] with a room. I can probably acquire the job as [chef] and [innkeeper]."

Alexis looked horrified. "Meela, if you fuse with a tree, you can't get job levels. Job levels are for humanoids only! My skills, so far, are all because my creature-type was research tree spirit. So, no!"

"Eh. TreeTree, can you make a tree decorated with multiple hotel-like rooms, kitchen, dining, and café area?"

"I-I can try." Huh, forcefully decorating a tree such that I get a different tree type. That's like the playroom and training room. It might just work.

"Okay, TreeTree, I've decided on my career path! If you can make one where I get the right type, then I'll fuse with it," Meela said.

"You serious?" Alexis flew up and down. "You won't even know if there were tourists. We have no data on tourism and travel traffic! How do you know it'll work out? How many people even eat out?"

"What's the worst that can happen? I'm a tree! It's not like I'll starve to death if the hotel and restaurant fail."

"Meela!" Alexis shouted.

"It'll be fine, Alexis. Of all the options offered to me, this actually seems like fun! Chef and hotelier! That's a whole lot more interesting than looking at a lab all day. I could even open branches! Hotel-tree branches! Get it? I could be a moving tree hotel. Or a popup store! The wandering treehotel-restaurant! Maybe even add a convenience store!"

Alexis slams her head into the trunk of her biolab. It didn't really hurt her.

"If trees can move, then I could be a coconut hotel and restaurant tree by the beach!"

Hey, that's an interesting idea. Giant treants but actually a walking hotel.

"TreeTree, can I name my hotel and restaurant? I can, right?"

"Uh, sure." Hey, Meela wanted to be useful, and if naming rights was all she wanted...

"I'm gonna call the hotel the Meela! And the restaurant the Fried Mee! And if there is a café, it's gonna be the Café Meelatte. Oh, TreeTree, you should totally get coffee beans."

Alexis smacked her face into the trunk multiple times. I was sure she was just doing it to vent her frustration with Meela's insane choices.

"Alexis, you can name your lab, too. I'll give you an idea. You can name it A-Lab-is. It's like your name, but with a lab in it. Or Labalex. That's cool, too."

YEAR 79, MONTH 1

Roots, the subterranean network of trees. Through them, I was connected to the tens of thousands of trees within my valley and beyond.

These roots, they covered vast lands, serving as the forest's backbone, carrying information, minerals, essences, and mana. These roots went through many kinds of soil, so they picked up the subtle shifts of the mineral composition and—a feature of my various subsidiary trees—acted like little sensors, collecting measurements.

When it rained, when it snowed, when the earth shook a little, the roots and subsidiary trees all collected data. Data that my root-brains, Trevor, Dimitree, and Ivy fed on. Vibrations, humidity, magic. Together, all these sensors formed a vast array, so we could now triangulate the sources of tremors and unusual magics to determine direction.

Some trees in the distance would feel it first, a tug, a pull. Then, later, more trees picked up on the tremor.

An earthquake. A minor one. Even the volcano gave out little warning signs, the small tremors before it started to erupt, when part of the volcano spat out lava. This ability could have saved more beetles if we'd had it a bit earlier.

It was Trevor's newest skill addition.

[Tree-angulation]

Crunching all the data, telling me what's happening in a distant location without actually being there.

"If we had magic sensors..." Alexis was about to start with her usual marketing of magic labs.

"Let's start material labs first. I understand that's a prerequisite to the development of magic labs?"

"Ah...erm...yes. We would need to have the ability to analyze materials and develop mana-sensitive materials, then magical labs."

"So let's do it. What do I need to get to material labs? Once we have that, I'd like to analyze that dismantled airship again."

"What? Really?"

"Yes. I've decided to get magic sensors. I imagine that would be very useful if we had another case of that super-blizzard."

Alexis nodded. "Ah...yes...so, material research first?"

"Yes. Get to it."

"Sure." Alexis looked awkward, floating around, one part of her happy, yet another part of her quite confused. "What made you change your mind?"

"Am I changing my mind? I just wanted more time to mull over whether that's the right direction for us."

Alexis looked like she was about to bark some kind of retort before she seemed to realize something. "Do tree spirits normally take so long to think?"

"Hmmm. No."

"Well, it makes sense since that was a common kind of myth associated with tree-people that they tend to be sluggish and take forever to decide." Alexis was mostly talking to herself. "It's like that council of trees in *Lord of the Rings*. Took them forever to decide, didn't they?"

Huh. Was she complaining that I took too long to decide? But at least I did decide, right?

"Ah, never mind. Starting material testing and tree-lab varieties."

*[**Eye-Tree Stage I research option unlocked** - 2 months remaining.]*
*[**Beetle** - anti-magma armors stage 2 – completed.]*
*[**Beetle** - anti-magma armors stage 3 - 3 months remaining.]*
*[**Tree** - volcanic adaptation stage 3 - 2 months remaining.]*
*[**Roots** - Volcanic mineral harvesting - stage 1 – completed.]*
*[**Roots** - Volcanic mineral harvesting - stage 2 – completed.]*
*[**Roots** - Volcanic mineral processing - stage 1 - 5 months remaining.]*
*[**Materials testing** - stage 1 - 3 months.]*
*[**Tree-lab varieties** - stage 1 - 12 months.]*

Research took longer as I'd predicted earlier. Magic was necessary, and though I had to take precautions on who and what got access, I was starting to lean on the side that it was an eventual step I'd have to take, one way or another. I couldn't face the threats this world had with one hand behind my back.

A necessary risk.

I would have a long conversation with both Meela and Alexis about magic and the sort I would give them access to. Though, with Meela, I had less ability to control her. My hope was that they would be able to contribute to the defense against the next demon king as they had more experience in magic as heroes.

Meanwhile, New Freeka had a small boom in terms of growth. The era of peace and the reputation of stable, secure food supplies attracted more refugees, even from other nations, not just Salah. It was a busy time for the council of New Freeka, and they'd been hard at work to expand their town premises and prepare new farmlands. More people, more food, and more homes meant public services needed to be expanded. Of course, there was a need for refugees to 'buy' their way to 'public' services, such as the right to use some of the new housing.

At the same time, there had been more focus on security and screening, so the NFHC hired the laid-off soldiers to work as guards. Ivy said some of the councilmen felt a need to bolster their forces now that they were actively 'threatened' by the presence of the Valtrian Order as a 'competing' political power, what with Jura and the Valtrian Order's secure, legally protected position.

A faction in the council emerged that wanted to assert 'independence' from the Order's growing influence, and this faction somehow managed to coerce Yvon, such that she voluntarily resigned from her position as the chairperson of the council. Her position had been tenuous and under scrutiny for some time, as it was an open secret by now that her soul was contracted to me. That led to a whole lot of whispering and rumors about Yvon being 'compromised.'

But to the layperson unfamiliar to the nuances of New Freeka politics, her statement to the public at large sounded voluntary enough.

"I'm resigning from my post as chairperson of the New Freeka council effective immediately. I've led and held this position since New Freeka's founding, and finally, after almost five years, I believe this fledgling nation is in safe hands, and I can hand the reins over to someone else and spend time with my son."

How sweet. Spend time with Roma, who was now almost six years old.

The pressure to 'counterbalance' Jura's growing influence meant the person holding New Freeka's chairperson role had to be more than just seen as independent. In other words, the chairperson must be seen as a force that stands against the Order, against me.

Frankly, it's just silly political struggles. A large faction within the councilmen themselves understood this. After all, they knew I could crush them. So they were left in this uncomfortable situation where they yearned to be the ruling group but acknowledged that, without me, they had nothing to rule.

Anyway, silly, silly things, those jostling for 'authority.' So long as nothing 'unreasonable' happened, I'd let them be. Ivy had all of them monitored, and retaliation wouldn't take much time at all.

"Lady Yvon." Jura was one of the few she met after her voluntary withdrawal. "I heard the news. Frankly, it's disappointing, but the Tree Spirit expected it."

She laughed. "Hah! Well, that's life."

Jura shrugged. "So, really, retirement as a mother?"

"Why, do I not look like I have motherly desires?"

It was Jura's turn to laugh, and he took a small alcoholic beverage and offered it to Yvon. "Frankly, no. You're the warrior-queen type."

Yvon sipped the drink. "Well, to be fair, it has some truth. I admit feeling a little jealous that Roma's a lot more attached to Eriz than me. All these times I've been trying to get this town in order, Eriz has been more like his mother, more than I ever have. So, yes, a bit of it was a desire to make up for what I have failed to do."

"Really? I really didn't see you as the actual mother type, though most of New Freeka regard you as the 'mother' of this city." Jura laughed, holding up his small cup, and the two cheered softly. They both took a sip.

"Anyway, my time's up. And time management has never been my strong suit. There was never enough time to do right by New Freeka, or by Roma."

"Time's never enough. It comes with the job. Look at me or Laufen. Both of us are so busy these days we only have a bit of time to spend with Lausanne and the kids. I try to make dinner happen, and at least we still meet up. Lausanne's been bugging me for combat practice every time we meet."

"Oh, yes. I have heard a few captains sing praise of her talent. She's really good for her age. My son's not showing any interest yet, though."

"Well, that may not be a bad thing. Laufen constantly worries she'll injure herself. At least Roma's just playing chase or spending time with wooden toys. I just hope Lausanne didn't find someone who doesn't know how to hold back and injures her in practice."

"You know, I could offer to spar with Lausanne," Yvon offered. "Now that I have free time."

Jura smiled. "I would appreciate that. It will be good for her growth that she fights someone with a different style."

"So I take it that's a yes?"

"Yes, yes. Please, tell Lausanne you're her new sparring partner."

Yvon nodded. "Great!" By then, their cups were both empty.

Jura leaned forward. "Ah, all of you, can you leave?" The guards nodded, and so they departed, leaving Jura and Yvon alone in the room.

"Huh. Something important?"

"Yes. I'll cut to the chase, really. It's about Roma. Was he related to the royalty?"

"Damn. The Tree Spirit saw through that, too?" Yvon's fist smacked her other palm, and Jura just shrugged at her statement.

"Does the Kingdom of Salah know about it?"

"I sure hope not. We forged a fake marriage arrangement with one of Galen's knights, one of the other elves. It also helps that Roma doesn't manifest any of the human traits yet, so no one will know whether he's part-human until he's much older."

"But he will. It's only a matter of time before he asks about his own heritage. How many know of this?"

"Maybe ten?"

"That is too many. Where are the ten?"

"I-I don't know."

"In which case, you better start preparing Roma. If you're lucky, he'll be forgotten by the kingdom as just one of the many bastards the royals have. If not, there is going to be a group out for his head."

"Well, now that I have some free time, it looks like I should get started on his practice."

Jura nodded. "You should. He needs the ability to protect himself. You're good, but you won't be able to stop all of them."

"Can I count on you to protect him?"

Jura paused and shrugged. "Maybe."

Yvon smiled weakly. "Ah, well."

"If you're going to start preparing him, then have him practice with Lausanne. I can permit access to the training rooms or use the one near the main tree."

"I will. Thank you."

"Take care, Lady Yvon."

Yvon nodded and left.

Now that the room was empty, Jura leaned back and spoke out loud. It was quite obvious he was talking to me.

"Royalty. As you predicted."

"It's obvious, isn't it? She sent her baby so far away with protectors. If it's not royalty, I doubt she'd take such precautions. It's such a…cliché."

"I thought it's just a motherly thing to do, to keep your child out of harm's way. But I'm happy she offered to practice with Lausanne. That'll really help me and Lausanne. If only the others would show any interest in learning how to defend and protect themselves."

"They'll be fine. So long as they remain in the valley, the beetles will look out for them. What do you think about her replacement?"

"Smart, but a little greedy. The position he takes isn't one he truly believes in. He's only taking it because it allows him to be in a greater role. I believe he's just saying what everyone else wants to say but doesn't have the guts to. He's a mouthpiece for the anti-Order faction, so he's going to try to stonewall a few of our initiatives."

"Well, it is normal in politics. The opposing party will try their best to stop us. So long as it's not too annoying, let it be. If you run into trouble, let me know, and I'll crush them."

Jura nodded. "I figured you would say that. Oh, yeah, my [Diplomat] and [Warrior] classes merged last night. It's now [Warlord]."

"Sounds like an upgrade."

"It is. I feel stronger already. Cumulatively, I'm level eighty! I think it's due to your influence."

"Great." Well, it was good that Jura was getting even more powerful. All that [Power-leveling] and [Learning Aura] helped after all.

He sighed, and it was a loud, long sigh. "TreeTree. I think...I think this was my limit."

"Huh?"

"I can feel it. Even though my classes merged, I have a sense, a feeling in my chest that this...this is as far as I can go. My body and soul are at its limit of growth."

"Strange words. Don't people grow and gain levels so long as they push themselves, fight monsters, and gain experience?"

"Well, in theory, yes. But other than heroes, most of us plateau at some point. For those who are not so gifted, we experience multiple plateaus. That's why I'm worried about Lausanne. She might be doing well now, gaining levels and all, but there is a point where our body and our souls level off."

I thought Jura had mentioned something similar in the past, but it hadn't registered as anything significant.

"We were not born heroes, so we have a limit. They say—"

I cut him off. "Rubbish. Are you sure you're not just feeling tired? Rather than talk about limits, take a dip in the biolab and let me have a look at what's going on. Come back to the main tree."

"Ah..."

Jura somewhat reluctantly put himself up for examination.

And first things first, I noticed the arrangement of stones near and around his mana spring. The core of the soul was different from last time. I recalled it looking like a few scattered mounds of rocks, but this time, the mounds were shaped like a proper wall, a bit more like the ranger would do. There was a better structure and organization to the rocks and stones. I supposed it was what the class merger did to the layout of the rocks.

Next, I looked at the mana generation. It was healthy and quite good and didn't look like there were any blockages or dark spots that sucked up mana. The spring spewed out mana very well, and the supply of mana and life force was good. Not as much as the heroes, of course, but it was healthy for someone like Jura.

Then I looked at the body, finding it healthy, too. Jura wasn't a young man anymore, a middle-aged man by elven standards. Despite that, his body was in good shape, strong and fit. The shores on the body took up all the mana it could offer, and there was no blockage to the mana flow to any part.

Hmm, so why would he feel like this is his limit? Was this something different than mana? I drew on the power of my [Soul Forge] and channeled it to my main tree's biolab pod, hoping to get a better look.

With the [Soul Forge]'s power, more data appeared. First, it showed the rate of production of mana from the spring and then the passive mana consumed to sustain each level and skill. It was denoted as two bars, mana produced and consumed.

"Is this the mana we're familiar with or another kind of mana?" Alexis asked. She'd also been looking at Jura.

Well, as it turned out, it sort of was the normal kind of mana. Each person produced a certain amount of mana, but it was 'allocated' into two pools, 'active' and 'passive.' Active went into the person's actual mana pool used to cast spells and activate skills; Passive was directly consumed to sustain the body's stats, power, and all the other 'passives.' The passive was commonly referred to as the body's vitality or life force.

It was then the data finally answered the question.

Jura's vitality was maxed out. And his body's consumption of that vitality was as well. Though nothing was wrong with him, he was right to say something *felt* wrong. It was like a car pushed to the limit, unable to go farther. A car that hit its speed limit.

"Sounds simple enough. Can you tweak the soul such that it produces more vitality and less mana? It sounds like he didn't really need that much mana as a warrior. Maybe some of his skills and abilities consume them, but I think a higher level would be better. Or maybe you could just give him an upgrade? I wonder whether you could upgrade souls."

"It's something I want to think about. There may be other ways to go about it."

I could tweak the soul, but I needed to be sure it worked. The soul forge, if used incorrectly, could cause great damage.

YEAR 79, MONTH 2

I finally received the skill. We needed to decorate a subsidiary tree's customizable rooms with beds, complete with partitions, segregated washrooms, a reception area, and a dining area.

[Tree Lodge]
[A tree with a whole lot more space than it looks! Each tree lodge has ten rooms, a restaurant, a cozy lounge, a reception, and a kitchen, all while looking no bigger than any other tree! Need to hire workers to work.]
[Limited to five, and each lodge must be a distance away from the other nearest lodge.]

Uh, odd. It was the first time a tree skill had a minimum distance requirement. I couldn't cram all the tree lodges in one place?

"Meela, I got the skill. I can make you a tree lodge." Once it was fused with Meela, the slot would free up again. Meela was her own person, and she didn't use my tree lodge slot. It was like Alexis's own independent biolab-thing, which was now a weird, crazy-looking tree with lots of vials, tubes, and other contraptions.

Strange blobs flowed up and down its sides. It was so weird that I had to use beetles to guard it.

"Awesome. I have ideas for names again. Want to hear it?"

"What?"

"Hotel Treevago." Hey, I knew that joke from the two girls. It made me wonder whether they all come from the same generation as me? Was there a kind of speed difference in time between this world and ours? Because if it's the same jokes, it felt like we're from the same time period.

Alexis facepalmed. "Meela, that's lame. And it sounds kind of wrong. Like a bad reproductive disease."

Meela laughed. "I know, it's a joke. I'm probably going to call it something a bit more proper. Perhaps, the Faraway Home-e."

"That's not much better!"

"The Palms, then? I think there was a luxury hotel by that name, wasn't there?"

"The Palms...but we're not at the beach!"

"How about the Pinewood?"

"Oh, okay, the Pinewood sounds better." Alexis put her spiritual fingers on her chin. She was thinking rather seriously.

"Or the Oakwood. I think that sounds quite classy as a hotel."

"Meela, you sure you want to be a hotel?"

"Hell yeah. Alexis, stop questioning my decisions. I know what I want to do."

"Ah, I know you won't change your mind. Fine, fine. You'll need to hire workers, and you will need money. And where can you get it?"

"TreeTree, can I get a loan? You're rich, right? I'll pay you back when I start to make money."

"Okay. Thirty gold for now. Consider it my investment."

Alexis smacked her head. "TreeTree, you're being awfully generous."

"Great, thanks, TreeTree! Let's totally do this. Uh...but wait. If the soul forge merges me with the tree lodge, does that mean I take the position of the current tree lodge? That's not a great location. I would prefer one right in New Freeka!"

"Ah...hmm..." I mentally connected to the soul forge, and then a little prompt appeared. Alexis and the tree-minds didn't have this issue since they were located right next to me, so after the merging was complete, I could just 'spawn' them there. But New Freeka was outside the range of the soul forge, so I had to use the Carrier Drone.

*[**Carrier Drone**. After a soul is merged with an object, skill, or person, it can choose to become a 'deployable egg.' The carrier drone will then carry the egg within it to the desired location, where it will spawn into the merged structure! But beware, the carrier drone is vulnerable, and destruction means death to the cargo as well.]*

"Once again, the system to the rescue." A little too convenient but, hey, that was life.

So I initiated the soul forge. Meela's soul left my [soul realm] and went into the forge, together with the tree lodge, which melted into a greenish liquid. The soul forge then spun the two together. Meela's soul took the form of a white light, and together with the greenish liquid, it mixed into a mild green light.

Lightning struck at the branches of the forge tree, making an electrical connection to the heavens above. It periodically pulsed, and the thickness of the lightning increased.

The spinning within the forge sped up intensely as more power and mana were drawn through the roots. Activating a soul forge resulted in a lot of mana and energy flowing through the roots, especially from the leyline. It felt like having a whole lot of water flowing, spinning around me, like I was stuck in a whirlpool.

Zap!

One large lightning bolt struck the forge tree, and then it was complete. The merging was done.

A small greenish egg appeared from the forge tree, containing a sleeping Meela as a hotel-spirit-tree.

A drone beetle appeared, its hard shell opening to reveal something resembling a small but very long limb. It lifted a small egg the size of a dog (relatively) and placed it in a compartment on its body. Then the shell closed.

"Wow. It even has a little storage space."

I commanded a dozen beetles to quickly escort the drone to the marked place in New Freeka, a place Meela chose beforehand, where she wanted the 'hotel' to be. It was nighttime, and Jura had already made arrangements for the beetles to enter the town. Once the carrier drone arrived safely, the drone beetle dug itself into the ground and started to…melt?

It's melting? The body of the carrier and the egg liquefied into a greenish goo, and it seeped into the ground.

"Whoa." Alexis was quite amused by it. "Magic?"

"I-I think so?" Well, I had no idea. I didn't know how the deployment worked, either.

It was actually an empty plot of land, owned by the Order, and now a wall appeared around that plot of land. The ground expanded, inflating upward but still entirely covered in earth.

It continued inflating, and the bulging earth took on the shape of a cuboid block made of dirt and roots. It was like somebody took a hardened cube of dirt filled with roots and placed it where the empty spot once was.

Then, suddenly, a sign appeared on that large mound, on the frontage that faced the town's streets.

Under Construction. Grand Opening Soon!

"Meela, you there?" Alexis asked, a little worried. Meela was her only friend.

"Yes, but I'm very busy!" Meela replied. "I'll let you know when I'm done! I got tons of options before this thing opens!"

And Meela vanished, merging into the wooden block, and she didn't speak a word for the rest of the month.

The odd mound of earth that strangely managed to remain 'cube-shaped' drew a whole lot of curious onlookers, but most people didn't think about it too deeply. Just one of those strange things that happened in a world with magic: "Oh, look at that strange earth-block... Must be some magical shit happening in the Valtrian Order again." Compared to trees that spit fire, relatively mild as weird things went.

"She's busy in there." There was some kind of noise coming from that wooden block. I thought it sounded a bit like construction work, but it was a tree-structure. There would be no actual construction going on. Maybe it was just some kind of sound effect.

"Running a hotel isn't going to be easy, and after lazing around for so long, it'll take some time before she gets the hang of it." Awww, Alexis was worried. "Hey, take your time, all right? Yell if you need help. I'll try to help out."

Meela didn't reply. The noise grew louder.

Alexis sulked. "Meela, you're okay, right?"

"She's in there. I can feel it. Just give her space."

"Okay...Meela, let me know if you need anything, all right?"

Meela didn't respond, but I thought the message got through. She said it so many times she was almost nagging.

———

"Is it something you're working on, TreeTree?" I'd told Jura to set aside that plot of land for me, but I didn't really tell him what exactly it'd be, so now that there was a cube of dirt there, he had to ask.

"Sort of. It's going to be a project by Meela."

"Meela? Tero?" Oh, wait. Jura didn't know about Meela's soul. Even when he was in front of Alexis's biolab, all he saw was a glowing blob and not Alexis's ethereal form. So he hadn't spoken to them at all.

Come to think of it, nobody knew about Alexis and Meela's second life as a soul.

Now, I hoped they didn't accidentally expose themselves as former heroes.

YEAR 79, MONTH 4

Oakwood Hotel was finally ready to open for business!

Meela's block of wood revealed itself to be a mountain wooden-lodge-like structure, the logs usually making up the lodge still part of a large living tree that formed Meela's combined body. She was the lodge itself, a living structure, and her present appearance, which Meela said was a cosmetic choice. She described it as playing in a sandbox, a 'game' where she could choose the decor of everything. I couldn't help feeling like it was some kind of mobile game that commuters loved to play, to earn points, unlock décors...

"Inside, fifteen rooms!" Meela beamed. She took the form of a treefolk-ish creature within the hotel, her legs constantly melding and merging with the floor itself. This form somewhat resembled her human self, but her skin color and texture were that of walnut-colored wooden bark.

"You've got a physical body!" Alexis was most impressed, probably because she unfortunately took the form of a ghost surrounded by levitating vials, tiny petri dishes, and other similar lab equipment.

"Cool, right? I'm like a treefolk, only...well, I can't step more than ten feet away from the hotel." Unlike Alexis, who'd been flying around the entire valley, occasionally scaring some of the townspeople who saw her glowing blob.

"Ah, don't worry about it. I'm sure it's a level thing like me. I was stuck to the biolab at lower levels, but now that I'm level thirty-four, I can travel quite far! Or ask TreeTree to help! The range limitation doesn't work if you tap into TreeTree's [Soul Realm]. But I'm not sure whether that's because I'm soul-contracted to him, though."

It was then the wisp pulled me into the soul realm.

Ah, I may have forgotten to explain this. A tree spirit had the ability to 'share' and 'connect' souls together, and it was that ability that allowed all the souls a platform to speak and interact, and through it, they could see what I see. The [Soul Realm] was that platform, and it was independent of where their physical 'locations' were. I believed the locals referred to it like being in a 'mailing group.'

Well, I knew they could see what I could see, but I supposed it didn't occur to me to wonder why Alexis, Horns, or Bamboo were able to share their thoughts while they were out there traveling. I supposed it was like a video conference facility for souls.

"Do you still have the skill? The [Heroic Meld]? Did you see your status?" Alexis's spiritual body floated over Meela's little wooden lodge, exploring the rooms. Meela had spent a lot of time arranging the décor. It was rather...cozy?

"Nah, almost all my skills are gone, and I no longer have the [Hero] job. I'm level one all over again. All I have left is [Goddess's Blessings]." Meela shrugged. She had a wooden body to properly do so now.

"I was wondering whether our circumstances would be different, but it looks like death removes all our skills."

"Well, I really don't mind starting over. I'll get a ton of skills running this hotel. I'm gonna be awesome!" Meela smiled and walked around. "Besides, now that I'm restarting, I'm better able to think through my levels and skills."

"Good luck, Meela. Hope you don't get strange skills like [Compendium of Research Failures] and [Emergency Shutdown]."

"What were you looking at that the system made you get a skill like [Emergency Shutdown]? Were you trying to clone dinosaurs?"

"A biolab of giant dinosaurs..." Alexis wasn't insulted. Rather, she rubbed her spiritual chin.

It was Meela's turn to shake her new tree-head. "Oh, no. I gave you an idea."

"We have giant beetles. Dinosaurs are just giant lizards or giant birds."

"I like that idea," I chipped in.

"You know what dinosaurs are?"

"Uh...didn't you say giant lizards or birds?"

"Oh, yes. Yes, I did say that. Never mind me, Meela. How's the hotel?"

"It's a 'lodge' at the moment. I think there is going to be an upgrade at level thirty. Strangely, I seem to be able to see what sort of upgrades to the lodge are available between now until level thirty."

"How come?"

"I have no idea." Meela shrugged. "But I need to start recruiting workers to man the kitchen, the reception, and the restaurant. I'm planning to hire treefolk to complete the 'feel' of the lodge. An inn by the treefolk. TreeTree, is that something you can help me with? Ask perhaps Jura or Laufen to put out a recruitment notice?"

"Sure. You'll need to give a lot more details, though, like... what's your pay and working hours like?"

"Oh. Can I talk to someone? Maybe some of the locals?"

"I'll ask Jura to come see you. Also, are you still going to call yourself Meela, or are you going with another name?"

Meela paused in a thinking pose. "Good point. Should I still call myself Meela, and would that get me in trouble?"

"Depends on what you want to achieve. Do you want people to

know you were once a hero? That said, I doubt everyone will associate your name because, well, it's really quite common to name their children after heroes. Though I'm not going to call myself Alexis. I'll go with a different name, maybe...Ritz, or Ambrose," Alexis told her.

Meela clapped her two wooden palms. "I've got an idea! I will call myself...M. Lady M."

Alexis smacked her head. "Meela."

"I will be referred to as...M. You can call yourself A."

"Ugh."

"Don't you think Lady M is a classy name? I think it is, and it fits my role as the lady of the hotel," Meela said. "Aaaaaaaaaaaanyway, TreeTree, I need your help! Can I speak to Jura or the rest of the Valtrian Order? And are there any permits or permissions I need to get?"

If I had a head to shake, I would, but I could only lightly sway my branches to indicate my lack of knowledge about New Freeka's bureaucracy. But I could give her a hand. I wanted to see her succeed. "I'll arrange someone to meet you."

"Great. I'd like to know before I accidentally commit a crime or infraction or have to pay...unnecessary bribes."

"Bribes?"

"Uh, it's actually common. The nobles throughout this world ask for bribes all the time. Even enforcement agents regularly ask for money. I heard from so many innkeepers and blacksmiths throughout our journey..."

At this point, I turned to Ivy. "Any idea if that happens?" Given Ivy's earlier bombshell that everyone committed some kind of crime, I thought of course bribery happened.

"Paying small sums of coin to avoid complete, thorough legal enforcement? Yes. One of the more common transactions to occur was intentional understatement of tax collections. In exchange, the enforcers get paid."

"Ah. Does that happen to our people?"

"Yes. I've ignored it as the coins exchanged were minimal." I wasn't shocked. People there did what they had to do. That was just how it was.

"Uh..." I recalled telling Ivy to ignore most of the petty crimes, so I guessed she classified that as such.

"It lubricates commerce, and my calculations indicates most traders would be bankrupt if they had to comply with the actual tax rates and the full extent of the law."

"That's a problem with the New Freekan Law, is it not?"

"Perhaps. It's heavily inspired by wherever the lawmakers are from, so the mishmash of laws gives rise to a whole lot of loopholes and possibilities for abuse. It's compounded by the fact that the justice system refers most rulings to the High Council, of which the lawmakers themselves are the 'judge.'"

"Ivy, has New Freeka's justice system always been so screwed up?"

"I think it functions rather well. There is a clear acknowledgment of authority that flows up to the councilors. The people understand that, so they obey the councilor's demands and whatever the city tells the people to do. The councilor's role as the adjudicator and arbitrator of peace is incredibly important to allay the citizens' fears and address their needs. Even if it often lacks 'justice,' it is a kind of 'order' the people here have come to accept and respect."

"Really?"

"Indeed."

"Isn't there a written document? A constitution? What were they updating when they revised it to include the Valtrian Order?"

"Constitutional documents only list the major items, the 'key' issues and matters the High Council wants to have formally documented. But, outside of that, the councilors issue proclamations all the time, and their decisions over time get stitched together into an informal 'law.' Furthermore, punishment for noncompliance isn't specified, so that's left to the jurisdiction of councilors."

Ah. Whatever, I've gotten a little sidetracked.

Now, to get Jura to send some people over.

YEAR 79, MONTH 5

Meela eventually hired some treefolk, paid taxes for all the necessary permits, and got started with business. I just kinda let her do her own thing. There was really no need for me to interrupt and watch over her all the time. I felt I could trust Meela, so I was gonna let her play her sim-hotel while I did my shit.

So I turned my attention to my own priorities, my big three threats: demon king, other nations, and monsters. In dealing with demons, I was fairly confident in my abilities. Regarding the other nations, I needed the assistance of the people around me, so Jura's leveling challenge was something I needed to solve to help him. As for monsters...well, I'd just let that be.

Actually, looking at it, I'd reduced the relative threat level of monsters generally. So far, I hadn't yet faced any truly difficult monsters, though we did have golems that were territorial, but as a threat, I thought their territorial 'camping' nature made them less of a concern than I initially expected.

It was the demon king and the other nations that were the most immediate dangers.

Looking at the other nations, I was relatively comfortable with where things were at the moment. I had a large army of beetles, and that was enough to deter the threat of small armies.

As for the demon king...he was about four years away, and I'd asked Madeus to do more research on when the rifts will start to appear. He said it was usually two to three years before the demon king arrived, so I might have only another one to two years of 'peace' before we were back to war with the demons.

"Master, we're at the north sinkhole." Horns' delegation of beetles and Alexis's probe finally arrived. I'd soon start deploying subsidiary trees to the location, once they'd surveyed the area and found where exactly I needed to go.

The sinkhole was massive, and I really wondered how no one had found it all this while, but then again, it was probably just magic. There were multiple entrances that led into the sinkhole, and the area around the entrance was now filled with camps. One of the larger entrances even had a small town that catered to the adventurers' needs, clearly run by opportunistic merchants trying to purchase the collected materials. Apparently, snakeskin and snake-bile had various uses, some of which could be sold for a huge amount of money.

"Which location should we pick? All the entrances were taken by the adventurers, and honestly, we'll attract unnecessary attention. We are, after all, a delegation of beetles, and the adventurers will immediately assume we're hostile."

"Horns, suggestions?"

"Somewhere farther away. We're beetles. We don't need to use the ledges, so we can climb down vertical walls just fine."

"Good point." Alexis nodded.

If needed, I could use my roots to form new 'ledges' for the beetles to crawl down, or even the roots and vines as a kind of 'rope.' So, after a bit of scouting, we picked one side of the hole where there was already some shrubs and trees. That way the beetles and trees could blend in naturally.

"Could you spawn a biolab this far away? The sensors the probe has aren't as good as the ones on the biolab."

"Oh, why?"

"The probe-etle can connect to it to amplify the sensors."

"Fine, the trees were some distance away. Just hold position for a day or so. Spawning the roots to reach such distances takes time. So what kind of monsters?"

"Snakes? I see snakes. And spiders. A lot of snake-like slithering monsters. There were a lot of them down there. A lot of big ones, too. And colorful ones." Horns, once again, with not exactly helpful descriptions.

Alexis looked at them. "I wonder what's attracting the adventurers…"

"The usual, I suppose? Money, glory, power. Anyway, I'm here for power. Once I get the trees there, then we'll start exploring the sinkhole, too."

―――

Meanwhile, in New Freeka…

*[**Class seed obtained** - Dark Knight x 1]*
[Experience seed obtained x 1]

Huh! It's a joyous thing, to find an unusual seed from a death ceremony. Since this ceremony started, I'd 'processed' about three hundred dead bodies, half of them from plain old age, the other half from injuries, fatal work accidents, murders, and fights. Most of them did not produce any of such seeds, but so far, about six bodies, or about point-five percent, seemed to produce something, either a skill seed, which was the most common, or a class seed.

The rarest seed was the Experience seed. It made sense, since they gave a level.

Essences, though, were a whole lot more common. Almost all dead bodies, when 'absorbed,' produced a few essences. Usually simple essences, like essences of knife, or essences of lesser courage, or essence of water. Unlike seeds, essences were mainly used for 'infusions,' their effects mild.

"Who's this half-elf man?" I asked the priest handling the ceremony. After all, for this dead man to give me a [dark knight] class seed, he couldn't be ordinary. There was a young boy who looked to be a half elf, along with an old grandma next to him, attending the rites. Strangely, they didn't feel like family. The man who died looked to be relatively middle-aged, in his forties, and the cause of death was a stab to the heart.

"A recent refugee from Nung. Got into a scuffle with some of the guards and one of the guards stabbed him to death. Came with the boy and the grandma, in the same caravan, so the old grandma and the kid came to pay respects. Apparently, the kid and the man shared some kind of connection, so the kid insisted to come... That's all I know, sadly," the priest clarified.

"I see."

The priest picked up the compressed bones and passed them to the young boy. "Here, something from that man, for you."

The boy nodded and accepted it. "Thank you. I'll take good care of Uncle's remains."

"Is anyone looking after you, kid?" The priest smiled at the boy.

"Ah, I'm living with that granny there. We're working for a bakery now."

"Ivy, can I ask you to start surveillance on this young boy and the grandma?" I asked. "He's ticking quite a bit of the 'potential hero' tropes."

"I'm a bit overwhelmed at this point. There were too many newcomers to the town. I'm struggling with six to seven thousand people simultaneously." Ivy had a massive list of people to watch —at this point all the politicians, all the guards, and then the Valtrian Order's people.

Well, I was out of artificial souls. I'd collected quite a bit of soul fragments but not enough, not yet. "Ah, well...drop monitoring some of the Order's people then, those who do not appear to be undertaking any high risk or who aren't acting suspicious."

"Okay."

Ah, I got quite a bit of class seeds: ranger, archer, soldier, merchant, trader, and various other trades. So, dark knight's a rather...unique class type. Classes were available only to the humanoid races; monsters or the monster-like creatures usually didn't have 'classes.' Instead, they had racial or type levels. A person could gain as many classes as they wanted, but depending on the race, only some of the benefits from the active few classes manifested.

So...dark knight.

"What's a dark knight?"

"Oh, knights who tap on the power of darkness? Knights who fight at night? Night knights?" Jura shrugged and laughed. "Sorry, TreeTree, I've never heard of it."

[Research Status:]
[Eye-Tree Stage I - completed]
[Beetle - anti-magma armors stage 3 - completed]
[Beetle - anti-magma armors stage 4 - 24 months]
[Tree - volcanic adaptation stage 3 - completed]
[Roots - Volcanic mineral harvesting - stage 2 - completed]
[Roots - Volcanic mineral processing - stage 1 - 1 month remaining]
[Materials testing - stage 1 - completed]
[Tree-lab varieties - stage 1 - 8 months]
[Magically attuned materials Stage 1 - 6 months]

[Basic Tree-Eyes obtained. Limited to 10 'selected' trees. Place on trees to obtain multidirectional vision. Can actively look through two sets of eyes at any one time, view limit can be increased with root-brain complexes.]

Oh, I had Tree-Eyes. Obviously, I put one on my main tree and saved the rest. I'd need to think where to put the trees properly, since it was limited.

In terms of research, I'd decided to relieve Trevor from active research duties, so that brought my concurrent research topics down to four. That was because the valley was growing, and Trevor's energy and focus was needed to manage the larger valley. The forests now extended far beyond the valley itself, and there were now multiple patches. The total number was ninety-four thousand normal trees, some four hundred eighty thousand shrubs and bushes, and about five thousand subsidiary trees. He needed his full processing power to handle such a large valley, even with his higher levels.

Next, I cycled through my domain. The volcano's activity subsided, but we were not attempting any invasion into the inner volcano for the moment. Although the beetles were tougher, thanks to more anti-magma armors, it didn't resolve the golem problem. The golems were still too powerful, and deeper still, we spotted a larger golem. They were not 'aggressive' until we encroached on their area, and so, for now things remained as status quo. I did intend to have more research completed, a different army type, and more 'tools' at my disposal before attempting my next invasion of the volcano.

Then, the ginseng plant. I was on a good streak, it was the longest continuous time I'd protected the ginseng plant, so it was starting to attract stranger monsters. Together with a large army of beetles, both Dimitree and Trevor playing the role of the alarm and surveillance system, we'd held off many greedy, ginseng-stealing monsters. I hoped I'd get something for Jura to use, since ginseng, like herbs, was supposed to be good for supplementing vitality. Between Level Seeds and Ginseng, I thought I'd be able to push Jura up to the next level, but first, I needed to make sure the Ginseng worked. I feared that giving Jura the levels, without the vitality to support it, may weaken him instead.

Emile and Belle, as part of the Order's many business ventures, ran the various crop factories and processors, such as the olive press, the cotton factory, the herbal juice makers, the fermented or dried fruits and healing fruits. A plot of land near my main tree and another near the outskirts of New Freeka's town had been converted to grow all the different kinds of crops that the Order needed to operate these business ventures. I was hoping Brislach or Wahlen could participate, but they seemed content with their lives as ordinary elves living in New Freeka.

Speaking of business ventures, the New Freekans for now still made the wines for export, one of their most successful ventures so far. Even Salah bought from them. Their master winemakers apparently gained quite a few levels from this project and were even famous regionally. It helped they had the right kind of levels and skills, since there was a farmer with skills focused on growing high-quality fruits and also infusing them with a certain kind of flavor, so together, they made wines that had interesting taste profiles.

I still wondered whether Yvon thought it was worth it to trade her soul for grapes, but hey, she'd gotten lucky with Salah calling off the truce terms and instead offering an unconditional truce.

She was supposed to die and then I could use her soul for my own schemes! Oh well. She'd die eventually. Wars, demons, diseases, something would eventually get to all of us, and I thought she'd get killed somehow. Eriz, too! Eriz was still working as a 'maid' and 'minder' for Yvon, even though she was so free now that she didn't need a minder.

Yvon's routine now mostly consist of practicing, teaching Roma various things, and then sparring with Lausanne. Other than that, she was at her home in New Freeka, idle, receiving visitors, mingling in public spaces with an adoring populace. She was to some the 'mother' of the nation, the de facto 'queen.'

"TreeTree, can I ask for something?" Lausanne dropped by after her usual combat practice. Thankfully, she'd gotten over her Tarzan phase, and she wasn't swinging from tree to tree all that often, except for 'practice.'

"Hmm?"

"This special familiar...is there a price I have to pay? Like...Mom used to tell me that few things in the world were free...so...I'm just wondering whether there's a catch."

"Huh, why?" Surely it wasn't a statement like that that prompted this sort of question.

"I see it in my dreams when I sleep these days. There are days I forget that we're separate...things. It's like...it's like it's me. Part of me. And it's strange. Some days, I know what the vines are touching, I feel it, like the vines are like my fingers. It's...really, really strange and a bit scary."

"Uh..." Was that supposed to happen? I had no idea. I thought it might be an ability that the special familiar had. Did familiars meld with their hosts? "Don't worry about it, Lausanne. The familiar means you no harm," I lied. I was not sure, but I thought the familiar should not have such side effects.

Alexis butted in during the conversation. "And what's that familiar powered on? It feels familiar. Like...a kind of mana signature..."

"Magic. My magic."

Alexis shrugged. "Is it?"

"Okay, I believe you, TreeTree...but if someday I want to remove the familiar, is that possible? Can the familiar contracts be cancelled?" Lausanne, of course, couldn't hear Alexis's voice.

"Yes, yes. I can take the familiar back, so don't worry. How's practice? Was Yvon a good coach?"

Lausanne paused, and then she flashed her usual big, chubby smile. "Okay, TreeTree. Lady Yvon, she's good, but I think Uncle Jura's a better fighter." Well, Jura did gain more levels, and his recent class-merger made him really formidable.

"Oh. You don't like fighting her?"

"No, not that. I like her. I just have not gotten used to how she fights. It's...a different style. But I mean, Uncle Jura's a better fighter in a...erm...a bigger way."

"Well, you should get used to different styles of fighting. Heroes need to fight all sorts of monsters."

Lausanne nodded. "Oh, yeah. I didn't think of that. You're right, TreeTree, I should adapt to different styles!"

She walked into the playroom now turned study room, and she grabbed a small bag of wooden toys and some small, kid-size wooden swords. I thought she intended to distribute them to the kids in the orphanage, now her friends. "I'm going to train my friends. Is that okay?"

"Sure, don't go easy on them."

Lausanne frowned, her lips pouty. "Uhm, I can't. They're really weak, so I need to train them slowly. TreeTree, do you think one day you can use your powers on them, too?"

Well, Alexis did suggest a larger sample size. "Maybe?" I'd been monitoring the orphans for some time, and none of them, so far, showed anything...extraordinary. The regular checks using the biolab in the orphanage didn't indicate whether any of them would be special, but then again, Lausanne wasn't special, either.

I was in a bit of a dilemma. Lausanne was where she was now, a 'genius' because of years of consuming essence, dream tutor, and power-leveling such that she gained knowledge. If Lausanne was ordinary, then what if the others were special? But my dilemma wasn't really potential, but...maybe I thought what was really stopping me from trying was 'trust.'

For Lausanne, she had been with me since she was a baby, and that strong bond was why I had invested in her and she was my guinea pig. Maybe someday she'd betray me when she finally went to see the world. But still, it was a mutual benefit. I learned something, and Lausanne got stronger.

So, for these other kids... If I started young and molded these children, maybe I would build such a bond with them, too.

Most of them. Maybe, just maybe, I could link it to the 'familiar,' such that all of them must take the familiar contract, and the familiars would then also help to monitor them? Act as my eyes and ears, such that I could learn more about these children and, in turn, build a stronger bond?

>*[**Skill upgraded**: Symbiotic extension]*
>> *[**Skill learned**: Minder-Familiars. Maximum Minders, 20]*
>> *[**Special tree type obtained**: Dreamer's Treehouses]*

"Lausanne, would you have any of your friends who would like to…have a familiar?"

YEAR 79 MONTH 6

I chose five.

Five young girls, around age six to eight, from the orphanage for the first batch of the minder-familiars. I'd decided to use the minders in batches so I could spread out my sample size over time. Why girls? No real reason for girls, it just so happened that Lausanne's friends or playmates were mostly girls.

Their reaction to having a minder-familiar contract was mostly shock; to them, all they could see was 'familiar.' The status as a 'minder' was hidden, or else they probably wouldn't accept it. Amazing, they said. But these were young girls, their magic just starting to bubble out of their tiny souls.

I had conditions, of course, things that Laufen helped me explain.

1. Regular dips into pod, twice a week, so I could track changes to their body and their soul.
2. They had to stay in a subsidiary tree I placed next to the orphanage quarters. It had room and beds for twenty children, though they were all densely packed together like a dorm. This was because my [Dream Tutor] only worked when they slept either next to me or inside 'me.'

3. Practice. Once they accepted the familiar, they would go on a structured education and training program so that they'd become competent soldiers.

I had twenty slots, so I planned to split them into four batches, using the first five as guinea pigs and refining the process as I went along. There were things I wanted to identify, such as how the essence used influenced the creation of 'skill' blocks in the soul realm. By looking at them frequently, I hoped to gain some idea about how effective essences were and how much I actually needed to use for it to start having an effect.

For the education program, I tasked Jura to appoint some of the Order's militia to start these girls on simple exercises and drills. This world did not shy away from sending young children to fight wars, so I thought it was better to train them before they got sent to their deaths.

The girls took to training and education with much enthusiasm, showing up promptly and listening to the various trainings and teachers intently. It was a small, focused class, one teacher to five girls, and it was drawn out of my personal budget. The Order's budget allocated a discretionary sum to me that I could do whatever I wanted with.

Anyway, the girls were really enjoying the structure, which I found quite strange, as I remembered being a rebellious young child in my youth, but for orphans who never had structure, it must have been a welcome change of pace.

———

Next, I followed up on the hole. Further down, there was a bit of a 'space-warping' present, similar to almost all dungeons and, to some extent, my own [secret hideout].

"Dungeon?" Horns suggested as the small squad of beetles ventured down the hole.

"Magical presence was fluctuating, which seemed rather consistent with the presence of a dungeon core of some kind."

"Not a leyline?" I asked.

"Didn't seem like there was magical energies of a leyline. Do you detect any?"

Sadly, I knew the answer was no. When we conquered the earlier dungeon, the presence of the leyline was clear. My roots, as magically insensitive as they were, could pick it up because of how overwhelming the leyline's presence was once we got underground. None of that overwhelming magical presence here...unless it was somehow magically concentrated and hidden.

"A core, then."

"It's deep, I think." Alexis's probe walked down the cliff walls. Some snakes and flying creatures started to engage the group of beetles, which the beetles fought off successfully.

"Master, were you able to place your trees on the cliffs?"

"Farther up, yes. But once the dungeon's influence touches the cliff, no. There was a 'barrier,' which my subsidiary trees cannot pierce." I could use roots, though, to create a path.

"At this point?"

"I'm afraid that's in the dungeon, already." The good thing was I could see into the dungeon because, unlike the earlier dungeon, it wasn't blocked. Perhaps this dungeon didn't learn that sort of ability? Or not all dungeon cores had the same kind of power?

"Ah, could you put a tree right at the very edge and then lower a bunch of vines down? Something for us to grab on if we need to jump and fight."

"Ah."

The beetles had no problems walking on the cliff walls that led deep into the darkness below. The darkness itself didn't scare them, either; their vision was naturally adapted to all light levels. But fighting while trying to grip onto the walls was not so easy.

"...your presence was getting faint, Master," Horns said.

"Hmm...I'm still connecting to my probe. Looked like my

connection was stronger than yours. It's just really crazy dark down here."

"Tell Master I'll talk through you," Horns said to Alexis's probe. Horns' communication was also a kind of 'telepathy.'

"I know. I can still communicate, but that means you've got to protect me."

Snakes. These snakes had rough scales. Perhaps it helped them move and hold onto the jagged cliffs. Some of these snakes were like nagas, part-humanoid, with four or six arms and a long, slithering body that helped them navigate the cliffs. The nagas were tough opponents to fight, and they could easily take on five or six of the beetles before dying.

"TreeTree, your beetles were not suited for dungeon battles. They were tough, and their bodies strong, but their way of charging and fighting was not really appropriate in this environment. I would say only Horns with his skills was suited."

"What were you telling Master?"

"Nothing."

After another two to three hours of descending into the abyss, they'd decided to stop and retreat, as the attacks from the snakes became relentless.

"Master, I suggest a full-scale invasion of the hole. Maybe five thousand beetles, and fifty of the large beetles, all of us go into the abyss and attack everything we see. The dungeon's structure is deep, and wavy further down, and there are a lot of monsters, but unlike the earlier dungeon, it's still big enough for a large amount of beetles. A large attack force will work a lot better than a small, elite squad."

"I agree with the assessment. This dungeon seemed to favor large, wide caverns and hallways. Ideal situation for a large force to just march in."

"Very well. Let's do it. Horns, you're in charge."

"Ayy! This beetle army is gonna kick some dungeon core backside! Beetles will be the very best!"

A week later, the adventurers nearby were treated to the view of a massive army of beetles descending into the abyss. It caused a massive panic, but as the beetles did not attempt to engage the adventurers, cleverly, the adventurers took the hint and left the army of beetles alone.

And Horns's suggestion was working like a charm.

Within three days of the invasion, like an unstoppable tide of destruction, the beetles charged in and flooded the dungeon, slaughtered all the snakes that had the misfortune of being in their path, cleared most of the dungeon and, most importantly, reached the core.

The wide layout meant a large force could penetrate all the way in, even if we were outmatched one to one. And the space allowed our superior numbers to gang up on the individually stronger snakes.

The core was trying its best to defend itself, spawning and summoning as many snake monsters as it could, but with three thousand beetles left, and despite two thousand beetles that died fighting all the snakes and snake-like monsters, it was unable to muster an army large enough to fight back the tide of beetles.

"Bring it back." Horns and the army arrived at the core room, and with a strong nudge from the giant beetle, the dungeon core rolled off its pedestal.

And that was how we beat the dungeon.

I found it quite funny because what the dungeon core needed to do to successfully defend against our invasion was choke us off, but strangely, this dungeon core's design choice was wide-open spaces, large openings, and big walkways. Big spaces, big walls, all allowed for a large force to rush in and clear everything. Perhaps it was an architect with a thing for big spaces.

And why snakes?

Ah, perhaps the dungeon core rolled the dice and got snakes.

With that, the army of beetles returned with a dungeon core taken from its home. Strangely, without the dungeon core, the deep hole continued to spawn snakes, although to a lesser frequency.

"Dungeon core." It was a large, circular, crystal-like structure, about the size of a basketball. I recalled the earlier one being larger, though. Or were there many variants? Perhaps it wasn't something with a standard size.

"What were you going to do with it?"

"I would like to study it, of course. But between now and when I get that magic lab, it's going to sit in my [treeasury]."

"...fair enough."

Other than that, the beetles also brought back some interesting abyss vegetation.

*[**Tree-type obtained**: Cave Trees]*
   *[**Plant-type obtained**: Deep Moss]*
   *[**Special Tree-type obtained**: Cliff Bonsai]*

No levels for me, sadly. Horns and Alexis did get some levels. Sucked being a bystander.

YEAR 79 MONTH 7

"Tree Spirit, an audience, please." Yvon came marching to my main tree, alone. She didn't seem very happy.

"Yes?"

"What's your plans with the orphans? I heard from Lausanne that you've given them familiars and started them on some kind of training."

"It was as you heard, training. I intend to train them into warriors."

"Warriors? Is that all there is to it? Surely there is more going on, what with the strange things you have been asking them about."

Hmm, she was being rather aggressive. "What are you alluding to? If you have something to say, get to it."

Yvon took a step back, but then, she quickly adjusted her posture, such that she faced me head on, her eyes staring at my tree trunk. "What I hear is there is constant dipping into your... pool. That healing pod thing, with all of your feelers. So I want to know are you also meddling with their bodies? Are you...altering them? And are you meddling with their minds as well?"

"Meddling, yes. Altering, maybe." Well, yeah. I did plan to meddle. That was the whole point.

Yvon shook her head. "That...that's not right. These are children."

"You seem to think there is a reason not to select children. Wrong. It's because they are children. Children can be easily molded, shaped. Their minds are flexible, receptive to change. And seriously, why now, Lady Yvon?"

Yvon paused. Maybe when Lausanne started to tell her what I'd been doing with the five girls, it just flicked a switch. "Why? What do you mean why? Is it not wrong to start using children for some kind of war plot? As your future war potential?"

"Many nations do so, choose young children and prepare them for war, in some cases from the day they are born. What I want to do is similar. If you ask me why, ask all the nations before, and present, why. Fighting, war. Destruction. It's a way of life in this world. Preparing these children for that way of life so they—we— have a better chance of survival as a whole, is there anything wrong with that?"

Yvon nodded. "It is your altering of their bodies and minds. Is it something that's irreversible? Such that they may lose their ability to have children?"

"As I currently plan it, no. And seriously, you know better that the whole matters more than the individuals. Some must be sacrificed, and experience pain, for the whole to succeed. It is, as I said, strange coming from you, Lady Yvon."

Yvon's face was complicated, a mix of worry, perhaps disgust, and fear. "Would you deprive them of a childhood, of friends? Would you isolate them, make them...inhuman? Would this sacrifice that you ask of these young girls, would it be too much for them?"

"Maybe. Maybe this burden is too much for them. Maybe asking them to sacrifice their childhoods to be my warriors is too much. But there is no one else, Yvon. These orphans yearn for a purpose in life, and I give them one. To answer a greater calling, to fight for me. For the valley. For all of us."

"That—"

"I find it strange that you are suddenly concerned for these young girls. I don't recall you being so caring of orphans when you were in a position of power, so these words coming from you...sound...hollow."

Yvon's eyes were a bit watery. Was she trying to pull the crying lady trick? Sadly, I was a tree, and such crying antics did not trigger a protective urge within me. "Yes, I didn't do what I could. I had the power, yet I was too crippled by politics, too confused by all the competing priorities. But now, I have to speak up. I heard what Lausanne said these girls will go through, and I fear for these young souls. You're sending them into a life of only war."

"And so what? This is how the world is. Why do you want to speak up? Are you doing so to satisfy some kind of conscience that you suddenly discovered you have?"

"Uhm. No. I am trying to care for these young orphans. They deserve a life better than war now that we are at peace." I thought she was lying. And that was hogwash, really.

"Peace? You mean this peace that we have because our overwhelming might suddenly scared the shit out of our opponents? This was no true peace, Lady Yvon. It was a peace built on fear. A fear of our power. And if you know better, this peace is maintained by power. Lady Yvon, if you truly care, and want to care, I would like to suggest you participate in their molding as warriors. Be their support, then. These young girls, they will need a matron to watch over them, to guide and advise them where I can't, to be a 'wise elder' to these sheep, our future warriors."

She froze, and her eyes twitched. "Again? You...you want me to be a part of it?"

"Yes. Since you suddenly have a conscience, come, join the training. Join me in shaping our future warriors, our...future generals, our future knights. Perhaps you can then see for yourself what I am trying to do."

"Ahh..."

"So? Or were your earlier words just...something you wanted to get off your chest?"

Yvon finally nodded. "I'll do it. I'll help you with these girls."

"Good. Make them strong. We will need their strength one day."

"Alexis, do you have any results from the treefolk study?"

"Ah, yes. I got the dead treefolk, and I'm starting my investigations. So far nothing, but I'm mainly interested in the kind of flexible muscle-wood that they have on their joints. Their body is fascinating under scrutiny. It's both plant-like yet they also form muscle-like structures. It's like somebody just blended a tree and a person together to create a treefolk. Replicating that muscle-like structure would mean we could make stronger creatures overall."

"How long do you need?"

"According to [research planner], probably twelve months just to understand the treefolk's bodily structures. There was a lot to unpack. The treefolk's brain was also interesting and worth another twelve to twenty-four months of study, and I reckon would have a benefit to your [root-brain complex]."

"Are they not a communal mind structure, like forests are?" It was said that forests formed an intelligence through the interconnected roots, like each tree was a neuron. In this world, large, ancient forests often appeared to have a will of their own, and over time, this would often pool together and create a [spirit tree] or [soul tree]. It was one of the many ways tree spirits were said to come to existence naturally.

"Not exactly. Though treefolk have a head, their brains are actually distributed throughout their body, kind of like jellyfish. It's like a neural network, but with a few large hubs in the head, the heart..."

"They have a heart, yes?"

"Yes. Well, their heart is actually more like this main vessel through their body that runs from their leg to their head. In a way, it's like a large, muscled pipe..."

"Ermmm...never mind the details."

There was news from a distant land, as Nung, Takde, and Salah eventually settled on a peace treaty. Though culprit of the massive blizzard was still at large, the blizzard itself had been successfully dispelled, and the weather had returned to normal.

That said, ground zero of that spell was now a quasi-dungeon area, the presence of such blood sacrifice distorting the area such that it spawned zombies and monsters. It would take some time for the remains of such magic to decay.

So trade got rerouted around the now-cursed land, and the three nations reached a kind of awkward truce. Still, that meant less [essence] for me from this battlefield.

Further out, my traveling [soul harvesters] continued to bring back more souls, more [essences of death], and more skill type [essences]. Throughout the entirety of this continent, death remained a constant thing. Many small battles, many little monster attacks, little rebellions here and there. More death, more essences. And that was good for me.

One good thing about this peace was now I got more knowledge about our neighbors. And as more and more such little snippets filtered through the grapevine, I learned interesting things, like there was a vast sacred forest on the edge of Salah's capital where the kings hunted. Or near one of the large cities of Nung, there was a large mountain where people claimed ancient giants wandered.

Well, personally, I thought it was time to take the war to Salah. They may be at peace, but I still had a small score to settle.

The Salah kingdom's capital was really far away, so I had to undo my subsidiary trees that stretched to the abyss. It was the furthest I was going; if I measured the distance in beetle, it was about two and a half weeks away, so I was going to need a lot of subsidiary trees to create a line that connected the entire distance.

It was a process that took about fifteen hundred subsidiary trees to create a line to bend with the terrain and, eventually, the capital. I made it a point to hide the presence of the trees from plain slight, such that they appeared 'natural,' and this endeavor took me the whole month, every day, putting a tree, altering its appearance, and then moving on.

And there it was, the capital.

*[**Skill upgraded**: Local rootnet access upgraded. Longer distance between subsidiary trees unlocked.]*

*[**Special trees type obtained**: Root Relay Trees]*

[Max Quantity of Relay was Level x 5]

[Root Relay were special trees with the dedicated purpose of expanding your root network. A single root Relay can create a simple root network that extends 10x the diameter of a regular subsidiary tree. Does not have other functions. Looks like any other tree. Appearance is customizable.]

YEAR 79 MONTH 8

Salah's capital. It'd gone by many names throughout its history; many kings had changed its name. The most recent name of the capital was Ransalah, after the king's beloved but deceased wife, Queen Rani.

Next to the capital was a forest, Salah's Royal Grove. In fact, most large kingdoms maintained a grove or a forest for the purpose of having some supply of highly valuable herbs or plants for the manufacture of unique potions or medicines. Some temples, such as the temple of Gaya's headquarters, also had a large forest that it cultivated for its own use.

Now that my chain of subsidiary tree had finally made the long connection needed to arrive here, I paused for a moment to take in the view.

It was a large capital, not as populous as it used to be after the non-human exodus, but still, there was a lot of humans in this city, perhaps four hundred to five hundred thousand, maybe more, and the city sprawled to accommodate its large population. There were two rivers that ran through the river, and it merged further down, which split the capital into three parts.

The central southern chunk was where the palace, priesthood, mages, and wealthy mostly lived. Infrastructure was good, the roads were paved, security was top notch, and patrols were regular, staffed with the best-behaved men. It was a place where, to be frank, people behaved nicely because of the overwhelming presence of the royal guards and the Archmagus. It was home to the official trader's market, though in reality, it was more of a hipster market catering to the needs of the wealthy and elite.

Then there was the east side, where the army's main quarters, the river ports, and the warehouses were. This was also where the Royal Grove was. There was not that many dwellings there, as space was few and far between, the Royal Grove off-limits.

Then there was the west side, a large flatland where most of the citizens resided. Sprawling, messy, and infrastructure spotty, it was the definition of a large city where the plans failed to keep up with the population growth. As a result, it was a space where citizens often took things into their own hands, so there were multiple enclaves where there was some form of 'local rule.' Vibrant, energetic, and a space of constant change, the supervision from local authorities minimal, so long as the tax monies continued to flow into the right pockets. Half of the merchant corps existed here, and the true trader's market, where the trade volumes were high and the shouting constant.

How did I know this? Well, it was not hard for Jura to ask a Salah merchant to speak of their capital at length. Apparently, the merchants were incredibly proud of the peon's market, one of the largest markets found in the region.

It was a nice city.

A shame, really.

SIDE STORY - LAUSANNE 2

Sometime after the orphanage started...

"Where's the captain? We want the captain," the boys shouted.

"They're busy today. I'm here to be your practice partner."

"You're not a soldier. You're just a little girl. No, worse, you're a noble," the young boy accused. "You're one of the nobles, and we don't want to practice with you."

"I'm not. And what's wrong with practicing with me?" She didn't understand it; she'd never been a noble. Her father may have been the village chief, but he passed away, and the village was destroyed. Growing up relatively sheltered from kingdoms and their societies, she wasn't too aware about the negative emotions associated with nobility, even though Jura and Laufen did tell her about what nobles usually did in other nations.

"I know you! You're a noble, and we don't want to practice with you!" the young boys shouted, some of them really unhappy. The rest of the boys didn't like her, either; they all looked at her with disgust, which made her feel a little sad.

She didn't expect this. Laufen and Jura asked her to help out at the orphanage, to help teach the other children, those about her age, to be their sparring partner for a while. The captains were out on a mission. *Why were they so nasty to me? I'm just trying to help*, she wondered, but she didn't understand their hostility. "Uh..."

"Don't come here acting all high and mighty because of your mother!"

What? Where did that come from? Why? She just couldn't answer. *Isn't Mom the one who set up this orphanage?* The boys started going out of the hall. Lausanne felt that her presence was unwanted by these boys.

All she wanted to do was practice some sword fighting, since Uncle Jura was busy. He said to help out at the orphanage, practice some basic moves with the kids in the orphanage; good heroes did that sort of work all the time. And she agreed. She wanted to be a good hero.

But why did these fellow children, who were just around her age, treat her with such hostility? She didn't even say much; all she did was walk in, say she was helping out with the sword practice, and then this huge tirade of insults resulted.

One of the caretakers at the orphanage noticed the insults and rushed into the training room. The caretaker, an elderly lady, walked to Lausanne and pulled her to one side of the room before it escalated into a fistfight. "Forgive them, Miss Lausanne. A lot of them have a lot of animosity, a lot of anger, so when they see a young girl their age coming in to teach them, they...they can't deal with it. Please, come this way with me."

"They're really angry at me." Lausanne nodded, looking at the wrinkled face of the elderly lady. She held Lausanne's arms and leaned in to speak to her with a warm, grandmotherly voice.

"It's a complicated feeling. These boys, they've got things to deal with inside them, and so these boys want—no, they have a need for respect and recognition, a yearning to learn 'real' skills. So when adult soldiers come and practice with them, they feel they... they are respected."

"Hmmm...so they don't want to practice with me because I'm a young girl? Even if I have real skills?" Lausanne sighed. There was nothing much she could do with those kids who were bigger if they didn't like her. *I'll have to tell Uncle Jura and Mom about it later.*

She looked at the caretakers, most of them elderly women that her mother hired to help run the orphanage. There were about two hundred kids in this place, of various ages, and many of them were there because they'd lost both their parents, mostly during their earlier escape from the slaughter of Salah. The group was around aged nine to twelve.

She was sad, but she did promise Jura to help, so she asked for something else to do. Maybe if there were other girls? "Uhm...well, Uncle Jura did ask me to help out. Maybe I can play with the younger children? Any girls I can play with?"

"Ah...yes, okay. Girls...girls..." The lady smiled and led Lausanne to another room, where there were about ten to fifteen young girls, probably four to six years old, playing catch. It was a relatively empty room, and they didn't have many toys, so they mostly played with each other. "Maybe you can join this group?"

"Hi." Lausanne smiled. They were all younger than her, and a part of her felt happy. It was nice that she wasn't the youngest for a change.

They smiled back at her and welcomed her into the game. *Ah, this group's a lot more pleasant*, she thought. Maybe they were too young to feel much animosity, or perhaps this group was a little sheltered. It was a simple room with a few chairs, but it was well lit by natural lighting, thanks to multiple large windows; thin streaks of sunlight filtered through the leaves outside. There were a few wooden blocks here and there, but that was about all the toys they had.

A small girl with a short bob cut walked up to Lausanne. "Hello, elder sister. I'm Jien." She was shorter than her. Lausanne smiled and gave her a hug.

"I'm Lausanne. Can I play?"

"Okay. What do you want to play? We usually play catch. Or we throw the blocks back and forth."

"Okay, let's do that."

They played together for the rest of that afternoon, until it was about evening, and she learned their names. The biggest girl there was Sammy; she was about six. She didn't know when her birthday was because her parents both passed away when she was still a baby, and that was actually fairly common among those who lived there. Because the girls didn't know who was the eldest, they went with the biggest.

Jien was a year younger, and like the rest of the girls, her parents had died. Or maybe they'd somehow gotten separated. Most of them weren't very sure whether their parents died or got lost, but this detail didn't bother them much.

Lausanne felt happy after an afternoon of playtime and felt maybe she should help them out. *I should ask TreeTree for some more wooden toys. I remember we have a lot in the playroom.*

———

"Did you practice with the other kids?"

"No, Mom. They didn't want to fight with a girl. They wanted the captains."

"Oh." Laufen nodded and put down the reports that the other employees had prepared. She had a lot of assistants these days as the head of the public services. She honestly didn't like paperwork all that much, but there still needed to be reports to tabulate spending and income, and these were still made by actual administrators or the priests. "Why?" Laufen squatted to look at Lausanne eye-to-eye.

"One of the ladies said it's because they want to fight with an adult." Lausanne sulked. "Maybe it's because I'm not good enough."

Laufen gave Lausanne a hug and then started to pat her daughter on her head. "No, no. I'm sure it's not like that."

"The ladies told me so. The boys said they want the captains."

"Lausanne, my dear, they don't mean it. I am sure they like you."

Lausanne shook her head. "Mom...they don't."

"Really?"

"Really." Lausanne's face was serious and a bit sad.

"Well, they will like you someday."

Lausanne shook her head. "Hmph." She leaned in and gave her mom a kiss on the cheek. "Good night, Mom."

"Sleep well. Don't let it bother you."

Lausanne shook her head again. Maybe it would bother her that night.

Sometime later...

"Thank you for practicing with me, Lady Yvon."

"You're welcome. I always look forward to sparring with such a talented young girl."

They both gave each other a quick bow, and they started their practice spars, simple swings and strokes, moves meant to warm the body and get ready for the real thing. Yvon was still leagues ahead of Lausanne in terms of skill, but Lausanne's growth was outstanding as she was almost level thirty.

"How's things?" Yvon asked casually, ducking a horizontal slash and then parrying a follow-up horizontal slash.

"TreeTree's starting a small class of students. He calls them his chosen warriors."

"Huh?"

"Yeah...he says he plans to train them and maybe give them special powers like mine someday, but before that, he needs to prepare them."

Yvon blocked a flurry of slashes and retaliated with a body slam. Lausanne activated [Evasive steps] and managed to avoid it.

"He says maybe he'll have to fix them if they're not compatible later on. Like how he uses his powers to cure Uncle Jura's curse..."

"Really, why does TreeTree want to do something like that?"

"Hmmm...he didn't tell me a lot, but maybe, maybe he just

likes us to grow? He says he wants to watch our growth closely, as he'll be using some kind of 'essence' on us, though."

"Essence? Isn't that like condensed energies?"

"I don't know, Lady Yvon. But TreeTree says he has a lot of essences and some other things like his minerals and mana that he wants to use."

"On the girls?"

"Yeah. He told me it'll be good for them."

"Did you get those as well?"

"Uh...I think so? I frequently have dreams where I am training or where there is someone teaching me things. And TreeTree tells me to dip into the pod every week, too."

"And your mom was fine with it?"

"Mom thinks TreeTree knows what he's doing. She says it's how I get so good at fighting."

"Wait. You were not naturally talented at fighting?"

Lausanne smiled. "If you ask Uncle Jura, he'll tell you I was absolutely horrible at it when I started. But TreeTree's been helping me by giving me these...dreams."

Lausanne blocked a few more slashes from Yvon and tried to land a kick.

"Dreams?"

"Yeah. It's like I'll take a nap at home, and TreeTree's feelers will somehow touch my forehead, and I get the dreams."

"Tell me...more." Yvon charged and unleashed a flurry of slashes. Lausanne tried to parry them but failed to parry a few, so she took a hit from the wooden blade.

Lausanne staggered back from the impact. It hurt, but she had pain resistance. "Oh...it's different every time. Sometimes, it's like there is a voice in my head, and we will talk. About things, about a topic. Sometimes it's language, like I'll get a lesson on it. Sometimes it'll tell me about people, about places..."

Yvon listened intently, and they took a break.

"Some dreams were really, really fun. It's like all these colors and all these images of really strange things, weird monster-like things and shapes, but they don't attack me. It's like I'm on top of a mountain and fall down."

"That's like a vision. A...hmm. A hallucination."

"A what?"

"Never mind, continue."

"Oh, then like last week, I had a dream where I was fighting a giant demon. I had really strong powers, and I had to use those powers to fight the giant demon."

"Fighting demons doesn't sound like a fun dream." Yvon shook her head and took a drink from her bag of water. "Anyway, continue?"

Lausanne nodded, and they both stepped back into the ring. "Well, I think TreeTree's trying to teach me something."

"Sounds like he's making elite warriors."

Lausanne smiled. "Well, he's just helping me be a hero."

Yvon frowned, and Lausanne ducked, then jumped sideways to avoid a bunch of slashes. "Is it? I'm not aware he did so much to you."

"Oh, he's been fixing my body, too, like repairing a bone here, a bone there. And he's got this thing that can help strengthen the bones and muscles, too. It's all in the green pod."

"I am starting to think the green pod isn't all that it seems..."

"That pod was amazing, Lady Yvon. It sustained a hero suffering from a demonic curse."

"It did?"

"Did Uncle Jura not tell you? One of the previous generations of heroes was afflicted with some kind of curse, and TreeTree kept her alive until a cure was found."

"Before we came..."

"Yeah, yeah! I was still a tiny toddler then. But I do vaguely remember a lady constantly being in the pod."

"All right, let's stop." They had some more basic exercises just to cool their bodies down. "How were the girls receiving this news?"

"They're excited. It's the first time they've been chosen for anything, so they were thrilled when they got the familiar contract. They'll need to sleep in a special tree and have regular dips in the pod. It's like they're going to be transformed into something amazing, so all of them really, really want it."

"They should be careful. Tree Spirit probably has his own plans for them and may not be what they think it is."

Lausanne smiled. "We believe in TreeTree. He'll help us."

Yvon sighed. "I-I'll need to speak to TreeTree."

Dreams, physical alterations. Hallucinations. A need to consume strange liquids. It all sounded a bit like what tribal shamans gave to their warriors to whip them into a war frenzy or the work of some alchemist testing out strange potions. She had heard rumors of creatures that gave strange, mind-altering substances to enslave minions, and though it didn't seem like TreeTree was doing it, she needed to be sure.

Yvon was one of the modernist elves who had a rather defensive, cautious view of Tree Spirits, that Tree Spirits weren't exactly domestic animals that could be tamed, unless one happened to be a hero who focused on spirit control.

The modernist elves believed the benign, friendly myth of the tree spirit was actually a unique characteristic of the Great Tree Spirits of the Elf cities, and one should not assume all wild tree spirits to be similarly benevolent. Like the dryads, faeries, and other forest spirits, these avatars of nature share a common trait, that they were occasionally ephemeral, flighty, fickle, and manipulative. Though often their goals were aligned to what most elves desired, they should also be treated with caution, for the fury of a tree spirit was often subtle.

Lausanne, though, didn't think that way. To her, TreeTree was friendly and all he was trying to do was help.

In their own ways, both of them were right.

YEAR 79 MONTH 9

"Did you hear? One of the mage guild's private gardens near the Royal Grove was robbed last night! A lot of valuable herbs and plants were lost." I eavesdropped on some of the locals of Ransalah.

"Oh? Any idea who the culprits were?"

"The mages suspect a mage, so the royal guard has been deployed. But there were no traces. It's as if the plants all just... vanished into the ground."

"Can't it be just some thief with a magical bag? Or some kind of plant-manipulation artifact?" The locals had all sorts of speculation.

"I think it's just an unhappy mage taking revenge. There was a lot of politics going on in the mage guilds. This was just a reaction to the mage's council votes!"

Ransalah.

It was a large city, and there were a lot of high-leveled people around, strong adventurers, powerful generals, and mages. Their very presence permeated the air, and I occasionally picked up the effects of their skills, despite me being mostly magically insensitive.

A direct confrontation was not ideal, not with the distance penalty I suffered at long distances.

This might be the first time I had 'seen' a city. Moton and New Freeka couldn't compare to the scale and sprawl of a capitol city.

It was also the first time I encountered 'enchanted' roads. Around the capitol, these roads had some kind of 'anti-vegetation' effect, and as a result, I couldn't spawn my subsidiary trees near them. Even underground, the capital had a sprawling network of sewers and tunnels, and they were strangely also 'enchanted.' I suspected it was the effect of some masonry skill or builder's skill, which prevented decay and damage to these structures because logically, using magic on sewers just didn't seem to make much sense. These enchanted sewers prevented my roots from spreading that deeply, and so that greatly limited the extent of my spread.

In the city, multiple structures, such as the army's fort on the riverbank, were enchanted with strong defensive magic, which I was yet able to identify but I presumed to be a kind of 'warding' magic. The magic on the fort walls created a forcefield that repelled my presence and prevented me from placing subsidiary trees and also stopped my roots from approaching.

I frankly didn't know all of these, whether it was skill or magic, either. Or whether it was the powers of a local lord or king that granted such passive benefits to the city that he or she ruled.

These protections, whether from magic or skills, were clustered mostly around the old castle, the palaces, the eight forts around the city, the mage's main towers, the old cathedrals, and temples to the gods. The usual places of interest.

All of these, together with the layout of the river, meant I had very little access to the inner city, where all the royals were.

Still, there must be something I could do.

First was the Royal Grove, which, despite its royal status, lacked magical protection. I guessed that unlike the places where the royals lived, the Royal Grove wasn't worth much protection. So I extended a few subsidiary trees into the forests and soon discovered that its earth did have some magic. There was also a lot of new herbs and plants that I had not seen.

The royal guards and rangers were always on the lookout for monsters or for thieves, but when they spotted a new tree, they just went, "Eh." All I needed to do was disguise my tree to look like a small shrub and I could slip through the patrols like nothing.

The best reaction I got from a ranger was, "Oh, when did this tree pop up?" And then he promptly proceeded to ignore that tree. Like, not even an investigation?

In fact, the most legit confrontation I'd gotten was from a woodcutter. I had attempted to expand into the new part of the city where all the regular citizens lived. But the presence of a tree just stuck out like a sore thumb in the messy, dense mess that was the west side of Ransalah. So a woodcutter came up to my tree that popped up at the edge of town and, without any hesitation, chopped me down.

Chop. Chop. Chop. And timberrrrr.

My subsidiary tree fell just like that. I bet that woodcutter had special [woodcutting] abilities that made my tree's defenses absolutely useless. Those poor subsidiary trees didn't stand a chance.

Maybe that axe was enchanted to be super effective against trees. But honestly, other than the woodcutters, no one really noticed an unusual tree in a forest. I mean, I was discounting the fact that anything green just stuck out in a place filled with houses, roads, and shops.

Did this world not have tree-monsters? Did nobody disguise themselves as a tree trunk? Did this world not have ninjas?

Anyway, as my [subsidiary tree] connected to the other trees and the earth, I got a notification.

*[**Gained a passive buff**. Connected to an enchanted forest. Herb effectiveness increased by fifty percent.]*

Oh. Funky. Enchanted it is.

"What's your plan?" Alexis asked. She was obviously a huge

fan of seeing new places. "I've been there, that city. But we've only stayed a few days. It's nice, looking at the city from your point of view."

"Hmmm...I plan to first gradually infiltrate the capital, have trees and vines throughout the city...then I need to find the culprits. I want to know whether the commanders that ordered the burning of the village are still alive."

"That's it? If they are alive, do you plan to kill them?"

"Hmmm...I guess so. I should kill them."

"Is this for revenge? I mean, they burned down the village, so it's revenge, right?"

"Revenge, yeah, I think so."

Actually, that was a good question.

Why was I doing this? Was I just carrying the fury of the burning of the village of Freeka in my heart? Kind of silly that I was asking myself that now that I had made the entire journey there. I even invested all these subsidiary trees to establish a connection, a chain of trees that spanned a country.

So that question prompted me to think about what exactly I wanted to achieve, and because I could not answer the question myself, I turned to the elves, my fellow survivors, the seven elves that had suffered the consequences of the army's brutality.

"Lausanne, what would you do if you found the one responsible for killing your father?"

"Slap him. A few times."

"That's it?"

"That bad person, he made me grow up without a father. It was a bad thing. Bad people do such bad things to me. But it was so long ago. I was still just a small baby, and I do not know what happened. So...somehow, I'm not really, really angry. Maybe angry, but it's not burn-me-up kind of angry, you know? I should be angry at these bad guys because they did a bad thing, but it's not in here, you know?" Lausanne pointed to her heart, or was it her gut?

She had a point. She was a baby, and she hadn't seen it happen, though she suffered the consequences of it. But that'd been her life since.

"So, were you angry?"

"I think I am. But not much, really. Maybe Mom will be really angry. Wait. I should be angry. I am angry."

"You...don't sound that angry."

"I am angry because a group of bad people did bad things to us. But that's it, I guess. I am angry because I should be, but not angry because I feel it like a fire in my heart."

Okay, confusing.

Laufen.

"Laufen, what would you do if you found the man that ordered the burning of the village?"

Laufen sat and kept quiet for a while.

"Laufen?"

"I heard you, TreeTree. I-I need to think. I just did not expect such a question from you, suddenly."

Oh. Laufen kept quiet for a good fifty minutes, maybe an hour? Just alone, thinking. I honestly didn't notice the time.

"Honestly, TreeTree? I don't know what I would do. Maybe I will kill him. Or maybe not. But me...I-I think I probably won't be able to do anything. It's been so long, TreeTree... I...I don't know."

Laufen looked really uncomfortable, and she sat down on the large chair in her office.

"They took my friends, my husband, my home from me."

"So you will retaliate?"

"Yes. Maybe yes. But I tell Lausanne not to let it cloud and consume us, that this was a cycle of how the world renews itself. The world is full of this, you know, killing. People always kill each other. They always find excuses to. If it's not humans, it'll be royalty, or money, or territory. We have always been killing or getting killed. I sometimes wonder whether maybe it would have been demons that got us instead, if it wasn't the army."

"I'm confused, Laufen. Why were you talking about that?"

"Me too. I don't really know what I will do, what I should do. I like to think we have all moved on, succeeded in rebuilding our lives. A part of me takes the stand that living a good life is the best revenge. That not to be consumed by vengeance is the way to move forward with life."

Laufen paused and took a deep breath.

"But the loss, somewhere, it still hurts. When I look at Lausanne sparring, I wonder what Ricola would have said. When we celebrate her birthdays, I wish Ricola and all others were here."

She looked really sad then.

"But does my sorrow, my sadness, allow me to seek vengeance? I know Casshern once told me that when you've lived through so many years of death, you learn to accept it. But I can't. So what should I do, TreeTree? What's the right thing to do?"

She stretched.

"Like I said, a part of me thinks the right thing to do is to forgive and forget. But I don't want them to get away scot-free, either. I feel like a statement needs to be made. I'm so torn between those two feelings! TreeTree? I want both. I want to let go. Only with letting go I will have inner peace. But I also want to have vengeance, a statement, some way of slapping these idiots for fighting us when their attention should be on demons."

Well, I could actually share that emotion. I too thought I knew, but now that I was at the point where I was able to retaliate, I actually didn't really know what I wanted to do with Salah.

Should I slaughter the Salah kingdom, many of whom were similarly unaware of the evil their military committed? Or should I just focus my goal on the true culprits? But let's say I did find the true culprits; was death the right punishment for them?

"Jura, what would you do if you find the culprits behind the burning and slaughter of Freeka?"

Jura leaned back on his chair. "I would have the true culprit stripped naked, hung upside down in a public market, and starved, whipped, and burned for a few days, but without dying, without sleep."

"Huh, why?"

"Because he deserves shame and pain. For someone who crossed me personally, I feel to just let the person die was too lenient, too light. He should experience my terrible days, when I was hiding, running, my skin still scorched by the flames that engulfed the village, my feet bruised, my skin bleeding, but I had to keep running. All of us ran like crazy for days. So, yeah, he should have a taste of that."

"Okay..."

"But you know, now that I'm the Counsel of the Valtrian Order, I can understand how it got to that point, why the military did what it did. The burning. Even if I disagree with it."

"Jura?"

"I mean, look, a king exercises his authority through his institutions and his subjects. What good is a king if there are no subjects that obey his command? So when a king gives an order, there must be a weight to it so that citizens learn to obey them. We clearly disobeyed the order, so we were punished. Sure, the punishment on us was really extreme, but then, I sometimes wonder, if the punishment was light, who would put their lives on the line and fight for the king? I have heard of death for traitors, death for those who desert the battlefield. What we did was similar, no? We refused to fight when we were clearly asked to."

I thought there was more to it, so I let Jura continue.

"Eh, it's just some things I think about, sometimes to rationalize why such a tragedy happened. It's...it's a way of coping, to try and understand why it happened. A part of me learns to come to terms with that reality, by accepting that we deserved it."

Well, dissecting and rationalizing was a way of coping?

"Sometimes, maybe that's just fate, the way the gods of this world continue to play their games, and we were just puppets."

Jura stretched on his nice, comfy seat. It was custom made; after all, he was the Counsel of the Order. He kicked his legs a bit and then swung his two arms around. There was no one else in the room. Jura didn't actually like having other people in the room when he was working. Besides, he was a level eighty [Warlord]. If somebody could kill him, the guards probably wouldn't stand a chance anyway.

"But you know, despite all of that, I saw my friends die, so I think I really would skewer the guy. Cut him up and hang him for all to see. But then I'll probably look like a vengeful person, and public vengeance isn't something other elves appreciate."

"So...will you kill him or not?"

"Oh, yes, I will kill him, throw him in the gutter, let no one remember him, and be done with it."

Heh. I somewhat liked that, but then again, I felt death was too cheap. "Didn't death feel too cheap?"

"Life was cheap, so death should be cheap. Always has been. But I just want to settle those loose ends and be done with it. We've got the living to worry about, future enemies to think of, rather than enemies of our past..."

"You...sure?"

"No. I think I will only know what I will do when I hold the executioner's blade and the culprit's head is on the chopping block. Maybe those deep emotions will come back."

Hmmm...somehow those answers didn't satisfy me all that much, so I ended up speaking to Belle and Emile. I, too, asked both the girls the same question, about what they would do if they found the person who asked for the burning of New Freeka.

"Honestly, I kind of got over it and accepted that the gods let it happen. Been what, nine years?" Belle scratched her head.

Emile similarly looked confused. "I think those humans were evil, but they're mostly dead, right? Have you been thinking about it, TreeTree?"

"Eh...come on. None of you care about it anymore?"

"Uhm...Salah's so far away, and we're just regular elves, looking to lead regular elven lives. For me, I've not thought of vengeance at all. The only thing on my mind was to return to normalcy, which we have!" Belle smiled and sat on her bed. "And now we have you to protect us, so that won't happen ever again. So I won't do a thing."

Ah...

"I agree with Belle. I think after the first three years or so I stopped thinking about the slaughter. Having a job and a new town like New Freeka, we feel normal again. Well, our actions will not bring back the dead."

Seriously, these two girls could be a little too happy-go-lucky, even with the destruction. Well, there was Brislach and Wahlen.

Wahlen sat. "Erm...I would kick the guy in the groin. And publicly cane him."

Brislach scratched her cheeks for a while. "I'd have him apologize for ordering such a hateful, horrible thing. I want a sincere, heartfelt apology. And then I will slap all of them. And yes, I like Wahlen's idea. Cane them. Cane them! Use the biggest whip and cane their butts until they bleed."

Ah, an apology, that was a good point. An apology, a remorseful one would be good. But if I found the guy, how did I even get an apology out of him?

"What would you do, TreeTree?" Brislach turned the question around. "You were there when it happened, too. You watched the village burn, and you saw the rest of them die to the swords and fires while we hid inside you."

"I, I actually don't really know. I'm still thinking what I should do." I was confused now. It seemed these elves lived actual nine years while the past few years didn't feel all that long to me. They seemed to have mostly moved on, which I supposed made me happy. But then...

The two girls laughed. "Even the wise tree spirits can feel anger and know not what to do, eh? TreeTree, what do you feel they deserve?"

"I..."

I thought I must have vengeance. But what kind of vengeance?

What would satisfy this itch? This little scar in my heart?

I looked at Ransalah. My vision was incomplete, as my [subsidiary trees] could only see so far. The location of my trees wasn't very strategic, unlike how New Freeka was a town built around and with trees, so what I could see and hear was limited.

It'd been so many years. If I wanted to be specific about my vengeance, could I even find the person responsible?

What if the guy was dead?

What if something already killed him?

Where should my vengeance go, then?

Feeling stumped, I focused on my usual activities. Which was finding more types of trees to investigate. It really wasn't hard for some beetles to sneak in using the [root tunnels], especially in poorly defended places like the mage's garden. It wasn't even the garden with the most valuable herbs.

The real prize, I thought, were those within the usual suspects, the multiple large gardens within the palace compounds, a few other gardens in the three large temple complexes, and those gardens that were actually in the mage's guild.

It wasn't easy to infiltrate a city as a tree, what more with its generally enchanted paved or tiled roads, and there was really very little vegetation in the town area, except for little spots, little gardens here and there. Didn't help that because it was a city, demand for wood was high, so there was frequently a lot of workers going around the city to harvest trees.

That meant I had to frequently regenerate my [subsidiary trees], else I'd lose a connection to the trees I had inside the Royal Grove.

"Strategies, anyone? For both the vengeance, and for the maintenance of trees?" I asked my artificial minds.

"Obtain military records. Commands to burn a village should be recorded somewhere. Unless their recordkeeping was horrible." Ivy was the first to suggest the obvious.

"How do we do that? None of us can read, so if we do, it'll be with the help of the elves. And I predict the records will be kept in the main military installations, which were magically protected. Sending beetles there was unfeasible as well. The beetles won't be able to beat the high-level individuals in these installations."

"Ask?" Dimitree's views were more...direct.

"How, and who? We have no allies in Salah."

"The New Freekans were formerly from Salah. They must have allies. They were all migrants, after all. Perhaps they even know the structure of the army and bureaucracy inside out," Ivy responded; she did know their background quite well.

"If so, would they not be able to know who would have ordered such an action?"

"The fact that they don't means it's not common knowledge."

Feeling like I was getting stonewalled, I spoke to Jura again. Perhaps he had some ideas about the ways to proceed.

Jura mused, "I have an idea. Let's just ask Salah to surrender the officer responsible for the burning. We are an independent nation now, and if they see why we're not exactly favorable to them, they will appreciate that this is something they can do to repair that relationship."

Did his [diplomat] levels make him think of such an idea?

"Don't worry about it. Let me handle it. We will send out the request, TreeTree. I've been wanting to give the New Freeka High Council a jolt for some time."

YEAR 79 MONTH 10

The request came from the Valtrian Order, directly from the Counsel. The letter, with the Valtrian Order's official seal, went out to Salah's envoys and then to their king.

The letter, which was written with unnecessary legalese and noblesse verbose, could be roughly summarized to:

Dear King of Salah,

On year so-and-so, one rogue platoon of the Salah's army murdered the villagers of Freeka and set the entire village on fire. We humbly request for the assistance of the Salah Kingdom to investigate this gruesome slaughter and turn those responsible over to New Freeka, such that these criminals may face justice for the murder.

Jura, Counsel
Laufen, Vice Counsel

Signed and marked with their personal seal, along with the Valtrian Order's.

The informal networks were abuzz with chatter, trying to figure out what this letter really meant.

How many people knew of the burning and slaughter of Freeka? Certainly not many, evidenced by the sheer cluelessness displayed by so many.

With so many deaths in the world, such things were just a footnote, not worth a mention. Why should a village be any different?

Why did the Order bring this up? Was this request really something to remediate an offense of the past? Was the Order testing Salah's resolve and sincerity for peace? Or would Salah's refusal to assist be the precursor of future war?

It was the task of various envoys and diplomats to sieve out the true intent behind a request, to separate fact from propaganda.

Even among the councilors of New Freeka, there was a whole lot of guessing and subtle questions, trying to figure out what Jura and Laufen wanted. Laufen just shook her head, smiled, and said, "Oh, please redirect any of your questions to Jura."

Jura himself just smiled as he responded to the questions from the other councilors. "It's something close to our hearts. We lost so many friends and family then. With justice served, we can then face the dead with peace of mind."

―――

Anyway, I left that aside for now. Justice should be precise, after all.

I turned to my five new recruits, the five girls, a coincidence, I swear. I gave them a special title, the Valthorn Initiates because they would be the thorns. It was kind of inspired by the old saying, "rose among the thorns," only these roses were going to be the thorns. A part of me felt like I had unintentionally made this into an equivalent to those game of training little shipgirls.

Anyway, I was digressing. Their training was…slow. Firstly,

these girls had a lot on their minds, as they had to get used to me speaking to them every now and then.

The dreams via [Dream Tutor] that I had been giving them also made them a bit unsettled, even though it was just dreams made from [essences of sword] or [essences of spear], regular common essences that I frequently collected from my [essence generators], or from [soul harvesters] and [memory collection] of the dead. It seemed these five, they saw different things despite getting the same kind of essences, and their 'trainers' were somebody they didn't know. The dreams' lengths were also different; one girl said it felt like she'd been practicing for hours. Another said hers felt like just minutes of talking.

That was the routine. They were all excited, and eager, wholeheartedly embracing the change, but it still took some time to get used to it, and their young bodies couldn't take the sudden change, even with my biopods feeding them nutrients. The extent of the workouts and education pretty much overwhelmed them.

Even stepping into the biopods was scary, their first time dipping usually accompanied with struggling against the vines and feelers.

So, slow progress it was. Maybe it took a while, like a small sapling. I couldn't rush their growth. Strength came from true understanding and a strong foundation. It was like planting. The amount of nutrients, sunlight, and water must be just right, else you would kill the plant.

So maybe I needed to adjust my expectations.

YEAR 79 MONTH 11

A group of druids recently applied to New Freeka, and they wanted to open a Druid's House in the town. From what I understood, they were invited by the councilors, perhaps in an attempt to use the druids to counter my presence.

Indeed, using the druids' power over nature was a good strategy. If I were faced with a Tree Monster, I would find ways to weaken the opponent or find a hard weakness.

But it'd been a long time since I faced a druid, and my levels were much higher now. So I really looked forward to my future interaction with druids. I too wanted to know where I stood.

The elves once spoke of a reincarnated hero, Roana, who controlled tree spirits and nature. I wondered whether I would bend to her will, if a hero like that came around. These druids, they would be a fascinating entry-level test case.

"Wouldn't that mean druids were using some kind of mind control on trees?" Alexis wondered aloud. "I didn't think of it before, but it is a kind of mind control, isn't it? The taming of beasts by a beastmaster is similarly a kind of mind control if beasts are sentient, intelligent creatures."

"Well, I wouldn't know, but they can try using it on you, since your physical body is that of biolab, which is a tree. Then you can be a test subject, and we can find out exactly how it works."

"Eek. You were right, they might! They totally could." Alexis gasped, putting her hands to her spiritual face. "I need to gain more levels!"

I suspected I would have some resistance to such mind control or tree control, perhaps as a function of my levels. I would think mind control had a level modifier.

Ah well, still, I let the druids settle in and ordered both Ivy and Trevor to keep watch and to watch each other. My fear was that they may notice Ivy or Trevor's presence and then attempt to control them instead. These two were of a lower level than me, so I would think the chances of druid skills working would be higher.

Other than that, Meela's hotel seemed to be doing okay. She'd gotten customers, and she was spending money on decorations and materials. A few of her hired treefolks acted as her runners, doing all the buying and collecting for her. I thought she mentioned she planned to add an extra wing to her lodge.

Then there was the Salah issue.

Salah Kingdom responded with a 'holding' letter, saying they would look into the matter and provide an update when they had more info. Essentially, it was the diplomatic equivalent of 'I have no idea what you are talking about so I need time to find out.'

Which was fine. I doubted people remembered things like that, especially so far away, so I focused on gathering more intelligence on the Salah Kingdom. I too needed to know a bit more about Salah, its people, its structure, and its defenses should I choose to attack them.

[Inspection], as a skill, didn't seem to reveal much of the enchanted tiles and roads, other than they had been enchanted. It seemed it was more tailored to monsters, so perhaps I would need either a higher tier of inspection or a more specialized inspection skill to discern the true nature of these roads.

Stumped, I turned to experimentation. I found one of these enchanted roads in a quiet, less-traveled part of the capitol, far from the city itself, where I could place a few subsidiary trees near the road.

And I did my experiments on the road. No matter how I tried to make something grow on these tiles or rocks, the plants just wouldn't grow.

I then attacked it with my roots, and it was much, much tougher than any regular rock. It took a few hits, then it started to crack and break.

So, conclusion one: it was resistant to most kinds of attack, but not indestructible. Either that or these roads had some kind of plant-source damage reduction.

I would like to meet the person who built all these roads and structures.

"Perhaps we could talk to the locals in New Freeka. I believe one of Yvon's confidantes was a builder, of the magical kind." Ah yes, the group that used magic to build houses, perhaps they might know a bit more about these kinds of enchanted roads. Maybe all these builders knew one another, like some kind of builder's guild? Or, perhaps, contractor's association?

"Must be my luck, Counsel Jura," one of Yvon's followers said, now also one of the councilors of New Freeka. "So to what do I owe the honor of being before the few true natives of the valley?"

Jura grinned and tapped on the chair. "Ah, nothing too serious. I asked for you to borrow some of your...knowledge. I've got some questions. Tell me about...construction-related skills and abilities."

The room was empty save for the two of them, both seated on a chair. Jura had a pot of tea made from my younger, tender leaves. It was still steaming; there was a small firestone under it, used to keep food warm. The councilor moved, adjusted his body slightly. He was a man of average height, but his build was bulky, stoic. Since his election to the council, he'd changed a builder's attire for something more formal.

"How strange. May I know why?" The councilor leaned forward; he didn't touch the tea.

"I'm thinking of building a new building, so I thought I'd ask an expert on what kind of crazy skills would a builder have. It would help me in assessing what I can build and how long it takes. So tell me about the great builders of our world."

The councilor paused, smiled a little to himself, then shook his head. "Surely there was more to it, Counsel. Well, there were no builder-heroes."

Jura sipped his tea. "Oh, that's something I didn't realize. I thought there were heroes from almost all the classes. But that's another conversation. I want to know about builder type job classes today."

"Firstly, there were all kinds of builder-related job classes. There were the entry-level versions of the jobs, such as the draftspersons and the regular workman, and there were the stronger variants, the architects, the foreman, the master-builders. Their passives run the gamut from weak to incredible. A true master-builder can build a house out of hay that can withstand a typhoon, a house out of wood that will never rot or spoil, a wall that can withstand a dragon's flame, and roads that can speed up the domains trade."

"Am I right to assume the materials were the same, or do these master-builders use their skills to change the materials?"

"Yes, and no. A builder, a farmer, a blacksmith, they all have skills, and these skills influence the materials they work with, and it persists until the materials are unmade. A plank of wood processed by a master-builder can be many times stronger than one made by a regular builder, just like a blacksmith can work with metal to make a sword multiple times stronger than the work of a regular apprentice."

"But then what happens when the maker dies? Do these skills disappear?"

"You really were a warrior, Counsel Jura. It was basic knowledge that non-combat skills have longevity. The effect of a non-combat skill persists longer than the burst-one-off nature of active, combat skills. The great castles of yore, made by the master artisans, the effects of their skills on the shine of their walls, the foundations and strength of their ramparts, they remain till this day, with little decay, even after the deaths of their makers."

Jura rubbed his chin and hair, looking a little embarrassed that the councilor called him out on his cluelessness on such things. "True, else they wouldn't be handing down enchanted artifacts and heirlooms. Ah, but let's say I want to know about roads and walls. What kind of skills have you seen that work on walls and roads?"

"Thinking about building walls around the Order, Counsel Jura? Where do I start? Think about it: there are kings with powers to create nigh-impervious, indestructible fortresses and walls; kings who amplify the effect of roads on travel in their domain; or mages who can enchant walls with defensive buffs. Highway markers that speed up travel on those who travel along them…"

"Ah, fine. I'm asking about builders?"

"We would have many kinds. Most builders worthy of building anything more than a wooden house would gain some variant of the skills [Enduring construct] or [Low-maintenance structures] so that they last longer and need less upkeep and repairs. I would think walls and roads would gain the effects of such skills."

"Are there dedicated roadbuilders in the world? What kind of skills would they have?"

"Yes, of course there are. The world's skills were as vast as the stars in the sky, but…I don't know their skills. I'm a magic-augmented builder, I construct things using earth magic, and sadly I have not met a true roadbuilder."

And, well, that was all the councilor was willing to share and Alexis had a postmortem.

"A metaphor I would use was that these passive skills are like… paint. They stay on the object until they are removed." Well, Alexis was willing to share her views on such things. "Usually, the benefits of such skills are that they are close to perpetual, they usually can interact and stack with other such 'passive' skills, and the drawbacks are that they're not that strong."

"So, what's your take on what's happening? Why do the roads resist me?"

"You're a pest, I suppose. I doubt the road knows how to differentiate between a tree and a weed, so it just repels all of them. Have you seen roads destroyed by roots that grow underneath them? Roots destroy buildings and roads, so I would expect any good builder would want to prevent his things from getting destroyed."

"Fine, let's say what you're saying was true. Then how about New Freeka? Why don't the roads that were built now, in this area, 'reject me,' if such passives are so common?"

"Maybe because you're part of the native ecology, so the buildings built here are used to your overarching influence and do not regard you as an invader. Or maybe your main body is so overwhelmingly powerful in this area that such skills don't work in close vicinity to you. Or maybe you have some kind of ability invalidating all these skills. Frankly, it could be a million things."

"I learned nothing from that conversation."

Alexis chuckled. "I am glad to have wasted your time."

Ah, well. I turned my attention to the herbal varieties found in Salah. There were little spots of greenery throughout the city. The issue was clearly getting there because of all the roads and buildings that impeded my progress.

The Royal Grove was actually rather boring, other than being 'enchanted.' The herb varieties were mostly common, but they were more 'effective.' There was some herbalists and druids that regularly tended to the grove, mostly just healing sick trees and stuff like that.

So, back to New Freeka.

YEAR 79 MONTH 12

New Freeka's population was close to sixty thousand. There had been a wave of new migrants, apparently coming from the north.

There was another conflict emerging there, between two countries, and it was a plain old war, apparently over a lady. Turned out princes from both countries fell in love with the same lady, and now they were fighting some kind of war over her. I mean, seriously. Couldn't they just have a duel or something?

And it was winter! Why'd they pick winter to fight a war anyway?

"It's warmer in their part of the world, a strong warm current and breeze keeps their two shore countries warm, so their winters...pretty much feel like fall. So they can still fight," one of my advisors explained.

Well, food supplies were doing well. The Order's 'rituals' for births and deaths were becoming something of a tradition, which made me happy because more deaths mean more essence for me to feed the six young girls that were now in my training regimen. According to data provided by Laufen, about two in every five deaths were now taking the Order's 'melt-in-a-pod' method of disposing the corpse. Of course, the actual name that went out to public was more...pleasant. Euphemisms, euphemisms.

The population boom came with its own challenges.

Clean water. Sewage. Public health.

Previously, the Council's workers dug wells and with some magical help and blacksmith tools made pulleys and pumps that brought out water from the ground. At sixty thousand, even with close to one hundred wells throughout the entire city, there were still long lines, and the water levels in the wells were running low, so newer wells had to be deeper.

And that exposed one huge flaw in choosing this valley as a spot for a town: water. Unlike a place with a large river, or a large lake, there were a few small streams through the valley, and unless the council was willing to dig really deep, providing clean water to sixty thousand was going to be a challenge.

The local builders constructed deeper and deeper wells and also larger, deeper latrine pits. Apparently, one of the ways poop and sewage was processed in this world was via magic, and strangely, the temples of the world usually played a big part in water and sewage.

One of the abilities the priesthoods and nuns learned was an ability called [Purify] and [Cleanse], which worked on people and also worked on sewage and water. So the city actually paid priests and nuns, or those with the relevant [cleanse] skills, to regularly 'process' the latrine pits.

The poop got converted, via magic, into regular dirt. Magic was amazing.

The process of cleansing the latrine needed to be done quite regularly, else the poop would start to contaminate the groundwater. Again, the priests then used [cleanse] on the wells to 'sanitize' the water.

So there really was a thing like [purified] and [cleansed] 'holy water.' I wondered whether they felt like a quack when they sold such things to regular citizens.

In larger cities, there were high-level [cleaners] or [mages] who could do similar functions or in some cases, meaning the wealthy, powerful cities, use artifacts that processed or decomposed sewers. In certain elven cities, their poop was usually processed by a kind of poop-eating worm, which, apparently, enjoyed poop and pee as its main food source. Centaurs and lizardmen tribes tended to spray a kind of 'yeast' or 'powder' that converted the poop and pee into fertilizer, which led to an odd behavior of them having multiple outhouses in their farms, but strangely, these centaurs here didn't have such habits.

Treefolk didn't have the issue of poop or peeing; it seemed their bodily wastes just...evaporated from their body or got discharged via their legs into the earth.

The fact that magic and magical monsters existed gave a wide range of options on how to process such issues. I wondered how large dragons dealt with their poop. And did they poop midair like birds did?

Anyway, enough of my constant off-tangent ponderings. Population consumed resources and also produced waste, and both needed to be managed. Assimilating this growth and managing it as part of the valley's overall population while balancing and caring for the health of the valley's florae was my personal duty as the Tree Guardian of the valley.

With Trevor's constant replenishment of the valley's resources and my powers of growth, the valley's treecount was growing steadily. Lately, though, the growth rate was slowing again, partly because of consumption from a larger population.

I had [Timber farms], which the Valtrian Order sold to the local businesses, who then made furniture and built houses and other products. Increasingly, demand was starting to catch up to supply. The speed in which the timber grew was easily ten times, maybe more, than that of a regular tree, as a regular seedling reached maturity within two months, yet there was a size limit to the farm.

The idea of stone beds or stone furniture was unappealing to the citizens; even centaurs preferred wooden furniture to stone. Perhaps there was something unappealing about purely stone homes. Centaurs, for example, cultivated small patches of a certain grass, which, when dried, were woven into rugs and paddings, for them to lie on, and these woven rugs and carpets were a must-have for any centaur dwelling.

At first, I was unaware of this, but it seemed as New Freeka's 'economy' and 'safety' stabilized, the centaurs started yearning for little luxuries, and mixed cotton rugs and carpets started to proliferate. Which meant a market for the [Cotton]. Sadly, Laufen said it was a break-even business, as the selling price barely covered the cost of processing and paying workers to work on the cotton, and then making the carpets. I thought this cotton business needed industrialization.

There was probably a better way to process the cotton, and I vaguely recalled studies and visits to the textile museum. So even though a machine like that must exist, and should exist, I was no master of mechanical objects.

So I couldn't recreate it. Maybe there was some magical solution someday.

Oh, yes, where was I?

Poop. And water.

The reason I was also rambling about poop was some of the ordinary, normal trees felt sick. My main tree, roots, and subsidiary trees were almost immune, due to the effects of my skill, [rhizofiltration], so it didn't absorb all the other shit, literally, that got dumped into the ground that contaminated the groundwater.

But my fellow normal trees, normal as they may be, were sick! And sick trees grew slower. And some may eventually die. That was bad.

Dead trees were a big no no. I felt for my fellow trees.

YEAR 80 MONTH 1

With data from the root sensors on subsidiary trees spread out throughout the valley and also the city area, Trevor helped to map out an overlay indicating the pollution problem.

I firstly needed to know how bad the poop situation was.

The source was, of course, the city.

There were multiple latrine pits, which the frequency of sanitization by those responsible had been a bit lacking. The priests and workers were supposed to cleanse the pits once every three days, but it was an incredibly unpleasant task, so they only did it once every two weeks.

That meant some of the sewage accumulated, and the extra period for it to stew in the pit meant quite a bit managed to contaminate the ground. Furthermore, the effectiveness of the [cleanse] spell was range-limited, so it didn't cure the sewage accumulated deeper in those pits.

The first issue was, like I said, the priests were not doing their jobs. They generally viewed this duty as demeaning for these self-proclaimed servants of god, to literally [cleanse] the filth of others. Even the priests, those in the Order's employ, abhorred the task.

"I hate that part of the job," a priest would routinely say.

So usually the most junior of priests, those who possessed the skill, would be sent on the toilet duty.

That meant the strength of the [cleanse] skills were poor because skills scaled with levels, and because of how deep and massive the latrines were, to accommodate sixty thousand citizens, the skills of these low-level [cleanse] just wouldn't do. At most, it just created a superficial clean and dry layer on top of the rest of the sewage, deluding the priests that the job was done.

But I had no cleaning skills myself, even if I did have the ability to filter such toxins and other unfavorables out.

"Huh, the most senior priests on toilet duty? No, no amount of money will make that happen. We were servants of god, not the city's sewage cleaners. The fact that we send our most junior priests to do it was good enough!"

The task was seen as dirty, disgusting, and demeaning. Money wouldn't fix it.

"Can we import the worms? Or the cleaning artifacts?"

"Artifacts were ridiculously expensive. As for the worms, I will reach out to the Elven kingdoms whether they were for sale. Transporting those worms will need special arrangements, as they rarely survive outside their sewage environment." Jura was rather amused by the sanitation issue; he didn't really feel it. In fact, most of the citizens were not even aware of the contamination of the groundwater, since those things reached deep, not floated up above.

Trevor's map of subterranean water flow indicated the groundwater flowed toward the valley, so as the latrine pits tended to be close to the forest's edge, the New Freekans were lucky that their own drinking water was clean.

Perhaps if somehow it stunk up the entirety of the town, then it would make them realize the gravity of the situation. Or maybe I should somehow reverse the flow of groundwater such that their wells got contaminated with poopwater?

Ah, maybe I shouldn't be so nasty.

Solutions, solutions. Relying on the priests to constantly use [cleanse] on poop and sewage was not exactly what I considered a scalable and reliable solution. These priests were going to hold the skill as some kind of 'ransom,' eventually, if they discovered what it meant to the regular trees. And the idea of having an army of priests going around town sanitizing all the latrine pits in a big city just felt...lame.

So I needed some kind of natural solution, something I could manage. Something I could 'create.'

"Jura, are you familiar with plants that survive in sewers or other such wastelands?"

"Uhmmm...no. But let me get the herbalist?"

"We do not have any plants that are capable of surviving in sewers," the herbalist responded to Jura's question. "Most plants have a natural state, and while these differ slightly, I am not aware of any plants that survive entirely in sewers. We do have plants that can somewhat tolerate sewer waters, though."

Hmmm. How about algae? Fungi? There must have been something that lived in sewers. I recalled trees destroying sewer pipes back home because the roots were drawn to them, so the trees must have some tolerance for wastewater.

I found it strange that the normal trees here were unable to process the sewage. They were native, they should have been adapted to native waste from the native population. Was it because the type of toxins or minerals in the sewage?

"What do large cities do with their waste?"

"Other than what I told you, no clue. Honestly, sewers are not something I pay attention to, and our village was so small a few pits were sufficient." Jura shrugged. He was really quite amused by my recent fascination and questions around waste, and he didn't really get my frustration with dying trees. Trees died all the time; not all of them could be healed.

Which was true.

But I was a tree, and it offended me that I let a fellow tree die from something as stupid as sewage intolerance.

"Are you even sure it's sewage?" Alexis shrugged. "Not a bug? Or sickness?"

And that was how I ordered the beetles to gather multiple wastewater samples from all the different latrine pits.

[**New beetle species unlocked**. *Dungbeetle*]

"No, fuck you, TreeTree. I am not analyzing poop." Alexis absolutely resisted letting the poop anywhere near her. "I am. Not. Touching. Poop."

"TreeTree, why were the beetles carrying poop?" the elves asked.

Analysis, duh.

"Can the poop not drip everywhere in the hideout?"

Uh.

Despite much resistance, I eventually got the poop into the biolabs for analysis. I did feel disgusted, but only mildly. I thought saving the rest of the trees to be a far larger and more important goal.

I doubted my feelers and vines felt a thing when they prodded and dug into the poop. Well, they did feel kinda moist and sticky.

But it was just poop. I was pretty sure the dirt all around me was poop some point in its long, ever-changing lives.

[Testing in progress]

I supposed feces and poop were considered biological matter as the biolabs ran through a range of tests. It took some time to actually know what was happening since there were so many tests to run for so many different samples.

I needed a 'control' group.

"You want our poop now?" Jura, Laufen, and the elves were all appalled by my request.

"Yes. Fresh samples. Just to measure change in fecal composition versus that of the latrine. All of you are healthy, clearly, so your fecal matter should be, too."

"Uh...how do we give it to you? Poop inside those pods?"

Hmm. The pods weren't meant for pooping.

*[**Biolab upgraded**. Biolab now has multiple extra rooms, functioning as a 'toilet,' 'bathroom,' and others for collection and harvesting of biological wastes.]*

"Well, you poop in this place that looks kind of like an outhouse, and the biolab will do the rest."

"Ewww." The elves were generally quite disgusted, but still, they eventually did proceed to do their business in the special poophouse designed for collection of their poop.

"Why are you so disgusted? Don't some societies use cow manure as fertilizer?"

"Uh...it's still poop."

Anyway, poop or not, the tests must go on.

And speaking of fertilizer, would minotaur poop be fertilizer, too? Since they were part cow? Or did I need some kind of bacteria to degrade the poop first? Had I seen a minotaur?

Tests. We needed more tests. The culprit of what exactly in poop that caused the trees to feel sick was still unclear. Could it be some kind of disease transmitted via poop? Was it some kind of metal? Some kind of mineral, or some kind of bug?

I needed to get to the root of the problem.

So, more tests. One of the other things I started Alexis on, since she refused to look at poop, was to look at the filtering nature of roots instead.

My body, due to [rhizofiltration] that I learned long ago, was able to filter out all these bad things, whatever they were.

There should have been some membrane-like structure to the roots, either that or the skill created some kind of filtering/extracting effect.

If I could do it, maybe there was some way to filter the poop and ring-fence the latrine pits such that their contamination was contained, and perhaps in the future I would find some ways to convert the waste into something more usable, like fertilizer.

As of now, the contamination was spreading, ongoing, as people continued to poop and pee every day, so the first step was, of course, containment. The source of these pollutants needed to be restricted.

[Research status:]
*[**Roots** - Volcanic mineral processing - stage 1 - completed]*
*[**Tree-lab varieties** - stage 1 - completed]*
*[**Magically attuned materials Stage 1** - completed]*
*[**Beetle** - anti-magma armors stage 4 - 17 months]*
*[**Material labs** - stage 1 - 6 months]*
*[**Magical sensors** - 6 months]*
*[**Normal Tree** - Root filters stage 1 - 6 months]*

YEAR 80 MONTH 2

"Did somebody plant these trees around all the outhouses? It makes it feel like I'm doing my business out in the jungle or something."

"Must be the druids."

"I think it's the tree spirit. He's a bit fond of meddling, after all."

"It's kinda creepy if you say it that way. Is the tree spirit watching us take a shit?"

"Uh…I doubt tree spirits are interested in us taking our shits, though. I mean, only perverts like that kind of stuff, and we aren't exactly the most attractive old men around."

"It's a fetish for some people? A fetish for trees?"

"Ewww."

"Ewww."

Anyway, I had to implement a stopgap measure. I couldn't get the priests to do their jobs, and I wasn't inclined to threaten them because it revealed a weakness about me.

So I decided to surround most of the larger latrine pits and outhouses in New Freeka with [subsidiary trees] and use my roots to then form a subterranean wall to block the fecal matter from leaking into the wider valley's groundwater.

I couldn't process the shit, but I had to deal with the shit. So blocking the shit was my temporary measure. The findings from my first round of analysis of the collected samples revealed that there was no particular culprit.

The problem was, well, there was just a whole damn load of shit. There was a lot of minerals that were generally not well accepted by trees, and there was also a whole mix of fungi, bacteria, and other stuff, all of which the normal trees normally could tolerate in small quantities.

Small quantities. Normally.

It wasn't a result I wanted.

"Well, I suppose you could have some kind of waste treatment plant before it's discharged? Like, you know, split the sewage into components and treat them separately? I can't seem to recall the water treatment process, though..." Alexis rubbed her head.

"Never mind, focus on researching the roots. That's probably going to help minimize the damage."

I was guessing it was going to be something like filtering, sedimentation, adding chemicals to kill bacteria or take out certain types of metals. I also couldn't remember the details, it'd been so many years since school, and honestly, I wished I could google 'wastewater treatment' and find the answer. But then, even if I did, I'd have to find ways to develop actual skills or tools suitable for the growing city.

For now, the poop was contained by the roots of my subsidiary trees, and because there was just a whole load of poop, even my subsidiary tree's root filters occasionally failed and it absorbed some of the poop, and it made the subsidiary tree weak and sickly, which Trevor or myself had to step in and use some of our tree-healing powers.

Important lesson: skills could fail.

And because the roots kind of stopped the poop from escaping the pits, the pits got filled up faster, so the city had to build more of these pits.

Ugh.

Not. Sustainable. They couldn't constantly be digging new pits all the time.

I needed to figure out a way to decompose the poop.

"You could maybe, erm...separate their components? Then store them separately? I think some plants can consume or extract certain kinds of elements in the wastewater sludge."

Thus I ordered some beetles to bring back some of the trees near the sewers of on the outskirts of Salah. Salah's got a vast network of underground sewers, some of which piped their waste for disposal somewhere further, far from the city.

There, the beetles brought back different types of plant samples, collected from near the sewer outlets and the sewers itself for my biolab's analysis.

I wondered whether I could make a plant able to eat poop.

Meanwhile...

"I-I want to drop out," one of the girls said. She was tired and frustrated, even if she was making progress. "It's too hard. So much fighting and so much studying. I-I can't. I can't do this."

"But what will you do, then?" another of the girls asked. "We don't get chances like this. We're just orphans..."

"Er..." The young girl didn't know. She only knew she didn't actually want it as much as she did.

Lausanne nodded. "It's intense. If you really want to drop out, please let Tree Spirit know. It's fairer for everyone, so that someone else who wants it can try it out. Let's not force yourself. I think now you know what you truly want."

The young girl cried and covered her face with her palms. She didn't know what to do, actually. Yvon sat next to her. "I spoke with the Tree Spirit. If you drop out, you will return to being a regular orphan, so you can still stay. But you will lose the benefits you have, like the stipends you get."

The girls got some pocket money for their participation. I

thought it was fairer that way, since this was like an apprenticeship or internship. I thought of it as being a reward for their hard work, since their routine was literally a whole lot of combat and studies, some eat, sleep, poop, and repeat. Rest days were few and far between, perhaps a day in a month.

Honestly, my expectations were not very high, but I wanted dedication and a display of effort from the girls. They needed to at least try.

"Are you sure?" Yvon was sort of their counselor. I thought she was probably suspicious of my activities and didn't trust my intentions, but because of that, she'd taken a personal interest in the girls and was now quite close to the girls, acting like their mother.

Or maybe Yvon was just bored.

"I-I don't know. This was so hard. My body hurts everywhere, and I feel overwhelmed. I'm tired. I thought being a warrior, a fighter would be nice, and I'll be those super cool adventurers who defeat monsters and all. I just didn't expect the work to be so...so... much. I don't even have much time to play anymore."

Yvon tapped her on her shoulder. "I understand. This program is rough. I told Tree Spirit as well that it's extremely intense, but he insists on it being this way."

The young girl sobbed. Her friends gave her a hug.

"If you are sure you want to drop out, we'll go and see the Tree Spirit."

She nodded.

The next day, I cancelled her familiar contract, and she lost her status as one of the Valthorn Initiates. I was down to four girls.

Though she cried, I thought she'd be happier just as a regular person.

Ah well. Not everyone made the cut.

This was a good thing. In the future batches, the girls would do some self-selection, and only those who truly wanted it would participate.

YEAR 80 MONTH 3

Salah had yet to provide an update on our request, though from the intel sources Jura had, it seemed they were discussing it in great detail.

According to the grapevine, it seemed that they wanted to find a scapegoat for the incident, someone related but junior that they could throw under the bus. If that really happened, I would be very disappointed, but for now, more intel needed to be gathered.

After that string of conversations with the elves, I felt a bit magnanimous. I wondered whether I should look past this incident, and maybe what I did next should not be out of vengeance.

But I should still send a message that such actions had consequences. Even if the consequence was ten years later.

"Please. Take care of my children and my wife. Protect them from the demons...and these monsters, too."

I recalled feeling angry, these humans, killing the elves, when there were demons out there, something as scary and overwhelmingly powerful like a demon king, and yet the Freeka villagers all slaughtered and burned alive.

If I descended into a war with the Salah again, would I be doing what they did to me? Fighting amongst ourselves while a demon threat awaited?

It wasn't going to be long. This month, I began to feel strange fluctuations in the star manas, and they made my leaves tingle. It was a familiar feeling, like that strange dream I had before the previous demon king. I could feel it, the looming presence of the demons.

The first of the many demonic rifts would soon open.

YEAR 80 MONTH 4

I had my first material lab. It 'deconstructed' what I inserted into its underlying components, and the level of deconstruction was proportional to the energy supply and the level of the material lab.

I inserted a wooden plank.

First, it stripped any skills out of it, and there were many skills. They appeared as little blobs of light, and most of these 'skills' appeared as 'unidentified.' I knew the blobs represented skills because one of those blobs was actually readable [Fine-cut wood], and so I drew the conclusion that all the blobs were skills. Besides, what else could those formless blobs be?

After that, what was left was raw, 'unskilled' wood in the shape of an ordinary plank. The lab's energies slowly broke the wood apart, strand by strand, strip by strip. The plank peeled off, layer by layer, along the grooves of the plank.

Then the separated layers, or strips, got further broken down into smaller pieces, almost little specks. After that, it split up into its constituent components, like bubbles of air, blobs of water, blobs of...unidentified things; it appeared like a piece of plank was flash-dried and drained of all fluids and air bubbles, and then one of the last components was...mana? Or maybe that life-force thing that the souls generated.

First revelation of the day, unlike our world, mana actually existed as part of things, even things as simple as wood. Maybe mana replaced one of the primary fundamental forces? Or did it become an additional fundamental force?

Somehow, I thought I should've known this.

Anyway, the remaining strips of dried, airless, manaless specks could be further broken down. But I needed material labs of a higher level...

"Well, do you want to further develop materials labs or work toward magic labs?" Alexis asked.

"I don't know. It's kind of cool that it breaks things down to these components. And actually, I can use it to analyze the poop samples."

"Ugh." Alexis rolled her eyes at the mention of poop, and she floated away, back to doing her own thing. She was busy anyway.

The materials lab took the form of a single tree outside my inner circle of subsidiary trees, its appearance like any other, but its internal structure contained multiple little bubbles that stored the separated materials. It was power intensive, draining quite a bit of energy from the normal trees, with each 'separation' process. I supposed it was kind of like those labs where they spun stuff until they split apart.

Anyway, back to the poop samples.

I used the materials lab to test out the poop samples, and... well, the first thing that surprised me was that there were also some blobs of skills. Unidentified, of course, but seriously, who used skills on their poop? Either that, or it was...some kind of passive that got applied? Rhetorical question.

Moving on, I ran the tests through few more different samples of poop, and then seriously, quite a few of them had skills. All unidentified. At this point, I was wondering whether it was unidentified because I didn't know them or whether because the amount of it was so small that I couldn't tell it apart. Maybe I couldn't identify it because the quantity of skill was too small?

The poop split apart to more components, like water, air, and the type of 'materials' that made up the poop...and also...mana? Oh great. There was mana in poop, too.

Now that the poop had been drained and dried, it started to break apart and easily separate into different kinds of metals without requiring much energy. What was left was a collection of mostly unfamiliar metals and some of the usual iron, copper, and stuff.

Was this normal?

Deciding that I probably needed a bit more of each type of metal to be identified, I broke down more of the poop, including some fresh samples from the elves, and I got about a handful of each 'unidentified' metal type, at different ratios.

Next, I asked Jura for any professionals who might be able to assist on such samples.

"I'll probably need help identifying these metals..." There were about thirty small plates of different metal types on top of Jura's desk, all from splitting up the poop samples.

A blacksmith and a merchant came along. It was rather easy for Jura to ask for help. These people were here to curry favor anyway, and he was the counsel, so he could give them big deals someday.

The two quickly went through the samples, easily identifying them. All of them were just some kind of local metal mineral, our world's equivalent of sand, or tin, or iron, and stuff like that. This world's metal types didn't exactly match ours, since they did have iron-like things that were stronger and also some that were weaker. Variants, but different metal types.

Maybe they were alloys?

"Metals and elements in this world exist in a spectrum, rather than distinct types in my world...or I think they have a larger, more granular version of the periodic table." Alexis was nerding out; she was paying attention to the descriptions given by the merchants and smiths. "You should buy some books, then I can explain this better."

"You can read?"

"Uh. Yeah? Why wouldn't I know how to read?" Wait. Did I know she could read? "Ask the merchant whether anyone published any guide or summary on the metals and minerals of the world."

I placed an order for three different tomes on materials and resources found in the world. I wouldn't want to make basic research from scratch; there should be some body of knowledge already in tomes and books.

Back to the poop analysis, that material breakdown of knowing what the metals were kind of did...nothing? Though the merchants were able to identify the metals, it still didn't give me an idea whether those metals were harmful or beneficial to the plants, since their knowledge was more of use for trade and metal-working. Also, I couldn't rule out that there was most likely an 'optimal' level of each metal, and exceeding that would result in some kind of poisoning, and a deficiency may result in stunted growth and other kinds of problems.

So, there was to be more studies. More tests. I ordered the beetles to take samples of the dirt throughout the valley, around healthy trees, and around sick trees, to compare the composition of the dirt in the ground. Maybe there was some minerals appearing in different ratios that may lead to something more conclusive.

"Frustrating, isn't it? There was no skill that just tells you what's wrong, other than something's wrong."

"On the contrary, I feel happy that at least I need to use my head. And because of it, I'm getting you, Trevor, and Dimitree to run more tests."

"Ugh, I was just thinking wouldn't the druids know the answer?"

"Asking the druids..." Hmm...that was a good point. Why not use this chance to test out the druid's abilities?

So, with a bit of backhanded string-pulling, Jura managed to get the newly settled-in druids to pay a visit to a small patch of sick trees, somewhere on the edges of New Freeka. "What do you think? I was told something's wrong with these trees, but I can't tell what."

There was four of them; all of them looked middle-aged and were dressed in robes. They knelt over the ground. They all had a wooden staff of some kind.

"[Natural diagnosis]," a druid called out, and his wooden stick glowed. A spirit-like wisp appeared and entered the ground, and then after a while, it came back out.

"Hmmm...the wisp tells me there seems to be groundwater contamination. The ground's concentration of metals is all too high. Particularly Whitetin and Green Iron."

Oh I knew that— *Eh?!*

Another of the druids touched the ground, picked up a bit of dirt, and tasted it. I thought he used some kind of skill there, but I couldn't quite make out what it was. He looked a bit puzzled, and then he spit. "Agreed. Groundwater contamination, likely to be from the city. Counsel Jura, I suggest we move all the trees somewhere a bit further away."

"Can't you heal the trees or the ground?"

"We could, but usually the sickness will come back after about a month, unless you find a way to stop the groundwater contamination. The earth itself was contaminated due to exposure to the city. Healing the trees was just a temporary fix."

"What do you normally do in such cases?"

"We move the trees. There is usually no way of convincing the populace from changing how they live, just for the sake of some trees." The druid shrugged. "Trees are just...resources to most normal people."

Jura just nodded, looking around. The druids continued to touch a few of the normal trees.

"So...do you want us to move the trees, Counsel?"

"I don't think it's necessary," another druid spoke up. "They were just mildly sick. At least, they look better than they did a few months ago."

Jura shook his head. "Well, leave them here for the time being. We'll know if things get worse if they start dying. Thanks for your time, druids." Jura passed the four druids a bit of coin to thank them for their time.

As the druids and Jura walked back to New Freeka, one of them asked, "Council, may we have an audience with the Tree Spirit? I understand you speak to it often."

"Oh, why?"

"Erm...well, we are druids. We make it a point to meet and greet with the tree spirits of the land. Kinda comes with the job class."

"Ah...that was a druid thing, no?"

The druids grinned. "Yeah, kind of."

"I see. I'll have a word with the Tree Spirit."

In the meantime, I was still trying to process what I'd just see, i.e. the druids actually having skills able to diagnose the problem without the need for experimentation. And why did I not have a similar skill?

I had a few theories on that, but I wanted to see what they were up to.

As for the waste situation, it was sort of under control. With my subsidiary trees' roots acting as a barrier and filter, the sewage's leakage to the greater valley was now limited.

The druids clearly could identify the problem, though their solution was meh. Moving the trees was a solution, but I didn't like being moved, and I thought the trees wouldn't like it, either.

Personally, I thought it wasn't really an issue about meeting the druids, but I had to prepare, so I called Madeus and the Order's top guys back in for explanations on the druids. "I'll get straight to the point. I've met druids, many times in fact, but I don't know much about them. So let's start from the beginning. What do they do? What are their powers?"

The leaders stared at each other, and they shifted a little uncomfortably.

One of the priests went first. "They're tree-lovers. They tend to go around healing the land after the destruction left behind by the demon king. The druids are famous as the major supporter of the Restorers."

"They can summon trees and animals, use wood magic, earth magic, and water magic. They also usually have some animal companions as well." The captain was pretty much reciting the norm; it sounded like the usual myth around druids. Did the makers of this world somehow start off as dungeon masters?

"Anyone know the specifics of their jobs? Like...what do they do?"

"When I was a young child, a druid came and gave simple tips on farming. He tried to teach us the power to boost fertility and speed growth, but none of us picked it up..."

"Fine, clearly they have some ability to have earth and restoring powers. Were they like some kind of generic mage but with more of a focus on earth, wood, and water?" I asked.

Madeus nodded. "Close, though pure mages like me think druids are...erm...a bit of a hack, since druids mostly borrow powers from their surroundings and neglect their own physical and mental training. So druids pick their battlefields, such that they have more power and things to tap on, but that's kind of predictable."

"Okay, they have some kind of connection to the surroundings, too. Anyone know the history of druids?"

Everyone shook their heads. One of the priests tried to answer. "Some say they learned it from trees. Some say they learned it from treefolk."

"Fine, how many types and groups of druids were there? Who exactly were the druids in my valley?"

"They're from the far southeast, and they were under the Hutan, one of the three largest groups of druids. The other two were the Tarimba and the Mulfic. The three druidic councils are just...well, kind of like guilds. They are separate but work together for common goals, like restoring the land and focusing on training. The councils themselves are neutral, but their druids are free to work with any kingdom they want, though they generally speaking, most druids will avoid participating in the kingdom-wars."

Okay. "What do they want?"

"I don't know, really."

"I think they're just interested in you, Tree Spirit."

"What do they want with me?"

Everyone shook their heads.

"Trevor, Ivy, what've you got?"

After my discussion with them, I consented to the meeting a day later.

The next day, the four druids came without their apprentices and assistants. They came fully in their druid-ish attire, which included some kind of headwear that resembled an antler's horns, or a wolf headdress, elaborate and fancy carved woodstaffs, armor, and all the rings they could wear.

"Dressed for combat, druids?" Jura chuckled. He was dressed up for the purpose in armor, sword in hand.

"It was but a tradition of druids, to show our best to the tree spirits, especially when we face the tree spirit's true body," one of the druids said, but he looked nervous. My seeing eye noticed the subtle shaking in his hands.

The four stood in the inner circle of subsidiary trees before my main body. Jura was on one side, and I had Horns hidden in the corner, but I thought they could sense his presence.

They looked around, and they sweated. They whispered a bit, so softly, or perhaps a skill, that I couldn't make out what they were saying.

"State your business, druids," Jura prompted the guests to start.

The four bowed. "We are druids of Hutan, one of the many caretakers of the land and those who live on it, protectors of the forests and trees, and we...uh...humbly seek an audience with the great Tree Spirit of the valley, as we...come to seek an understanding of the needs and wishes of the valley and its true guardian."

"Flowery greeting." I chuckled. It sounded like they practiced it.

"They sound nervous," Alexis whispered into my mind.

"Their body was tense. They might be up to something," Ivy advised.

The four druid's eyes started to glow green, and I felt my defensive instincts kick in. "Tree Spirit, we come in seek of your name and hope to gain your blessing." Oh well, my roots were ready to strike at any time.

"Oh? I'm TreeTree." What kind of blessing?

The four druids glanced at each other. I thought they gulped, but I wasn't sure.

"Is that all you're here for, druids?" Jura sounded a bit amused.

"No...we'd like to acquire the Tree Spirit's blessing."

"Uh...what blessing?"

The four druids shared a glance. "Surely the Tree Spirit is testing us. We mean *the* blessing."

"Well, I've got no idea what you are talking about, so explain what this blessing is." I really didn't know what blessing meant, yet the four druids seemed to take the question a bit...negatively? They didn't seem particularly keen on answering the question.

One of the druids stepped forth; he looked to be the youngest, but his staff and headgear were the most flamboyant. "O' great Tree Spirit, the aspect which we ask, we will give our share in return. We offer our services, and that of the Druid Council of Hutan, which we represent. Our oath, as druids, as guardians, is to come to your aid should you ever find yourself in peril."

"Okay, but what's an aspect?" I wondered. "You introduced the concept of blessing and aspect. Can you explain?"

The first one knelt, his staff embedded in the ground. I felt a bit of magic swirl around me, it felt kind of pleasant, so I didn't feel a need to react. I later would realize this was when I made a mistake; I should have stopped them there and then.

The second druid stepped forth, standing next to the first. "O' great Tree Spirit, behold the oath of mortals and the true mother, a promise as ancient as the world. Give us your aspect, and we shall give you ours." Green glowing lines started appearing throughout his entire body, and then he knelt. The green glowing lines then flowed into the ground and formed a greenish glowing circle around the four druids. It still felt rather pleasant, and then I noticed I was starting to get a little sluggish, like I was drunk.

"Ivy, Trevor?" I tried to prompt my tree-minds to help, but then I noticed all of them, including Alexis, were in a daze. They were struggling to fight off whatever the druids were doing.

"What were you doing?" Jura and Horns noticed, so they quickly jumped in, attempting to break the ritual or spell, whatever it was. They were both unaffected by the effects of the ritual. Maybe because it only worked on trees?

They charged in, but a barrier of some kind repelled them, pushing both of them far back.

Despite feeling like I had too much alcohol, like a happy drunkard, I managed to collect my will together to activate my anti-magic aura, which sadly didn't really work on that barrier or the 'ritual' that they were using.

Still feeling dizzy, I pulled my mind together and used [Root Strike]s on the two druids. A glowing wooden shield magically appeared and blocked the root strike. The third druid stepped forth.

"O' great Tree Spirit, for the land requires us, requires all of us, all our worship and care." The third and fourth druid were both covered in green lines, and this time, I noticed that their familiars were out—two massive wolves, also covered in similar green lines, and a small wood-like bear appeared.

I was starting to shake off that drunken feeling, just a minute into the ritual, and so I unleashed more root strikes. One of the druids called up a large, half-wooden totem with a beetle-head, and it created a shield that blocked my root strikes. Each strike cracked the totem instead of the shield, and the totem needed about five to seven hits to crack.

Meanwhile, Jura was easily stronger than the two wolves, yet despite how much pain or damage they received, they just kept getting in his way, the two wolves really determined to stop Jura from interfering with the rituals. "DRUIDS! What is the meaning of this?!" he shouted while trying to shake off the two wolves.

The druids focused on their ritual.

Two minutes in.

"O' great tree spirit, we seek your power to complete our oath to the true mother." The fourth druid stepped forth and entered into a kneeling position as well, just as the earlier ones did. To protect the four druids, more familiars and creatures appeared, two tiger-like creatures, a cat, and an owl. They were all large, easily the size of an elephant, their bodies covered in the green lines, and their job was to block Horns from entering the circle.

The two wounded wolves now received backup from the tiger and the cat. Jura then unleashed some kind of sword-skill I hadn't seen before, and it instantly diced up all the four animals.

Yet the druid wasn't done. Another wooden staff appeared; this one had the head of a tortoise, and it glowed. The glow restored the diced-up animals and made them whole almost instantly.

Three minutes in.

The four druids were mumbling, singing some kind of hymn. Whatever ritual this was, it was really quite fast. They certainly prepared for this.

The totem cracked and broke apart as my [Root Strike]s landed a few hits.

TING.

It was then I got a notification.

[Four druids have each entered into a non-cancellable Druidic Aspect contract with you.]

*[**New familiar contract type obtained**: Druidic Aspect Contract.]*

[Druidic Aspect contracts allow druids to use lesser versions of the master's abilities.]

[You've received 8 Druid Class seeds.]

EH?

The glowing green lines on the four druids faded, and along with it, so did the barrier. The four kneeling druids stopped kneeling, and one of them almost jumped. "We did it!"

"It's not over yet. We still need to run!" The one druid clearly realized they were not out of the woods just yet, and so they quickly started to run.

You four are not going anywhere! A wall of roots appeared around them, and the four druids attempted to use their druid powers to interfere with the roots...but it didn't work. Not this time.

But the root strikes got to the familiars and skewered all of them.

Jura charged in, furious, and the druids attempted to dodge.

"Don't kill them yet," I mentally pinged him.

Oh, I was gonna interrogate them before I did.

Maybe I should torture them.

Hang them on trees in the city for attacking me.

The tip of Jura's sword closed in, now on one druid's neck. "Take a step, and I'll slit your throat."

"All you four wanted was this...druid-style familiar contract?" I asked aloud.

I thought I had a massive communication problem with the natives. Why did so many of my encounters with the natives end up like this? Why didn't the druids just ask nicely?

Seriously. I liked to think I was a reasonable person. I could be negotiated with!

Right?

Did I have a sticker somewhere that said, "Pushover. Just take whatever you want," written on me?

Jura, his sword still at the druid's neck, said, "Answer the Tree Spirit's question."

One of the druids nodded. "Yes. We made a contract for the Tree Spirit's power. It—"

Sigh.

"I honestly didn't know what you meant by blessing. Why didn't you just have a bit more patience and explain? All of you wanted this familiar contract-like thing? This was the blessing?"

One of the druids mumbled, "Yes?"

Ugh!

I was annoyed. Sad. *Angry*.

The roots formed a cage, trapping them all, thorns and barbs closing in. They attempted to use their druid powers to move the roots, but it wasn't working.

The four druids realized how much shit they were in. Immediately, all four of them knelt... No, they literally prostrated themselves on the ground. "Our sincerest apologies, O' great Tree Spirit! We...we thought we'd never get a chance to get this close to a Tree Spirit of your level of strength! We apologies for our...recklessness. Please, don't kill us!"

"What sort of stupid assumption is that?"

"Access to the true body of all the great tree spirits is heavily restricted and controlled, and here we are, four mid-ranked druids, getting the chance to meet a great tree spirit. We had to jump on the chance!" one of them started to justify what they did. His hands and head were on the ground, prostrating. "We thought we would never get a chance!"

"Fools!" If I could yell like a villain, or an evil angry emperor, I would. "Give me one good reason why I shouldn't kill all four of you right now."

The cage's roots closed in, the thorns on the roots making little cuts but nothing lethal.

I mean, how'd they think they'd get away with it? Come up to me, use this ritual-style spell, which gave them some level of protection, but did they think they could run away from me? Seriously. My roots spanned the valley. Even if they succeeded, I'd still be able to kill them.

They would have to knock me down for at least an hour or two for them to even give themselves a chance.

"We...we really mean no harm. We really mean what we said during the ritual. We will come to your aid should you need it, us and the Hutan."

Rubbish. I could protect myself as it was.

"We...we offer you our services. We'll revoke whatever arrangements we had with the councilors! Anything!"

"I still plan to kill all of you. Not good enough." One of the roots pretty much poked the druid's skin.

"I...*we*...can arrange the archdruids to provide you with unique items. We can arrange for you to be in contact with other spirits!"

Oh.

Other spirits.

The druids picked up on my pause. "There are other great tree spirits, too. We...the druid council of Hutan, our senior archdruid is in contact with the Guardian Tree of the Elf Capital, and also the Giant Lilypod City's Spirit. If we tell them about you, we can make some arrangements for the spirits to commune."

Well, meeting other similar tree spirits was something I always wanted.

"Please, please spare our lives and forgive us."

"I recall the four of you saying you were but ordinary druids. How can you arrange for us to meet with the other spirits?"

"We can't, but our archdruids can. I...I'll do my best—no, I'll give everything to arrange for it. Please, don't kill us."

Hmmm...fine.

"I suspend your punishment. On a few conditions!

"All of you will remain under house arrest in New Freeka and the valley. Make any attempt to leave, and all of you will die. If you need to, call for more druids to come assist you with all the necessary arrangements for me to communicate with the other tree spirits. If any of you try anything funny, all of you die. You all will remain in Freeka as my guarantee, until contact with the other spirits is established. If I don't have contact with the other tree spirits within a reasonable amount of time, of perhaps three years, all of you will die. And I want you to cooperate with me fully, and you will revoke your arrangements with the councilors. Double-cross me or attempt to use any kind of ritual or spell on me ever again, and I will not hesitate to put my roots through all of your skulls."

The four druids breathed a sigh of relief. "Certainly, certainly."

"Go."

After I let the druids go, I called for a meeting again. I wanted to know what was causing all these people to react so recklessly in front of me.

"Why did the meeting unfold in that manner?" I complained to the audience, the senior leaders of the Order, and when Jura explained how it went, Madeus pretty much facepalmed.

"To be fair, your main tree was really intimidating and scary. Even walking in the woods feels intimidating." The priest seemed able to relate to the feeling.

"Lausanne walked in and out without a problem."

"Lausanne's not a good example."

It was the Order's captain that offered a bit of honesty. "Counsel Jura, Lady Laufen, and Lausanne were natives, and so they were oblivious to its appearance, but for the rest of us, being before your main tree was like standing before a council of monsters. The presence of the various ghosts and wisps around your main body, the crackle of magic radiating from every root, branch, and leaf, how the surrounding trees feel like a prison… those strange trees around you, or that few trees that look like they've been burned and charred by thunder… Seeing it for the first time, I had nightmares. It's a place for monsters, for…gods. The druids probably panicked, overthought, and probably did what they thought they needed to do."

Oh.

Well, the layout of my main body was surrounded by the two

tree-minds and their [root-brain complex], the soul forge and all its extensions, the labs and pods, and then a ring of subsidiary trees, home to the beetles and spiders. The canopy was covered in webs and vines, and because of the effects of [soul forge: black], there were all the [soul collectors] floating around. And maybe Alexis's body as well, which appeared like a deformed, mutant tree.

"Fine. Next time, all meetings will be held here. Only those truly deemed worthy will face my main body." I guessed that was why access to a tree spirit's main body was restricted. If they were all similarly high level, their presence was going to be incredibly intimidating.

Now, I was really curious what the other tree spirits were like.

YEAR 80 MONTH 5

Back to the sewage issue. Containment by way of subsidiary tree worked, for now. A long-term solution was still in progress. Broadly, the idea we had was to use plants and algae to digest the sewage. I couldn't help but feel that I was a tree, so all solutions I developed must involve trees, kind of like how everything looked like a nail when I was a hammer.

I let Alexis take the lead on the plant samples, so she conducted research on all the different kinds of collected plant samples. The hope was to develop some kind of poop-processing hybrid plant. There were some plants with slight tolerance, so the idea was that tolerance level could be amplified such that the plants were able to obtain some kind of resistance.

There were promising results from algae and trees, but as with all research, more time and more samples were needed. Well, it was just time. I had plenty now.

Meanwhile, Trevor was in charge of the materials lab, with a focus on creating filtration systems, whereby the different 'elements' of the sewage was separated. Different plants had different tolerance of elements, and if there was no single sewer-eating miracle plant, then it'd have to be multiple plants working together. To do so, splitting the toxins was critical!

At the same time, Jura and the Order lobbied the Council to actually build a proper sewage system. The sewage system would then connect to a sewage tunnel, and that tunnel would move all the sewage to a designated spot out of town. That spot would be where my future 'sewage-processing' plant would be located.

Jura phrased the argument to the council using 'pride' as the main emotional hook. I admired that.

How could any self-respecting capital city still rely on primitive poopholes? Could you call yourself a developed nation? If New Freeka wanted to be respected as a kingdom, it had to have a proper sewer. Think about all the adventurers it would train, all the secret passageways it would create!

Sewers were a source of revenue! A source of jobs and experience for newbie adventurers! No more poopholes! More time for priests! Less regular [cleansing] needed because the poop could pile up out of town!

And so the Council debated the New Freeka Subterranean Sewage Project.

YEAR 80 MONTH 6

Demons.

News of their presence spread through the merchants, through communication spells, through artifacts.

Demons, humanoid demons. They were humanoid and yet had appendages that resembled weapons, some in the form of spears, some in the form of swords or axes. They also seemed to have particularly strange behaviors, building 'fortresses' and 'camps,' which had never done in recorded demon king history.

The news of the multiple rifts sent all the nations into high alert. When did the rifts appear so quickly?

Unlike all other occasions, the number of rifts were significantly more.

"TreeTree, you'll protect us, right?" Lausanne asked.

"Yes, Lausanne. But if you have to fight them, will you?"

Lausanne paused. She was eleven now, and it'd be another nine years before she was mature physically. If I could, I'd like her to stay out of it. "Yes. I'm not as strong as I'd like to be, but yes, I will protect my family and friends."

"Good." I didn't think she was ready yet. But sometimes, you had to throw them into the water.

YEAR 80 MONTH 7

"We need to talk about defenses." The council gathered in the large meeting room. Some of the councilors sighed. "First up, we need walls and more soldiers."

"We already have walls."

"Not enough. The news coming from those near the rifts was quite concerning." The meeting was led by Yvon's replacement, a guy called Arza. He'd been in the job for some time now, but really, he was just a very clever coordinator and spokesperson for his faction of councilors.

The other councilors looked at him quizzically. "Is there something that's on your mind, council leader Arza?" Council leader was an informal title, since all in the council were theoretically equal, but there was always one taking a chairing role.

"Yes. Demons. Our defenses are inadequate for demons, with their numbers and their strength. We need to urgently improve our defenses."

"Walls don't work against demons. They've got crazy numbers, and they've got those large monsters."

"Not this time. The news coming out from the nations facing the demons is that they are like..." Arza paused, and then he took a deep breath. "They are like us. They're using our tactics and strategies."

"That's absolutely crazy. Are we talking about demons?" one of the councilors said. "In recorded history, demons have never adopted our tactics."

Arza nodded. "I think it's crazy, too, but...but...it's our chance to bolster our military. We needed this excuse."

"You mean..."

Arza paused, then whispered, "We've lost the druids. We've got to find something else, and this is it."

"Ah. Then we must!" One of the councilors spoke.

"We'll take this excuse to raise taxes and train more soldiers and mages. We need the Order's money, and this is a good excuse to force them to collaborate. If they don't, we'll shame them publicly for being selfish!" The other councilors added fuel to the flame.

"I see!"

"But didn't... Wait. Why would that work, Council Leader Azra? The Order's strength is the Tree Spirit, no? The tiny militia and force they maintain are nothing compared to the amount of warbeetles they can deploy." One of the more skeptical councilors asked Arza.

"Indeed, so we have more to gain! We need to use this excuse to adjust the revenue rate that the Order gets, so here's the message I want everyone to spread. 'The Order's not spending enough on defense! We need the money to defend the city!' Arza emphasized to the group.

"AH! So the idea is to make the Order seem like they are spending money on frivolous things like collecting plants and animals, gifts for babies, and unnecessary rituals!"

One of the councilors objected, "I wouldn't talk about the rituals. They're quite popular among my electorate, and many find them meaningful. Stick to the collection of plants."

"Agree, wouldn't this move backfire?"

"Maybe, but we must be subtle about it then. First, we need to expose how the Order spends their tax money and then tie it to our defense needed. Show the people that they are not doing what they can to defend the city."

"Uh...they have beetles, Councilor Azra."

"I know, then we must explain to the people that beetles are not trustworthy! We need our own strength! The strength of our people! Inspire them not to rely on a secretive power, like a tree spirit. We don't even know whether it will protect us when it really matters or if it will only choose those it cares about!"

"Ahhhh!"

"Think about it. We embed a belief in our people that we must rely on our own mortal strength, with powers within our control, ideally, with us, the councilors in charge. We represent them, whereas the Tree Spirit is unelected, and it is a magical being, not mortal, not one of us! Now we suffer the whims of a magical creature! Where is our dignity?"

A murmur rippled around the councilors, mostly in agreement.

"So, we must have more walls, more soldiers, more mages. We may not be stronger than the army of beetles, but I'll be damned if we are beggars, begging for mercy and protection from a magical creature!"

"Our founding documents say they would protect us..."

"Myths! Tell the tale of when the great cities who suffered the wrath of dragons who no longer wanted to protect them, tell the tale of the city who fell when the sacred beast turned on the royal family!"

"Isn't the message of that story about doing good because the royal family was evil?"

"Doesn't matter! It's about self-reliance, strength! We are refugees, and if we fled Salah to be subservient to a magical beast, what good was that?"

"Councilor Azra, is this something your faction thought up?" a centaur councilor said, an independent in the sense that he was unaffiliated to either the Order or the independence faction. That was partly because his voting district also comprised the slopes of the valley where the 'rural' centaurs lived rather happily.

Azra paused. "Well, yes."

"I agree on the need to bolster the city's own strength with more soldiers. I also agree on the need for more defensive walls. Yet, among the centaurs, treefolk, and even the lizardmen, Aeon's presence is a reassuring force. So tone down the rhetoric. It will backfire on your faction's election chances."

"Hmph. We'll see about that. But more importantly, I'm glad to see you agree with our need to improve our own military prowess."

The centaur shrugged.

———

Meanwhile, the druids...

The [Druidic Aspect] familiar was clearly a double-edged sword for the druids. On one hand, they got to store about three to five percent of my power, depending on their own level, for their own use, but because of the link and how it was magically entangled with me, I could see them clearly, wherever they went in New Freeka, kind of like how Lausanne glowed like a lightbulb in my overview of the valley. In other words, I could observe them through the Aspect.

The Aspect stole their experience and mana, too. I did recall that the familiars took a portion of the experience, too, which was why I leveled up when the contracted warriors died, but in the Aspect's case, the ratio was even more skewed. I could also see their skills and also mark two skills of my choice as targeted for collection on death. Oddly, there was a time counter on those marked skills. I thought it meant it took some time to 'mark' the skills.

So much for 'blessing.' Were the other tree spirits also secretly taking skills from their believers? After all, how would they know that their blessing was actually not free? But if so, why did the tree spirits not give it freely?

[Aspect contracts were limited to Level divided by 10. You were allowed up to 13 Aspects.]

Ah, limited again. Just like familiars, which I could give out about 132, since I was level 132, or the [Possession of the devoted], which I could give five. I supposed there was a mana-maintenance cost to it, which was why these were limited.

The four druids just used up four valuable slots. But they were called druidic aspects, so only druids could use them?

[Druidic Aspects can be awarded to druids, herbalists, farmers, and gardeners (and variants). Can also be awarded to treefolks, with no job class requirements.]

Confusing! System, you need a massive cleanup!

Anyway, I did somewhat regret letting the druids go, and I realized I was not very good at making high-quality decisions when I was in a spot. The druids could read my interest in meeting the other spirits and managed to, therefore, save themselves.

So what do I need to do?

Being able to make good, high-quality decisions? That was something I needed to try to do, but if I failed, what should I do then?

"Honestly, I wanted to help you, but their spell made me feel so drowsy and weak that I couldn't."

Should I kill and drain the druids? Ah, well. I thought of looking, studying, and learning from them first, since I had them under my custody.

"Pods." The druids gulped. "Go in."

"Are...are you planning to drown us?"

"You were not making much progress on arranging the meeting. It's almost three months. *In.*"

"The archdruid was coming. He...he needed to assess the situation. Please don't do this!"

"*In.*"

The vines and roots pulled the druids inside, and all four of them were now in the biolab pods. They struggled a lot for adults, compared to my four girls, who were getting rather good and used to the biolab. One of them even said it was quite relaxing.

Under the scope, the druids' bodies were actually rather ordinary. They had a spring like any other, and a collection of stones around the lifespring, which were the skills and levels of the druid. What was quite unique were the animal head–shaped stones, which were the 'links' between the druids and their animal followers.

Then there was the Druidic Aspect. The Aspect took the form of a vine-like plant, it grew and made a space around the spring, and its vines and roots spread around the stones, growing into the gaps between them, like a well that was partly abandoned and now reclaimed by plants.

Some of the stones around the spring had more vines around them, but most of them just had little roots at the sides, like small climber plants.

The Aspect's main body, a large central flexible 'trunk,' was like a parasitic plant living on the wellspring of his soul. On the aspect's plant body, there were three large, gourd-shaped organs, and from a little prodding, it reads, "Aspect's storage organ. Stores energy from the main body."

Strange.

I thought back to Lausanne and Jura's souls. In Lausanne's case, the familiar appeared like a separate plant in the shape of a sunflower, growing at the side of the well, but it didn't have vines or feelers growing like crawlers on the well. Instead, her special familiar had a strange, swirling portal.

In Jura's case, the eidolon Bamboo didn't even appear as a plant in Jura's soulspring. Instead, there was something in the shape of a Bear Statue that had a small waterspout on its mouth, and it was located outside the Soulspring. It seemed the relationship of the druid's familiars would be similar to Bamboo, since they too appeared as statues or stones.

I would later discover, from the druid's mouth, the druid's familiars weren't familiars, but actual animal spirits that had agreed to become their companions. These animal 'spirits' were somewhat similar to artificial souls. They formed from the collective energies of many animals of their kind, the remnant outer shells of animals' souls. Druids and beastmasters had an ability to 'separate' the outer shells of their slain animals through a ceremony of some kind, where the inner soul was sent forth to reincarnate, leaving the outer shell in their service.

That said, it was also possible for druids and beastmasters to form lifelong bonds, a kind of 'soul contract' whereby the animal served them for as long as they lived. These sorts of bonds were rare but also way more powerful.

It was also why the animal companions of druids and beast trainers were usually able to independently gain levels, due to them retaining a part of their 'souls.'

Back to the four druids, I decided to let them be. The Aspect's presence in their soulspring was fascinating and was something I wanted to watch.

So, rather than let them do as they please, I tasked them with training my four Initiates and Lausanne.

The four young girls were doing well, though I should be looking for five more new 'recruits' soon. They were now about level ten and had gained basic proficiency in the usual sword, dagger, staff, and shields.

They were just six to eight, though, so they practiced with wooden weapons and wooden dummies in the [training room]. That formed the bulk of their combat practice, on top of spars against each other.

Still, a very long way before they could enter battle. I would reckon they needed to be at least twelve before they would fight any real battle.

The [minder] familiar kept me updated on their levels; the moment I focused on them, a game-like panel appeared and showed me all the skills and levels, their mental state of mind, whether they were happy or sad or stressed, and also their health, whether they were hurt or healthy.

It was helpful and allowed me to tailor my [Dream Tutor] and the nutrition I was feeding them; when they were stressed or frustrated, I would have a bit of that calming fruit tea on the menu.

Lately, my control of [Dream Tutor] improved. I still couldn't control the exact specifics, but I could use the [essence of summer] in dream tutor so that they got rather pleasant ones, like beaches, warm suns, things to help them unwind.

I also regularly talked to the girls, but they were young, so it was usually silly things, like how far did a tree see or how high did I go.

YEAR 80 MONTH 8

More rifts were spotted.

Apparently, there were a few rifts near Salah, but they were on the other side, so it'd be some time before they came near me. Their army had been dispatched to deal with the demons coming out from the rifts.

So far, only heroes had the power to close rifts, so the rifts remained open, and the army stationed a garrison force near the rifts to fight the demons that came out.

"If only we had our star mana powers again, then we could close the rifts." Meela had popped by after so long.

"Do you want to go back into battle?"

"Ugh, true." Meela shrugged. She'd gained a lot of levels since her hotel started operations one and a half years ago, so like Alexis predicted, her mobility had increased, though she still mostly stayed back in her hotel.

"But maybe we can help, somehow…"

"We are stuck here. What do you have in mind?" Meela's body was like a treefolk, and frankly, it took quite a bit of effort to figure out she wasn't a treefolk. She had a dress that was formed from wood, and for her, changing attires meant changing how the wood was shaped around her body.

"Hmmm...maybe we should try to help the next generation, perhaps research? The materials lab should count for something, right?"

As they discussed, I turned my attention to research.

[Research status:]
*[**Beetle** - anti-magma armors stage 4 - 10 months]*
*[**Material labs** - stage 1 - completed]*
*[**Magical sensors** - completed]*
*[**Normal Tree** - Root filters stage 1 - completed]*
*[**Metal hyperaccumulator trees** - Stage 1 - 12 months]*
*[**Phytoremediation process** - basic - 12 months]*
*[**Dedicated Filtering Blackwater-Plant** - stage 1 - 6 months]*

We had some normal trees gain filtering abilities, and this allowed them to reduce the effects of the poop-contamination.

But the materials lab was more of a properties kind of lab, which identified the components and the qualities of materials and also 'distilled' the different types of materials. It looked like there were further upgrades, which allowed me to design specific materials and forge special alloys, but that was a whole lot further down the road.

Next was the magical sensors.

The magical sensors were instantly installed on my material labs and gave me a reading of the mana flowing through the air and the composition. Mana had many types, after all. It also detected spells and area-of-effect skills. Together, with sensors in multiple material labs, they formed an array able to triangulate sources of unusual activity, like sudden surges of energy in the air.

At first, there was a whole load of false positives. Spells were being cast daily, in many battles throughout the world, some not very far away. Adventurers of New Freeka constantly traveled the region, slaying rogue monsters and bandits. Or priests and healers taught in Madeus' academy for the junior students.

All these false 'positives' had to be removed.

So we had to set a very high threshold to remove all the lesser spells from detection. My assumption was they probably wouldn't be much of a threat.

"TreeTree, can we help the next generation of summoned heroes?" Meela asked. "Alexis has some ideas, and she thought, well, we need your help."

"Hmm, honestly, I'm not sure why I should help the next group of heroes. From what I hear, heroes are pretty dangerous. They have a whole lot of magical power and are extremely idealistic."

"But isn't protecting the world from demons aligned with yours? Protecting the valley means also protecting it from demons."

"They certainly overlap, but what are the benefits of helping the heroes?"

"Uh...protecting the valley?"

"Honestly, if it's just demons, I don't need heroes."

Alexis paused. "True...but would you permit me and Meela to aid them?"

"Hmmm..." I couldn't control Meela, since she was her own independent soul, so... Frankly if she did, and it wasn't against me, I wouldn't stop her. "Fine."

"Great!"

YEAR 80 MONTH 9

An uneventful month in the valley.
Training, practice, observing the druids and citizens. Eavesdropping on conversations about battles from far away against the demons.

The humanoid demons were appearing everywhere, and the battles were getting more and more intense.

Unlike all recorded history of demons, this time, the demons had brought a special item that spawns demons, and it took the form of a camp. Larger variants had been spotted in places where towns and villages used to be.

And so, it could be said that overnight, all mortal wars ended, as the focus turned to face this new era of demons.

Demons used to be a 'continental' affair. Only a few rifts would open, and when they did, it was usually not far from each other, at least, until the demon king came.

Not anymore.

And for me, the big question was why?

Why did the demons, after what seemed to be years of taking the same strategies, finally trying this sort of carpet-bombing technique?

YEAR 80 MONTH 10

I chose another five children, this time two boys. Overall, due to the relative peace in New Freeka, the number of new orphans was trending downward. Still, accidents, fights, and death were inevitable, and there were also migrant orphans.

In certain communities where there was no capacity to support another orphan, it was better to send them off to a place where they would be cared for.

Anyway, the first four girls were around level twelve; the highest level was level fifteen, with eight levels in [soldier]. This job class thing was fascinating and more for me to learn.

As for Jura, he was still at level eighty and stuck.

Which was why today I harvested a three-year-old [ginseng plant], leaving two others to continue maturing.

[Three-year-old magical ginseng root]
  [Permanently improves lifeforce (faster mana, stamina and health regeneration)]

"So...how do we use this?" Jura held the ginseng root; even though it was three years old, it actually looked like it was a one-hundred-year-old ginseng root from my old world. I thought it was its a mana and probably my influence and bounty.

"Do you want me to cook it?" Meela offered. There was a cookhouse in her lodge.

"No." I was trying something more direct. "Please step into the soul forge."

"Uh, okay." Jura looked at the lightning-burned tree and then stepped in.

I'd thought about it for some time, and essentially, what I wanted to do was try to inject the ginseng into his 'soulspring.' It sounded like some kind of cultivation novel when I described it like that.

I attempted to start up the soul forge and start the merging process...

I got an error message when I put the ginseng roots in.

Ginseng roots needed to be further refined before they could be used in the soul forge. Refining required access to an essence concentrator.

Essence concentrator?

At the same time the soul forge was still active, Jura was still inside, his body 'sleeping' in a special 'altar' within the forge-tree. A prompt appeared.

[Do you want to remove some of Jura's skills or job classes? Doing so will free up lifeforce to learn other skills or gain levels. Removed skills have a chance to be converted into skill seeds. Skill seeds made this way can't be reused on donor.]

Eh.

I suddenly recalled the day, some six years ago, when the Wisp told me about surrendering of levels and skills.

"Why didn't it work when I captured the ranger?"

"It's called surrendering. If Jura's willing, you will be able to remove skills he doesn't want. And as I recall, you partially succeeded since you received a few skill seeds and class seeds. The conversion odds are higher if it's a voluntary surrender of the skills."

"Huh, so surrendering skills isn't exactly all bad, either." Was this like that pocket monster game again, where you unlearned a move, and somehow there was a chance the move you unlearned got transformed into a TM? In a way, the soul's ability to support the person's level and skills was limited, and this ability technically...technically allowed minmaxing. "Can a hero surrender his hero class or blessing?"

"What comes from the gods can only be removed by the gods."

INTERLUDES – AKBAR
SOMETIME AROUND YEAR 80, MONTH 9 (TREETREE-TIME)

Every demon king was slightly different, every generation of demons usually a variation of the previous. Scholars, inquisitors, and demon-hunters had often wondered why it was so, but since these invading demons didn't seem to be able to communicate, no one knew for sure.

Still, the inhabitants facing the demons could still observe and make a note of how subtle differences existed. The first demon rifts revealed little hints about the characteristics of the demon king they faced and the sort of battles they would have to prepare for. Usually this meant elemental and/or monster variants, like how Andraas had earth-golems, earth centipedes, and fire hounds, and as time went by, its larger versions of such monsters.

Spotting a demon rift was something every warrior learned by experience. Once they'd seen it, they would remember it for life. The way reality itself warped and broke, a tear in reality that linked to another world, it was an unforgettable sight. The portal to the demon world.

―――

"General Akbar." A human knight rode up to central camp; there were about five thousand soldiers there.

"Commander Akbar," the older man emphasized. "I've been demoted, and you need to remember that. Had it been in the city, you could get in trouble."

The knight shrugged. "You're still my general. Anyway—"

Commander Akbar frowned and gave the knight a stern look. "Get to it. What's the status? How many demons did you spot?"

"Twelve hundred. Surprisingly easy to get a count now that they look like humans. They made something that resembles a large house or camp. Still no sight of the rift yet. I'm waiting for the other scout to report back."

"Demons, making camp." Commander Akbar scratched his chin. "What has the world come to? I must see this."

The force of five thousand men marched toward the site of the reported demon camp, and what they saw was indeed a demon camp.

"There it is, Commander."

The demon camp's surface resembled a dark-reddish hue, its existence as if magic itself was forced to form the fabric.

"What's it doing?"

Akbar started counting, his eyes looking through his portable telescope, right at the demon camp. He watched intently for about thirty minutes.

"It's making more demons, soldiers. Get the mages. I want a magical reading on this area right now."

Akbar's hunch was right. The camp's location had slightly stronger natural mana and energies. There was only one decision to make: the camp had to be destroyed before it spawned more demons.

They crushed the twelve hundred or so demons easily.

A few days later, they were back at the camp.

"The news is unsettling." Akbar pored over the news coming in from all the other continents and kingdoms. Demonic news didn't have the usual diplomatic embargo and political filters, and frankly, Akbar enjoyed fighting demons. It was just plain fighting, without the bullshit of politics or the worries over the unnecessary death of others. It allowed him to be a true military man; the only thing he had to focus on was crushing this faceless, demonic enemy.

"There were so many..." Both of his aides nodded, and they looked over a rough map of the world. It was one of Akbar's personal collections as a general. Akbar placed a small red flag wherever they received reports on rift sightings.

There were multiple rifts in every large continent, and even in smaller continents. In earlier demon kings, the rifts were concentrated, most of the time on a single continent. Maybe two, at most, and even those, the bulk of them usually formed on one continent.

It didn't take much for Akbar to conclude the obvious. "This demon is planning to overwhelm the world with sheer numbers by attacking everywhere simultaneously."

One of the aides shook his head. "But does it matter? If they come with us with that tiny force, scattered throughout the world, they won't be a threat! And the heroes will come around and save the world when the demon king arrives." Akbar frowned a little at the aide's statement.

Two knights and a mage walked into the war-planning room.

Akbar looked at his aides. "True. But between now and the Demon King was at least a few years. This tactic may potentially destroy the world before the heroes even appear."

"So what? We can stop them. The quantity from the rifts reported so far has been small."

Akbar paused and remembered the demon champions. No reported sighting of the champions yet, though they often arrived before the king.

The other aides answered before Akbar got to it. "If the demons can build camps that generate more demons, their quantity won't be small for very long. How many rifts do we know nothing about? How sure are we all these are the only rifts out there? If the rift and camp were made in a secluded area we know nothing about, they could suddenly surprise us with a large force!"

"True, true."

"How's the analysis on the camp and the demons?" Akbar asked.

The mage shifted uncomfortably.

A soldier ran into the camp. "Gene—sorry, Commander! The mages, they...uh...they turned into demons. We had to kill one of them."

Akbar's eyes widened, and he stared. "When did this happen, and why did I not know about it?"

"It just happened, General," the soldier shouted, trying to catch his breath. He'd been running. "The mages, they were just meddling with the demonic staff, and suddenly it started to absorb one of the mages! So we had to destroy the staff, and we couldn't save the mage."

Akbar stopped. "You know about this?"

"No, sir." The mage in the room shook his head, but then he walked over to the soldier to talk.

Before Akbar could ask more, another person came in. He was a mage, too, and he looked younger than the other mages. "General."

"Commander."

"We have the report you wanted."

Akbar glared at the young mage; he was unfazed. "What happened?"

"Accident. It was quite unfortunate that I could not save him. But we now know that the staff seeks magic and consumes it to create demons."

The two aides paused.

"So, my guess is we should probably seek out major magical locations and dungeons and seek to take over them."

"But how does the demons expect to beat the dungeons with their tiny force?" Dungeon, generally, had a respectable defense force and multiple boss-level creatures within their base.

"Maybe not immediately, but over time their force will grow."

"We must let the world know," Akbar acknowledged. "This fact may be helpful for the other nations."

"Commander, we must first report this to high command. The king will want to know before this is shared," one of the aides said.

Akbar nodded, but inside he just felt annoyed. Politics. He could see it coming; the king probably wanted to sell this information for money. The awkward truce with the Nung and Takde wasn't something the king enjoyed, especially since he wanted his reign to be one of glory.

And so, Akbar and his retinue returned to the capital, Ransalah, leaving the rest of the force behind. The rest would continue to hunt demons and look for the rift.

The journey took them a few days, and soon Ransalah entered their view. The massive sprawl of the city, the faint stench of human activity, the smell of the forges and factories, it was a sign they were getting close. Even at night, one could see the dispersed glow from the city's lights.

The aide cheered. "Civilization! I can't wait for a hot bath!" The captains were relieved; one of them was from the capital, so his family was here.

Akbar just sighed. As a military man, he never felt like he had a place in Ransalah. Earlier in his career, he lived fortresses and camps, and till this day, that was where he felt where he belonged. Ransalah just reminded him of all the politics of the court, unnecessary reports to various nobles who wanted to build 'rapport,' and bureaucracy.

"Don't look so glum, Commander. Let's have some good food. And good wine! I hear there was quite a good vintage coming from New Freeka, something we've never managed to try before!"

One captain nudged the aide, signaling him not to mention New Freeka.

Akbar just shrugged. Perhaps he shouldn't be so upset. The capital did have a whole load of good eateries. "Well, let's do that. I do miss having properly cooked food from a good chef."

The group passed a damaged set of roads, some trees, and shrubs. "Ah, I notified the city that we were arriving soon." The aide messaged the city using some kind of [message] spell. At this distance, the spell didn't cost much mana, and the message decay wasn't bad.

Akbar's mind was still occupied with the strategies of this generation's demons. What would the champions bring this time? Was the demons' plan to split the heroes?

He distracted himself and looked at two rings on his fingers, one made of a greenish gold, another just regular silver. "Anyone coming to greet us?"

The aide shook his head.

Akbar smiled. "Best news I heard all day, then." He hated the whole greeting and welcoming ceremony, frankly, the best thing since his demotion from general. Even his aides knew how much he hated it. "Let's eat some good food!"

Since they didn't have a welcoming ceremony, that meant he also didn't have to immediately go and face the king or the senior ministers. Not that the king was eager to see him.

So the group went for one of the many famous eateries in Ransalah, this one located on the commoner's district. Despite being the commoners' district, there were many such eateries, serving adventurers, or wealthy merchants, or just some young men looking to impress a woman.

They had a spread of grilled and roasted meats, mostly from the nearby farms and also some of the edible monster meats, and a few different dishes of potatoes and yam, accompanied by wine. They had wine in regular wooden cups; though glass was available as a material, it was far too expensive for restaurants to use regularly, given how often glass things broke when an adventurer brawl happened.

Akbar, his aides, and the two accompanying captains took their time and dined, their conversation beginning with demons because, well, that was their job, and it was an easy thing to talk about in a dinner with colleagues.

Most of them wondered when the demon champions would start appearing; demon champions were still the single-highest risk outside of the demon king, and there were usually multiple champions. In terms of actual destruction, the champions were probably ahead of the demon king. The captains joked about running if they ever saw one, and Akbar just nodded. "I would run, too, if I saw a demon champion."

And they all laughed. Demon champions were difficult; even a general like Akbar would need a strong mage and healer team to defeat one.

But once all of them were progressively drunker, the conversation turned to less serious topics, like how everyone's love life was and whether Commander Akbar would ever remarry. Or other silly things, like what some of the soldiers were doing when in camp or stupid manliness challenges.

One of the aides talked about his failed dates with the local girls whenever they went on expeditions, and the rest of them just laughed, but they all also admired his guts for trying to date girls from all the various villages.

As they were about to leave, two men approached Commander Akbar. "Are you Commander Akbar?"

Akbar was a little tipsy, but he still managed to turn and face the two men. The two looked like plain, ordinary villagers; their presence honestly didn't seem anything special.

One of Akbar's aides, probably drunker than Akbar, tried to step in. "Why were you bothering our commander?" The aide was usually a little more timid; maybe it was alcohol-fueled machismo.

"May we talk to the commander, just for a while?" One of the men smiled politely.

Commander Akbar looked at them from top to bottom. If they wanted to rob or kidnap him, they did not need to ask. Though, even while drunk, Akbar could easily fight off two men, his [alert] passive did not trigger, so he had a good hunch that these two men didn't mean to harm him. Besides, he had a [General] class, and that meant he could hold two men down, easy.

The aide's attempt to respond on Akbar's behalf was stopped by Akbar's hand.

"Yes, let's talk. Back inside?" Akbar pointed back to the eatery.

The two men nodded, and they walked back inside. "Yes, inside is fine, but without your aides, please? Just something we want to ask you personally."

Akbar smiled. "Let's use one of the private dining rooms, then. They can wait outside."

"Commander, no...General Akbar." The two men sat. It was a small room with one round table and chairs for six. Akbar sat opposite them. "What do you think of the demons?"

Akbar chuckles. "They were bad, of course." What kind of question was that, anyway? Demons caused tremendous destruction and death, couldn't be negotiated with, and didn't have any useful functions. The only possibly positive thing about them was the daemolite left behind when the demon kings died.

"Do you think the heroes were doing a good job of fighting demons?"

"...not as well as I think they should." Akbar spoke his mind. He had a hunch they were leading him somewhere, but he'd see.

The two men grinned. "Great. Do you enjoy fighting demons?"

Akbar paused and stared at the two men. Enjoy fighting demons? In what sense? "I'm sorry?"

"Have you ever thought of joining a cause dedicated to fighting demons?"

Akbar's stern eyes met with two others; the room felt heavy then. "I'm afraid I need a bit more than that. What exactly was your cause?"

At that time, a third man appeared in that small private room, he materialized from the two's shadows.

Akbar, though, still didn't react and just took a sip out of the wooden cup of water. "I was wondering when you would come out."

"As expected of a [general]. Proper introductions now. I am from the Laenza Alliance, a secret society. Allow me to do the full explanation. The Laenza Alliance's main purpose was to support the heroes in their quest to defeat the demon king, and we would like you to join us in that quest."

Akbar didn't react; he just took a good look at the man. "Have we met?"

"Yes. But that matters little. Our issue was the coming demonic conflict. We believe you've realized the gravity of the issue, and so we'd like to invite you to join us." He felt familiar, but Akbar couldn't pin it down.

Akbar sipped from the cup of water and said, "When you say, 'Support the heroes in the quest to defeat the demon king,' what does that actually mean? You want me to put my life on the line and fight the demon king myself, together with the heroes?"

"Well, no. You won't be the ones actually fighting the demon king. Ultimately, the heroes received the gods' blessing, and only with the blessing can the heroes hope to stand toe to toe with the demon king. Our presence in that fight would be unnecessary. We may even be a hindrance. I would say we would be throwing our lives away."

"So what do you do?"

"We, the Laenza, aim to support the heroes by spotting them early, guiding them, removing the barriers to their growth, and giving them what they need to progress."

"Barriers..." Akbar looked at the three Laenza men.

"Politics. Bureaucracy. Think about it: these otherworldly heroes, they arrive in the world with very minimal guidance from the gods. They are lost, despite their gifts, and when they meet the locals, they need time to find their way. If it so happens they come under a nation's protection, kings and rulers often have their own political agenda. Every step of the way, they face resistance and unnecessary barriers, from locals who have no idea whether they really are heroes, to politicians and rulers who seek to manipulate them."

The man paused to catch his breath, then continued.

"Our role was to offset those resistance, help them discreetly, and where we can take them away from politics. We try to be the first or among the first to find and contact the heroes and to offer them assistance, guidance, training. And if the heroes need any special equipment or items, or need to get somewhere, we try our best to help them along."

Akbar sighed. It suddenly occurred to him that the heroes had it rough. They started off weak at first, thrown into a world they knew nothing about, they were still young and naïve, and that usually made them gullible, and nobles usually tried to manipulate them. It suddenly made sense how things usually did work out for the heroes, especially if there was a secret organization that supported them in the shadows.

"So, would you be interested?"

"I have a feeling that you already know I would be."

The shadow man offered his hand. "We must hear it from you."

Akbar nodded, and they shook hands. "Yes. Let me be a part of it."

The shadow man took out a ring with a single red stone surrounded by various smaller red stones and passed it to him. "Drop your blood in the ring's inner stone."

Akbar gently pricked his finger, and a single drop of blood touched the inner stone. It glowed gently, a soft reddish hue, and then the shadow man walked over, and he too pricked his finger, adding a drop of his blood in the same ring. The two bloods mixed, and the ring released a red flash.

"The ring, it's invisible to all but the rest of us who also have it. It marks the Laenza and is how we communicate."

Akbar put the ring on, and he could feel its magic mix with that of his own. The ring fit nicely. "Intricate carvings."

"Made by our magesmiths, from where we are from, Rhongo."

Akbar nodded. "That's far."

"The demons' rifts are everywhere. And we follow."

"True."

"Welcome to the Laenza. We have taken too much of your time, Commander Akbar. We will not keep your aides waiting any longer." The three gave a gentle bow, and the shadow man vanished into the shadows again.

YEAR 80 MONTH 9

"The fact that I'm here means it's not good news for the four of you." A lady arrived in New Freeka and quickly found the four druids. There were many other ladies looking like her, and she didn't emit any visible presence or magical energy, so her arrival didn't even trigger any of my sensors.

A mature-looking lady, in human terms, she looked like she was in her fifties, though I suspected she was probably older. Despite her petite size, her very presence sent the four druids into a tense combat stance.

"The enforcer..." The four fumbled over their staff and called out their familiars. They were right in the middle of town, and the citizens cleared a space. It was common for brawls and fights to break out in town, and citizens generally knew to just give way. When there were fights among adventurers or people of that level, everyone would just let them fight.

"I've been busy, and I wish I could've come sooner. But you know how it is. Investigations take time. A crime would be committed months ago, and only now the sentence was meted out. Such was the speed of justice, always lacking." The lady shrugged; she was dressed in a loose-fitting shirt and pants, but they were clearly woven with high-quality materials. When she took out a scythe from nowhere, all my alarm bells started to ring.

She wasn't exactly tall and probably on the older side, but the way the massive scythe swung around her, I knew she was trouble.

An intense aura spread around her. It even made the subsidiary trees around New Freeka feel heavy. It was some kind of suppression aura.

"On what crimes?" The druids put on a brave face, attempting to feign ignorance in the face of the lady.

"Oh, this trick has been done many times. But fair, the one carrying out the punishment must repeat it, just so that the offender may drill it into their souls for their next life."

The lady stepped forward one small step.

"For lying to the council, jail time. For forcing a high-tier spirit tree to a spiritual contract, the four of you have contravened one of the core tenets of the Hutan Council. And for that offense, the Hutan Council has empowered me to bestow your punishment. Death."

The four men summoned their wolves, armor, and whatnot, and whatever they had. All the familiars charged at the lady.

But the battle was awfully short.

The lady swung her scythe, and it glowed in a dark-greenish color. "[Druidhunter]."

A dark wave spread out, and the familiars of the druids all just turned into dust. Then, from the earth, four black roots emerged and stabbed them each in the heart, killing them instantly.

She then walked up to the four impaled bodies of the druids.

"Children, everyone, please don't watch." It was in the middle of town, and the announcement of the execution sent a lot of younger children and their parents running away.

And her scythe beheaded all four of them. Their heads fell easily, like harvesting hay. She chucked their heads into a gunny sack and then into her magical pocketspace.

"Should we do something?" I wondered and asked my tree-minds.

"She's scary. I suggest not," Ivy said. "She's got the ability to sneak in and find the druids and then kill them. She might use it on us."

Well, the lady quickly went and met Jura.

"Supreme Counsel Jura, I apologize for my sudden, unannounced presence. My name is Leithia, a conducts enforcer of the Hutan Council. I've been informed that I may be able to seek a meeting with the Tree Spirit through you?"

No? I didn't feel like I should meet her because she was dangerous! Jura seemed unfazed, though; he even managed to sit comfortably in his chair and took a sip from his tea. He was really into tea these days.

"I understand that the Spirit is probably apprehensive to meeting another druid, and that's fine. I would like, on behalf of the Hutan Council, to apologize for the acts of our rogue druids. It was a great disappointment to us as well, that our druids acted in such manner in the face of a chance to get power."

Jura nodded and offered her tea. "Well, glad to know that laws are being enforced after all."

"Indeed, I would like to assure the Spirit that we will still fulfill its wishes to commune with the other great tree spirits, and we are in the process of arranging that. It's not easy to convince other tree spirits to participate, and we will need specialized items to allow the tree spirit's thoughts to be transmitted. In the meantime, the council will send someone over as compensation."

Eh? Wait. Was there really a need for such things? Couldn't I just erm...chain my subsidiary trees all the way to wherever the other spirits were? Or was this 'subsidiary tree' skill rarer than I thought?

"So, please assist us and manage the spirit's expectations."

Jura nodded. "I think the Tree Spirit will...give some concessions on this. Though I'm not sure for how long, I will try my best to convince him."

Leithia smiled back at Jura and nodded a little. "That's the most we can ask for the offense the council's poorly trained druids have caused."

They both sipped on the tea. It was an awkward silence, but Jura looked more comfortable than the lady. "Would there be anything else?"

"That's all we wish to say, Counsel. I'll take my leave and will leave your town in a few days."

"Enjoy your stay."

[Druidic Aspects failed to collect the chosen skills as the period of the contract was too short.]
[Received 24 x Essences of Druid]
[Received 4 x druid class seeds]
[Received 1 x experience seeds]

Aiks. Oh well, I would have to use the essences to teach the girls then, but twenty-four essences might not even lead to a single skill. Sigh.

Anyway, I was happy that the druid enforcer didn't push to see me, and so I turned my attention elsewhere. Ivy was still keeping tabs on her, though, and as she said, she spent her time in town. Thankfully, she left after two days of eating and meeting.

I'd decided to reward one of the girls, the one who reached level fifteen, by giving her a choice of the class seeds to take and one skill seed for [archery].

The choice was actually just between [Druid] and [Ranger], since I'd like to keep [Dark Knight] for later. I also had some random jobs from the deceased, like [farmer], [merchant], [scribe] and stuff like that, but since the Valthorn Initiates were meant to be a combat unit, it'd be combat skills and jobs. They also already had [soldier], which I found quite strange, but I supposed that was the result of being trained by soldiers?

The problem about the [druid] class seeds was that the trainers were now dead.

"Can't we learn from you?" the girls asked. Good question. If I was playing a game, I would think going to the 'source' was a good way to truly learn a skill.

But no. Druids and tree spirits understood the same kind of abilities differently.

The way I sensed and commanded trees was different because I was a Tree, and I had access to certain kind of senses that elves or centaurs, like these girls, did not have. So, even if our powers looked and felt similar, the mechanics of how our powers worked, at its core, were different. The way I commanded and used [Root Strike] was different from how a druid would. I could move my roots as if they were...a button I could press.

For the druids, they had an incantation to call on the earth and trees to obey they commands. It was like I was the wheels, whereas the druids moved the wheels through a steering that went through the transmission.

"I am afraid it would be very challenging for me to directly teach you druid magic, though I can use the [essences] I have to give you lessons through [Dream Tutor]."

And the druids magic actually covered a wider scope; their field extended into earth magic, water magic, some air magic, and also some animal-mastery. Whereas mine so far was rather wood-focused and a mix of tree abilities. In a way, they were generalists.

"But you are a tree. Are you not superior to druids?"

"Superior's not a fair way to say things. Our natures are different."

"Why?" the young girls asked. Perhaps to them, everyone could be placed on a spectrum from weak to strong, and that may be true from a strictly combat perspective. But there was a nuance to abilities that extended beyond pure direct combat. "But why? You're a giant tree with strange powers. Shouldn't you be better than them?"

These young girls could be strangely naive.

"Well, there are some things you can do when you have hands, and there are some things you can do when you have roots."

They have job classes. I don't.

YEAR 80 MONTH 10

The Hutan Council sent a strange person to serve me. "Compensation," they said, accompanied by a beautifully written letter.

An [Arborist] by the name of Zhiga.

"Uh...why did the council send you?" Jura looked a bit puzzled.

"I am here to make the Tree Spirit feel better, of course!" Zhiga smiled. He was an old man, but there was plenty of spring in his step. He came with a bag of tools, like little scissors, small shovels, and multiple bottles of dirt.

"Uh...after the recent incident, I am afraid that the Tree Spirit is a bit reluctant to meet new people."

"Nonono, totally understand. I shall remain in the city and take care of the trees here." The [arborist] remained in the city, with Ivy watching his every move. The city was open to visitors, it was peacetime after all, and so long as he obeyed the rules, he could stay in city.

―――

Jura had a lot of time to think. When I offered to remove some of his skills, especially those from his earlier days that he may no longer need, he needed some time to think about it.

His levels and skills, experience as a villager, and also a fighter—some of those held certain memories to him and may have saved his life back in the day. Some skills made the difference between victory or death, and although they seemed weak now, they had special meaning.

"I'm not sure whether I want to remove my [villager] skills. I have like...fifteen levels in them." Well, Jura's overall level was eighty, and it comprised of sixty levels in warlord, being a combination of forty levels in fighting and twenty levels in diplomacy and administration. "What if there was a way for it to merge with Warlord? Maybe I will be Village Warlord?"

Hmmm...

If such merging was possible, it would improve the organization and presentation of his soulspring, but I wasn't sure whether that freed up lifeforce to support new skills and levels.

Was there a way to assign a 'lifeforce consumption/drain' value to skills and levels because perhaps there was some skills that used up more lifeforce than others? I would imagine these skills had a 'slot-value.'

"What if someday I need those villager's skills again? When I grow older and I can no longer fight?" Wasn't that a long way to go?

"Uh..."

"You said I won't be able to relearn the skills?"

"No, I mean, I can't use the skillseeds on you, but I suppose you could learn it on your own again?"

Jura paused and sipped his ginger-tinged tea. "Hmm. I think I'm fine. TreeTree...I appreciate you trying to push me past level eighty, but...I think I value my existing skills, they have meaning to me, and I'm not willing to let go of them."

Inwardly, I felt like sighing. I guessed skills were like scars; they punctuated certain moments in a person's life. Jura knew what it meant to be higher level. It meant he could fight stronger monsters, do more, but he had somewhat decided there were certain things he wouldn't do to get there.

"I can respect that, but if you ever change your mind..."

Jura nodded. "I think rather than that, maybe let's get back to basics, and erm...figure out how to restore my hand?"

He flexed his wooden hand. It was made using his mental link with Bamboo, his 'eidolon'/familiar. It'd been wonderful since Bamboo obtained the skill [Extended Self], which sort of functioned like a power armor, and because how frequently Jura used it, it was really like having a hand again.

The challenge about lost limbs was that, well, the soul itself lost the blueprint and memory of the limb. Essentially, when healing magic attempted to heal a person's body, it accessed the soul's blueprint. That blueprint was then used as the basis for restoring the body.

When a limb was cut off, there was a crucial period during which the limb must be healed. After that, the soul lost the 'blueprint' relating to that limb, and then healing the limb became impossible, and what was left was a stump.

In my earlier days, I didn't have the soul forge when I saw Jura; he had already lost his hand. I didn't have any ability to heal the lost arm.

But I'd changed, and altering his soul to recreate the 'blueprint" was certainly something I was now willing to try.

At least, I would first need to do some...experiments.

Animals.

If all souls were reincarnated, sometimes as animals, I probably should not be doing this. These poor animals could be me, in my next life.

Alexis and Meela clearly felt disturbed by what I was doing, even if they understood the rationale of what I was planning to do.

I had the Order gather stray animals in New Freeka and those further out: dogs, cats, deer, wolves, cows, any stray animals that were injured, amputated, limbless.

If I was to alter and recreate the limb, I needed some practice.

And then, I went to do my testing on these animals, using the soul forge to 'repair' their souls.

The first animal died from the magic overload instantly. A gruesome death, best not to be described.

"What you are trying to do seems to require precise tools, beyond just what the soul forge normally does." Alexis was curious, of course. I thought she was attracted to such gory things, even if she was disturbed.

"I healed the princess many years ago. Her soul spring was wrecked. Why do you think is this different?"

"The fact that you are doing experiments tells me you know it is different. The princess's spring was wrecked, but the body was still there. It's like her house collapsed, but the components were just a mess. I think in Jura's case, the component is lost, and you are trying to rebuild it. You need to do something in the soul so that the left arm can regrow."

"...okay." To rebuild that 'soul blueprint,' I would have to alter the form of the outer shell of the soul.

"Maybe something like a massive mold? Like those casts people make?"

A mold, eh? But let's see.

For the second animal, I planned to put the animal inside the mana soaking facility, wait for a day, and then start up the soul forge. I put two subsidiary trees with biolabs right next to the [Forge tree] and attempted to use the vine-tools from the [Biolab] to make the changes.

The [Soul Forge] did have some default tools, but unlike the biolab pods, the array and precision of the tools were lacking. At least for the augmentation I was thinking of.

During the test run, the vines from the [biolab] burned once they entered the forge tree. It was more like...they started to darken and turn to ash. Details were a little lacking when it came to the [Forge Tree].

I thought it looked like I had to get something with more mana resistance. Something that did not burn from mana or allow the mana to flow around it.

I had some ideas there. But I would need to buy some jewels.

At the same time, I asked Jura for his oldest belongings, ideally something before he lost his hand.

Like the princess, maybe his belongings had a remnant, a shard of his soul that I could somewhat work with.

"I think they all burned down during the burning...except my sword."

"Your sword it is then. Give it to me."

"Uh..." It was precious.

"I'll make you a new one."

The sword went into the [forge tree], and there were some 'shards' of his being, but because he'd been using it even after the incident, the shards and fragments in there were all without his hands.

"Sorry, I really have nothing else."

Perhaps these items were like loose memory cards, and contact refreshed their memory to the latest version? Or did they merge?

"So...my sword was gone?" Well, the sword was still there, but in order to analyze the shard, I had to break it down, and unlike people or souls, the soul forge wasn't designed to put them back together. It was quite strange how the soul forge knew what to keep and what to break. I mean, why was it that a person inside could survive, but a steel sword got broken?

"Uh...kind of." It wasn't that great a sword anyway. It was really just a basic steel sword, despite the fancy design.

"Ah..." Jura sighed. But he understood why I did it. Even now, I had an inkling of how to do it, but I still needed to test it out on animals.

YEAR 80 MONTH 11

The merchants delivered a bunch of ores containing various unprocessed jewels and metals.

The idea was simple, really.

Some of these metals should be able to strengthen the biolabs and their tools, via [mineral augmentation], and together with [woodshaping], I could make the tools necessary to perform more precise adjustments in the soul forge.

Should.

Or maybe... Could I use [star mana]?

Anyway, that was also worth testing. First, the ore and jewels test.

Before the second animal test, I fired up the soul forge, put the ores in, and measured how long each of the ores lasted before they melted into a puddle. Some would last longer, and if so...some of them should last?

Nope.

All of them melted, some a little bit slower than others, but all melted into a puddle. It was as if they were stripped apart, bit by bit. Or maybe I just didn't have the right kind of ore.

Maybe I should use my main body? Wouldn't that work? My

main body should be more resilient than using it via subsidiary trees.

But I would have to move things around.

"Can I have a forge tree inside my main body?" I asked the Wisp. The [Forge Tree] was created to minimize the pain of using the soul forge; that was why it was...outside.

"You certainly could, but you will feel quite an intense pain when you use it." The forge tree received lightning and vibrated like mad when the mana spun. "It will feel a bit like when you were evolving. And you will feel like mana-poisoned, but then again you were an evolved tree...maybe you can."

"Let's try it anyway."

So, in my body, within the secret hideout I set aside a space and made it into a forge tree. It came easily' after all, I already had the tree, and this was just internalizing it.

[Secret hideout modified: Internal Soul Forge Chamber]

And I fired the internal soul forge up.

whooooooooommmmmm

It spun.

It was kinda like a really bad stomachache, the mana spinning in my metaphorical tummy. But not as bad as I thought.

"Uh...you okay in there?" Alexis asked. She couldn't see this part, inside here, deep inside the secret hideout.

"Yeah."

Using [woodcrafting], I created layers of wooden walls around the chamber, which formed a barrier, to protect myself from the swirling mana. The space here was flexible in sizing, after all.

And I fired up the soul forge, again.

These protective walls were in a state of constant regeneration. The gathered mana swirled and sped up. As it did so, it expanded and burned the protective wooden walls.

At higher speeds, and at full power, it felt like I was surrounded by fire. Like I was in a sauna.

But my initial theory was correct: my main body, vines, and feelers were more resistant to the mana-burn, and they did last longer. Not only that, thanks to [Self-awareness], I was far more aware of what was happening.

Zaaaaappppppppp!

A lightning bolt struck my main tree, followed by loud thunder.

Ugh. I felt it travel down from the branch to the trunk, leaving a streak. It burned a little while, but my fire resistance and healing power quickly kicked in and put it out.

The mana in the forge spun, and it sped up. As it sped up, it quickly took the shape of a spinning ball. Time for another test, so I put an ore in with a feeler. The ore started to disintegrate into a puddle, levitating in the middle. My soft, green, viney feeler started to disintegrate as well as the swirling mana bombarded it.

Hmm. There must be something. Maybe just starting up the soul forge wasn't the complete process.

I needed to see how the [Soul Forge] did it normally.

I decided...to test it out on an animal.

The animal was one of the many stray ones, a small hamster-like animal. It'd lost its tail. This time, I observed it intently instead of letting the 'skill' do what it needed to do. And partly, being inside me also allowed me to truly 'see' it, perhaps through my skill [Self-awareness], since my vision of the separate [Forge Tree] wasn't as 'holistic.'

And I saw it. The mana-dispensing feeler in the soul forge.

The moment the animal stepped into the soul forge, a small layer of mana was applied to the creature by a tiny feeler. As the soul forge started to spin, the body was protected by the mana funneled by two vertical magical connections, and then...the soul was pulled out of the body.

Even the tiny hamster had a soul.

Were you possibly human in some previous reincarnation?

Sorry I have to do this. It's for...science. May your soul move to a better place, reincarnated into some other form.

The soul was in the shape of a hamster, too. It...it didn't have a tail. I could see the soul, it had multiple layers, and the soul forge started to split those up. One layer representing the spirit-body, and one multi-sub layered spirit representing the skills and outer soul.

Seemed like all these details were omitted when looking at the [forge tree]. With the princess or the artificial souls.

The body was moved aside, and the two spirit layers moved to the center of the soul forge.

What did I do at this point? How did I recreate the 'tail'? I tried to look back at all the other animals that the Order gathered, and yes, there were a few samples of this animal. Some of those animals had tails.

I pulled up the data, stored in my biolab, and cross-checked to the body.

Ugh. Firstly, the data from my biolab was in a different format, presented in the form of the soul spring and its extensions.

This meant my biolab wasn't collecting data suitable for the [soul forge]. The way things were presented and the information was different. It's like one was an X-ray photo, and another was a 3D MRI scan. The information was different, even if the body was the same.

Still, the creature was in. No point stopping. I tried to use the data I had to 'recreate' a tail. Using soul fragments, which I had plenty of, I formed it into a rudimentary shape of a tail. Ugh. My difficulty in shaping the soul fragment into the tail was partly because my feelers only lasted a short while before the swirling mana burned their tip up.

The soul forge spun, and another lightning fell. It felt like when I touched a light switch after a shower, only stronger, more intense, and it traveled to my belly, where the soul forge was.

The tail slowly, clunkily merged with the spirit-body, my burning feeler clumsily trying to adjust its position, and then it merged with the layered spirit. The real body now came back and rejoined the spirit, and then the hamster-creature was whole again.

The forging complete, I put the hamster-creature back into a healing pod.

And I used a healing ability.

The creature's bottom started to heal; indeed, there was a small dot that was regenerating, and it resembled the shape of what I made. It was somewhat mispositioned, like...the root of the tail started a little too low.

A rough tail shape appeared, like an engorged balloon stuck on the creature's bottom.

Then the tail expanded...and exploded in a massive splatter of blood. The hamster-creature died instantly.

I'm sorry, hamster-creature.

Looking at the remains of the splattered body, the cause was simple: the tail lacked all the details of the blood vessels, muscles, and bones that were needed in a real tail. All it had was a layer of skin in the shape of a tail as a result of my poor drawing of a tail.

The healing accelerated the blood flow into that tail, so when the skin could no longer take the pressure from the blood inflow, it exploded, and the creature died of blood loss.

Ugh.

Looked like it wasn't going to be easy to 'rebuild' a limb when the soul had forgotten what the limb was like. And I wouldn't want Jura to go through that sort of miserable death.

The barriers?

The first challenge would be to get a good soul forge level imagery of what a hand should be. I would have thought I could fix this by taking a good scan of Jura, again, this time in a biolab pod inside my body, using the soul forge's power. Something of a similar resolution and detail as what I had now seen, preferably more. Maybe create some kind of soul forge–biopod hybrid. Maybe, if I could somehow flip the image of his existing hand, then I wouldn't have to start from scratch.

Next barrier, a way to recreate that image in the soul forge, using soul forge. My expectation was that a full 'soul-copy' of the limb would be extremely detailed and would need a lot of work to recreate such a thing with soul fragments. Even if I had a lot of soul fragments, my concern here was whether I had the correct tools and means to recreate it, and how long would it take?

And lastly, even if I could recreate the hand in a 'soul form' using the soul fragments, I would need to figure out a way of accurately joining it all together and then heal it in such a way that he would have a functional arm. I still didn't know even if I created the hand correctly whether healing would somehow 'regenerate' a hand with all the necessary bones, muscles, blood vessels, and stuff. I had taken the assumption that magic would handle it, but I did want to minimize that risk.

Lastly, what if there were things I didn't know? Maybe there were other details that I couldn't see because I was not using the right equipment.

*[**Skill upgraded**: Biolab healing pod]*

Jura thought healing his hand was going to be easier than breaking level eighty, but I thought both of these challenges were equally difficult.

YEAR 80 MONTH 12

The news of demons from the distant lands trickled in. More rifts had been spotted, but the military remained fully in control and had been suppressing the demons from the rifts, though perhaps the military was greatly downplaying the threat of the demons. So, for now, our part of the world remained safe.

The reason we were all generally suspicious of the good news was because the kingdoms were stockpiling resources; whether this was due to habit as a precaution from all prior demonic wars, or a sign of true distress, we still did not know. In past instances, trade lines got disrupted, and sources of food became unreliable, so it could be that there was really nothing, and some of these kingdoms were just being prudent, preparing for the worst.

Still, it was infectious. New Freeka was also in a mood for preparations; the council hired more soldiers, conducted extensive training for their militia, and stockpiled food. They also tried to run a campaign to smear the Order's name, especially on the way we spent money, and to some extent, it did convince the regular citizens.

But we didn't part with the Order's money. Instead, we decided to spend the money on new walls and defensive towers.

This was partly because I had a good range of defensive skills, and I wanted to make use of them. We built an outer wall a short distance away from New Freeka, and it was filled with trees on both sides of the wall. The skill [Reinforce Defensive Structure] created a vine-based structural reinforcement with sharp thorns on the outside of the wall and [carnivorous plants] and [cactus defense system] as traps.

The walls were separated into segments by defensive watchtowers. Next to that, I had [subsidiary trees] filled with beetles, and they functioned as 'watchposts' and the beetles patrolled the walls. In front of that, we placed some subsidiary trees with [shield generators] to block large projectiles.

This whole thing was Trevor and Ivy's suggestion. Ivy listened in on military defensive strategies from other nations and collated the information and put forth this suggestion.

Which I thought worked for the large hordes. If it was going to be a large army of hounds, the wall would work swimmingly well.

Still, the core issue with demons was their demonic champions. Like the massive golems, or the large centipedes, with opponents like that, these reinforced walls were not going to last very long.

On that front, the plan would be anti-demon weapons. It'd been something I'd been hatching since the previous battle with the champion.

Magical wooden spears were filled with all the anti-demon abilities I had, also made with damage boosting essences, and all the holy enchantments I could get from the priests and mages in New Freeka. I would use them to cap my [super anti-demon root strike]. I even managed to weave a bit of [star mana] into it, and hopefully that'd make the difference. It worked before, so, I thought it'd work again.

This time, I was going to stockpile a whole load of these anti-demon weapons. If the heroes were going to come around, they'd probably do crazy tricks like that again.

"You could make a sword like that?"

"Huh?"

"The anti-demon weapons you were making. Could I get one? You did take my sword...you know."

"Oh." Ah yes. I needed to make a weapon for Jura. "But these were wooden...spears?" I showed him one of the spears, and well, it was massive; after all, it was made for me. It was bigger than a lance, and so it was really heavy. It worked for me because their wooden nature meant my roots merged with their other end, and this was the largest size my roots could handle. The size helped because you could fit more spells into bigger things without having to increase the complexity of the spell or use more magically compatible materials, which may not work with my roots.

He touched them, and he looked quite impressed. "So, this was what Madeus and the group of priests have been doing for the past week...enchanting this?"

"Yeah. I can make a wooden sword, but I doubt it can carry the same quantity of enchantments as these large, multi-layered, wooden uh...bolts."

"I'll take it. I would like it to have anti-demon effects, too. I might need it."

Well true. Maybe I should outfit Horns, Lausanne, and the rest with anti-demon weapons as well.

So, I went and made wooden weapons for them.

"Ooh, this is new. You didn't show me this before." Meela poked her head when I was growing wooden weapons using [woodcrafting].

"I didn't?"

"You didn't use it much, or if you did, I wasn't there."

"I used it to make toys and furniture. I made Lausanne's toys with this, and the playpen was made using this."

"Oh, true. Come to think of it, that explains where a lot of your tools come from." Meela stared a bit too closely at the little growing sword, and she poked it. Now that she'd gotten a physical body, she was frequently walking around New Freeka.

So, I made more wooden weapons, swords, spears, and stuff.

The process of making wood weapons was actually quite time consuming because for them to have a comparable strength to a regular metal weapon, I actually cheated, meaning I used irons and other metals harvested via my roots and infused them into the wood itself, the wood using them to form a kind of metallic 'frame' in their structure.

But that wasn't enough, so I then infused [essences]. I had elemental essences, strength essences, and life essences, and adding essences strengthened the overall weapon. The best part of essences was that they could coexist with magical enchantments; for small weapons like a sword or a spear (relatively speaking), they could take one or two enchantments, more if I embedded jewels in them.

But since I didn't have many magical enchantments, I used the only one I had, [lesser holy enchantment].

"Cool weapon." Meela nodded, looking at my completed wooden sword. It was almost black in color because of the essences used. In terms of sharpness and strength, it was above a regular steel sword. It was no super-sword, but eh.

Jura tried to swing it around, nodding. "Hmmm...the weight distribution feels a little weird. Probably need a bit of getting used to. But I suppose it's good enough."

He still liked his own steel sword.

Meela was also examining Jura's new dark-wood sword now that it was done.

"Mika, you like swords?" Jura asked. Mika was Meela's name in New Freeka, and Jura thought Meela was one of my artificial souls, like Horns. Meela didn't want to be known as a former hero. There was just too much baggage, hence the new name. Alexis's new name was Alix, but for now, nobody could see her except me and Meela.

"A bit. I think they're quite cool. I generally like things made of wood."

Jura nodded. "I see. It makes sense. Treefolk like wood stuff, too. But don't you find it weird, in a way? It's like an elf admiring a weapon made of elf-bones. I would be somewhat creeped out."

"Eh, I don't see it like that. If your entire life you were brought up that this was what your species does, you wouldn't think it's strange."

Jura paused, nodded. "I see."

The two chatted for a while, mostly talking about swords.

"TreeTree, you should fuse an artificial soul into a sword. You could make a talking-sword!" Meela casually said; she also took a swing of the new sword. It was a little too heavy for her, so after a swing or two, she gave it back to Jura.

Eh.

I felt like I'd had a stump rammed into me.

That...that was...actually quite a good idea. But then the poor, artificial soul was stuck in a sword, and what if he didn't want to be in there? What if the sword broke?

But those were minor challenges. It was an idea worth exploring. It'd been two years since I'd made Ivy, so I already had enough fragments for more artificial souls. I just need to check whether I had enough potatopower...

[59,400 normal trees. 5,630 subsidiary trees. One leyline. Currently have enough power to support a total of 11 artificial souls.]

Oh. There was really a lot of trees now, since...well...it was peaceful.

Now let me think...

———

Back to Jura's arm. I had Jura sit down and go for a full scan in the biolab again, this time specifically the one inside my body. And then, when he did, I pulled the power from the soul forge and used it to get a scan.

Now that I had some idea what I needed, based on my experience with the hamster-monster, I was trying to recreate that sort of data.

And it worked. But it was a far longer scan that the usual biolab, which took about two hours. I had to sedate Jura and put him in sleep, since the mana from the soul forge had to 'scan' the arm.

To use my earlier analogy, the biolab was an X-ray, and the soul forge was an MRI, and now, the mana from the soul forge was 'entering' the hand to collect 'data' on what Jura's existing body looked like. And because it went section by section, it took Jura the whole day.

When he woke up, he was not too pleased.

"I was asleep for a day!"

"Sorry, didn't expect it to last so long…"

"I mean…you should tell me first. I had work back in the Order!"

"Uhm…"

Laufen, who came to check on Jura, smiled. "No worries I postponed all your meetings and briefings to tomorrow. I figured they understand that you've got a personal life, and that involves seeing your healers. Honestly, some of those issues, I told them to deal with it themselves…"

It's just a day, I thought. I slept for weeks sometimes, and I had my three lovely artificial minds running things on my behalf. Looked like the Order needed to delegate more.

Jura nodded. "Fine, fine."

"Let me look through the results. I'll let you know."

The scan was a lot more detailed than the ones from the biolab pods, but it was missing something.

Maybe this too was incomplete.

So I tried putting my two scans together, the one from the biolab pods and from this soul forge–powered scan. I needed some additional processing power from the root-brain complexes, so I had to temporarily tap on their root-brains for a bit more mental juice.

Suddenly, a string of notifications appeared in my head. It seemed there was a whole load of upgrades available for the internal soul forge chamber, but they would require me to build or grow certain things.

*[**Secret hideout**: Internal Soul Forge Chamber upgrades]*
　*[**Upgrade** - Dedicated root-brain complex - to support higher resolution data-analysis of souls & storage of scan output]*

Wait. This reminded me of something I didn't finish...

"A ton of gold and a ton of quartz? And all these crystals and stuff?" The men looked amazed at the order.

"That'll cost us quite a bit of our revenue," one of the treasurers said. "We'll need to dig into our reserves, then..."

The master of ceremonies opened his arms wide. "Our reserves were meant for moments like this, when Aeon calls on us to meet his demands. Do you not answer?"

The men gulped. The treasurer shook her head and nodded. "Certainly."

"Go before Aeon finds us lacking."

YEAR 81, MONTH 1

"How are the preparations?"

"Shouldn't you not care about this anymore?" Jura asked. He parried a vertical slash from Lausanne and then ducked to dodge another Initiate's horizontal slash.

"I can't. You know I care," Yvon answered. She was sitting on a bench, watching Jura spar with Lausanne and the Initiates.

"Didn't see the walls?" Jura jumped, and he elbowed the young initiate on the chest. The initiate wore a wooden breastplate; all of them did. It made them look a bit like a wooden knight. It cracked. The initiate was out.

"I did, but you know walls alone do nothing."

"Haven't visited them?" Jura ducked, and Lausanne momentarily vanished and emerged behind him.

But Jura blocked it anyway.

"Good move, [Shadow stab]. But you tend to appear right behind me. It's predictable."

Lausanne's sword bent, and it curved toward Jura's head. He grabbed it with a reinforced wooden hand and, with a strong yank, pulled the sword out of Lausanne's hand. Lausanne protested. "It's a spar!"

"You used two skills, so I retaliated."

"It's a handicapped spar!"

"Rest. We can continue later." Lausanne was still a bit upset, but she did as she was told. She was close to the initiates now.

Jura walked to Yvon and grabbed a drink from a wooden flask.

"Where were we? Oh yes, the walls. I thought you would have visited them. Didn't you?"

"I did." Yvon looked at the girls. All of them were young; Lausanne was the oldest at eleven. The rest were between six and nine.

"Not enough?"

"Yeah. My own sources tell me nasty things. About massive armies in the southern continent popping out of the hills, ravaging cities and setting up camps. I fear for us, whether we can survive that."

"I wouldn't worry too much. The Order's making preparations, and so is TreeTree. He's making a whole load of preparations. Even the council's busy preparing for the demons. As a whole, we're doing fine."

Yvon paused, breathed a long sigh. "Is there something underground?"

"Oh? Is there?"

"You don't know about it?" Yvon looked puzzled. "Then...is TreeTree...doing something? All these tremors and shaking. Is it not him?"

"Didn't sound like it's related to what I know." Jura shrugged. He motioned to the initiates. "Anyway, time's up! Three initiates this time. Lausanne, you sit out and watch!"

Lausanne raised a fist.

More spars. The girls and Jura would spar a few times that day. The initiates benefited the most, since they lack combat experience. Lausanne, on the other hand, was starting to plateau. I wasn't sure how it worked, but it sure seemed like there was a limit how much one could gain experience from fighting the same person over and over, even if the gap was huge.

Yvon asked during one of the other breaks, "Do you think we can beat a demon champion?"

"What?"

"You, and me." Yvon pointed to herself.

"Hmm... No." Jura shook his head.

"Why not?"

"Have you ever faced one in battle, Yvon?"

"...no."

"I have. We're quite good. Both of us. But a demon champion...I don't think we are there yet. Not without TreeTree's powers."

"How is it that TreeTree is able to defeat demons, anyway? I've never heard of a Tree Spirit that's able to defeat demons. It's... unlike their nature."

Jura paused. "That's a question I do not ask."

"You should. There was something, isn't it? Maybe he's some kind of unique anti-demon variant sent down by the gods?"

"This is a conversation that I don't want to have, Yvon."

Yvon hmphed. "Fine. But you are his spokesperson. You should know."

"I am fine with other people having secrets, Yvon. I am not a young teenage elf who's obsessed with everything anymore."

"It's not the same. You could lose your life."

"Lives have been lost for far pettier things, Yvon. Let's leave it at that."

Yvon sulked.

---

*[**Research Status:**]*
*[**Beetle** - anti-magma armors stage 4 - 4 months]*
*[**Metal hyperaccumulator trees** - Stage 1 - 6 months]*
*[**Phytoremediation process** - basic - 16 months]*
*[**Dedicated Filtering Blackwater-Plant** - stage 1 – completed]*

With the blackwater filtering plant research complete, I now had a specialized tree type, derived from the trees near the sewers of Ransalah.

New Freeka's sewer project was still under construction, so this tree was a bit early. Thanks to the budget reallocation to the military, the New Freeka Sewer Project was now crawling, with less than half the original workforce and artisans.

Meh. But I didn't want the Order to fund the project, so I deployed some of these new [Filtering Trees] near the present latrines. These trees helped segregate the contaminated water, such that only filtered water passed through.

Poop was generated daily. Daily. It grew. And it must have some way of being recycled or processed. Reluctant to use the Order's funds, I decided to get the newly obtained [Dungbeetles] to dig a subterranean tunnel to act as a 'wastetunnel' for a designated spot, where the poop was aired and sun-dried. My hope was the sun and air could kill or allow natural microbes to partially process the poop, and my future poop-processor trees would be able to do the rest.

The [Dungbeetles] rolled the poop into balls, and over the month, they pushed massive balls of rolled-up poop to a field outside town, where they remained. It kind of resembled a futuristic art installation, a field of round balls of poop.

Thankfully the rain didn't break it up. Seemed like the poopballs had some water resistance.

Or maybe I could use them as a weapon, roll these balls of poop into the enemy, like a bowling ball.

Oh well, this was a temporary measure, while research continued.

"Okay, we decided on helping the heroes...but what are we going to do? I am already eavesdropping on my guests, and it seems like the heroes are not here yet." Meela frowned. She was sitting on the bar in her hotel-tree; Alexis appeared as a ghost on the other seat. There was no one else in the bar.

"I've got magic sensors, so that's going to help a bit when they do appear. I've used what I remember of our own magic to calibrate the sensors, but they keep having false alarm, so I'm still trying to tweak it..."

"But seriously, even if we do locate the next batch of heroes, then what? I'm a hotel, and you are a tree-lab. What can we do? Without TreeTree, at least. He's got subsidiary trees!"

"Can't you get subsidiary trees like TreeTree? Like...hotel chains?"

"Yes, I can, but it's like a level eighty upgrade. I'm only level forty-one! And even then I'm limited to two branches initially."

"That's pretty fast, considering you just started...but yeah. It was a bit risky...if the demon king pops out in another year or so, and the heroes three to six months after that... We've only got like...two years to gain those thirty-nine levels." Alexis twirled a drink. It seemed Meela's bar was ghost-friendly.

"I can make drinks and foods that makes my guests stronger. And as part of a hotel's hospitality services, I do have some healing abilities. I have a [VIP escort] unlock at level fifty, but I'm not sure whether that's any help to the heroes." Meela looked at her upgrades. It seemed she had visibility of what skills she would gain, up until level one hundred. Something that I had yet to figure out why, but I was guessing it was part of the hero-blessings.

"Hmmm...fine. Let's do a recap. Maybe we can figure something out. In terms of potentially useful abilities, I have [probe beetles], [magical sensors], [decipher runes], [copy biological ability], [life-scan], and multiple versions of [heal]," Alexis said. "We have a lot of healing."

"Our physical forms were both derived from TreeTree, and TreeTree's got incredible healing powers."

"Ngeh. You should've taken the beetle. Or the wooden body." Alexis frowned.

"But that [copy biological ability]...what does that do?"

"Pretty much transplant an ability native to a living thing, to another entity. But copying is one thing. After copying, I get an [ability seed]. Then I need to create a [fruit] with the [ability seed]."

"So...what can you copy?"

"Native racial abilities. Like the beetles, that would be [armored body], elves, [nature-affinity], centaurs, and [centaurion endurance]."

"Cool! You can give that to the heroes!"

"You could be right, but then I just realized the heroes don't lack overpowered abilities. They lack..."

"Experience. Knowledge. Other people to take the heat off them. True friends, not scheming nobles and greedy adventurers. People...that won't backstab them." Meela sipped from her wooden cup.

Alexis paused, and she looked up at the chandelier. It was weird having a magical chandelier on top of the bar, but it was one of the aesthetic options Meela had to decorate her hotel. The chandelier comprised of almost twenty little glowing lights, and multiple merchants had inquired about it to buy it from her.

Meela waited. There was no one else in the bar, but a few autonomous Tree-servants, cleaning the rest of the tables and adjusting the chairs. It was quiet; the bar was quite soundproof.

"You're right. They don't need more power or abilities. They need friends."

"Didn't have to be us, though. And they won't trust us just because we come from Earth, and frankly, I don't think I want to tell them that we are from Earth. Maybe...we need to narrow our scope. As it is, helping the heroes is probably out of our league."

Alexis tapped on the bar countertop. It was ghost-friendly. "True. But we do need to find them. They will be most vulnerable at the start. It'll be horrible if..."

"Don't say it." Meela glared.

Alexis nodded. "I know."

"Your probes, can they communicate?"

"I'll find a way."

"But if they don't spawn in this continent…"

"Then it's out of our control. They won't be the last batch of heroes. This plan can be used for all subsequent generations if it works."

Meela nodded. "Ah, true. I would have more branches by then. If I have branches on different continents, they could be like assassin safe houses, like you know, that John Wick film. I'd be a brand name, like the Continental…"

"That wasn't something I expected you to reference, Meela."

"But heroes do need a safe house of some kind. A place to keep their stuff. I've got a niche I can fill!"

Alexis frowned. "How…how about me?"

"You…you could make weapons? Or be like those skill-editing NPCs in the safe areas?"

YEAR 81 MONTH 2

Spring began, and a strange structure was spotted emerging from one of the rifts in our continent. Massive, it resembled a giant walking tortoise with a castle on its back.

Any attempts to approach had been met with stiff resistance from new types of humanoid demons.

"Uh...what do you think?" Jura read the circular from the merchants guild. It advised alternative routes of trade. Somehow, the merchants guild's trade routes circular was one of the best updates on the demonic invasion.

"Sounds like a champion," Meela said.

"A large walking castle."

"If TreeTree could walk, we'd have a Walking Tree versus Walking Castle fight."

"Ugh no." I groaned. "Not keen on that." Besides, I'd lost a lot of power and my consciousness the moment I was no longer connected to the earth, so not exactly keen. "But it does sound like a...champion?"

"How far was it?" Meela asked.

"Not far enough." Jura smiled.

"According to the circular, they predict...maybe four months?"

The merchant guild circular came with a map, and it had a shaded heatmap, resembling a hurricane path kind of map. The merchants used this information for trade-route planning, and there was a small disclaimer saying the information was not guaranteed and demonic movements were unpredictable. The merchants guild bore no responsibility for any loss or damage arising from the use of these maps.

"Should we do anything?" I asked the group.

"Against demon champions..." Madeus paused. "We would need to get the temples' aide. Else we stand no chance."

"The Gaya temple and the other large temples were already mobilizing their best priests and paladins to the capitols. I doubt we will get much aid from them. Their resources are limited," Wesley, the senior priest, responded. "And for them to aid another...uh...faith was weird."

Yeah, we were kind of like a faith now, with me as the 'deity.' I still found it weird, but apparently that was what the temples said, since I had rituals, priests, and a focal point. I hoped I didn't get classified as a cult, though for now the temples classified the Order as a 'folk-faith,' a kind of animistic 'religion.'

"So, we were on our own."

"Oh, well, nothing different, then." I had been making my own preparations for demon champions. I just did not expect it to be...a walking castle.

Madeus then went off tangent. "Ermm...if I may, Aeon? I would like to request we offer refuge."

"To whom?"

"Uh...somebody from Baroosh got in touch with me yesterday. The demonic forces were very close to where they are, and although the army was trying their best to hold back the demons, it seemed the presence of this monster has tipped the scales in the demons' favor."

Ah, Baroosh. That was where Madeus was from. They exiled him, didn't they? Looked like he still had some positive feelings for his former state.

"Many of them are still friends. And they want a backup plan if the Barooshian army can't hold them back."

"Jura?" I wanted to add some conditions, but I thought of asking for views.

"We could accommodate, but they are guests, so they will be expected to behave themselves and follow our rules." Hmm, looked like Jura had similar thoughts.

"Certainly, I will relay the message." Madeus nodded.

"Back to us, what should we do?"

"The walls are not going to hold if a massive monster like that can just...walk through it."

"TreeTree, that...dungeon we attacked. Is it still there?"

"Yeah."

"Can we convert it into a shelter? And I recall there was a deep tunnel from the giant demonic centipede?"

"The tunnel is now home to beetles and fungus, but I can make some space. The former dungeon is empty. I think there are rats, but that shouldn't be a problem."

"Then it's decided. We need to start convert these two locations into fortified shelters. If we can't fight, we need to hide."

There was an uncomfortable look around the group, a realization that this was going to be it. Demons were real.

"Should we tell the people?"

Vice Counsel Laufen nodded. "Yes. If this was going to be hideout, it's best if everyone knows about it."

"Even those outside the order?"

"Yes. We're not going to pick survivors when demons come around," Laufen insisted before anyone could respond. "Whoever gets to the shelters deserve a chance."

The group discussed other matters, usual administrative, trade, and training stuff, and they left when the sun was starting to set.

"TreeTree. The...[secret hideout], you're not willing to let anyone go in."

"Yes. As I said before, it's only for all of you. The most I'm willing to accommodate is in the outer [subsidiary trees], and those for the people I trust." It was a risk, and frankly, after what happened with the druids, I felt I should be more careful with whoever got to come near me, what more inside me.

It was unfortunate that some lives would be lost this way, but I thought my own self-preservation trumped that. I couldn't save everyone, and I didn't plan on trying.

Laufen sighed. I wasn't sure whether she was happy or sad. "Your [secret hideout] was probably one of the safest places this valley has, though."

"If I still stand. But I believe the two options are pretty good. The tunnels don't require me, and the dungeon's been reinforced." The root networks should last for at least a few months before the spatial magic started to collapse on itself. It was probably a good idea to get the builders working on it.

One of the things when disaster happened was that people prayed. It wasn't my first time to receive prayers, but there was something about impending death that caused more people to pray. Some of those citizens prayed to every god, even if they only professed to one. Some even prayed to me.

Not all behaved this way, of course. Some became more devout in times of crisis, putting in a more offerings, going for more blessings and masses.

But this...behavior led to something that was new to me. Throughout New Freeka and the valley, there were about seven trees of prayer: one in the treefolks' village, one up on the slopes of the centaur camps, and the remaining five in New Freeka itself, mostly in the Order's compounds. These functioned as mini-shrines.

[Tree of prayer upgraded]
[Tree of prayer's calming presence significantly improved. Those around

more likely to express their grievances. Tree of prayer gained ability to extract some negative emotions and convert them into essence.]

I mostly listened. After all, there was no real need to interact. I thought to a certain extent most of these citizens knew what they wanted to do with their lives, but anxiety, fear, and worries just clouded their minds, so...they needed a place to vent, to relax, to just think in peace. So if I could talk back, that wasn't exactly something pleasing.

Instead, the Tree of Prayer just bobbed its branches, the leaves shook, and occasionally a small fruit would fall down on right on the person's lap, kind of like, hey-I-heard-you-have-a-fruit. The fruit was just a regular fruit, it was sweet, though, so...most of them ate it, and some of them actually displayed it in their homes. Which was creepy.

Anyway, the amount of too-much-information when people poured their hearts out in their prayers and whispers was...well, immeasurable. Seriously. Elves, centaurs, treefolks, all still had their emotional problems, their professional challenges, financial and money issues. It may be a magical world, but problems were persistent across worlds.

The [Tree of Prayers] had an odd side effect, which was...it remembered the prayers. Especially those who prayed often, regularly over the same thing.

It was an annoying side effect. Because I'd suddenly remember who-and-who cheated on who-and-who and I didn't need that sort of telenovela in my tree life.

I told myself that it was a public service and it helped to keep the citizens pacified. Like my other services, the birth and death services—

"We should have more," Ivy suggested.

"Huh?"

"They're good intel. It helps me with my dossier." Ivy's like a real spymaster now. "If you could create one in Ransalah, that would be ideal."

"...that's a great idea."

On the Salah side of things, they'd finally responded to Jura's letter. There was a follow-up letter sent two months ago, just lightly reminding the kingdom of the official letter sent a year ago.

So it seemed they picked someone to be the scapegoat.

An unfortunate administrator and some of his subordinates were identified as the mastermind of the massacre, and he would be transported to New Freeka.

"A scapegoat."

"Could really be him. We have to interview him to know for sure. The prisoner convoy will be escorted, and they will arrive in a month." Jura shrugged. "Let's see what comes out of this."

"Perhaps he has a passing involvement."

"I would think so. Salah isn't that stupid to surrender someone with totally no involvement. The point was to sacrifice the tail to spare the head, so the real mastermind of such slaughter was spared."

"It could be it's just some prince up there, who just goes, 'Burn the rebels,' and everyone down there just carries it out," Madeus chimed in. "It's very common for royalties to say things without actually thinking about the lives lost."

"You say that like it's...an everyday thing." Meela/Mika frowned.

"Yes, Mika. That was indeed how the kings and royalties are. Our role as their servants and subordinates was to understand our liege and guess what they truly desire. We cannot always take the words of our king for what it is."

At that point, I thought, *That sounds like insubordination or treason.*

"After all, our king has a wish, a desire, and sometimes the words he has cannot communicate that will, though some kings have [skills] that help with that."

Jura raised a hand, and everyone quiet down. "Let us not speculate. We will wait for whoever they sent. TreeTree, I must trouble you to help us in our interrogation. Would you happen to have those...tree saps from long ago? The ones that make them...delirious?"

"Of course. I'll make some." It wasn't hard to make different kinds of tree saps; regular plants made poisons and allergy-triggering saps all the time, so it was easy-peasy for a magic tree. In fact, I should totally infuse more magic into it.

Anyway, back to Ivy.

"Ivy, you suggested having a [tree of prayer] in Ransalah?"

"Yes, master. These people seem to confess their challenges to the Tree so easily. Why go through all the trouble of spying when they are more than willing to tell a tree? There is nothing to lose, and if anything, we gain insights into the human mind."

"...fine. But where and how should we do it?"

"New Freeka can make a goodwill gift, since they gave this scapegoat to us. Then manipulate the officials to plant the sapling in a public park, which we can then replace with the [tree of prayer]. Call it the [New Freeka - Salah friendship tree]."

That sounded like something politicians did back on Earth, but I thought it could work.

"I could make a sapling-sized [tree of prayer]."

And so Jura arranged for a small sapling of a [tree of prayer] to be sent as a gift. It was sent, planted in a large vase so the [Tree of Prayer] didn't die, escorted by the [Arborist]. Since Hutan sent a tree-caretaker, it made sense to call on his services for such transportation duties.

The merchants completed their big deal, and the demanded goods were finally delivered.

"Good job. Now, leave them here." Wesley and the master of ceremonies pointed to a place. The workers started to unload.

"Just...leave them here?" the merchants stuttered. The master of ceremonies nodded, and the jewels and gold were unloaded.

"Yes." Beetles started to emerge from the woods, and some

started to tug at the shipment. The merchant wanted to say something and pointed to the beetles, and the master of ceremonies smiled. "The shipment was for the Tree Spirit, and it was time for us to leave."

The master of ceremonies and a few of the Order's men started to walk. The merchants were still a bit shocked by the beetles that were pulling the shipments into the tunnels that suddenly appeared. "Uhh...uhh...this was fine?"

"Have you not done business for tree spirits before?" Wesley grinned.

"Aaaa...of...of course, I have." The merchant tried to straighten himself up. Procuring the gold and hiring a large escort, only to put them in an empty spot for beetles...it was a first, for sure.

After everyone leaves, the beetles continued unpacking the goods in the network of tunnels underneath my trees. I created these tunnels recently because realizing how vulnerable I was, I wanted some of the structures to be underground, and that was... the ten new root-brain complexes and the Grand Mind Tree project.

> *[**Grand Mind Tree's construction has begun**. 18 months to completion]*

YEAR 81, MONTH 3

The updates from the merchant network increased in frequency, especially from the Western Theatre head office. Two towns were lost in a month, a large army of demons escorted the walking demon castle wherever it went, and throughout the continent, the demons had been spotted in more locations.

"One of our merchants was attacked. Half his convoy was destroyed, but luckily a party of riders managed to come to their aid!"

"Are we not far away?"

"Well...it seems the demons now have small raiding parties, targeting weak spots and gaps in the nation's defenses. It's a very... uh...kingdomish tactic."

The raiding parties were one to two hundred demons strong, populated by mounted humanoid demons on hellhounds.

"Don't kings and many generals have some kind of [Watcher] ability?" Jura asked. "I had the impression kings have ways of watching over their territories."

"Well, yes, but such skills are not exactly...detailed."

The Council deployed multiple two hundred–strong militia patrols to help protect the trade routes, but honestly, I would know. My [subsidiary trees] functioned like my watchtowers; failing that, there was the [rootnet] so if there was anything, I would like to think that I would be the first to know the presence of demons near New Freeka.

But with demons, one could never be too careful, so I spread out my beetles to a few locations around as an additional protection force.

This month, I added more to my anti-demon bolts and more weapons for the elves and the Order. In fact, this occupied most of my time, my preparations to face the demon champions. And made a whole load more bolts and weapons.

[Woodcrafting upgraded]
  *[**Skill learned**: Wooden Anti-demon equipment-crafting]*
  [Essence infusion upgraded]

More! More bolts. Spears. Shields. More!

"What if it's the demon king?" Jura asked.

"Then we die." If I could shrug, I would. The demon king was as close to a death sentence, wasn't it? If the heroes could die, how could we face it? I didn't think some anti-demon shield was going to survive a nuclear explosion.

Anyway, demon king was not here yet. So that was not something to worry about.

"Heh. I guess we will all run."

"Yes. On that front, maybe we should be preparing like Madeus's friends. Tell the Hutan council druids to grant you safe passage as compensation. Just in case."

Jura paused. "Okay."

"I will be fine. I want you to take everyone as far as you can if a demon king comes our way. Arrange for some kind of teleportation…"

"I'll speak to Madeus about it…" Jura sat on his chair. "This feels…morbid."

"Why? Staring death in the face sounds morbid?"

"Not that. We villagers used to live and let live. Things happened, and then we reacted to it. For me, having to predict what might happen and then try to prevent or prepare for it..."

"Unusual."

"Yes. It's a strange thing to do. Plotting and planning. The most we planned for was when to plant our crops and when to build houses. And even then, we defer to the wisdom of our elders or tree spirits."

"It is the burden of those who lead to see what lies ahead and to guide them. Know that your actions will determine whether your friends and family lives or dies." Was that me? Where did such TreeTree wisdom come from?

Jura slumped on his chair. "That is a mindset I am still coming to terms with. Truly, only when faced with demons I realize how heavy this burden is."

"Everyone prepares for it. This is just on a larger scale, with more players. It was once about how much stronger you can be, but now, it is about how much stronger the Order is."

Jura paced the room and had a sip of ginger-flavored tea. I thought he preferred ginger tea over the other flavors. Meela had been experimenting on tea flavors as a specialty drink for her morning and lunch crowds, so she had funky flavors like Garlic Tea, Herbal Mint Tea, and Grape-Ginger Tea.

"Ahhhh." Jura stretched, tired.

A knock and then a voice from outside the door. "Counsel, the suspect is awake." There was a small prison in the Order's compound, located beneath one of the buildings. It was lightly guarded, just two beetles there.

Salah's scapegoat.

"Yes. I ordered the burning. I was the officer in charge of the military draft for that region," he said when interrogated. He tried to put up a brave face, but it seemed like he was hiding something.

Jura looked. So did everyone else behind the bars. The elves shared a glance, and one of them, Emile, started to cry. Somehow, it brought out a strange emotion in her heart.

A vine administered the hallucinatory sap I'd prepared.

Jura sat, facing the officer. "I ask you again, did you order the burning of Freeka?"

"Yes...yes, I did," he said. Something wasn't right.

So he went into the biolab pod for testing. Hmmm...

His soulspring looked fine. The skills were okay... If he was lying or being forced to, there should be something to hint at the truth. I would have to go deeper and call on the powers of the soul forge.

Once he was knocked unconscious, a few beetles helped to transport his body into the main pod in my main body. With it, I used the soul forge's power to pry into the outer soul shell.

What I saw was the usual human soul, semi-translucent, but in that soul's head, there was a small bluish blob.

As I attempted to alter or touch it, a strong force repelled me.

[Blocked by Oath]

Huh?

It seemed there was no progress here, either, and it looked like he wasn't under the influence of magic.

"Is he lying?" Jura asked.

"I have no clue." The oath could have nothing to do with the burning. Or it could be key.

It looked like I had to use other means of interrogation, so I subjected him to some more hallucinogens and relaxants.

With my vines wrapped around him, I used an authoritative version of my telepathic voice.

"You died." I spoke to the prisoner, now in a daze because of the crazy cocktail of hallucinogens, relaxants, and other stuff.

"I-I have? How?" he asked, flailing his arms.

"Poison. Died in your sleep."

"Ah...so that's what they were feeding me. Why am I looking at a scary-looking Tree? Is this hell?"

"Yes. This is the entrance to hell. You died near a Tree Spirit, so this is where you will depart to hell."

He paused and looked confused. "I still feel…a pulse?"

"What made you think hell would not have a pulse?"

"Ah…so I might not be dead?"

"It's a common mistake. When you die, your soul goes to this other [soul realm], awaiting reincarnation. During that waiting time, life goes on normally."

He paused. "Uh…okay."

"So, please wait. There is a long queue to enter hell, so it will take some time. Make yourself feel comfortable here." I didn't know how successful this would be, but I was going to overload his body with so much of these saps that he was going to lose his grasp with reality.

"Heh…there is a queue to hell?"

"Everyone's a sinner. So it's natural the path to hell is extremely crowded and why we have demons so often. Since we are on this topic, would you like to confess your sins?" That was a whole load of bullshit, but he bought it.

He paused, and he started to break down, shouting and weeping. I was not sure whether he realized it, but I increased the dosage a bit more.

He started talking about how many people he killed, the people he betrayed, the families he lost. It was kind of like we were having a session of [Tree of Prayer] confessions.

He talked for a good hour, alternating between breaking down, crying, and anger.

But then I got what I wanted. "I…It was just fair that I died this way. I sent the army to burn the village. I mean, the commander said that dissenters should be punished…but maybe I did go overboard. I gained levels in [Authoritarian] when I ordered all those villages burned. I-I was drowning in joy when I gained levels. The skills were powerful, too! I got a skill like [Submission], which worked so wonderfully with the commoner ladies!"

Oh. I'd expected a scapegoat...but color me impressed, Salah actually sent the right guy. And a scum, too.

"But could you fault me? The commander himself burned many villages to the ground when they rebelled against the king. All of us did. We did what we had to to enforce order. Fear was key to maintaining control. It was either that or we would be chopped for punishing the villages too lightly."

Hmmm...looked like maybe not. It was an institutional failure.

"We burned many villages. When there was a plague, we culled. When there was a suspected demonologist, we culled the villages. There was no time for proper justice, we lack the resources, manpower, and even if we did, there was no way of ensuring justice was properly conducted. Every kingdom did what it felt was right!"

Uh...

"Maybe...maybe all of us should just burn to the ground, you know?"

He sat, surrounded by the vines and roots.

"I... All of us were sinners. Maybe the demon king should just crush all of us."

Did I overdo the tree saps?

Uh...

"Say, would I be able to meet the commander here? Or is he already on the other side? How long a backlog are we talking about?"

I definitely overdid the tree saps.

*[**Skill upgraded**: Tree saps]*
　*[**Skill obtained**: Condensed Tree Psychedelics]*
　*[**Dream tutor variant obtained. Skill**: Psychedelic dreams]*
　*[**Dream tutor variant obtained. Skill**: Mystical dreams]*

YEAR 81 MONTH 4

The war in the Barooshian territories deteriorated. The presence of the walking demon castle greatly hindered all attempted progress, and even with high-level individuals, the demons had now deployed 'knights.'

These demons had been described as elites, capable of standing up to a level forty elite soldier toe to toe, and were described as humanoid, horned demons, usually with one large, unnaturally crimson wing. They had been seen wielding spears, swords, axes, and many other types of melee weapons.

"No rifts near our location yet," the captain elaborated. It was a once every other day meeting to gather data on the demons. They were coming, and everyone was feeling a little tense.

"That's of no comfort. We are just waiting." Jura sighed.

"One of the merchants wants to meet, Counsel."

"Huh. Sure."

A merchant walked into Jura's office chambers. "Salutations, Counsel. I'll get to the point. The merchant guild is trying to build a coalition force to protect key trade routes, especially those that cut through the kingdoms nearest to the spotted giant demon walker. In exchange for the various nations' contributions to the force, led by a group of senior military men, the merchants guild will offer preferential prices on goods well below market rates, and also the rights of first purchases on goods passing through these routes."

"You sure didn't mince words there." Jura sat and thought for a moment. "How many men were you talking about? Have you spoken to the High Council?"

"Yes, I have. They are keen, but only if the Order also participates. They will match every person you put in."

"Heh, clever of them. If the Order doesn't participate, then we look like scum." Jura sat and twirled a wooden pen. "Back to my question, how many men does the guild want?"

"Ideally, we want high-level individuals. Elites, if possible. Numbers, while they do have their own quality, are not the most suitable countermeasure against a demonic force-of-nature like the giant demon walker."

"I-I need to have some discussions. Come back in two days." The merchant bowed and left.

Jura turned and called in the management team. "Madeus, would you be keen? I'm also planning to talk to Yvon. If anything, I would like both of you to participate..."

Madeus shook his head. "I'm having fun teaching the kids in the orphanage."

Well, turned out Yvon also had a similar idea. "The Valthorn kids need me. I'm not leaving them alone with TreeTree, not without my supervision."

Also, now that we knew quite certainly the Salah guy was the 'right' guy, I was a bit stuck with what to do.

"Y'know, if he wasn't the right person, it's not cool to drug him and make him think he died. How did you plan on integrating or undoing the effects of such a powerful hallucination?"

"Hmmm, I had a hunch he was hiding something."

"He could be hiding other things."

"Too bad. I'll just make him think it's all a dream. You know, like those exceedingly vivid dreams that you wake up from wondering what in the world just happened."

"That sounds like the kind of essays I used to write for school." Meela grinned.

When I delivered the message to the elves that he was the right guy, Laufen stormed up and went to one of the Tree of Prayers to gather her thoughts. Somehow the reality that she faced the person who indirectly caused the death of her husband made her…angry.

"I want to slap him many, many times."

"Okay." So the drugged delirious prisoner was 'freed' from his biopod prison, and Laufen slapped him many times. In fact, the other elves joined when they saw Laufen started to slap the man.

"You! You evil man! Our lives lost just because you felt like it!" Laufen slapped. "I had thought that maybe you had a vendetta, but no." She slapped again. "We were just." Another slap. "Another village to burn." Another slap. The guy was delirious. The overdose of hallucinogens had massively distorted his sense of reality.

"Is this like purgatory? Where I meet those I have sinned and answer for them?" he asked.

Which only made Laufen even more mad. "Hell yeah, it is." She slapped him some more. The other elves, like Emile and Belle, both just gave him one slap. One big, fat slap. And that was it.

They walked away. Because although they were angry, watching Laufen's ugly chain of slaps made them feel like they needed to be above this.

"All because of some stupid levels! Were our lives all so meaningless and insignificant to these nobles and lords?" Laufen slapped.

The guy just laughed. He'd lost it, really. "Yes, my dear. Yes. Actually, even lords and nobles were meaningless. We all die in the end. Everyone's just out for themselves and we make life difficult for everyone that is not us."

Laufen slapped him in between those words, so it was actually not so coherent. "AGGGHHHH." She slapped him a few more times, until she stopped, sat on the ground, and started to weep.

Lausanne watched and gave her mom a hug. "Mommy...it's okay...it's okay..."

The guy's face was red and blue from all the slaps, and I thought it's time to end it. So some vines pulled the guy back into the pod. "I'll keep him for now."

Laufen still cried, so she didn't respond to my statement. Jura just watched, and he walked away.

"TreeTree...just kill him already. Him being insane and mocking us with that insanity just makes us feel worse."

Hmm. Well, I kind of figured he was gonna die anyway, but to kill him would be a waste of valuable 'mortals.' He would join the other criminals on death row that I'd reserved for my soul-related experiments.

I mean, if the justice system said who was to die, might as well contribute to science while dying. It wasn't as if the manner of death made a difference. It was a position opposed by Meela and Alexis, of course, but they couldn't stop me.

If I was going to figure out how to fix Jura's arms, I needed more experience with all the sophisticated meddling in the soul forge.

In the past month, in between creating more of those anti-demon bolts and weapons, I'd been experimenting with creating an arm, and indeed, the first thing I needed was to reverse-engineer the thing that protected a body while undergoing the forge process.

It seemed there was a specific frequency to the mana, kind of like a state in which the mana was able to hold its form despite the maelstrom within the [soul forge], and mastering this process would allow my feelers to 'interact' with the exposed soul fragments in the soul forge.

So, firstly, the process required the creation of more 'mana-tuning' organs. It took quite a few tries, but it was a whole lot easier once I used some of the jewels as regulators. I knew this because it was part of why jewels were so commonly used in magic items because precious gems and jewels had a kind of mana-storage, mana-stabilizing quality to them.

Essentially, it was like a ball of roots organized along a few jewels as nodes, with two feeler ends. Kind of like a large tuning fork, and the length-width of that fork determined the 'frequency' and 'spin.'

With it, I was then able to coat my feelers with a 'tuned mana,' which protected it from the effects of the [soul forge] by about ninety to ninety-five percent. Pretty good, I thought.

Next was to make simple organs. Using animals as my test case, I tried to make small tails and whiskers, repair ears, and repair skin.

Most of them failed, but I was getting better at the smaller stuff. Relatively speaking.

I judged my performance by the size of the little animals' explosion when 'healed.'

YEAR 81 MONTH 5

My first encounter with this generation's demons, a pack of humanoid demon riders spotted passing through one chain of [subsidiary tree] that stretched up to the previous dungeon hole. The chain of subsidiary trees, with New Freeka Valley as the center, was kind of like a 'spider net.'

They didn't attack my trees. But I moved some beetles to the area as I watched their actions.

These demonoids were clearly more intelligent than before. There was a visible leader, giving some kind of instruction, in a language I couldn't fathom. They were setting up an ambush.

I watched them camp there for five days until a trader caravan approached the area.

Their ambush was countered by an ambush from my beetles. It went well. Despite their intelligence, their ability to fight was just about...average. A regular demonoid was at the same strength as a regular hellhound. Which wasn't much.

Their leader was much better; it took two beetles to take him down.

"The merchants are struggling to keep certain trade routes with the demons employing such guerilla tactics."

"I'm impressed that demons have the concept of attacking supply chains."

"Impressed? This was horrifying. We could spot demons a mile away thanks to their unfettered destruction! Now we can't! That's not a good thing!"

"Hmm...I think we shouldn't overreact. It seems the precautions needed will be similar to bandits, if their raiding parties are so small. A small group of adventurers would've been able to defeat that raiding party."

"The threat of the raiding party was small, but the thought that there is potentially sophisticated intelligence behind the demons..."

"TreeTree, you said your trees spotted them?"

"Yeah."

Jura paused and sat. The captain then asked, "Can we have a perimeter of trees? Would it be possible?"

"Uh...no. I can't make that many trees." Four lines as it was almost maxed out my [subsidiary tree] quota. Unless I gained levels or the skill got an upgrade, I didn't think I could spam more [subsidiary trees].

I did have my basic tree-eye, but there were only ten of those, and I wanted to keep those for special places where I wanted to see things for myself.

Trevor interrupted.

Demons.

"There was more of them," Trevor said to me.

"What?"

"A pack of three hundred demons appeared. North. Mostly regular demonoids, but this pack had about ten of the 'captain' grade demons and one mounted 'knight.'"

"Beetles?" I looked at the map, and Trevor pointed me to the nearest group of fifty or so beetles. There was another group of thirty beetles further away. "Okay, let's group them together."

"They won't make it in time to save that convoy if they do." What? A convoy?

Trevor changed my vision to see a convoy of eight carriages and about twenty merchants. "Recommend we send the fifty beetles now, and hopefully the thirty beetles can join the battle midway. Or if you want to intervene directly…with root strikes."

"Heh," Well, I was itching for a fight.

[Rooting field].

Roots emerged from a field of grass, and they quickly entangled the group of three hundred demonoids. The leaders of the group were able to cut the roots off, and then my squad of fifty beetles arrived. The beetles' charge easily destroyed quite a bit of the regular demonoids.

Except the knight. It had a black sword, and in a single slash, it cut one of the beetles in half.

"Noooooooooooooo." Horns was upset. "Kill that enemy."

The demon knight cut down a few more beetles. I recalled seeing demon knights during the previous war, the 'demonized' humans. But this knight was pure demon, and I would say he was about level…forty? I wasn't too sure.

Heh. No point delaying.

[Serpentine Rootstrike].

Multiple roots appeared and pierced through the demons, like a multi-headed hydra. The knight dodged and cut through some of the roots, but the roots, when cut down, instead split into more roots, which attacked the knight.

The knight cut down more roots, but it kept breaking up into more roots. And then one root speared through the knight from the back.

And it turned into ash.

"Huh." If the demons could create more knights at that level, the kingdoms were going to have a whole lot of problems.

Turned out, shit was already pretty bad. News from the Southern Continent came, and it wasn't pretty down south. Another walking castle had been spotted, and they'd overrun a few kingdoms. The Southern continent was essentially in a pure-war mode, every nation in the region combining their forces, where they could, to delay the demons' advance.

"These numbers…"

The captain started to read out the merchants' guild report. "Are they trying to ask for help?" The report had a whole load of numbers on the size of the demon armies. In the southern continent, they'd spotted six different armies with at least fifty thousand demons.

"Sounds like it. The merchants' guild can't formally request for aid without the consent of the local kingdoms. At best, they will try to build a coalition with the local kingdoms, but it's something they were already doing…"

"Is it normally this bad?" I asked the captains. They shrugged.

"I don't know, but…it's sure messier this time around."

"How many have been displaced?" Jura wondered. "Are we going to get more refugees?"

"A lot. With all continents facing some demon issues, the refugees don't really have a lot of choices on where to go."

"What about the islands?"

"Hmmm…sounds like they won't be able to run away from the south that easily. So, if anything, we're still going to get Barooshian refugees…"

"The elven kingdoms were up north, right?" Laufen suddenly asked.

"Yeah. Why'd you ask?"

"If Baroosh was in trouble, how about the other elves?"

Madeus paused. "I-I believe they would not be in any better shape. The demon walker is a massive size and the army's not been defeated yet."

"We need to figure out how to hide," Jura pondered. It was only six months into the beginning of the demons, and things were already not great.

And that was how I spent more time on the underground

tunnels. The farmers did already have 'warmed' farmhouses and underground chambers, but I didn't, and I thought I may be able to do things...differently.

The underground tunnels were humid but had no sunlight. Any plants that needed to survive here would have to have long roots and somehow have 'tubers' that stored their food in the tunnels, which the refugees could use.

Using [root tunnels], we built a network of tunnels, with rooms, and with some wood magic and [woodcrafting] made wooden furniture and flooring to make the rooms somewhat habitable. In the event the demons overran the surface, though, they would need a source of food and water. It was fairly easy to create roots that stored some water and food as emergency rations, since I had the [tuberous storage], which, when not storing 'energy,' could be converted into a massive edible potato and a high-water content potato.

"Preparing for the apocalypse?" Meela seemed quite interested in all the preparations. I thought she recently added a few underground chambers to her hotel, so I thought we were aligned on that part.

"Yeah. This demon king feels different."

"I doubt it'll be that different. Maybe it's just a change in the minions. The previous demon king we faced was a floating castle."

Alexis then butted in. "I like all these preparations. Reminds me of the kind of nuclear bunkers we have, preparing for eventual doomsday."

"I should add something like that to the basement of my hotel, huh?"

"Of course, if a disaster happens, a hotel must have a safe space for its guests! It should be reinforced and close to impenetrable." Alexis laughed, and Meela nodded.

"True...I guess if I wanted to make a hotel like the Continental, it better be a battle-ready hotel."

"You can start by adding a vault, a strong room, an armory..." Alexis rattled on a list of things to add.

"Uh...I think we're getting sidetracked. I'm trying to make habitable hideouts for the citizens in case things deteriorate." I had to bring the conversation back on track. "And if both of you want to help, help me with it."

Alexis stopped and thought for a moment. "Hmmm...it'll need some artificial sunlight. Perhaps mana-powered lights, and then with it, grow some kind of vegetables under those lights?"

"Oh." That was kind of like the greenhouse idea again, but indoors.

So we tried it out. I got Trevor and Dimitree to help, since I was really kind of tired of doing things on my own; there was just so much to do, so many things to manage.

We upgraded the tunnels into canister-like compartments, each canister a self-sufficient setup, with a water storage plant, fungi and plant growing area, food storage, and wooden beds. It had metal-reinforced wooden pillars and walls, for additional strength and toughness.

It was kind of like segments and sections in buildings.

*[**New skill acquired**: Customizable Roots]*
[Customizable Roots function like the underground equivalents of your customizable branches. Each subsidiary tree now can support one customizable branch and one customizable root. Choosing the customizable roots will shrink the [Tuberous Storage] of that subsidiary tree.]

Oh. Cool?

"How does it look?"

Jura and the elves looked around at the new network of underground housing cum hideouts.

"Just needs some more lights for additional brightness, but for a war-time hideout, absolutely luxurious."

"The food supply may be insufficient, though, since these things depend on you growing your own vegetables. But at least there is water, and the potatoes on the wall are still growing..." The potatoes on a segment of the wall were still linked to the roots. It was like the 'seed' of the potato, so the refugees could pluck the potato and a new one would grow.

"Good enough. I suppose next will be fortification and security."

Alexis and Meela added, "How about air? Is there sufficient oxygen down there? Ventilation is super important in underground spaces! People could die from choking and smoke!"

"Good point..." I had thought of using the plants, but the plants probably didn't produce enough oxygen.

"Could you use mana to create oxygen?"

"Uh...is there a spell like that?"

*[**Natural Tree Ability**: Water, oxygen, carbon cycle - converts water to air, or air to water. Uses mana.]*

Oh. That was easy. Turned out I had that ability all the while.

But it didn't solve the problem if I wasn't there. How did the refugees get air?

"Do you have plants that create air?"

"No..." Maybe there were, but I'd need to find them.

It was Madeus that gave the solution. "We'll get some 'Gems of breathing.' Those gems can produce air at a mana cost, and with that we can breathe. It doesn't require much mana that ordinary folks with some magic should be able to operate."

"That's quite expensive." Jura nodded after the Treasurer told him the expected cost. "But we'll get a dozen. And the 'gems of sunlight' as well, if we plan to grow these plants underground."

Ah, turned out, there were some off-the-shelf solutions already.

Alexis paused. "Can you ask for some of those gems? Ask Jura to buy a bit more?"

"Our coffers are a bit low after my recent spend on the gold and jewels for the Grand Mind-Tree, so..."

Alexis frowned. "I could use some of those for research."

YEAR 81, MONTH 6

The magical sensors went crazy. Across my many subsidiary trees and biolabs, the array picked up multiple large surges of energy.

"Something's happening." Alexis was the first to be disturbed by the sensor readings. The air seemed tense, and a sudden gust of wind followed. A while later, my network of roots started to detect tremors from afar, the sign of a massive explosion.

"Jura, any idea what's going on?" Jura was oblivious to it because, well, unless you had a built-in magical sensor in your body, you wouldn't notice it.

"Uh..."

It was Madeus who ran in, along with Yvon, to the Jura's Counsel Chambers. "A massive magical explosion has been detected. The demon walker was attacked with some kind of projectile weapon."

"Oh, isn't that good news? Who did it?" Jura asked.

"The Barooshian court gathered their mages and the voluntary sacrifices of a few young men and women. It's...forbidden blood magic. And it didn't work. Instead of destroying it, the magical projectile heavily injured the demon walker, and now it's marching for the Barooshian capital."

"Blood magic." Jura looked at Madeus suspiciously. "Baroosh has blood magic? And sacrifices?"

"...there was a hidden faction in the wizarding academy studying blood magic. Secretly. But the king gave his consent to do this."

"The blizzard may have links to Baroosh..." Meela said. "What's Baroosh's relationship with Nung, Takde, and Salah?"

Madeus shrugged, a little bit ashamed.

"Okay, I don't know. But whatever it is, that magical disturbance came from Baroosh."

The magical sensors went off again. But this time, it wasn't from Baroosh's general vicinity. It came from further north, from the coast.

"Uh...any idea what's going on?"

We didn't know. Until news came about a week later that the same Blood Magic Ritual was repeated in another kingdom south of Salah...with more sacrifice.

And the worse part? The second projectile missed the demon walker and left a crater filled with an unpleasant miasma.

"Madeus...is there a cult practicing blood magic throughout the continent?"

"Uh...there are all sorts of cults out there, practicing all kinds of obscure magics. No one really knows, but I would say...yes?"

"The demon walker changed direction. It...it's now heading south."

"What?"

Another magical disturbance. My sensors were starting to become quite attuned to this. It was the same country, and they did the ritual. Again.

"How many times can this ritual be repeated?"

"I-I don't know?"

This time, we all saw it, because the dark purple and red magical projectile flew overhead. Even with my spiritual vision, I could see it. It was a missile made of condensed magics, sacrificed lives, and a whole load of unknown energies.

"It's from a country called Gila." The array of magical sensors could now track the movement of the magical energy. A kingdom led by a new king? There was little I knew of them that wasn't outdated.

This third blood ritual bullet exploded at the edges of Barooshian border. Scrying revealed half of the castle on the demon walker's back was destroyed. The regular demons died. But it didn't stop the walker.

Oh no, it didn't. "Uh...it's still headed south."

"Are they planning to use this against the demon king?"

Well, it turned out Gila and Baroosh were not alone. In the southern continent, a few similar spells were used to great success. They destroyed a demon walker.

The demon walker, though, now moved as fast as it could toward Gila, devouring every single town or village in its path and, with it, a growing army of demons.

"Uh...it's coming here."

"This is insane!" Alexis screamed. She used the readings from the magical sensors and her own sensors. "It's pretty much a magical nuclear weapon, tuned to cause immense destruction in a narrow area."

News indeed spoke of the location of the missed shot turned into a corrupted, haunted, poisoned place, where everything died and strange alien monsters emerged from it.

But, despite the costs, the fact that there was a reliable weapon against these demonic walker-giants gave great hope to many kingdoms. A weapon that could fight back! So it seemed there was widespread propaganda that the magus had discovered a potent magical spell able to defeat the demons. No longer did they have to fear the champions.

"TreeTree, I hate you," Alexis said one evening at the news that more such rituals were being used throughout the world.

"Why?"

"You were preparing for underground hideouts. Did you have a spirit vision or epiphany that you somehow saw this coming? Hex

Bombs?" Alexis called them hex bombs because they left a hex on the land.

"Honestly, no. I was preparing for the possibility that a demon champion would defeat me. But this feels too coordinated. Who's teaching the process of this ritual to all the different kingdoms? The speed this ritual spread was unreal."

"The kings won't hear naysayers now. They all bought the story that this spell can defeat the walkers, and they have two success cases now." One in the Southern Continent, and one in the Eastern Theatre. People celebrated, ignoring the reality that there were sacrifices needed for each shot, which numbered between hundreds to thousands, less if the person was of a high magical power and level.

"But one was still walking our way." After Gila's two shots, they stopped. The demon walker was wounded, with a strong hex on its body, but it was still headed this way.

Deep inside, I just knew that it was going to come through here. I didn't need a messenger running inside the room shouting.

"Demon walker was headed for New Freeka…expected to be two to three weeks away. With an army of forty thousand demonoids."

It was just how it was. I was a magical tree, and somehow, I would always end up fighting demons.

Which was fine. Demons were my natural enemies.

I just didn't appreciate being potentially in the line of fire of a Hexbomb.

YEAR 81 MONTH 6

The demonoids came over the hills, the giant walker with the body of something resembling a mutant giant tortoise with a castle on top. The castle consisted of multiple reddish spires with jagged edges, resembling the teeth of a monster.

It wasn't hard to tell that it was approaching. The demonic army would cut down the trees in its path, and I could feel the walker's energy; with each step, a bit more of its energy pushed back on my 'bubble' and caused the effective radius of my [lesser demonic suppression aura] to shrink.

But whatever that was, it only worked on the outer area. At this distance, in this valley, the aura from my main body was strong, and here, it overlapped against whatever that demon walker emitted.

Together, with the walker, the fifty thousand or so demonoids crossed the rolling hills. By the scouts count, the army increased by ten thousand, and this was due to the 'bases' and the walker itself being a mobile demon production factory.

Or as Alexis called it, a 'hive.' Like a beehive that made more bees.

The past three weeks, along the expected path of the demon

army, we built a few more layers of walls, filled with traps and places for the soldiers to retreat, and tunnels for the beetles to spring a surprise attack.

Honestly, I felt confident. A defensive battle was pretty much how I could fight, and it was something that I was good at. And we had been preparing for this fight.

And when the demon walker emerged, I felt ready.

The demon walker's spires somewhat recovered, the damage from the blood hex magic was no longer noticeable, so we presumed they had some self-healing ability. Until we saw the other side of the giant walker, where a large chunk of its body glowed purple, as if it oozed a magical rot. This massive giant tortoise with a big castle on its shell stomped, and the earth shook. Luckily, the walls held. The roots and plants helped to absorb the shockwave.

"A zaratan." Alexis was the one with a wide general knowledge. "A walking zaratan, instead of an island on its back—"

A loud but deep roar shook the entire valley.

"Trivia will have to wait."

The demon walker roared again, and that signaled the beginning of this battle. The army of demonoids charged toward the first layer of walls into the [carnivorous plants] and [cactus defense systems].

And the sound of wood and demon colliding became the background chorus. The demons chopped the defenses down, but not before the carnivorous plants devoured some of the demonoids, and in doing so, gradually, but surely, reduced the number of demonoids. I reckoned about one thousand to two thousand demonoids fell before the outermost layer was breached.

Jura, Madeus, and Yvon prepared on top of the fourth makeshift wall layer. "Lausanne, stay with TreeTree. This is not your battle, not yet."

"But my level is already in the thirties! I should be out there fighting!" the young lady protested. She, too, was armed for battle, and she had two anti-demon wooden short-spears on her back.

"She's right. She's a valuable battlefield asset. We need her on the field, together with the girls," one of the captains said. The archers got into position. They'd been waiting for this moment. Many had a good meal last night, perhaps in preparation of death.

"No. Not Lausanne, and not the kids. The Valthorns stay back," Jura insisted. "Right, TreeTree?"

"Lausanne should be fighting, but let her take one of the flanks where it's less risky. Together with Horns, the beetles will cover her." The beetles were all hidden in the tunnels. All ten thousand of them. But I could spare some to act as Lausanne's squad.

The demon walker roared, and the demonoids all received a boost it. My [lesser demonic suppression] was effective, and the roar merely offset the effects of my aura.

Yvon nodded. "You can't coddle her forever. Fighting demons is a regular affair. She best get some experience—"

The giant walker had a large head, and its head resembled part-tortoise, part-dragon. It had spikes and horns, and it roared, revealing its fangs. It was a different roar; the vibration was different. And that roar sent out an energy blast.

[Steelwood barrier] [Woodshield] [Shield Generators].

The subsidiary trees that functioned as shield generators created a large wall of wood, blocking the energy blast—

Crack.

The energy projectile from the blast slammed into the shields, and it crushed the first barrier and woodshield and then cracked the last shield.

"Okay, fine. Go. Keep yourself safe." Jura sighed, turned, and faced the horde of demonoids. The demon knights led the charge against the first layer walls. "Remember what we discussed. We've got to take on the demon knights. TreeTree will focus on the demon walker."

Yvon nodded and then shrugged. "Though I would prefer to observe TreeTree in action, but I suppose we don't have a choice… Be careful of the knights."

Lausanne smiled. "Okay. Stay safe, everyone." Jura gave Lausanne a pat on the head.

"You, too. Retreat or ask for TreeTree's help if you're in trouble. Better alive than dead."

An armor of wood surrounded Jura, and in his hand, a dark-brown wooden sword. There were multiple wooden spears on his back and multiple smaller wooden stakes enchanted to weaken demons.

"And Yvon, you can watch after the 'knights' are destroyed."

The demonoid horde still charged. And in one area where the density was highest, I activated [Root Surge] and skewered about two thousand demonoids.

The walker stepped closer, and the earth shook. It roared another energy blast, this time aimed for the second layer of walls. I couldn't stop the full power of the energy projectile in time, and this time, a section of the second layer walls disintegrated and killed about twenty archers and the beetles hiding underneath.

"TreeTree, can you stop that blast?" Jura asked while running toward the army. The archers had started their volley overhead.

"I am creating shields right in front of it to deflect and absorb the blast. That should take the heat off you. But be prepared to run if I can't stop it in time."

"Great." Jura cut down a few more demonoids in the way. He was looking for the knights.

A roar and another energy blast, but this time, I stopped it. It took four layers of [steelwood barriers].

A special demon, one with wings, appeared, and it landed with a bang. The explosion from its crash crushed another section of the second layer of walls. And then it stabbed the few soldiers right in front of it.

"Jura, there was a winged demon elite. Look out for it. It should be on your left."

"Aye. I don't see it." Jura was deep in battle, fighting some more demonoids.

The horde breached through the new gaps in the second layer of defenses, like a pipe with holes.

The mages conjured their fireballs and spells. And the demonoids raised a shield made of their demon-matter. Since when did the demonoids have shields? The explosions from the spells still destroyed a few demonoids, but the shields reduced the damage.

Two knights closed in on Jura's position. Tall, dark, and honestly quite cool looking with that jagged-edged demonic body, one used an axe, and the other used a spear. I should create wood knights. They looked cool.

Rooooooaaaaaaaaar.

An energy blasted from the walker again. My shields blocked it, but there was still collateral damage from some of the deflected blast; a part of the third layer walls was destroyed. It was using the blasts to open a way for the horde. These makeshift walls weren't that tough, but the fourth layer was the one we built previously. The fourth wall was tougher, and where most of the men were stationed.

"So you're the demon knights." Jura was deep in battle near what remained of second layer walls, and his wooden sword glowed. "Show me what you can do."

[Speed slash]. Jura's sword flickered like streaks of light, and the first demon knight turned to mincemeat.

"Oh. Easy?" Jura looked at the other knight and closed in. Indeed, the level eighty warlord crushed the level fortyish knight within five swipes. Honestly, using his high-speed skill was overkill.

Rooooooaaaaaaaaar.

The walker stomped, and it interrupted the archers' and mages' spells.

Another energy blast, and somehow I got the angle a bit wrong. The projectile deflected and made a hole in one of the valley-cliffs.

The walker's large size meant it could easily walk over the

walls, and it did so. It stepped across the second layer of walls. He'd entered the range where my root strikes were at full power.

Something hopped off the demon walker's back and landed right in front of Jura.

A demonoid with wings, proper demon-like horns, and a sword large enough to cut a cow in half, he radiated a magical aura.

Jura smirked. "So, the demons now have tiers of elite forces, too, eh? TreeTree, you watching this? This the guy?"

"Yes." But my focus was on the walker. My three artificial minds were working really hard to help. Trevor, Dimitree, and Ivy managed the beetles, created root tunnels, and helped to activate all the [subsidiary trees], [cactus defense system], [shield generators], and provided battlefield intel to Horns, who was deep in the fighting with Lausanne. It was a good thing I could delegate some of my abilities to them.

Yvon landed next to Jura after killing one demon knight. "Need help?"

Jura shrugged. "I'll let you know. But I'll try to handle him myself, for now. I've got skills I've been itching to test out on... something strong."

"All right, I'll keep the demon knights from meddling."

"What should we call this demon?" Jura looked at Yvon, and the demon-elite looked quizzically back at them. Its large sword glowed red and then black. A black flame emerged from it.

Demonfire, again. How nostalgic.

The walker stepped closer. A bit more. I just needed its entire massive body entirely within range. Most of the horde of soldier-demonoids crossed the second layer of defenses. Those makeshift walls really didn't last very long, but it served the purpose.

"For TreeTree!" Horns mentally shouted. "Battle-beetles, let's go!" There was no new beetle type; it was just a name Horns came up with. It was punny, he said. Wisp said their personalities took after an aspect of their creators, so I thought Horns inherited a punny part of me.

Beetles streamed out of the tunnels under the second and third layer of walls, charging into the mass of demonoids from both sides, and the entire area turned into a massive brawl.

Strangely, despite the chaos of the brawl, all the demons had the sense to avoid the demon-elite and Jura, both in intense, rather high-speed combat.

The demon-elite or general could fly, but at that distance, neither could really hurt each other. It seemed that the demon-elite wasn't much of a spellcaster, so they went into a full melee.

Jura ducked, dodged, and sidestepped the demon-elite's large bastard sword repeatedly, often narrowly avoiding mini-explosions from the sword-blast.

"Demon-general's a better name?" Jura's sword cut the demon-general's wings, but the wings regenerated. It roared in response, its mouth shooting out a mini-projectile at Jura. "And screw this." Bamboo generated a massive wooden shield in front of Jura. The wooden shield disintegrated, but it seemed like the demon-general didn't have that many uses of that projectile, since it went back into melee.

Right above, the demon walker stepped even closer. Its feet now crossed over the third layer walls easily. It roared again, this time the energy blast aimed right at the forest, right at me.

"It can sense our presence, Master," Trevor commented. "It knows of the magical energies you are radiating."

In my mind, I didn't think so.

[Steelwood barrier] x 5. Thank goodness I seemed to have more than few hundred uses of these shield-skills per day. Multiple large wooden barriers once again appeared to block the energy blast. Four barriers disintegrated, but the last one held. "Well, what do you know? My shields at this distance can stop that blast."

Below it, the beetles and the demonoids fought it out in a massive brawl. The militia and the Order's soldiers kept up the volley of arrows, but in such state, there was quite a bit of friendly fire. The beetles' large sizes didn't help.

The walker roared again, and...the spires on its back glowed red, and another spire glowed purple. Once that started, the demonoids glowed red, too, and they went into a kind of battle-frenzy, and the 'damage' suffered by the demonoids seemingly regenerated.

"Oh. That castle's an aura-machine." I mentally smacked myself. Of course, the castle imparted passive buffs, like me.

The spires started to shoot out smaller, less powerful energy blasts.

"And it's equipped with laser-turrets." Alexis looked in amazement. "It's a walking laser tank."

For me, those glowing red spires reminded me of the Obelisk of Light.

"The blood-rituals don't look so bad now." I sighed. To be fair, without the walker, I'd defeat the forty thousand, even sixty thousand demonoids without a problem. Ten thousand beetles would've taken out twenty thousand demonoids, easy. Clearly, for regular humans without special anti-demon skills and weapons, they would need to gather a large group of high-level individuals. At least multiple level eighties.

It really made my multiplier against demons a great advantage.

Madeus, together with the mages of New Freeka, changed their targets to the giant walker, since it was hard to avoid friendly fire with the beetles fighting literally in the trenches. Lausanne was doing fine. She had a whip-like weapon that seemed to cut through the demons like they were made of paper, and it was only against the knights that she needed help from the beetles.

"We've got them held up at the third layer," one of the captains said. Well, the fourth layer was the last layer of walls, and after that, it was New Freeka's own town walls or the forest itself. I wasn't keen on letting the walker anywhere near the forest since the treefolk village was between me and them.

The walker stepped and kicked the third layer's walls with its large feet.

"Oh." I kind of forgot that it could just...hit things instead of using the energy blast. And it kicked again.

And that segment of the walls crumbled. Most of the men had retreated to the fourth layer; it was mostly just ranged combat, except for beetles. Some of the soldier-elites also tried to fight the demonoids. By now, the demonoids thinned to about thirty thousand, and I'd lost about half of my beetles, some losses of soldiers or the Order, mostly from the walker. But it looked like they would have to bear some more.

The walker stepped through the crumbled sections. It kicked the fourth layer walls with incredible force, and then, strangely, walked past the fourth layer of walls. It walked toward me as if it knew I was there. Waiting.

"Oh, it dares to approach TreeTree?" Alexis grinned. "Even though TreeTree has anti-demon powers?"

It roared. My wooden shields blocked the energy blast. *Good. Come.*

"Get as close as you need to so I can shove all the roots I have through your body."

Hmm, let's see whether there was going to be any collateral damage.

"Have the treefolk evacuated?"

"Let me check...yes," Trevor said.

Most of them were now in the designated 'safe houses.' Those that could fight were on the fourth wall and some back at New Freeka's town walls. The demonoid army was still behind it, caught up in the brawl with the beetles, though some were trickling past the third wall.

Jura and the demon-general fought toe-to-toe as Yvon focused on fighting the other demon knights that tried to come to the demon-general's aid.

Jura's still had an edge, but if there was two of them, he'd be in trouble. He took a few hits, but thankfully the armor bore the brunt of it. Yvon, on the other hand, focused on the other demon knights.

At first Yvon wanted to help, but her own level was only about sixty, so she changed her targets. Jura and the demon-general traded blows.

The demon general leaped high up, half of its wings torn from an earlier well-placed slash. Its large bastard sword cracked, and a massive wooden fist punched it right in the body. It staggered back, and Jura changed weapons again. The wooden swords didn't last long, but he had a whole lot stored.

"So, any tricks?" Jura's body was surrounded by Bamboo's wood-armor, and its flexible form meant it was also a weapon. "Or were you just faster, stronger, and hit a whole lot harder?"

The demon-general staggered, even with the aura-effects from the Demon Spires. There were three wooden spears lodged in its body, the wooden spears enchanted with holy magic and made from TreeTree's anti-demon wooden stakes. Its enchantment meant it drained some demonic energy out of the demon-general.

"Well, time to end this. [Speed Slash]."

A flash of light and the demon-general's body was cut in half, then it disintegrated.

"Just a faster, stronger demon knight. I'd be worried if they start having actual skills." Jura did a fist, and then he realized there was still a whole lot of demons to fight.

"Good, I'm going to be fighting the demon walker now."

"Is this what Godzilla looked like? It's massive." Meela looked in amazement. "Are we going to have a monster fight now? Tree versus demon walker."

Size-wise, it was larger than the earlier demon-champions. But it felt like maybe it was not as strong. Or maybe there was some trade-off. It certainly didn't feel as threatening, despite its enormous size.

A demon champion. I'd long awaited this day.

The special anti-demon bolts were ready. I'd gained twenty levels and many skills since I last fought the demon champions eight years ago, and I had more hero fragments, too. I had prepared for this moment, with skills and items. I believed I could take it, and now to see whether I could.

The giant demon walked, and now it was on the very edges of my forest.

And that was as far as I was going to let it go. A wall of wood shields appeared in front of it.

"You shall not pass!" Alexis shouted.

Meela did a facepalm. "That's lame."

[Super anti-demon rootstrikes] x 5. All tipped with the specially made demon bolts. One rootstrike for one of those giant legs. The roots shot out of the ground, a dense energy surrounding each of the bolts and the edge.

And it exploded right on the legs. The demon walker roared, and this time, it shot out a few energy blasts. I blocked three of them, but the fourth one left leveled a patch of forests and destroyed a section of the treefolk's village.

Still, I was happy. The rootstrikes did what I expected them to do. It stopped walking as large chunks were taken out of its five legs. It looked unsteady, as if it was going to crumble on its own weight. But it didn't.

It roared again, and this time it turned its head. It wasn't aimed at me, but at the fourth layer of walls.

Shit! I created the wood shields in the wrong place, and the blast vaporized a large chunk of the fourth layer walls. Some of the beetles and soldiers there were killed.

"TreeTree! Don't let it shoot at us!" Jura shouted. Some of the men were buried under the rubble.

Heh, all it could do now was shoot? The spires on its back glowed and shot out red beams, and it set a portion of the forest on fire. Its large head roared again and blasted one more energy blast.

My wooden shields caught the shot, but still, the impact caused the space right before the shield to burst into flames.

[Constrict]. Using vines, I attempt to force the head to aim only at me.

[Super anti-demon root strike] x 5. More bolts, and this time, before it could release another round of energy blasts, I took out its five feet. The giant crashed into the ground, and with it came a huge shockwave of smoke and dust. But it wasn't dead yet, the spires on its back still shooting beams.

Still, I was confident. Let's see whether it had any tricks left.

[Super anti-demon root strike] x 5.

More bolts. I had about ninety bolts left and had many more super-root strikes to go.

It struggled.

It roared again and more energy blasts. This time, I thought it used a special attack because it blasted through all of the defensive shields I had and then blew up three [subsidiary trees], and then the energy blast smacked right into my main body.

And I felt a chunk of my bark fall off. "Oh. I'm still alive." Thank goodness for all the fragments.

Well, let's retaliate.

[Super anti-demon root strike] x 10. The hard shell around the main body shattered on impact, and a few of my roots struck whatever was inside. I thought I hit something important.

The ground shook, like something exploded inside of its body.

Its head roared again, charging another energy blast. This time because of the poor angle, the shot went wide and flew into the sky.

No chances. I shot out another ten [Super Anti-demon Root Strike], aimed at the giant head. It cracked, and then the entire head crumbled.

The spires of the castle collapsed. A humanoid giant appeared in its place. Its...body was half-hexed, as if the demon-flesh was rotting, and each step, chunks of it fall off, as if it was melting. If this was what the hexbomb did, it felt like the future was gonna be quite...grim.

"Uh..."

The giant humanoid demon stepped forward, and more parts fell off. Yet I saw it struggling as it attempted to regenerate the destroyed parts. It was an ongoing battle between the demon's regeneration and the corruption of the hexbomb.

"Uh..."

It was a demon, and there was no time for caution.

[Super anti-demon root strike] x 2.

Two roots shot out of the ground and impaled the giant through its chest and what I suspected was the head. Seriously, a humanoid demon.

And then it disintegrated, along with the rest of the demon walker body.

"Uh...is that it?"

"The walker is down! The walker is down!" Alexis shouted and clapped her spirit-like hands.

I mentally made a fistbump. I'd finally reached the point where I could take on a champion by myself.

As the body disintegrated, the aura from the spires faded, too. The elves, centaurs, treefolk, and beetles who were busy fighting the regular demonoids suddenly found their opponents had become far weaker than they originally were. The energy that was resisting and offsetting my [lesser demonic suppression] was gone, and now, they felt the full effect of the aura.

What was left of the twenty thousand or so weakened humanoid demons fell to the might of the remaining forces or were skewered in the flood of root strikes that followed.

> [**Level up**! You are now level 137! (+5 levels)]
> [**Skill acquired**: Healing Aura]
> [**Skill upgraded**: Subsidiary Trees - 15,000. Subsidiary Trees gains a share of main body's environmental adaptations and auras. Only applies to subsidiary trees within 100km of main-tree.]
> [**Skill upgraded**: Woodcrafting]
> [**Skill upgraded**: Steelwood Barrier]
> [**Skill upgraded**: Root tunnels]

YEAR 81 MONTH 6 (CONTINUED)

"We lived." Yvon sat. "I thought that was...not the hardest battle I've been in."

Jura tapped her shoulder. "We've still got work to do." He pointed to the many, many injured soldiers and the dead. The energy blasts from the demon walker still killed many, and there was a portion of New Freeka that was blasted wide open. A whole load of repairs had to be done.

"But...but...the demon walker was defeated. We deserve a celebration!" the captains said.

Jura smiled. "Perhaps. Though I would give credit to TreeTree's exceptional anti-demon weapons. The demon general would have lasted a lot longer without his demon-draining weapons."

"But you would still win." Jura just smiled and looked at a young girl running over, her short hair fluttering.

Lausanne was covered in dirt, blood, and a whole load of demonic shards. Mostly unhurt.

"Uncle!" She landed right in front of him. "I destroyed eighty-seven demons!"

"Good job." Jura smiled and just rubbed her head. "Hope you gain a level!"

"I hope I gain many levels!"

Jura smiled. "How was it, your first true battlefield experience?"

"Oh, it was a lot less bloody and messy than my dreams. I think TreeTree exaggerated how gory and brutal it is…"

"TreeTree been giving you gory war-dreams, eh?" Jura frowned a little. Using the essences, and my own memories of wars, I could somewhat mold the general direction and types of dreams Lausanne got. I honestly didn't know what exactly happened in the dreams; [Dream Tutor] was kind of like a random map generator where I put in the parameters and ingredients, and things just happened.

"Yeah. I told him I wanted to feel like—" Lausanne then paused. "Oops."

Yvon frowned, too. "I better check what dreams the other kids are getting. It's not good to have visions of death and destruction at that age."

What, I needed to start parental guidances for dreams now?

Lausanne shook her head. "TreeTree was just helping so that I know what to do when it's the real thing."

Jura sighed. "Anyway, not a good time to argue about it. Let's get the wounded to the healers, those seriously wounded to the biopods, and the dead to the morgue."

There was a lot of wounded and dead soldiers, despite my interference. About eight hundred soldiers and close to seven thousand beetles still died in the fight against the demons, the soldier deaths mostly from the demon knights. But then, my new [healing aura] kicked in, and for the injured, their wounds began to heal even before the healers got to them. And my new aura even improved the effect of healing.

"New skill?" Jura asked, noticing the unusually quick recover of his own cuts and wounds and those injured suddenly finding their strength returning to them.

"Yup."

The mood all round was mixed but getting better. Some groups were upset and mourned the deaths of their comrades. Some were just incredibly amazed that they survived a battle against a towering giant, and of those that survived, a lot of the soldiers would gain levels from this battle.

The citizens also got the signal to leave their respective bunkers and hideouts, and there was a big blast that wrecked a portion of the city. I also had to get the mages to help put out the fires, since I didn't have my own water magic.

Beetles closed in on what remained of the demon walker. I had a quarantine zone established, and Madeus, our resident wizard, was tasked to investigate the remains. There was massive rubble where the main body of the walker collapsed, and most of the demon walker's body disintegrated into nothingness, but there were still some remains.

The rotting thing was the hex. Like a sludge, it now pooled on the ground.

"Aeon, can you see this?" Madeus poked it with his wooden stick. It kind of latched on, like a slimy thing. Madeus likes to refer to me as Aeon, since he felt it was inappropriate to refer to me as TreeTree. He poked it. It was not exactly...a slime, but it sure radiated a kind of energy. "I don't feel too good being so close."

"Hmm, then stay away."

[Inspection].

A hex, made from the sacrifice of souls.

Uh. Didn't tell much.

"Can you do anything about it?"

"Uh..." Madeus tried to use some spells, but the hex kind of just...stayed there. It didn't react.

"Can you blast it to smithereens or something?"

"Nope." Madeus did a fireball. Hex remained. It was not exactly...destroy-able. It kind of just got splattered.

"So...we just leave it there?" I asked. This was new to me.

Madeus looked at his staff. The hex had damaged the wood somewhat; a section that had come in contact with the hex was rotting. "Yeah. I think it's best we just seal off this area and let the hex dissipate naturally."

"Uh." Hmm...I wasn't sure whether I should get near the hex, though. Alexis's nuclear description somehow made me suspicious that this hex might be 'radioactive residue.' But I had to know for sure. "Can you take a very small sample? Just one cup?"

"Oh. Okay." I had one of the beetles carry the small wooden container. The almost-black hex-slime seemed to have a purple glow, and really, Alexis took a glance at it, shook her head.

"Disgusting."

As a precaution, I created a biolab some distance away, such that if anything happened, such as...rotting, I could cut off the biolab and I wouldn't suffer the consequences.

"This hex thing...it's created from sacrifices, eh?" I asked.

"Yeah. Blood magic's quite special in the sense that it powers itself and lasts really long. But of course, the cost of it is...usually someone's life. It's common in the countries with extensive slavery some time ago, but its practice and use has dwindled as the constant use of slaves is...unsustainable, and there is often a great deal of backlash from blood magic, such as the spellcasters suffering nightmares or perpetual hauntings." Alexis went into full nerdy magic mode. Even Madeus didn't know that much, but it seemed Alexis was a mage, and she did somehow manage to read such things.

"It's just bad." Meela frowned her wooden eyebrows. I thought they looked like little stems from a flower. She had an actual flower on her head now; she said it helped in the whole hospitality business thing.

"According to our modern sensibilities." Alexis frowned. "But blood magic is primordial. I recall meeting a shaman on one of the islands we visited, and they used to sacrifice goats and cows to the gods, and they say they've been doing for ages. Kind of like our ancient civilizations, Meela."

"Which one?"

"Most of the Mesoamerican ones. Even now there are some ritual sacrifices that happen in many cultures. I would think there must be some parallels with how blood magic is in this world. Perhaps they sacrifice and trade for some godly powers?"

I took a look at the blackish hex-liquid. Godly? Certainly didn't feel that way, but well, what did I know?

"How do you plan to investigate it? Biolab? Pour it into your pod and figure it out?" Alexis asked.

"Yeah. It certainly looked a bit...organic." Well. Yeah. Black, hex-like thing. Maybe it was like sludge, from like...a petrol spill? But there was a purple glow, so there was clearly some magic to it happening.

I decided I needed more time to think about what I was going to do, so I let the specimen sit on a little storage container in that lone biolab in a corner of the valley.

YEAR 81 MONTH 7

After a brief status check, New Freeka emerged mostly... unharmed. The site of where the 'hex-sludge' left behind by the massive demon walker, by order of the Council and Order, was to be quarantined. So it was now surrounded by walls and guarded by beetles. If reports were true, they would spawn monsters, though so far, I'd not seen any.

The 'sludge' kind of just pooled together into a large, blackish pool, and it seemed they were somewhat magically intertwined, like magnets, that they would naturally merge into one interconnected body. Not that anyone wanted to get near it. It seemed Madeus said he felt sick for a few days, and I had to check on him.

It wasn't a 'bodily' sickness, or maybe if it was, it wasn't something that [healing aura] or my powers did offset. It really did give credence to the whole radiation theory that Alexis had, but the idea of doing nuclear fusion or fission with souls just...boggled my mind.

"I think the [tree of prayer] does relieve the symptoms a bit. I think it's all the 'negative' energy from the blood sacrifice," Madeus theorized. Again, something worth investigating. Or maybe it could just be additional placebo from the calming effects of the [Tree of Prayer].

On the political front, the defeat of the demon walker was significant and greatly boosted the Order's standing. Jura was now viewed as a hero, and the soldiers, even those from the Council, now viewed Jura as a respectful, good man because he fought on the front lines, unlike the Council who hid or fled. That meant the council had to shut up on their anti-Order rhetoric, though I suspected this silence was only a temporary one.

The euphoria and memories of this battle would fade, and with it these power-hungry folks would rear their head again someday.

And the news of the victory spread quickly, drawing the attention of the guilds. "The Merchant guild has determined that we are a high-priority safe zone in the region, and they will send a fair bit of resources and manpower here." The Order's treasurer read out the notice. "The guild plans to explore the possibility of establishing a regional trade coordination and cartography center and also a collection of high-security storage warehouses."

Jura clapped his hand. "I must confess I don't exactly understand what some of those words are, but it sounds like a good thing."

The merchants' guilds were essentially like the world's shipping companies; they were the blood vessels that connected the world. So much produce and money changed hands through the guilds that they often were able to sway kingdoms into fighting wars for them. But I wondered whether this world had protests against banks and corporations. After all, capitalism could be pretty nasty.

The treasurer nodded. "It is. They will be having a proper office here, and an actual [merchant prince] or [guild trader], rather than just appointed representatives. This is usually followed with the opening of a guild's marketplace and exchange, and the regional contracts department. The council will be approached to discuss the regulations on the markets once they arrive to survey the location."

Jura nodded. Honestly, trade was not his strongest suit,

though he had improved. Laufen just smiled. "Don't worry, most of us will attend the meetings and will let you have the summary."

The recent battle also made the elves think about the future of their combat forces.

"We need more combat experience." Lausanne looked at Yvon. "The demons are coming, you know it, we know it, everyone knows it. All of us need to have experience." Lausanne referred to the rest of the Valthorn, especially the four girls from the first batch.

Yvon shook her head. "I spoke with TreeTree and Jura, and we're only letting those at level twenty actually join the battle. Until then, the rest of them are staying back." Only one of the girls had hit level twenty, so she would join the next battle, if there was one.

"But Lady Yvon! It doesn't make sense! We gain levels when we participate in battles. Holding us back is just taking away our levels! And TreeTree needs high-leveled fighters to fight the high-leveled enemies."

"I know, but they are too young, and they are not ready. They are not you, Lausanne."

"If they don't get chances, they will never be." Lausanne was now...twelve, so she had more opinions. "I gained seven levels in that battle. Seven! I'm almost level forty now." By most accounts, she'd be classified as a genius. "Wasn't it you that told us that during great battles, explosive leveling happens? Then why are they not given the chance?"

Yvon sighed. "I-I get your point. Let me discuss with the rest perhaps an arrangement depending on what kind of battles. If it's a smaller-scale battle, we can consider putting you and the girls on support."

Lausanne nodded.

For me, I did need to expand the Valthorns. It was true that I couldn't multi-task as well as I liked, and when I ended up focused on the demon walker, my ability to coordinate all the other fights on the ground had to be delegated to my tree-minds, and yet I needed my skills on hand against the walker.

So I needed more high-level fighters, multiple Juras and Yvons, to win such a fight consistently, with minimal casualties. Speaking of casualties...

There was a funeral procession for those who fell in battle. It was something one of the officers suggested, something they had from where they came from. A practice of one of the world's southern continental religions, the Urgama, to honor the dead, and the benefits of it was that the dead's spirit apparently enchanted the surviving soldiers to carry on the fight. The mechanics of how such a 'magic' worked was interesting, and as a Soul Tree that helped the reincarnation and passing on of the fallen spirits, it was...educational.

"Surely they don't have time to do such processions when a demon army is on their doorstep?" Alexis wondered. The Southern Continent was embroiled in massive wars with the demon hordes. According to the merchants, there were four demon walkers in that continent alone, and inland trade prices were sky-high.

"I wouldn't know."

Well, for us, the procession went on, and...we didn't get any blessings. Or at least, nothing I could see for now. It was all business-as-usual in my soul realm, too; people were dying all over the continent to the demon hordes, but thanks to the fall of the demon walker, it seemed the rate of death throughout the entire continent also somewhat dropped.

I wondered whether it was a coincidence or the walker had some kind of continental-boost ability. If it did, would the king have some kind of worldwide ability?

But anyway, it was still not the end. Now that the demon walker battle was over, I went back to making more demon-weapons and research. The whole schtick with restoring Jura's hand was still ongoing, so...more brutal animal explosion followed, but...I was getting there. *I think.*

I had to get some help in cleaning the room, though, since...

there was a lot of blood splattered everywhere. So I made a quarantine area where the specimen animals remained.

And blew up. Or lately, it was more like leaking pipes. Like the tail would regrow and then somehow a hole would appear, and blood just kept dripping out of it. And no amount of healing would fix it because it was a flaw in the 'soul.'

In a way, it was like...3D printing. I had to set up the template in the soul, and then the body would heal in accordance to that template. At the same time, I needed to make the 'soul-part' using my new tools, in a 3D-printing fashion, putting the bits and pieces in, piece by piece. All of this was from a sudden epiphany when I saw a key-duplication contraption one of the New Freeka's smiths had.

Essentially, I needed a tool that worked simultaneously, that read whatever scan results I had, and reproduced it in the soul forge.

Also, I needed to also build a 'library' of organs that I could use in the future. Kind of like playing Spores, the game. Honestly, I didn't know why it took me so long to figure shit out. Maybe there was mold in my wooden brain somewhere.

Oh and on research...where was I?

[Research Status:]
*[**Beetle** - anti-magma armors stage 4 - completed]*
*[**Metal hyperaccumulator trees** - Stage 1 - completed]*
*[**Phytoremediation process** - basic - 10 months]*

Ah yes. I had new accumulator trees. These Hyperaccumulators functioned primarily to absorb high levels of metallic content from the contaminated poop-ground, which continued to be something of a problem, even if a contained one.

But I supposed it was a good time to force the council.

"We're having the upper hand after the recent victory. The population sees us as the protectors of the valley, and TreeTree's position was close to unassailable. And we want to use that goodwill on...sewers?" One of the treasurers tried to debate with Jura in the meeting room.

"Yes. Sewers. We need sewers."

"Why not more seats? Have our own candidates on the council against the other group? Some of the independent-leaning councilors now feel they should lean toward us, given the Order's secure position as the defenders of the valley. No political power can change that."

Jura frowned. Sometimes, the Order's own officers got sucked into politics.

"Perhaps we need more resources for the Order's military?" Jura frowned, too. Between me and Jura, both of us generally felt that quantity was unnecessary. I'd need about three to four months to replenish the beetles, but my beetle army was tough and, for what it was worth, unlimited and expendable. The only drawback was that they couldn't gain levels, but who cared when I had so many of them? If anything, it was the Valthorns that needed to be expanded. There was really no point throwing more fodder at a monster like the demon-general or the demon walker.

The merchants delivered the gems that provided light and other stuff meant for the hideouts, and it came with an alchemist's contraption thing, so I requested for one of each for research, which led to an upgrade for my labs.

*[**Biolab upgraded**: Centrifuge]*
*[**Material lab upgraded**: Centrifuge]*

These gems were essentially concentrated 'light,' 'mana-sensitive rock,' and 'mana' that, via some fluke of natural magical forces, formed into a gem. There were apparently 'artificial' variants as well, but these didn't last as long as the naturally mined gems.

This new centrifuge essentially acted as a concentrator, creating for higher concentrations and enriched versions of... Ginseng. Okay, it worked for more than just ginseng. I meant things, but when I was thinking about the possible uses of this item...

Wait.

If I needed to concentrate ginseng, and concentrating them eventually made them into gems, that meant I should be able to use gems as [soul forge] components. But I tried that previously. When I acquired gemstones.

Running the ginseng through the centrifuge, I got...

[Concentrated ginseng - medium quality] that took the appearance of a brownish paste, kind of like those funky pastes used in exotic oriental massages.

Was this it? Maybe I needed to soak it in mana or something? Like how there was a layer of mana on the body? It was really not going anywhere, was it?

"Again?" Jura asked. Well, he was busy. There was still a lot of demonic movements to keep track off. It'd been a year since the rifts opened, so the demon king should appear soon.

"No, I just wanted to test something out..."

Infusing ginseng into Jura's soul using the soul forge took about an hour, strangely easy.

[Ginseng infusion successful.]

"How do you feel?"

"Uh...nothing? Did you do anything?" Jura woke up from the quick nap. "Or maybe not yet?"

"Maybe it takes a while."

YEAR 81 MONTH 8

"Will the Council grant us rights to grant us refuge, rights to purchase land and build a mansion?" A royal envoy from a nearby nation of Rajahskan came, with 'gifts' and money. They were not the only ones.

What was happening was quite simple.

The royalties of the nearby nation, now that they realized I could fend off a demon walker, wanted to set up a refuge. Essentially, they would buy land and build a small palace where their family could hide. Although the kings usually did not leave; there were some weird rules about king's powers being related to being 'present' in their kingdoms, but these kings wanted to protect their offspring and successors by sending them away to a safehouse. Kind of like what Madeus' allies did. But they wanted exemptions, special treatment, and the ability to 'rule' over their own properties. Which was absolutely ridiculous.

"It's politically advantageous for us to accept. But if we do, we must be prepared to accept most of them, except those who have crossed us," a councilor said.

A delegation from the Council and the envoys came to present the case. The Council, being the usual politicians, would like to agree. But Jura said, "This is a decision for Aeon. It is his protection to give, not us."

"I do not fancy the creation of a royal district where our laws do not apply." The idea that all these runaway princes came to my place and set up little outposts just frankly annoyed me. When I imagined all these stuck-up royals treating this little valley of mine as their summer palace, I just felt disgusted. "No. They may come as regular guests, but they will be treated in the same manner as any other refugee in this valley. If the Council wishes to extend any privileged treatment to them, let them know that I will not recognize that privilege, and if I so desire, I will not hesitate to crush them. In this valley, they are ordinary souls, like anyone else."

The Councilors froze. "But...but...Counsel Jura, surely Aeon can recognize the value these royals can bring?"

Jura shrugged. "I'm afraid the Tree Spirit was very firm about not giving royals any privileged treatment. And if I may add, accepting royals and granting them special treatment contradicts why New Freeka exists. Do you guys really want to put up with the whims of royalty all over again? Do you not forget that it was royal conflicts that brought all of you here? They can still come, should the demons ever threaten their lands, but they will be like any other refugee."

One of the Councilors stared at Jura. "The Tree Spirit has no concept of royalty?"

Jura nodded. "He is aware of it, but he does not intend to recognize their power in this valley."

Three of the envoys from three kingdoms were present. "Surely there is something that our kingdoms may provide to sway the Tree Spirit's view?"

It was one of the Order's head priests who responded. "Aeon's protection is a blessing, and one couldn't haggle or bargain one's blessing, even if you are royalty. Accept, or do not. When you stand before a local deity, what is a royal?"

I mentally cheered for the priest—good comeback. I was a bit embarrassed that they thought I was some kind of deity, but I was too far into that whole religious schtick to bother correcting it now. And if I gained even more levels, I guessed a deity wasn't too far off anyway.

The envoys frowned. One of the envoys, the one from Rajahskan, then said, "It's a shame that the Tree Spirit of this valley rejects our king's offer. I will relay the message, and I fear he will not be pleased."

I told Jura then, "Is that a threat? I don't like receiving threats." Of course, the envoys couldn't hear this.

Jura smiled at the envoy. "I am afraid your king must get used to it. Aeon's under no obligation to obey a king's demands—what more one of another nation."

"And Aeon didn't not even heed the views of his Council?" the envoy retorted.

"Aeon was here before the Council was born, and he may remove the Council should he so pleases." Jura smiled, but it was a creepy kind of smile, and the room's air suddenly felt heavy. A [Warlord]'s skill, [Heavyweight Presence]. He looked at the Councilors, and the Councilors somehow all took two steps back.

The envoy, too, took a step back. Then he drew in a deep breath and sighed. "I see. But surely...we can still purchase property in New Freeka?"

"You may, but your property will be subject to all of New Freeka's rules and regulations. There will be no exemptions. In short, you will be like any other wealthy merchant who invests in a property in New Freeka. And know this, you will be watched."

The envoys traded glances. They discussed with each other a bit, but then they all decided to leave. But I could still eavesdrop on them as they walked back to their inns.

"Who does this Tree Spirit think it is?" one envoy said. "Our king's adventurers can chop down a tree."

"But your adventurers cannot slay a demon walker," the envoy for another country said. "Or you wouldn't be here."

"Ugh."

The Rajahskan envoy said, "A powerful druid or monster tamer should be able to sway this Tree Spirit's mind."

"I wouldn't count on that. Any monster able to slay a demon walker has to be at least level one hundred, and you won't find many druids or monster tamers willing to even try taming a creature of that level. It's a life-or-death battle."

The Rajahskan envoy nodded. "Perhaps. Maybe a heroic artifact could."

The two other envoys eyes lit up. "Ah...that certainly changes things. Is there such an artifact?"

The Rajahskan envoy said, "The Elven kingdoms may still possess Roana's Staff. I reckon a level eighty druid wielding that can bend this Tree's will."

The two envoys laughed. "And I thought you have such an item! That staff was destroyed long ago!"

"Was it? I had the impression it was what they used to keep the Guardian Tree of the Elven Capital under control..."

"Hah. Don't tell me you believe some of that kind of silly propaganda. It's a myth to maintain the royal family's legitimacy."

The envoy frowned. "Well...the king won't be pleased with this. I-I don't know how to go back."

"Well, we're in the same boat. I bet the king's gonna have my head. He tends to do that when he loses his temper."

"I'm just going to fake my death. Demons killed me on the journey back. That's going to be my story."

The three envoys sulked together. Were there seriously no good kings around? Or do they just die because they were too nice?

YEAR 81 MONTH 9

Another demon walker had been spotted on our continent this month, and strength returned to the demonoid forces throughout the continent. Thankfully, it appeared far south, nearer to Gila. I guessed they could use their newfound sacrificial blood-magic powers and test it out. For us, we still saw small packs of roaming demonoids close to our territories, but they were easily crushed by the patrolling beetles.

It was a bit annoying that we were only free from demon walkers for three months, but then again, I was expecting the demon king within the next six months. Couldn't be helped that the 'escorts' would increase before the main character came along. We just hoped it appeared on the Southern Continent, where there were now six demon walkers. The nations in the South managed to kill one using the blood magic, but it took more than one shot to slay the demon walkers.

So it was really quite a miserable battlefield, the Southern Continent. I heard from Jura that they'd sent all sorts of requests for assistance.

Ah, too bad for them, that was their problem. For now, I focused on rebuilding my stockpile of anti-demon bolts.

YEAR 81 MONTH 10

Winter arrived early. Apparently something to do with moon-movements, according to Madeus—every thirty to thirty-two years or so, the moons changed position and somehow caused this world's winter to last a month longer. Not sure how that actually worked and why, or whether it was magic.

And fun fact about the world: nobody could agree on how many moons there were. Some said three, some said four, some said ten. The night sky, even with magic, sometimes revealed odd 'moons' that only appeared every now and then.

"Elliptical moons," Alexis said. She'd been sky-gazing almost every day. She'd even gotten a telescope recently. "I suspect some of them have century-long orbits."

"That's like...crazy." Meela was quite into the moon and star stuff, too, but mostly for astrological sign stuff. Some of her guests enjoyed that kind of service. "I thought even the biggest planets from our world orbit the sun in a few years. How can something orbit a small planet so slowly?"

"Or they could just be comets. Not strange for them to mistake comets for moons. Comets have crazy orbits."

"Could just be magic." Well, that was my view. I mean, there was really no reason why the astronomical rules that applied from one world should carry over into another world. The forces acting on interstellar objects could be different; maybe there was a fifth magic force, or maybe dark matter in this world comprised of aether or star mana. You know, weird shit like that.

"True." Alexis sighed. "TreeTree, how high can you grow?"

"Uh...why?" That was a weird, off-topic comment.

"I wonder whether it's possible for you to grow until well... space. Like a space elevator. Or maybe you could be like a super-tall viewing gallery and observation tower."

"That's going to be absurdly high," I said. "No way." The required height of a space elevator was dependent on rotational spin and planetary gravity; unless I had some kind of magical item or object that created some kind of 'levitation effect' such that it functioned as a counterweight...I doubted it. I recalled Earth's space elevator needed to be like...thirty-five thousand kilometers high. How could a tree ever grow that tall? Unless there was some really wonky magic.

"I mean, maybe you could be like...magically super strong that you could support the weight. Maybe you could even reach like... uh...what's the word for it? Geostationary orbit?" Alexis mused. "Or Low Planet Orbit?"

Meela shook her head. "I think you should just think about using magic. Magical rockets, Alexis. Magical rockets and levitation."

But why would I even want to grow so tall that I reached space? Was there something to achieve there? Fruit-satellites? Or would star mana harvesting be far more efficient because of the altitude and exposure to direct star-light? Or more solar power?

Seriously, growing so tall just sounded like...Jack and the beanstalk. Unless...

"You know, maybe ancient space elevators were how stories of world trees came around. You know, Yggdrasil supposedly connected itself to nine worlds, and if you imagined a modern, futuristic setting, a tree-shaped space elevator would be the 'gate' to those other worlds," Alexis said. "Oh, wait. Do you want me to explain what all those words are?"

"Yeah." And Alexis went on about space elevators, Yggdrasil, and stuff like that. I sort of recalled the story.

It was a fascinating thought, but I supposed there were magical...alternatives to a tree that grew into space. And why would I want to go to space?

A tree couldn't grow into space. Or could it?

Anyway, enough about space, and winter, and moons. Demon battles intensified throughout the world, refugee movements increased, and news of death, destruction, glory, and victories flooded the merchant channels. And that Gila country was crazy enough to actually use the blood sacrifice again.

And I thought Gila used three rounds of that blood sacrifice ritual. Because my sensors detected three surges of magic.

But it didn't kill the walker, though it did somewhat disable it. News reported two of the hex-bombs hit the walker's legs, so the walker was unable to move. Still, that didn't bring an end to the intense fighting, as the walker did what it could, which was to spawn demonoids and flood the area with them.

So it kind of sucked because...the walker was a walking demon-hive. It just vomited out demonoids when it didn't move.

And thanks to the merchants, there was increasing awareness that the demonic 'camps' were all hives as well, constantly spawning demonoids, and taking them down would be key to reducing their threat.

"I think they were like ants, despite looking like...humans," Meela suddenly said, giving a cleaning analogy. "How do you kill ants? Wipe out the nests, or the ants will just keep roaming the entire kitchen."

Turned out, she was not the only one with that idea. Jura had been asked to support a five thousand strong force meant to take down a demon fort found in the vicinity of a neighboring kingdom. A 'coalition' force, a common thing during demonic wars. I recalled that Lord Rajjiv Nung was also part of a coalition force.

"So...are you going?" Yvon asked.

Jura shrugged. "I'm not keen, and I told the merchants that my place was here. Joining coalition forces is for youngsters."

"I'm starting to think you spend too much time with TreeTree, that you're getting his stationary habits."

Jura didn't mind the jab. "TreeTree's got a point. Staying home's nice, and I've got better things to do. Like practice. Besides, they've got a general, don't they? Or some of the human elites. They don't need me."

Yvon sneered.

"They'll be fine. I don't quite trust this coalition force anyway." Jura felt these coalitions generally had ulterior motives, like getting a good sense of what his strengths were, and so on. *I thought that was his diplomatic sense tingling.*

"Heh." Yvon wasn't exactly trusting of them, either. "Merchants probably just want to clear that base for a trade route. It was between this side of the city and the other, and they can't be using their airships all the time."

The coalition was partly funded by the merchants, and they would handle the logistics and supplies and also provide reimbursement. Forces from various kingdoms would join, usually the lower-ranked ones. Battles were a good chance to gain levels, and usually such coalition forces tried not to take on challenging opponents, due to the political fallout from a failed coalition attack.

Throughout the world, there were multiple such coalitions, many based on century-old treaties for mutual protection or ancient commitments with temples and religions.

"But they will insist on someone, and the council will look to us to volunteer someone," Madeus, who was also in the meeting, responded. He wasn't keen, either, and like Jura, he'd prefer if he could just study and conduct magic research all day.

"I'll ask one of the captains to volunteer, then. He's about in his level forties and should see more battle experience."

"I'd send Lausanne if she was a few years older." Yvon shrugged.

"True, but she's not. So she stays. We have enough demons roaming the countryside as it is."

Well, Lausanne and the Valthorns were now attached to a mobile 'cavalry' unit. They rode beetles, in a way, as the proto-beetleknight squad, traveled the countryside, and hunted any demon packs that we spotted. Helped that I could telepathically communicate with her over the distances, for coordination.

A feature of her special-familiar contract.

"Maybe Roma can join if he's a bit older...depending on how long this demon king lasts..."

Yvon shook her head. "Roma didn't seem to have inherited our combat talents. He's more...into books. Perhaps a mage." Yvon's son, Roma, was about nine now, and he seemed to prefer being at home with his books. His mom struggled to get him to practice with her, and well, there was a bit of resentment between the two. Maybe he needed a father figure. In fact, Roma's relationship with Eriz was a whole load better, and Yvon frequently had to rely on Eriz to speak to Roma.

Jura nodded. It was between her and her son, not for us to intervene.

"Ah, never mind." Yvon diverted the subject. "I hope the girls come back safely."

Lausanne led four of the girls, together with a group of one hundred beetles. They were headed for a hundred-strong demonic raiding force. They should win relatively easily, and Horns was close behind with a force of another hundred beetles.

Even though New Freeka's territory was small, my subsidiary tree network stretched far, thanks to my prior expansions, and with my newfound Aura-sharing skills, the subsidiary tree network functioned like 'defensive' lines, a place where the intercepting troops could return should the battle turn bad.

Gradually, I am extending this network of trees further. They were, after all, a great early warning system. Trees had eyes, y'know.

YEAR 81 MONTH 11

Wars. Wars. Wars.

Battles and battles, seemingly endless ones. So much that my soul realm was filled with the souls of the recently departed. My soul harvesters were busy, battlefield after battlefield they visited, and each trip, they brought back more souls.

Even as the cold swept through the continent, the demons didn't stop fighting. And so the defenders were forced into battle even when they didn't wish it.

"I feel a little bad, being safe and warm here," one of the captains joked. The other one was out as part of the merchant coalition force.

Madeus laughed, and then he sipped on his ginger tea. The group decided to have something a bit cozier, so they brewed a few pots of fruit tea, ginger tea, garlic tea, and snacks, mainly some fried potatoes, chips, fries. One of Meela's kitchen projects was to recreate potato fries because part of the global-domination plans involved being a chain-restaurant, like...McDonalds. So she had to have fries.

Wesley and our priests sat around the meeting room, too.

"Don't jinx us. Appreciate that we can still huddle around in such comfort, even when there was a demon walker around."

Meela was happily playing the caterer. Apparently serving food contributed to her levels as a Hotel-Tree. Jura, Laufen, and Lausanne also ate the snacks. "Yeah. Never know when the good times come to an end."

There was a nod of agreement throughout the room. I wondered whether they felt it, that the demon king was coming. I certainly thought I could. The strange twitches to my star-mana leaves. The unusual fluctuations there...

"I'm just missing good chili sauce to go with my fries. Or ketchup, for that matter," Meela whined to both me and Alexis. "I need to get chilies and tomatoes."

Meela was clearly more focused on unlocking new recipes for her restaurant. I was starting to think she was playing hotel-tycoon or Overcooked, since the whole demon king thing was really just a 'distraction' for her.

"The council is of the view that we should be building more walls and have the sewer project modified," one of the treasurers said to the group. Even though it was cozy, it was still a Valtrian Order meeting.

"Four layers of walls was insufficient?"

"Well, they thought that some of the collateral damage could be minimized, and we do have the capacity to add walls. As for the sewer project, they're now thinking of adding bunkers and hide-outs to double its function as a safe zone from the demons. Should we oppose such a motion?"

Jura shook his head. "I think it's fine. It's aligned to what we wanted, and the city should be allowed to protect itself. But it should be funded by the Council, not from the Order."

Most of the other meeting attendees nodded, then went back to eating.

"Any other business?" Jura asked. Most of them had just completed regular updates and reports. Discussions on the demonic forces took up about half the time, due to the far-reaching implications of the demons on trade, funding, military, and infrastructure.

"The demon king, according to whispers among the temples, will arrive within the next three months," a priest said.

In my mind, that was what I thought, too. This meant the temples may have some kind of star-mana equipment.

"How reliable is this prediction?" Jura leaned forward. "And even if so, what can we do about it?"

One of the captains said, "I believe the best thing to do, Counsel, is to just keep watch. You were right to say that we have no way to stop whatever the demon king does. Be on the lookout, and move out of its way."

"Agreed." Jura nodded. I thought it was probably the best decision as well. "I'm personally more interested in when the heroes will arrive, what powers they have, and how we can spot them so that we can stay out of their way."

"We...don't like heroes?" Meela asked. The crowd here didn't know her true identity as a former reincarnated hero.

"If they are not humans, I will like them," a captain said. "Else these stupid heroes will buy into the propaganda the royals feed them and treat us non-humans as enemies once the war is over."

Meela did not reply. I thought she was trying to remember what the other kings and royalties had said to her in the past. She deftly served a plate of fried potatoes to one of the priests.

"Thankfully all the previous generation heroes died with the demon king." It was a priest that said it. "The post-war political jostling was usually...terrible. Heroes who see it as their duty from the gods to correct all that was wrong in this world."

Meela stopped. She sighed.

Yvon, who was invited for the food, nodded. "Indeed. We should do our best not to offend them. We stick out, with our presence as a non-human nation in this region. But let's hope the gods spread out the heroes a bit and that some of them are non-humans. If that's the case, the heroes will balance each other out. Or maybe all of them will die to the demon king."

Meela sagged a little.

"Never mind, never mind. Let's just wait and see what happens..." Jura munched on a piece of bread.

YEAR 81 MONTH 12

The Hutan druids responded that the meetup with the other tree spirits would be delayed because of the demons. Their efforts were dedicated to defending their areas against the demons.

Ah well, I didn't expect much from these druids anyway. I intended to reach out to these tree spirits without their intermediation, anyway. I certainly would prefer to have discussions without the eavesdropping of others. Somehow, I had a gut feeling that there would be things only we, tree spirits, should know.

Or should I say root-feeling? What would be a plant equivalent of gut, anyway.

After my recent level gains, and my recent subsidiary tree numbers, I might have just enough to extend one long chain to the Giant Lilypod City, but I would have to give up all the other subsidiary trees around, and that would leave the valley defenseless and without its early warning system.

Ugh.

I'd wait for my next subsidiary tree upgrade, then.

Or maybe…I could extend halfway there and see whether I gained levels killing the demons I encountered along the way. But

Giant Lilypod City was way down south of my continent. Hmmm, even past that Gila country where the legless demon walker was.

Hmmm...

Decisions.

YEAR 82 MONTH 1

A new year, but same old threats. The demons found the volcano, and now we were fighting a three-way battle: the native golems, the demonic forces who seemed to be interested in the same mana-source in the volcano, and my beetles. This to me was sufficient confirmation that the demons were looking for mana-rich sources, so maybe they would look to my [ThreeTrees of Mana] soon.

Without the walkers, it wasn't that difficult to defend these two locations, but I was having some trouble with the demon knights, so I did need to deploy Horns, Lausanne, and the Valthorns. I mean, I could root strike the knights, and I did every now and then, to delay and postpone the battle until I could get Lausanne and gang into battle.

The reasoning was really simple. I was way too high level that defeating the knights was really quite pitiful for my experience gain, even with my overpowered experience gain. It was far more fruitful to save mobs of this level to Lausanne and the budding initiates, such that they got to a level where they could be of some use against the demons.

At first, they were excited.

But after one full month of constant battles throughout the volcanic area against the demons, Lausanne and the initiates were beginning to realize the enormity of the task.

"Wars are not nice." One of the young initiates—*she's eight*—sat next to Lausanne at a campsite. She sipped on a small wooden flask containing a kind of healing fluid. There were a few subsidiary trees here, so they benefitted from my [Healing Aura] and [Demonic Suppression Aura], so it was a relatively good campsite.

One of the captains who'd come along nodded. "Good that you realize that when you're young. It's not a nice feeling going out to fight and realizing you might not come back. We're lucky our Tree Spirit watches over us in this area."

The volcanic area's outer area was mostly conquered by my subsidiary trees by now, effectively forming a ring of trees to block out the demons. I called it the volcano tree line. That didn't stop the demons from trying to break through, occasionally with five hundred to one thousand strong forces.

Lausanne sighed and massaged her left shoulder. A wooden vine surrounded her, an effect of the special tree familiar. She was level forty-two from a whole month of demon-fighting, most of it from taking on a few demon knights. "Doing it every day was quite different from fighting occasionally."

The captain smiled. "You may be a genius, Lady Lausanne, but fighting daily is a reality for most common soldiers and guards in small villages." There was a group of soldiers who also came along. It didn't look good to leave the fighting to young kids.

She nodded. Jura did tell her stories of the past, when Freeka was still the village of Freeka and the men frequently patrolled the woods to defeat monsters. But still, nothing beat the experience of active duty, to know what it was like. "If only we can stop this for good."

The captain smiled and patted Lausanne on her lean shoulder. "Honestly, New Freeka has it good. The protection of the Aeon's beetles meant we soldiers can fight more carefully and less frequently."

Lausanne twirled her right hand, and the vine formed itself into a spear. "Ah, let's not have this talk." She twirled her fingers again, and the spear unmade itself into a vine and then into a wooden sword. This was one of her daily practice routines, to hone her mastery over the flexible vines from the special familiar. She would alternate the vine's forms: a spear, a sword, a whip, a lasso, a bow.

The rest of the initiates watched. To them, it was a bit like a magic trick.

They would rest for an hour before continuing their journey home. Thankfully, the beetle army carried them. A few of the beetles had things resembling seats, and since each beetle was about the size of a large rhino, about two to three could fit on each beetle. Except for one of the centaur Valthorns. She was one of the younger Valthorns, from the second batch, but centaurs tended to be bigger despite having similar ages. She would gallop next to the beetles, and her stamina was pretty good.

The soldiers who returned did so to relieved family members, happy to see their family returning safe. The Valthorns would mostly be greeted by the ladies of their orphanage.

The orphanage was frankly overloaded. The number of kids aged three to thirteen was close to eleven hundred, and Laufen and Belle were tasked with supervising the expansion of two additional buildings. The population was generally supportive of the orphanage, so there really wasn't any challenge in terms of funding or land, though the politicians saw it like a private military academy, given the extensive combat training in their curriculum, so according to my people-watcher Ivy, there were little pockets of discontent.

In fact, the expansion of the orphanage meant about thirty percent of the Order's budget was now used to fund the charitable segment. Both the death services, orphanage, and birth gifts all did not generate money.

One of the priests suggested 'Tithes' or 'Donations,' but I shot down the idea. I felt if people started giving money to priests, that was going to just send us into a downward spiral of corruption. So, no, I insisted on the priests being paid a salary, and no donations or tithes.

Instead, the Order had to do work for money. We ran a vegetable market, food market, and herbs market.

"Herbal soup, herbal soup." There was actually a lesser variant of ginseng, grown by our herbalist. It didn't have the full effect of the [Ginseng Plant], and this variant's boost was temporary. We thought of using the term ginseng, but then that might ruin the branding of the real ginseng plant, so we decided just plain old herbal root soup.

"Ginger tea, ginger tea!" an employee of the Order shouted.

"Flavored olives!"

"Oranges!"

"Cotton! And clothes!"

Yeah. A market. I thought of having a more upmarket feel to the premises, but somehow it just organically transformed into this chaotic mess of a market that wouldn't feel out of place in any Asian or Middle Eastern metropolis. I wondered whether this was what the Grand Bazaars of Baghdad would be like.

I would usually tune out the shouting match in the markets. There was only so many times you could bear a middle-aged lady repeatedly shouting, "Potatoes for sale! Potatoes for sale!" Listening to it for too long, I found that those words ended up repeating in my thoughts, too.

Thank goodness, like the [rootnet], I could tune out all the chatter.

But Ivy liked the market. She said the gossip in the markets was her top five ways of getting information. The things ladies shared with each other while haggling over carrots and tomatoes was quite...interesting.

Ninety-five percent made up, by the way, but still, that five percent was worth it.

Oh. And the bigger orphanage kids were usually tasked with security. If they weren't in the orphanage, they'd be the ones stealing. I thought it was a good way to deter the food thieves—it took a thief to catch a thief.

Until we got some rather interesting comments from the general populace.

"Why can't we just give our surplus away?"

"Can we just run charity kitchens for the poor and hungry?"

Hmmmm...the council already did have some kind of community kitchen, a legacy of the New Freekans' origins as refugees. The generation that came and survived the move to New Freeka generally appreciated the community kitchen.

"Never mind." I decided to just stick to the plan.

The little tree of prayer shipped to Ransalah had safely arrived and was planted in a small public garden. A rarity in Ransalah, from what I heard.

Sadly because it was way too far from any of my other subsidiary trees, it was not connected by root to the rest of the rootnet, so I couldn't really communicate with that tree. All I knew was it lived, and it was there in that little garden somewhere.

My [rootnet] needed to get some kind of wide-area network service. I mean, did we have like 4G transmission trees? Or [Wide-Area Network]?

Ah. Nothing much I could do, except to find a way to extend my roots into that area of town, so for now, I hoped that [tree of prayer] was well taken care of. It'd take a few generations of rootnet upgrades before I'd get there.

In a way, my network of trees was essentially a subterranean cable line, kind of like those subsea fiber-optic cables that crossed oceans to form my homeworld's internet. Of course, the scale of my rootnet was miniscule in comparison, but I'd like to think, with all the research and advancements I was doing, I was like a precursor to DARPA, and my rootnet was like...root-arpanet?

So, I was TARPA? Tree's Advanced Research Projects? Wait. Wasn't that TARP? TARPANET?

Never mind. That was horrible. I mentally told myself that set of names was to be forever banished from existence.

YEAR 82 MONTH 2

[Demon King Sabnoc has arrived.]

The news came like a wave. An actual energy wave swept through the world, coming from all directions. I felt it, and I was sure everyone else felt it, too.

But the wave stayed, like some kind of background...disturbance. Buzzing. Like...white noise from a radio.

Jura gathered all the leaders. "What's going on?"

"We...we don't know. None of my [message] spells are working." Madeus looked afraid. "It seems like the demon king has somehow managed to interrupt all long-range communication spells."

I tried to check on my beetles and got no response.

I lost contact with all the beetles that wandered too far off from my [subsidiary trees]. Immediately, I ordered all beetles to stay close to my subsidiary trees.

"Lausanne's out on patrol." I spoke to Jura. Looked like here, near my main tree, it still functioned. I couldn't contact her.

"We'll have to do it the non-magical way. Couriers, messengers. Escorts." Jura looked, and the captains ran out to summon as many couriers and messengers they could get.

Madeus sat; there was another mage I rarely saw next to him. "This has never happened."

Well, times had changed. Certainly, this new demon king seemed to try rather exotic strategies. I wondered whether he was a reincarnator. That would be something very, very scary to think about.

In the past, dedicated couriers, messengers, or even scouts used to travel long distances to deliver highly classified messages before the encrypted magical means of communication were invented by one of the heroes a few generations back. These days, diplomats and merchants took over the role of official documentations and treaties, and the magical encrypted messages were the mode of communication for discussions. Magical obsolescence, I supposed.

But I supposed a return to the analogue ways had its...interests. "What do we know?" Jura sent out the couriers and messengers to all the nearby kingdoms, requesting for status updates. A new set of magical seals were made to facilitate these sorts of letters and messages.

The merchants were the first to quickly summarize the effects of the demon king. It seemed they managed to retain some form of communication network throughout the continent, though their intercontinental networks were now broken.

"Message spells are unreliable at ten kilometers. High-tier communication spells are unreliable at thirty kilometers. Warnings on summons, magically controlled monsters have a chance to break their servant-master link at a distance of five hundred meters to five kilometers, depending on the type."

Hmmm...all my subsidiary trees were still in contact. Rootnet was still online.

"Message integrity decays at five kilometers onward. Merchant's guild is still experimenting with supercharging magical messages."

The [Message] spell was essentially the communication 'backbone' of the present society. War, commerce, and trade all relied on it. A [message] spell was essentially a message wrapped up into a magical 'container' and sent like an invisible 'letter,' where it then arrived at the other side as a letter. It was possible to 'secure' the 'packet' by way of encryption codes, and similarly, it was possible to 'intercept' them as they passed through.

All [message] spells traveled along corridors high up in the sky, known as the Aurora currents. These currents helped to reduce the mana load required to travel long distances, as the Aurora currents had a positive, 'recharging' effect on these [message] packets. Apparently, and this was also something that was debated, the Aurora currents were created by some heroes a long time ago to facilitate their anti-demon efforts. Some said it was made by the gods because why else would the currents be so convenient? It boggled the mind that a supposedly natural phenomenon could be exploited to function as a global airborne [message] superhighway.

A mage learning how to use [message] learned about the world's magical currents and sent the 'coordinates' along the packets. The way I understood it, as Madeus explained it, was that the [message] network was essentially like a collection of email servers with some snail mail features.

For example, a mage who wanted to send a [message] from New Freeka to, say, Ransalah must know which 'current,' 'node,' and 'sub-node,' kind of like a traditional country-state-city hierarchy common in addresses and old-school mailing systems. The [message] packet itself was then wrapped with some 'identifiers' and 'locators' so that it could 'locate' the intended receiver. Or what most nations had was a magical artifact that acted as an 'anchor' to receive the [messages], sort of like a 'post box.'

But now, this network was unusable. The chaos was perhaps similar to what happened when the internet went out. Learning the intricacies of the [message] system worked, only when the system went down, was like how people started to study the intricacies of how planes worked after a flight crash occurred. A little too late.

Merchants, especially, scrambled to find alternatives to their usual sources. Trading prices for certain goods started to fluctuate because the merchant's ability to obtain market price information from other cities was now gone, and a merchant's willingness to purchase local goods dropped significantly because he was unable to guarantee his own ability to make a profit by locking in another deal in some other part of the world.

"How about scrying and remote viewing?" I observed the mages in New Freeka's mage guild in a discussion with the local merchants. Thankfully, this newfound magical interference from the demon king didn't affect my ability to see my own trees, and I believed my own energies were repelling that interference somewhat.

It really brought back memories. The guys banging on our IT admin's tables, demanding to know why the payment systems were down and how soon we could fix it.

"Didn't work, either...and we do not have mages who focus on such spells."

"Then what works? I've got a warehouse full of goods, and I can't find out where to send them or whether the route is even safe! There has got to be something?!"

"I'm afraid the best chance, at this point, is a messenger." The mage tried to placate the angry merchant.

"That's too slow!"

"We're still trying..."

Over at the military side, Jura attended a meeting with the New Freeka council, together with a lot of military guys. A strategist under the council's employ was present to give a quick briefing on the situation.

"One, our ability to coordinate our military with our allies is now significantly reduced. Two, our ability to locate the demon king and demon walkers on a close to real-time basis is also almost gone. This means the blood sacrifice spells used to bombard the demon walkers is effectively useless."

Ah. Shit. That was a bad thing. What use was a nuke if you didn't know where to shoot it?

"Also linked to that second point, we'll need to rely a whole lot more on scouts to monitor the demon's movement."

I supposed they needed to return to flares, fire signals, and stuff like that.

I still hadn't heard from Lausanne, so I decided to send some [subsidiary trees] toward her last known location.

YEAR 82 MONTH 3

Silence was eerie. Without the communication networks to inform one's decisions, most travelers decided to stay put and wait. Only those truly desperate, or daring, made the journey.

Throughout my network of trees, demons appeared more frequently and in larger numbers. Given my now-smaller effective range due to the interference of the demon king, it was also harder to move my beetles from one place to another as they had to travel close to my chain of [subsidiary trees].

"When are the damn messages going to get through?" Some of the merchants had started drinking extensively. It seemed they were in a limbo. Some of them started to band together and try to make the trip to the next town. A small minority sold all their inventory and decided to stay put.

"I'm not going anywhere. This town can defend itself against a demon walker. I'll just stay. It's a risk to go out there. You might not know if a demon walker was nearby!"

"We are merchants! We do not sit still in a place. We need to sell to make money!"

Anyway, back to the beetles, the attacks throughout my network increased, and so, with Trevor and Dimitree's advice, I'd split my beetle force into six squads of fifteen hundred each, all stationed in a different part of my network, the rest of them in New Freeka. I couldn't move the beetles as quickly as before because of the longer route they now had to take, and with lesser 'visibility,' I had a lesser amount of time to 'plan' and 'respond' to any incursion.

In a way, this was a hub-and-spoke strategy, mini-bases for my beetles.

Frankly, I didn't see this coming. I thought demon kings were just overpowered and had high destructive abilities. Utility or passive abilities wasn't something I expected. It really felt like there was a mind behind the demon.

"Would you think it's a reincarnator? A hero from your world?"

Alexis paused. "That...would be terrible, wouldn't it? If they brought someone from my world..."

"There was really no reason why the demon kings would change tactics this time. There has to be a trigger point. When you fought the demon king, what did you think?"

Alexis waited, and then she responded, off tangent, but very relevant. "...I wonder whether the demons accessed my memories."

"Huh?"

"When I was trapped as a fire-demon. Whether...whether the demons looked into my mind, just like how I saw their homeworld."

"You...you saw their homeworld?"

"I think so. I'm not sure whether it's a dream or it's their home world, but after the demon walker, it brought back memories. It's a massive desert with large spires, similar to the ones on the demon walker's back, but many, many times bigger, and more."

"Okay, now we have two suspects. One, the demons somehow brought a reincarnator or offworlder. Two, the demons took a look at your mind and decided to copy some tactics. Or possibly both were true. Or you may have let the demons in on where you were from, and therefore they can now summon their own version of heroes."

Alexis's spirit body rotated and twirled in the air. She looked horrified. "That...I hope not. We need to warn everyone if we were potentially dealing with an enemy reincarnator. All the nations must treat the demons as intelligent!"

"Hmm...let's not panic yet." I did suspect that this generation's demons were possibly intelligent or had some kind of thought process to their tactics, but the fact that they only had a small variety of units seemed to imply that there was some kind of 'migration-limit' on what they could bring to this world. Maybe the reincarnator himself wasn't here in this world.

"We need countermeasures. We need to do something!" Alexis spun. I thought her spiritual body was changing color. "Meee-laaaaaaaaaaaaaaaa."

Meela was happily in her inn. Now that the merchants weren't going anywhere, they needed a place to stay, so her inn was full house. And many merchants were drinking their worries away.

"Busy, Alexis. I've got a full house to manage." Meela waved her off.

"This is important, Meela, IMPORTANT!!!"

"After I'm done with my customers...which is like, really, really much later. Later, okay?"

"Meelaaaaa!" Alexis pouted.

In the meantime, I called Jura and Madeus to discuss the possibility of an 'intelligent' demon king.

"Demon kings were somewhat monster-like, at least in history. They seek out places with large populations and have an ability to sense the presence of heroes. Their instincts seem to drive them toward the heroes. They have some primitive intelligence, according to statements from past heroes, but in combat, and once provoked, they are like...monsters," Madeus clarified.

"So, how bad is it if the demon king is intelligent, say...like an average human?" I asked.

"On the bigger scale of things, it's probably the demonic equivalent of a very very nasty undead necromancer."

"Is that bad? It sounds bad," I continued with my questions.

Jura shook his head. His knowledge about such things was quite...shallow. Madeus had a better understanding of historical outbreaks.

Madeus nodded. "Hmmm...if the heroes can work with the kingdoms, it should still be possible to defeat the demon king. After all, the demons can't level, and the lower-level demons and demon walkers don't display the kind of intelligence that I would associate with 'sentience.' So...it's likely that only the demon king was 'fully' intelligent."

"I agree with that theory." Indeed, the demon walker or the demon general did not appear to be 'intelligent,' even if they had some tactical sense. Else, they would not have walked in a straight line toward the source of the Hexbombs. If so, all the thinking must be done by the demon king, and that was inherently a weakness.

Jura and Madeus looked at the map. There was nothing on it, now that we had no data on the demons.

Jura shrugged. "Nothing's actually changed, has it? The heroes still have a demon king to slay. It just means the process is harder for them. For the rest of us, the demon king will continue to wreak havoc. Our preparations just need to continue."

"True."

Alexis, on the other hand, said, "We need to send letters to all the kingdoms. The threat of the demons should be higher."

"That achieves nothing. For kingdoms already fighting for their survival, such as those in the Southern Continents, the demons are already their number-one threat. For those currently safe, all of them are preparing. By now, no one is treating the demon king lightly. I believe many other strategists and kings must have come to the same conclusion as we have, that this demon king is sentient and intelligent."

Alexis pouted.

"Our best course of action is hunker down and prepare for war. And pray the demon king isn't on our continent. As for you, what have you got from all your research? Can you research how to counteract or offset this demonic interference so that we can restore the communication with all our neighbors?"

"I will get started."

Lausanne came back at the end of the month. They had been forced into hiding to avoid the roaming demons. With the beetles 'asleep,' they did not have the numbers to take the demons in a fight, so their progress home was super slow.

Laufen was delighted to see her daughter again and gave her a big hug.

"Happy to see you, too, Mom." Laufen was worried sick, even if she put on a strong face in front of others.

"We need to stick closer to the trees from now on." Jura was relieved, of course. Lausanne wasn't alone; her squad had twenty others. Luckily, none of them died. Avoiding battle was a good choice.

YEAR 82 MONTH 4

"When will the heroes be summoned?"

"Usually six months to a year after the demon king." Maybe less? I hoped it was less.

If the demon king was smart, he would expand as fast as he could and crush all the allied kingdoms. That way, the heroes had less support; the kingdoms stood no chance against a creature like the demon king. If he was truly intelligent, he would use this headstart to cement his position.

"Aeon! A demon army in the distance!" I spotted it, too; they seemed to employ a scorched-earth strategy and were headed for the volcano. New Freeka wouldn't deploy itself, but I would have to defend the volcano.

After the demon walker battle, I had fifteen thousand subsidiary trees, about a third of which were beetle-nests. Each tree, with Horn's upgrades, was home to five beetles, so I had a total beetle force of twenty-five thousand. I was literally a one-tree beetle army, but I had to spread this force throughout my network.

Seven thousand were at home, in the valley as its defensive force, and I'd lost about four thousand beetles in various smaller skirmishes in the past months. That left fourteen thousand, of which spread into the six fifteen hundred squads, give or take a few hundred.

Twenty thousand demons. There were already fifteen hundred beetles stationed in that segment of my tree network. The rest of my beetles, the seven thousand stationed at home, would take about five days to get there. It was a battle away from my main tree. Not my ideal battleground.

"They...they are headed for the volcanic area?" The Order captains were surprised, of course. They presumed they would head here.

"The volcano was a natural mana source. A difficult one to work with, but a mana source. We must defend it, else we will have a demon factory as our neighbor," I told the Order, and Jura relayed the message to a clearly spooked New Freekan council.

The councilors were afraid, so they summoned their local supporters for views. Some of them wanted to participate; they saw why it should be defended. Some preferred to wait and hold a defensive line here, in the Valley.

So the choice was given to the councilors, and they gathered support: either send an army to fight a force near the volcano or tolerate a demon base next to New Freeka and die eventually, anyway.

In a way, it was an easier battle since it was just a large army of regular demonoids. There were no giant walkers. But the flipside was my ability to intervene slightly weakened by the distance.

"Jura and Yvon, I need both of you at that battle."

Lausanne tapped herself. "Me too." Well, I planned on including her, anyway.

"And you." Laufen gave her daughter a hug. "And the Valthorns. I need every high-level person I have at that battlefield. Go, and go quickly. The beetles there may not be able to hold the line for more than three days. And the demons were only two days away."

In a way, this could have been prevented had I created an outer perimeter of subsidiary trees, but even that would only give me one extra day's advance warning. Still, I made a note to further fortify the Southern forest and [ThreeTree of Mana]. Clearly that magic leyline would be a juicy target for the demons should they discover it.

To delay the demonic force while the rest of the forces got into position, I activated [rooting field] and [poison field] multiple times. Sadly, poison didn't work on demons, but the roots did manage to delay them.

The battle began as expected, five days later on the edges of the volcanic area. I had increased the amount of [subsidiary trees] I had so that I could keep control over the beetles, and with new [subsidiary trees], the present beetle force stood at two thousand five hundred. My seven thousand beetles were a day away, and the New Freekan army of four thousand soldiers were two days away.

The demons? Twenty-one thousand or so. The demons themselves were increasing. The demons charged, led by humanoid demons, riding on demon hounds, wielding long halberds and spears.

"Fucking hell, they have cavalry." They had demon knights that rode hellhounds some time ago, a small 'elite' brainwashed humans that chased the heroes, but this was my first time witnessing pure-demonoid cavalry as combat force.

Actually, how did the demons brainwash those humans? Could they be the source of this change in tactics, too?

Something wasn't right. If demon knights brainwashed by the demons existed, that meant the demon kings had always been sentient. Because you needed a certain measure of intelligence to utilize 'demonic-corrupted human knights.' And the previous demon king had manticores and wyverns, too.

Ah, I needed to come back to this thought later. Now I needed to focus on the fight to defend the volcano.

The demonoid riders smacked into my beetles; we were fighting defensively, using the trees as a kind of makeshift wall. Beetles could fight even when they were partly crawling on trees, the demonoids less so. I needed to delay them as long as I could, until the rest of my seven thousand beetles arrived.

Utilizing their ability to burrow, the beetles dug numerous trenches throughout the battlefield, all meant to delay the demons.

A kind of treench warfare, but these were mixed in between the layers of trees.

Some of my [subsidiary trees] were [carnivorous plants], and they chomped on one or two demonoids before they needed time to recharge.

Here, at this distance, the effect of my [lesser demonic suppression aura] was slightly reduced, and a defensive battle meant my beetles could still benefit from my [healing aura].

But these things merely served to delay the inevitable.

The number disadvantage was too massive, and they killed fifteen hundred beetles within the first few hours of skirmish. The remaining one thousand retreated back to the last line of trees. On the positive side, half of the demonoid cavalry had been killed, and the demon army was now about nineteen thousand strong.

"Jura, Lausanne, Yvon. Situation isn't good. We are likely to have to fight the demons after they breach the tree line. There are a few demon knights in the force." Indeed, the demon knights, with their various short-range weapons, made the trenches unfavorable to the beetles.

A mistake, on hindsight. Silly me, thinking my beetles were the only ones who had an advantage in the trenches.

The seven thousand beetles were still half a day away.

The demons continued their charge, and the fighting continued into the night.

"Master, bad news: another twenty thousand have been spotted in the north corridor. They are headed to the former dungeon, the naga-hole." Trevor flagged the news. In fact, by the time we spotted the demons, they were already at the dungeon's doorsteps.

"There was nothing there?" How did the demons spawn so many demons? Didn't they need bases for this?

With another battle ongoing at the volcano, I had to concede the former naga dungeon. I didn't have enough beetles to fight two battles at the same time, so the beetles in that area retreated.

Back at the volcano, my defensive line broke quickly. There really was no way I could stop an army of nineteen thousand demons with only one thousand beetles, even if I kept using my skills to thin their numbers.

I had to make a call then. I retreated with the five hundred surviving beetles and joined them up with the seven thousand that arrived a little too late. The demons had breached the tree line and entered the volcano area.

"The demons were in the volcanic area."

"Should we continue, then?"

"Yes. We must defeat the demons before they establish a base in the volcano. We cannot let them tap into the volcano's mana source."

"The men were not keen," one of the captains said. Some of the men didn't see why they should risk their lives protecting a volcano.

"Then die when the demons come along." It really wasn't a lie. A demonic base next to us? They could spawn more demons, more than the beetles I could field.

Still, keen or not, we had to fight. I was not planning on letting the demons get too far into the volcanic area, and already I saw the demons fight the native magma golems.

The native magma monsters didn't mount any extra defense; after all, they didn't even know an army was headed their way, but the giant magma golems were more than a match for conventional demonoids.

But the demons were focused. While some demonoids kept the magma golems occupied, they charged for the caldera. And I didn't plan on letting them get there and establish a foothold.

I spawned subsidiary trees, even in this hostile terrain, and the army of beetles and New Freekans chased after the demons. They had one day's head start, and the army passed by more casualties by the wayside. Some soldiers took this chance to collect any loot that the golems dropped, since the demons were not interested.

As the beetles and soldiers headed up, I felt it.

A surge in mana, a shiver in the magma and earth below. "Shit," I told myself. They might have already started. Demonic energy was starting to corrupt the volcano's energies, and all the trees in the area could feel the incursion.

After an hour of climbing up the volcano with this army, we saw the demon's fortress. Past a field of crushed golems and the half-skewered demonoids, right at the edge of the volcanic caldera, a fortress in the making. It was growing slowly, but it already had the shape of spires, similar to the spires of the demon walker. There it was, at the center of the under-construction fortress, a banner-like reddish object, the so-called demon-rod as told by the merchant guilds.

"This...this was a terraforming army," Alexis muttered. "They plan to turn the world into the factories of their homeworld?" We could see the demonic energy leaking from the rod into the ground, and it was trying to take control of the land beneath it. But the volcano would not be tamed so easily.

This scene somehow reminded me of a game I played, where the four factions used little magical rods to conquer the land, and with it convert the neutral land into the four types of racial terrains, hell, blight, frost, or bloom.

"No time to waste. The fortress was not ready, and we must destroy it now." Or actually destroy the rod first. If the rod was the source of the corruption, there was really no need to focus on the army.

In fact, I thought of cheating, so I created a few subsidiary trees as close as I could to the fortress and started unleashing [Root Strike]s at the rod.

But it all met a barrier of some kind. And that barrier prevented my roots from approaching, and it also blocked my subsidiary tree.

There were three demonoids standing around the rod in a mini-circular formation. They seemed to channel the energy from within the rod to create the fortress and the barrier protecting the rod. I needed to stop them, or by tomorrow they would start to spawn demons. The barrier blocked the roots attacking the three demons, too. *Ugh.*

"Jura, I need you to take those three demonoids down."

"What, where?" I forgot they couldn't see past walls, unlike my top-down visual through all my subsidiary trees. The demonic army formed up around the fortress, and now we had a better sense of what we were up against. The demonoid army had suffered losses to get to this part, a section so close to the top of the volcano.

No matter. Sixteen thousand demons noticed our presence, and they fought hard to hold back our seventy-five hundred beetles and four thousand soldiers. And once again, another larger scale battle.

Without a demon walker to focus on, my role in this battle was to prevent unnecessary deaths. This meant observing the soldiers and interfering when they were in trouble. At the same time, I also cleared a path for Jura and Yvon that led to the three channeling demons, so that they could quickly end the rod's corrupting magics.

They were my best combatants, and since there was a magical barrier, I hoped they could still physically pass through the barrier.

Jura quickly cut through tens of demon knights; Lausanne, Yvon, and some of the captains took out a few as well. The battle lasted three hours, and the beetles finally managed to punch through the wall of demons. A path was open, and Jura, Yvon, and some soldiers charged in. The barrier did let them through.

Yvon rushed ahead, and with a quick slash, she slashed through the three demonic channelers.

The rod was almost completely enveloped in some kind of demonic energy, and when the three demonic channelers evaporated into demon-dust, it just levitated in mid-air, unmoving.

"Is it done?" Jura asked. I sensed the corrupting influence of the demonic rod slowly subsiding.

"I think we need to hit it," another soldier said. Apparently other countries had destroyed such rods before.

"Uh…" Jura looked at it; it was surrounded by a black flame. "I am not touching that. Madeus?"

"Guard it. Don't let any of the other demons continue channeling the rod." The beetles and Order soldiers fought off the rest of the demonoids. We should not stay long. I saw a giant magma golem starting to form in the distance. The native monsters were trying to fight back, and they saw both us and the demons as intruders.

"TreeTree, can you move it or knock it out? The channelers are gone, so the barrier should be down," Jura asked. Madeus was busy blasting some demons. Jura continued to cut through demonoids. The captains reorganized the men into defensive formations, the beetles doing the bulk of the fighting.

I launched a few more [Root Strike]s, and there was no barrier blocking it. It hit through the demonic flame, my roots just lightly scathed by the black flame, and the massive banner-rod fell down. But even as it collapsed, cracked, I could sense residual demonic energies from it.

The rod fell to the ground, dark energies jumped out like an arc lightning, and it tried to create more demonoids. This rod was the 'spawner' of the demonic hordes, wasn't it?

"Destroy it!" Jura shouted. "It's trying to spawn more demons." That was obvious enough. The demonic fortress and the spires around the soldiers started to vibrate, and chunks started to collapse. By now, the demonoids had been defeated. We were only left with the rod.

But no, I didn't plan to destroy it just yet. "Take the rod," I said to Jura, but then I realized it was massive.

"What? No way. It's still emitting that black demonflame. You need to knock it out a bit more."

Ugh. That meant I was the only one that could manipulate it? A beetle approached and the flames burned the beetle.

I briefly considered leaving it here, but that meant the rod would spawn more demons, and that defeated the purpose of this incursion.

I decided to weaken the rod a bit more, so with some [Root strikes], the demonic energy dissipated, and the rod itself cracked. Still, I could sense some remaining demonic energy, and that was what I wanted. Good, I felt it would be better for me to hold onto it and subject it to some research, see what I could learn from it. If this demon king was 'intelligent' as I predicted it was, then I needed to know how I could counter him, whether I could use the energies from such rods against it.

No one wanted to touch the demon rod surrounded by the residual black flames, and only I had the necessary resistances.

I used a bit of my vines, and the black flames were unable to hurt the vines much, and I moved the rod. It took a bit of effort to play pass-the-baton with my vines, tossing the rod from one subsidiary tree to another, all the way down from the volcano, back to New Freeka. This baton-pass took two days for the rod to arrive back at the valley.

It must have looked rather silly, trees passing a cracked rod, swinging it from tree to tree. It took a lot of effort to get the rod to move correctly.

Wait. Why did that sound wrong?

"Okay, let's retreat before the golems respawn. There was no need to fight the natives." Meanwhile, Jura ordered the army to retreat home. I would rebuild my defenses around the volcano after this.

*[**You gained a level.** Level 138]*

*[**New Skill learned**: Vine-Ropeway Network. Vine-Ropeway networks allows you to move things and people from place to place, like a cable car or aerial gondola system. Must be part of the same connected network of vines.]*

*[**Star mana-variant**: Consumes 150 star mana: Creates a star-mana vine-network that temporarily folds space and time, and opens a portal between any two subsidiary trees or your main body. Allows movement of any one animal or item instantaneously from any subsidiary tree to any other subsidiary. Need not be connected.]*

[TreeTree presently has 300 star mana, and generates 30 star mana per month.]

Uh. Wait.

This was like that story Jura, or was it Casshern, said so long ago, of the twinned tree spirits that had a steady portal between one another. Like paired stargates.

YEAR 82 MONTH 5

Two moons, high up in the sky. One blue, one white. Alexis said sometimes they changed color, and apparently, the alignment of the moons influenced the power of certain magics and monsters. Back home, there were stories of how some werewolves gained power from the moon; in this world, there were also certain kinds of werewolves that gained different powers, depending on which full moon was in the night sky. It was certainly a fascinating mechanic to magic. There was a third moon that moved a whole lot slower, and for now, it stayed out of sight.

Anyway, my immediate focus was on the now-broken demonic banner-rod, and I put it inside a large lab-tree close to my main body.

This was because, unlike the lab that experiment on the hexbomb's hexsludge, which was located really far away for safety, I was a whole lot more confident fiddling with the demonic rod, thanks to all of my anti-demon resistance. In fact, it was better for it to be nearer since the [demonic suppression aura] was stronger.

There was a layer of extremely dense demon-mana swirling in the core of that rod, a crystalline object that resembled daemolite. In fact, I thought it was daemolite. The dense demon-mana protected the core from the probing vines, and I was in the process of overpowering the demon-mana by slowly draining it.

It tried to fight me. The demon-mana from the rod even attempted to latch onto my body, but as expected, my body was resistant and pushed back. I activated [natural mana overwhelming] and did what I'd done in the past, just like how I used the mana from me and all the trees to overwhelm the demon hounds, and Alexis.

So slowly, but surely, my mana began to break into the rod, untangling it, and bit by bit, in slightly less than a month.

And then...

[Your mana has completely taken over the demonic-presence rod. Demonic rod has now transformed into The Stick of TreeTree. The Stick Of TreeTree retains the mana-conversion and assimilation abilities of the original rod, will grow trees wherever it was placed, and will spread your influence.]

The strange-looking rod now resembled a large wooden spear, with overgrown vines all tangled up around it. The daemolite core, once purple and reddish, was now entirely light green in color.

But seriously, I didn't come up with such a name. Or maybe I did. Maybe it was my subconscious.

Deciding it was a horrible name, I decided to call it the [Forest Rod] instead. I was just too embarrassed to even tell my beetles to carry the [Stick of TreeTree].

Throughout New Freeka, news was rare. Most [message] services were not operational, and there were not many couriers or messengers in service; they were often employed, at great cost, to deliver the most important messages.

Some merchant groups decided not to wait any longer, and instead, they spent money to hire a large escort force. It was a well-reasoned choice, since the demon king would not die until the heroes arrive. How long could they wait, anyway?

Messengers, couriers were escorted by riders, and armed cavalry. At this point, speed was key.

"Airships. Where are the airships, anyway?"

"I would think they are reserved for the most important tasks, like patrolling the capitols, transporting royalty, or urgent expeditions. Smaller ones are used by adventurers, but charging the daemolite's usually really...costly."

I was starting to suspect the airship I downed so many years ago was somehow stolen. Or just somehow...airships just fell out of favor? Under such circumstances, I would think airships would work, unless something was interfering with that, too.

Throughout my network of trees, I was starting to see more 'travelers,' merchants, and others.

A courier from Salah arrived today. Jura looked at a letter and then casually placed it aside. "They must be truly desperate to demand that we all contribute military to their defense. What a waste of valuable couriers' time."

"Huh?"

"Well, just a strongly worded letter demanding that New Freeka provide protection to the royals of Salah and support the continental coalition army. Salah's part of the 'organizing' nations this time around, together with Takde and the eastern Nagra."

"Nagra. Where's that?"

"Further east of Salah. It's a coastal nation, and its capital is actually on a large island just off the coast of our mainland. Funny it decided to play a part..."

"Maybe demons found a way to sail across the oceans."

"Demons can fly, though. At least, elder demons," Madeus added. "If one of these giant demon walkers have some kind of flying ability..."

"The previous demon king was a floating castle, after all... But what's the point of the coalition army anyway, if they can't hold a candle to the demon king?"

"They can act as a big, fat decoy," a captain said. "That's what happened to the last coalition army. A decoy to redirect the demon king elsewhere."

"Ignore them, then." I thought all these royal schemes tended to fail in the face of the demon king.

Jura laughed. "I've never intended to respond. We've got enough on our own plate."

YEAR 82 MONTH 6

Now that I had this...stick, suddenly a whole load of ideas came back to my mind. Could I do what the demons did? To 'claim' the volcano as my own using this rod? The fact that it had that 'spread' my mana thing seemed to suggest, yes. I could. I mean, that was how it worked in that other game I played, right? Rods spread influence, and if I had a rod, I could do it, too.

And after dwelling on the idea for a few days, I decided to call on my beetles and Horns, and it was time for me to try to use the demon's tactics for myself.

The trees I had on the volcano had been destroyed, uprooted by the magma golems, but it wouldn't be hard for me to get back there again. Six thousand beetles charged up the volcano.

We fought golems, and giant golems along the way, and it was a little easier this time around, with [healing aura] somewhat offsetting the natural 'burn' damage from the volcanic environment. With stronger beetles, thanks to the upgrades, we managed to secure a one-way chain of trees up till the caldera.

And there we had it. The giant magma golems.

Defeating the giant golems was easy. But consistently holding on to it, while saving all the things that were dying? That was harder. I had to personally intervene every time the giant golems attacked, and that made holding onto the volcano exceptionally time-consuming. That was even before the issue of the volcano's raw natural mana, which I couldn't seem to access. My subsidiary trees also kept burning from the natural heat of the volcano, and that meant I had to constantly replace them.

Thankfully, after the past few upgrades, they were a little bit tougher.

I hoped the [Forest Rod] changed that. If this worked, I was going to start hunting the demons for more rods.

A torrent of [Root Strike]s later, the golems were down, and four beetles helped to insert the [Forest Rod] into the edge of the caldera.

One of my [subsidiary trees]'s vines and roots then tangled with the [Forest Rod]'s growing vines, and I felt a strange sensation. I felt like I was in a hot sauna, but I was a tree. Focusing on the [Forest Rod], I quickly saw that it was the natural mana from the volcano and my own natural mana mixing.

I thought this might work.

And more of those magma golems appeared. They seemed to have been riled up by the sudden shift in mana, and we, the trees, and the beetles now played defense.

I supposed it was like tree versus volcano, then?

And we spent five days defending the [Forest Rod] while it channeled slowly. There really was no way I could speed it up, since the rod itself seemed to just work...automagically once supplied with mana. Increasing it didn't work.

Maybe it was like cooking: you couldn't speed up a natural process. Not too much, at least.

So, we endured for five days, constantly healing all the damaged subsidiary trees from all the spontaneous combustion. The heat meant the trees were drained of all their liquids, and when they were sufficiently dry, they would just burst into flames. That on top of the attacks by golems.

To slow down the effects of the intense heat, I tapped on the waters from the rest of my network and constantly 'pumped' water to the subsidiary trees on the volcano. It worked, somewhat, but instead some of the trees started to 'boil.' Which killed them, too.

But we held our ground.

Five days of constant fighting against golems, and I lost forty-five hundred beetles after five days. Battling in this unfavorable terrain meant their effectiveness was low, and I'd seen it firsthand during the earlier battle with the demons. A beetle that was normally able to take on three, maybe four demons could only take on one demon because of the damage from the terrain itself.

For five days, golems attacked the subsidiary trees and the makeshift walls from all sides, and I had the beetles try to do some rudimentary digging. The beetles suffered much, digging through hardened magma, and didn't help that there had been a few...accidents. Some beetles accidentally stepped on a chunk of loose rocks and then slid to their deaths into the molten lava lake in the center of the caldera. Or some chunks of ground suddenly erupted and a geyser of lava torched a few trees.

Five days. Honestly, five days was just a blink of an eye, usually. But this long 'grind' of barely defending the [Forest Rod] really reminded me of the early days of the [ginseng tree]. At least the rod was pretty tough. It could take a few punches.

Five days. I supposed I wasn't as good at 'corrupting' the land since the demons were almost done in two.

And five days of magma-golem genocide later, the volcano filled with the burned trees, burned beetles, we completed the channeling of the rod.

The [Forest Rod] transformed into a large tree right at the edge of the caldera. It was massive.

And then, one of the longest skill notifications I had ever had.

And I meant it was really, really long.

[**Natural Feature** - *Volcano integrated. Volcano has now transformed into Verdant Volcano.*]

[Verdant Volcano will now spawn Giant Wildbeasts instead of Magma Golems. Giant Wildbeasts and other spawned creatures will recognize your trees and subordinates as natives.]

*[**Volcanic Minerals** - Passive - Must maintain connection to volcano - Subsidiary trees now share nutrients and minerals from the volcano to its surroundings. Provides significant improvement to crop output, tree growth and regeneration and crop health. Bathing and drinking volcanic waters improve overall health. Resistance to disease, plague improved for New Freeka inhabitants.]*

*[**Soul Forge**: Red unlocked]*

*[**Soul Forge**: Red increases artificial soul level caps to Level 50.]*

*[**Soul Forge**: Red unlocks additional repair options and allows the repair of souls damaged by psychic or mental attacks. Improves a soul's ability to withstand exposure to other kinds of mana and also improves skill harvesting rate.]*

*[**Dream Harvester Spirits unlocked.** Dream spirits harvest essences, soul fragments, and occasionally 'skills' from those having dreams, aspirations, and strong passions.]*

[As you have unlocked 3 Soul Forge colors, you've gained access to the [Titan Souls]. Titans were guardian monsters, protectors of incredible power, and summons of yore. You have sufficient power to support one Titan. To create a Titan, you must have a [Titan Frame]. Titans start at level 70 and have a level limit of 150. Once destroyed, they will respawn in one year in your main tree, until deployed again.]

[[Titan Frames] are collected when a level 150 person, or a divine hero, or a dragon (or monster of similar grade) dies in your vicinity.]

Trevor, Bamboo, and Horns, who were now at their level-forty cap, had unlocked new upgrade options. Taking these upgrades would allow them to level up to level fifty.

[Trevor]
[Red - blood-path - Requires 10 rubies, and three barrels of monster blood.]
[Bamboo]

[Red - Flower path - Requires 10 star garnets and two boxes of red flower petals.]
[Horns]
[Red - Scarlet Steel Beetle path - requires 1 ton of Iron and 10 rubies.]

And I'm not done yet.

*[**You have gained a level**! You were now Level 139.]*
*[**Skill obtained**: Main Body Environmental Adaptation. Your main tree body was now able to survive all environments.]*

Metaphorically, I felt like I had to sit down and digest all that. In fact, that meant just...doing nothing. A tree couldn't sit. I could move my roots to resemble sitting, but it was not sitting.

YEAR 82, MONTH 7

I had a lot to think about, particularly about the nature of my new powers. Firstly, the colors of the soul forge, how many colors were there? I had earlier suspected that there were at least five colors, similar to how some trading card games did it, white, blue, green, red, and black.

If there were five colors, would that imply a level limit of seventy if I had all five colors for my artificial souls? Or if there were more?

And acquiring more colors expanded the kind of souls I could create, so if three colors unlocked Titans, what would five colors do? Or if there were more, what would those functions be? These were things I thought I would discover in the future.

Then the Titans. Sadly, its effects were not retrospective, so I did not benefit from Alexis's death in my hands. I wondered whether it still counted if I killed the heroes when they were weak. Did it? Or slaying dragons?

And environmental adaptation. Uh...kind of lame of a level 139 skill, since...I was here. At least if somebody used a super-blizzard, I'd be fine.

Also, the rod worked.

To me, this rod was a great gamechanger. I couldn't make the rod, but I could find more. And then I could corrupt it to expand my influence. It even helped to expand my forests. More forests was good. I liked having more forests everywhere.

Even now, the volcano's surface was filled with small shrubs and trees, the once 'violent' mana now a whole lot less 'hostile' to vegetation. I should have more of these rods.

So it was time for me to turn the heat back on the demons. Because these rods were awesome.

And for that purpose, I created a new [artificial soul]. Too bad I couldn't have a Titan yet, but I supposed Titans were like endgame units. Like Khaine, or the Warboss.

"Stratreegy, online. Awaiting your instructions, commander." Damn, I loved the fact that the artificial soul could leech on my memories to shape his voice and conduct. I honestly modeled him after the adjutants and advisors in all the 1990s RTS games I used to play.

"Good. Here's our plan. Dimitree, Trevor, your roles remain. That is defense and administration of the southwest forests, the valley, and now also the volcano area. Ivy, your role remains to monitor the inhabitants of New Freeka. Stratreegy, your role is to be my war room and battlefield command. Your task is to find and hunt for these 'demonic rods.'"

"Acknowledged."

"As it is, our visibility and scouting range has been significantly weakened, thanks to the interference of from the demon king, and beetles are only able to operate within a specified range of our [subsidiary trees]. This will be a difficult task. But together, we will hunt down more of these rods."

Silence.

"As such, I am delegating control over four thousand beetles and five hundred unused subsidiary tree slots to you. Get me more of those rods."

"Understood, Commander."

And so, I let my new artificial soul on its way. I felt a bit like the Overmind, creating new cerebrates to perform specific tasked. It helped that my special project, the [Grand Mind Tree], was going to be ready in two more months.

What would I be called, then? I honestly didn't want a name with a 'mind' in it because I thought my mind wasn't really all there. As much as I tried to resist it, my mind splintered and went off in weird tangents. It was almost like my mind was some kind of multi-threaded computer, jumping from one train of thought to another.

I wondered sometimes whether I was still Matt. But then, a part of me just brushed that off and pushed me back to my duties, which was the valley and caring for all my trees and 'citizens.' I liked my trees. There were so many of them now, and I considered them extensions of me.

Yeah. My mind wasn't all there. I wondered whether the gods were playing tricks on my me like how they played tricks on the heroes.

How long before the heroes arrive anyway? It'd already been five months. It seemed that the courier services were getting more and more active, with more people taking on the 'job' of delivering messages to nearby towns.

We still hadn't received any news from the other continents, but we were starting to get a better sense of what was happening on our own. The merchant's guild had finally set up something of a high-priority courier network, using their best scouts and messengers to travel along specified routes.

The good thing was at least the demon king wasn't on our continent. The bad news was there were a lot more demon walkers. But that was a small matter. Now that I was aware of the value of the demon-rod, I wanted more of it.

So I needed to help Stratreegy along.

Jura seemed quite puzzled, but once I explained how I 'corrupted' the demon rod, he, too, saw value in it.

"Yes. Preferably ones where there are known 'demon rods.' Jura didn't want to explain too much but said that I have uses for them."

"Uh..." The captains seemed strangely appalled.

"You do not have to engage. You just need to find it and report back."

"We'd rather not, Counsel. With communication lines so limited, the men would prefer to remain close to home." The captains didn't like the idea of looking for demons outside our immediate territory.

I could sense their hesitation, and I decided to tap on another source of valuable talent. Adventurers.

Twenty gold for the first party that spotted a demonic bannerrod. And indeed, that helped to mobilize the adventurers. I mean, conventional military men weren't really looking to risk their lives unnecessarily. The idea of poking the hornet's nest was strange to most regular forces, and only those with high levels in [Scout] or [Spy] or [Infiltrator] would even think of risking their lives.

Adventurers, on the other hand, were more than willing to take on danger for simple, good old moolah.

I mean, at what point did money lose value anyway? In a world where monsters and demons were so insane, why should money have any value? Shouldn't 'protection' and 'safety' be more valuable? What really gave money value in a world with no certainty of value? I mean, theoretically, if you were more likely to die than ever be able to trade that gold for anything of value, the gold was essentially worthless once you stepped out of the city gates, no? Perhaps one of the gods somehow guaranteed the value of gold, then? Acting as some kind of universal monetary authority? Or did the merchant's guild play that role indirectly, functioning as a de facto reserve bank?

It was a rhetorical question. I needed to stop getting sidetracked.

I needed more rods. Maybe I could plant them at the lake. Or what if I used it on the large mound of daemolite?

How did I get green-and-white-colored soul forges?

YEAR 82, MONTH 8

The fact that the rod worked made me ask more questions about the nature of these 'mana sources.' Why were my normal subsidiary trees able to tap into the magical leyline, yet it didn't work on the volcano?

What made the rod special?

I made a few theories, but I must admit these were shaped by my experiences with my own games.

The first possibility was that there were compatible and incompatible 'colors' for mana, and so, if my base color was blue, then red was therefore an 'opposing' color. So I would have to go through a lot more steps and upgrades to assimilate an 'opposing' color mana, hence the [Forest Rod].

That, of course, was just a theory. I had asked the Wisp, but the Wisp was surprisingly clueless about such things, and I suspected only other Tree Spirits would be able to answer me.

The second but not mutually exclusive theory was that there were 'tiers' to the mana. In this theory, the dungeon core and leyline beneath constituted 'directly accessible' mana, and the volcano's natural mana constituted 'mana that required processing.'

The mental model I had for this theory was similar to the oil and gas industry, which had different types of rigs and mines, like regular pumps, deep-sea rigs, oil sands, or shale oil, each with different rates of recovery, at different kinds of technological difficulty. I built this theory on the knowledge that heroes and I had 'star mana,' and the sick princess was exposed to 'void mana,' so it may not be too hard to then theorize 'star mana' was like nuclear fuel. So, if we were to lay down the types of mana on a scale, there would be an increasing difficulty.

Of course, the fact that I had the ability to produce star mana challenged this theory, like...if I could make star mana, why was the volcanic mana a challenge?

Anyway...whether these were 'types' of mana or 'tiers' of mana, or even both, I frankly had no proof. Or maybe I was just imagining things.

The rod was able to circumvent the tiers, or whether it was the colors, but other than it worked, I had little insights into the underlying mechanics of how it took the volcanic mana and made it usable to me. So what I could do was keep expanding and growing, using the rods in different circumstances and then observing the outcomes.

Meanwhile, somebody important came. We knew it was important because that person came in a rare airship. Apparently, after some sniffing, daemolite-powered airships were quite sensitive to the magical interference by the demon king, and so many, many fleets had been grounded. This airship was powered by Quantium, an expensive and rare crystal. The fact that it was deployed meant a lot.

"The Kingdom of Takde summons all high-level individuals to assault a demonic fortress. It's located in the ruins of a once-large city. All individuals above level fifty are invited to participate, and Takde will bear all lodging and costs."

The demons had managed to take down a large city, and a rod

had been planted. In the ruins of a place that witnessed intense death, the rod's magical harvesting ability mixed with the residual death energy, and as a result, they started producing special kinds of demonoids.

The envoy described it as an upgraded version of demon knights, bound to the ground, without wings, but they were twice as large as any regular demonoid. The size of a troll or a large ogre, these demons were equal in strength to a regular demon knight, the equivalent of a level thirty to thirty-five captain. Not a problem per se, but the issue was really about numbers. This rod produced these demon ogres by the hundreds every week.

"Fascinating," Alexis mused. "It's like these rods have some kind of natural-adaptation ability to produce special kinds of units. Like an…adaptive breeder."

It was expected. The volcano's 'conversion' created special giant beasts. Looking at this sort of trend, the former snake-dungeon might be spitting out snake-demons very soon. I should look into that.

"But why didn't these sorts of special units appear earlier?" I wondered. Perhaps it was a condition for unlocking the next tier units that required the presence of the demon king. Or like queens in a beehive, it was the demon king who introduced genetic diversity into their population?

A few adventurers in New Freeka agreed to join. I had the impression adventurers avoided participating in such high-profile demon-related matters unless the heroes were involved, but I supposed some people were going to bite if the rewards were good.

"So…that snake-dungeon, were you just going to leave it?" Alexis asked. Well, no.

I looked at Stratreegy's overlay, showing a large map, split into numerous hexagons. It was an overlay and presentation resembling Age of Wonders, with my main body at the center. There were five straight lines of trees, one to the volcano, one to the south-forest, one that went all the way to Ransalah, one that led close to the former snake dungeon, and another one that was headed south, toward where the other demon walker was once spotted.

"I'm thinking." It took one beetle pod, one month to regrow one beetle. So, theoretically, I could lose about five thousand beetles per month with no real 'loss' to my force. I could consistently assault that location with five thousand beetles, but it was probably better to hammer it with a larger force.

Unlike the humans, or the elves, or any other nation who manned their force with non-renewable lives, my beetles essentially allowed me to fight the demons with their own strategy, a war of attrition.

Outside of my own extremely overpowered abilities against demons, this was my second advantage against demons.

"How about your spiders? They've not been seeing use. Outside making webs here."

"They're anti-air...and were campers. They're not suitable as an invasion force. Beetles, being a mobile unit, were kind of like...cavalry."

"Your other beetle-variants? The dungbeetles or the spearbeetles?"

I looked at the map again. Visibility was still crap. A comparison to age of wonders would be being able to see only one or two 'hex' away.

"So...TreeTree, would you want to send anyone to join the Takde's force?" Jura interrupted my thoughts; the envoy had met a whole load of other adventurers and fighters.

"No." I'd deal with them separately. "Get me a map of where that location is." I was still very happy that I could actually 'see' now instead of just 'spirit vision.' I could read maps! Apparently Takde's airship was already filled with other adventurers the envoy picked up. It was going to be a rather massive force, and the Takde High-King intended to use a large, collected group of high-leveled adventurers as a sledgehammer. "What about the coalition army that Salah's leading? Or was it Nagra?"

"It's participating, of course. But to minimize casualties, they need this high-leveled force. Every week delay increases the demon-ogre force by a few hundred," Jura explained.

Alexis magically created a floating, holograph-like map. "So either strike early with a smaller force or strike later and face a bigger standing army. Sounds like fun."

From Ransalah, a chain of trees up to the Takde Demon Fort wouldn't be too far. I wanted to see the demon-ogres for myself, whether they really were the threat that the envoys said it was.

"So...you're going to sweep in to save the day?" Alexis asked.

"The beetles won't get there in time. Not with that kind of distance."

"Even with your new ability?"

"It's a pulley system based on vines, it's better for goods, and it's not fast." Pulley systems existed in this world. Many ports had engineers who designed large contraptions to help with moving goods. It seemed one of the heroes, a long time ago, did manage to introduce some rudimentary container system, though the practice was competing with magical holding bags.

"So what's your plan? Just create a chain of trees and watch the battle?" Alexis didn't seem too impressed.

"Honestly, yes. I like seeing new types of demons. I think it's fascinating, and it gives us insights into how intelligent this demon king is."

Alexis frowned. The airship with the adventurers left. There was some information trading as well.

———

Some of the adventurers we hired did come back with some targets. And after a few battles with smaller demon bases, this was where I made a discovery.

The rods must be collected, either when they were unused or still under construction or in transport. Once fully channeled and transformed into a 'base,' or a 'fort,' most of that mana-corrupting ability was lost. Left untouched, the fully channeled rods could still continue to generate 'small' amounts of demonoids, but they lost most of their 'base-creation' ability.

In short, a single-use item. Ugh.

I had the idea of smashing some demon bases and stealing the rods, but it made more sense that the rods were mostly a single-use item.

Back to the drawing board.

YEAR 82 MONTH 9

[Completed The Grand Mind Tree project]

The grand mind tree resembled a bunch of walnuts stacked on top of each other. The entirety of the Mind Tree was wrinkly, with multiple branches twirling around.

Located just next to me, the moment it was fully completed, I could see it glow a faint greenish light.

And then I had a massive, massive headache.

For a good…one hour.

But only one hour. I'd had worse headaches.

[Mind Control resistance significantly increased. Each of your artificial minds will now act as 'counterchecks' against attempted mind control attacks. Mind control must now apply to more than half of your artificial minds to work.]

Ah wonderful. The blockchain node approach to mind control resistance.

Also, my awareness of soul matters suddenly took a giant leap. If I focused, I could now observe greater details in the folds of my [soul realm]. And most importantly, the processing power to alter souls was at a fine level. It'd been something that I wanted, something I figured might solve what I had been facing with Jura.

After a string of successes with smaller rats and animals, I tried moving onto bigger things, and realized...I just couldn't.

I had 'resolution' issues. Because I couldn't create a 'canvass' big and detailed enough. That meant I would work halfway and realized I couldn't copy more. Even with a live version as a reference.

It was like working with a forced 600x480 resolution when I needed ten times that.

This [grand mind tree] was kind of like a massive RAM and solid-state hard disk.

"Jura. Soul forge, now." With the grand mind, I now had what I needed to create a functional copy of the 'hand.'

He looked puzzled, but he wasn't one to challenge me that much. So he agreed. I had Lausanne and Laufen gather all sorts of materials and animals and place them around my main tree.

With all three [soul forge: red, blue and black], I drew the mana from all over my network of trees, and they appeared as three separate balls of energy, one blue, one red, and one black. This distinction was also made possible by the improved mana-manipulation ability from the [grand mind tree].

And from the [soul realm], I took a bunch of the soul fragments and started to form the shape of a hand.

Jura's now asleep inside, the vines pumped nutrients and mana. And three viney feelers, ethereal, both 'physical' and 'spiritual,' reached into his body and pulled his soul out. Just partly.

It revealed an elf-shaped soul, but with one hand gone. A gap. It was rounded now, like a soul-version of a stump.

Two more feelers appeared and touched the other still-present hand. The Grand Mind Tree glowed, and in sync, another feeler started to work on the floating hand formed from the broken soul fragments of the dead. With the mental processing and storage power of the grand mind tree we had the necessary 'mental' capacity to copy all the details of his existing hand. And we started to work.

Ivy and Trevor acted as my assistants. They helped maintain some of the mana flow and regulated the [soul forge].

Cocooned in mana, it took a good four hours, and the floating hand now resembled the other, with the necessary corrections. Previously I could only do three hours. It had all the vessels, muscle strands, and bone shapes, a perfectly flipped copy of the other hand.

Then multiple ethereal feelers appeared, and it cut into the stump on Jura's soul. It was a slow process using the fragments of souls to create all the components and joining the existing soul to this new hand. Bit-by-bit, vein-by-vein, bone-by-bone, strands of muscle joined their counterparts on Jura's soul.

This took another four hours, and day had now turned into night. There were people looking for Jura, but Laufen sent them off.

The three glowing mana balls entered the 'new' hand, and then the energies mixed and bound them together. Before I woke Jura, I checked.

And double-checked. I made sure I fixed every part of the connection. Trevor and Ivy helped to check as well.

Checking my own work took another two hours. I had to be sure. If I lost Jura to my own mistakes, I was not sure how I could forgive myself.

But after that, I felt I was okay. Jura's body was stable. Gently his soul returned back to his body, and then I used the [biolab] functions to check another time. Fifteen minutes. He was all right; his soul spring appeared stable. There was a new section in there.

I injected something and roused him from his slumber.

Jura woke up and shouted.

He felt immense, immense pain. Because what was once a 'stump' was now something he could feel in his soul. The loss, the lack of a hand, the pain that once was, all of it returned.

He shouted. But now, I could apply healing magic.

With more...surgery. And I sent him back into sleep. I had to wake him to check his response.

This time, with real physical feelers, inside a biopod, I cut into the physical stump on his body and started to apply [healing]. And instead of healing back to a stump, it started to form a hand.

I did it slowly, making sure the recovery of the hand didn't cause any cuts or gaps that would leak blood. Trevor and Ivy helped monitor his vital stats.

And after another two hours of slow 'reconstruction,' Jura woke up to find that he had...both his arms.

Jura was speechless when he saw his returned hand.

He touched it, and he felt it. And he just stared at his 'new' hand for a good fifteen minutes, just moving his fingers, his wrist, his muscles.

I decided to just let him have his moment. He sat, and he cried for a while.

"TreeTree...you...fixed my hand. Only gods and their miracles can do such things. Maybe...maybe heroes, too."

Great, I took so long to do something a hero probably could do in his sleep.

"I didn't know I could, too. So...uh...be gentle with your new hand?" I wasn't sure whether everything was fine yet, even though all the stats from [biolab] were positive.

"Yeah." He stretched it. "It...It still feels kind of strange to be having my own hand and not Bamboo's wood hand. I'll be careful."

When he stepped out of the biopod room, everyone gasped. Jura smiled. "Hey. TreeTree made a hand."

"So...that tree makes you smarter?" Alexis asked. "Is it like your brain, but...bigger?"

"No. It's just a special-tree type I have, increases research, and improves my mental resistances."

"Huh. For something that takes up so many resources, and almost two years to grow, I expected it to be more...impressive. Like, warp space-time or something."

"I believe there are abilities that I have yet to discover."

"But I guess you needed it to fix Jura's hand. That's pretty good," Alexis mused and looked at the magical labs. "Too bad you can't fix this magical interference. Could it create like a psychic bubble to push back the demon king's interference? You know, like erm...Professor X's."

"Why?"

"Well, you can fix this newsless world for a change."

"Hah." I was a bit torn. Should I care about the outside world? I liked just caring about growing more trees, spreading trees from place to place. I liked looking after what was mine, my forests, and my valley, the trees that I had.

Wait. Was that me?

But then, the world was never going to just let me be. A part of me echoed the words of Gewa, that I had great power, and I should use it to fight the demons. The lives that could have been saved if I did something.

Yet that earlier part of me resisted that notion. I wondered whether this was the 'tree' part of me that just wanted to mind my own business and focus on growing trees. Helping trees. Trees were my friends, my family, and they were mine, in a way these elves and humans could never be. Maybe a part of me felt that they, these trees, were...me. I sometimes thought about where all this came from, a yearning for self-preservation?

A collective instinct for self-preservation, drawn from the thoughts of all the trees?

Was this world, and all these artificial minds and grand mind tree, unknowingly influencing my thought processes? Was it deliberate? Or was there something like how the gods could subtly guide one's thoughts in a particular direction without one knowing?

Again, why did my mind wander like that? I was having a discussion on the demons, was I not?

"TreeTree, you...okay?" Alexis seemed puzzled. "You just stopped...talking."

"I...have a lot on my mind."

"Ah, because you actually have a mind, now." Alexis pointed to the mind tree. She laughed. "I was wondering where you did your thinking, like...is there a brain in your tree? Or were you like jellyfish and the roots in the ground functioned like some neural network?"

"Uh." Well, I was beginning to suspect it was some kind of neural network. Or was it overstimulation from all the data coming in from all those other trees?

"Never mind. I often make jokes that only I find funny." Alexis shrugged.

"Yes. Back to subject. Demons." There was a big fight with the demon ogres.

The Takde's force of fifteen hundred high-leveled adventurers and fighters was super impressive, and it managed to crush the force at the demon city. The battle lasted for about half a day, and they were successful.

Of course, I had some trees nearby to watch the action. The demon ogres were just giant versions of their own demonoid soldiers, nothing much to be afraid of, and their combat ability was less than a captain. The kingdom of Takde exaggerated the threat, but I supposed that helped to ensure a smooth defeat of the demons.

The adventurers and generals did have to work a bit harder against the few demon-generals, but they still vastly outleveled most of the demons.

And, as a bystander, I witnessed many high-level skills used by some of the higher-leveled adventurers.

Yet even the best of them were just about level eighty to ninety.

I supposed it was a bit of a letdown on both the adventurer and demon fronts, but hey, the variants the demon-rods made weren't that overpowered unless the source itself was powerful. Or maybe...there were more powerful variants?

Maybe the demons captured a dragon cave or cemetery and spawned dragon-demons?

That would be a hell of a sight.

YEAR 82 MONTH 10

After the demon base over the ruined city was destroyed, the 'captured' souls were gradually released. The city, a field of death of many, had many wandering souls, spirits, and the rod caught on to them and leeched off their energies. I could tell because now that my trees were nearer to this location, some of these lost souls entered my soul realm, and their condition looked pretty bad.

It seemed the demonic interference also meddled with the navigational abilities of souls. Would it be like Warp Immaterium? Now corrupted by the presence of the demon king?

Ah, well.

[Class seeds - Knight x 6 received]
[Class seeds - Paladin x 2 received]
[Class seeds - Ranger x 4 received]
[Class seeds - Mage x 4 received]
[Skill seeds - various classes]

The souls, as they returned to the [soul realm], gave me various class and skill seeds. Many of those perished in combat, many more in the chaos after the demonic army breached the walls.

These were the fragments; as they died, the things that held their soul spring together started to break apart. So I might as well pick them up.

After all, once they entered the soul realm, only the inner soul was needed for reincarnation.

"It's a horrible thing, for these souls, that even in death they have to serve the demons for a while."

"Different demons, or are we talking about the same demons?" I asked Alexis. If these 'demons' were extraplanar in nature, wasn't the term 'aliens' more appropriate?

"Yeah...but I mean, the native demons of the world are more of...djinns. Or like...dark faeries who make unfair deals. Any resemblance of the physical appearance is coincidental because what powers them underneath it all is very different. These demons...are invaders."

"That's because you've seen it. To most of the mortals fiddling with demons, I'm not sure if they know. But heh...too bad there aren't any demon-hunter classes."

"There are. I guess you're just unlucky. But then, paladins can gain skills that boost damage against demons."

But if they were aliens, why did they benefit from the same 'boosts?' The skill system clearly acknowledged that they were demons. Even my own skills considered them demons. Or was this some kind of godly classification?

"Hmmm..." I wondered whether I could just plant these class and skill seeds and let them grow, so that I had more such seeds. Each of these class seeds gave one level in that class to the person that consumed the fruit made from these seeds. But second helpings did nothing. Skill seeds, on the other hand, there were specific types, and generic types. Specific types would grant a skill in the type if the person had a compatible class. Generic ones would grant a skill from that class's pool of skills. In a way, generic ones were stronger, since it was theoretically possible to give someone one class seed and multiple generic skill seeds to let him have multiple skills.

They were seeds, right?

[You can compress ten class seeds or ten skill seeds of the same type into a 'class tree' or 'skill tree.' These class or skill trees produce 1-3 seeds every year.]

Oh. Was it theoretically possible to create an orchard of these class trees and skill trees?

I mean, if I had a hundred paladin seeds, I could create a hundred paladins, right? Level one, for sure, but still, a hundred paladins! What if I had crazy powerful classes like [kings] or [heroes] or [emperors]?

What happened if I gave a hundred people all [king] classes? Did they fight each other for a chance to be king? What if I had a hundred knight seeds and had them fight each other to level up? That was possible, right? A survival of the fittest gauntlet to produce a strong fighter? Sounded like something out of those mobages where one fused units together to level up.

Why couldn't I just fuse those class seeds together? Wouldn't fusing class seeds create hybrid classes? Or did this world's classes not work like that?

[Class fusion and creation requires a compatible class or creature type and the divine gift - Taskmaster, or the divine gift - Evolutionist]

What? It was possible! And divine gifts?? What was that?

"So...are you doing anything with those class seeds?"

I was sitting on a lot of class seeds, skill seeds, and experience seeds. I thought I had enough experience seeds for about twenty levels now. Too bad only class and skill seeds could be multiplied, else imagine a fruit that gave levels? That was really overpowered, wasn't it?

But skill seeds were pretty good, too, since they gave new skills. If I could create a skill seed-tree that produced a strong skill every year, I could have a team of very highly skilled fighters.

"Uh...nothing." For the experience seeds, I'd like to use it on Lausanne or Jura or Laufen, but Lausanne continued to gain levels from all the demon fights she participated in. So there was really no need to use it now. The rest of the Valthorn Initiates too were on the lower side of the levels, so they were still able to gain levels.

———

"Commander." A part of me felt happy every time I got called that. Really felt like the days when I was playing RTSs as a kid, only, well, I was fully immersed in it. Stratreegy had been really busy with all the demonic movements. He deployed another three thousand beetles and [subsidiary trees] to go with it to hunt for more rods.

He wanted to get his first rod. He was thirsty.

"Glory to the Countree. We will expand our reach." He even had a catchphrase, like what usually happened when a player selected a unit in an RTS.

Uh. Did he just invent a new name for the state? Countree of Freeka? Did that make me the primogenitree? Count-Tree Aeon?

Anyway, focus, focus. Stop getting distracted. Grand Mind Tree, if you can, help me stay on track.

Demon rods, well, the issue really was intercepting the rods before they were fully deployed. Maybe someday I could get the necessary powers to make my own rods rather than robbing the demons for their rods.

"Operation Rob the Rod status update. We are pursuing a small demonic base that's just been spotted. The beetles will attack the rod as soon as we spot it to disrupt its channelling."

Well. The attack failed to secure the rod. The demons were able to protect the base until it was fully channeled, and because it was located in an open space, there was nothing slowing down the channel.

The demon rod's channel time was correlated with the

ambient magic energy in the area, so using the rod in a regular plain didn't take very long.

Ugh. Next target.

"Please bestow your punishment on me for my failure, Commander." Stratreegy wasn't happy.

"Do a postmortem and tell me what you think. It can improve your chances for success."

"Maybe...maybe you should flip it around. Look for magical places, and lure the demon rods to them," Alexis suggested.

"Genius!" I mean, why didn't I think of it? All these minds and I couldn't get a good idea?

———

News from the southern states of the continent. A demonic walker had been spotted swimming across the ocean. The southern naval states were forming an armada to intercept the walker before it hit land.

"This means the southern continent was done for." Jura looked at the parchment. "Else why would the walker make the journey across the ocean?"

"Intercepting the walker before it hits land is a good idea. The regular demonoids are unable to fight on water."

"Could the demonoids be...I don't know...walking beneath the oceans? Like that...pirate movie where the undead marched underwater?" Alexis asked. "I mean, they aren't exactly living things, right, so...they may be able to function in water just as well as on land."

That was a good point, Alexis. So I asked Jura and the leadership team.

"Uh...there have been documented records that some generations of demons were able to function underwater or fly... But walking underwater is not something that has been observed," Madeus explained. He rummaged through a few massive tomes.

"But...Aeon is right. Nothing rules out the possibility that the demons can simply walk underwater."

"So..."

"Perhaps it is a trap? I mean, what can the naval forces do? Shoot cannons and fire spells at the walker until it somehow sinks? But if it doesn't breathe, that doesn't change a thing, does it?" Jura thought out loud.

"Whatever the outcome, I feel it didn't change that we're going to have more demons from the south, so we need to increase our southern-sector defenses." This did mean I needed to widen my net of [subsidiary trees], but I'd already deployed most of my subsidiary trees. I needed my next level up.

Fifteen thousand trees was pathetic compared to the kind of numbers the demons could put out. I'd like to be a tree supercluster with billions, no, trillions of trees. I mean, if I could somehow become a massive forest that covered the entire continent, I could take on the demon king myself. I could just keep throwing beetles and trees at it until I won by attrition.

That was what ants did. That was what invasive plants did. Outnumber and overpower.

I would like to see a world where trees ruled the entire world. Where there were all kinds of trees, from the north pole to the south. Maybe trees on the moon and other planets. Earth was once like that.

If I was back home, I could solve global warming by just spawning trees everywhere. I recalled reading some articles while working that a few billion trees would help fix the whole carbon dioxide emissions thing.

―――

Anyway, I wanted to gather my thoughts.

So much had happened, so many places to watch, a whole load of news from all over the world. I had had so many new skills and faced new foes.

Since the end of the year was coming, it was time for me to do a bit of a checkup. Maybe I should do such things once a decade, or maybe once every few years, since a year was really short to me.

Introspection, or I supposed intreespection, was very much overdue.

Wait! Didn't I assign one of the artificial souls to keep track of things for me? "TREVOR!"

"Apologies, master. I had minimized the task manager when the demon king spawned," Trevor noted. "Pulling it out now and updating. Volcano...completed. Airship...pending. Research and Upgrades...suspended due to demon king. Mineral hunting...suspended due to poor visibility and reduced beetle range. Rune deciphering...no progress."

"Is that all?"

"The task list remained what was given five years ago."

"You didn't add new things to it?"

Trevor didn't reply, but then I thought he either needed explicit instructions or he wasn't sure what needed to be included.

The artificial souls had quite a bit of ability, and they were able to make judgments in their fields of expertise. But I supposed being artificial, their ability to make judgments and self-organizing didn't apply to all fields and all kinds of tasks. Then again, even a regular folk had different parameters for tasks. Some people were better able to judge cooking ingredient sizes than others. Trevor was really good at forest management, and he could decide on the direction of growth of plants and decide when to cull and replace normal trees that had gotten sick or damaged due to animals or monsters. So, perhaps this issue of judgment was a matter of...unfamiliarity?

"Never mind." I wouldn't have been able to handle that much, anyway. "Where are we on the sewage issue?"

"The newer hyperaccumulator trees are performing well, and we are introducing layered trees to the area. However, utilizing one thousand subsidiary trees to contain and process sewage and high magical toxin fecal matter is honestly not the best application of the subsidiary trees. I would recommend further research into the hyperaccumulator trees, as the single metal/magic type restriction on trees means we have to utilize multiple trees adapted to different materials to remove all the toxins."

"Ah. Upgrades..." The demon king's interference meant most of the merchant networks were down, and intercontinental traffic slowed down significantly. What this then meant for me was that I was unable to purchase the materials needed to upgrade my three artificial souls without incurring significant spending and without the usual delivery guarantee.

"No progress, Master."

Of course, rare gems were rare. Even if I could mine some of the gems, it remained that there were other materials that would be located far away.

"Ivy, Dimitree, what else is being worked on? Anything of note?"

"Observation of the citizens is ongoing. Nothing to report."

Dimitree's turn. "Defense is strong. Preparations and traps for the southern demonic incursions are ready."

Winter was coming.

YEAR 82 MONTH 11

A fairly quiet month for the valley. Maybe it was the cold. During this month, Lausanne and the Valthorns spent a lot of time fighting smaller demonic incursions. It was good for their experience, and they did need it. The second strongest girl in that Valthorns was now level eighteen, and that was pretty decent at the age of nine. I recalled Lausanne had only reached level sixteen at age nine. It was partly due to a mix of starting early and being exposed to the effects of all the leveling skills. It was still a long way for them.

Stratreegy was also busy extending trees to places where the demons might want to establish a base. We wanted to lure them there, just as the volcano did. I did hope to mount an offense against the snake dungeon and retake that location, but I was waiting for more information to come in. Not easy when the cold reduced the operating range of beetles.

According to recent courier reports, another demon walker had been spotted in the south, on top of the one that was immobile. That made two demon walkers on our continent. And if we added in the demon walker that was somehow swimming across the ocean like some kind of massive island-turtle, that was gonna be three demon walkers in the southern parts of our continent.

"I don't recall having that many demon-champion equivalents during the last demon king?" I asked Alexis.

"You have a point. It's likely that the demon king delegated more powers to its walkers rather than holding most of the power. Even the demon champions were just a wee bit stronger than the walkers. But then again, this demon king was also harvesting energies and mana from the world itself, and it may be using that energy to create more demon walkers. If so, the demon king may be just as insane as my time."

"Insane, eh?"

"I mean, it did blow up a massive crater, did it not? A crater that still remains today and left all that stray daemolite embedded throughout, creating weird monsters."

"I wonder whether the demon rods work on daemolite." It was a thought, right? If these demon rods worked on mana sources, would it work on the demon king's remains?

"I wonder what happens when your captured rods are in the demon king's crater," Alexis retorted.

Had the demons taken control of where the previous demon king perished? From what I understood, after the 'defenders' of the valley were cleared, the nearby nations usually attempted to mine all the daemolite for sale, given how valuable it was. Maybe it was cleared out by now. Apparently most demon kings' corpses had been cleared out due to how valuable daemolite was as a store-of-mana. Maybe it was like this world's equivalent of a super-lithium-ion battery.

YEAR 82 MONTH 12

Winter's fury mixed with demonic attacks. With winter in full swing, my beetles were forced into a retreat, even with their upgrades. It was harder for the beetles to move in such cold, but at least around my trees, the effect of [heat transmission roots] meant I could keep the surroundings of New Freeka relatively warm and the beetles could still perform optimally in the 'warmed' areas.

Yet this also meant I couldn't attack the snake-dungeon. The cold affected my beetles more than the demons.

So we waited for this winter to pass. We fought mostly defensive battles where my roots provided warmth and worked on research.

Winter also meant traffic and news from the south came... really slowly.

On some days during the cold winter, the sky turned really, really clear. And we could see about multiple astral objects. The moons, the stars, and things that just seemed to drift in space. On days like this, my star-mana production was slightly, very slightly, better.

For the New Freekans, it was a month of preparation, hiding, and retreat. The subterranean hideouts were now popular, thanks to the presence of heated water from the volcanoes, a great way to warm up.

News also slowed to a crawl, thanks to the thick snow and occasional blizzards. With news being carried physically, almost all the towns would be in a similar state. It was only thanks to my network of roots that I could still see what was going on in my surroundings.

Midway through the cold, we detected the presence of blood magic being used again. Somewhere, somebody out there was desperate enough to use blood magic, perhaps the demon king?

"Triangulating...Southern Continent."

"That far?" The readings of the amount of sacrifice were insane. Trevor and Alexis ran through some calculations and calculated perhaps three thousand to five thousand were sacrificed for a spell this large.

With little else to do, we spent our time theorizing about the nature of blood magic.

How did Blood Magic even work, really?

What really was blood magic, and why was it so powerful?

I mean, I could see the effects of the hex created from blood magic, even at the few locations near to me. It was just corrupted by the hex, though it was slowly decaying.

Alexis's theory was that it was like was a nuclear weapon. The hex was a magical version of radiation. I mean, looking at the indicator's high power, fallout. It felt like it.

She wondered if the origins of blood magic would be similar, that it was the magical equivalent of weaponizing the...soul? Perhaps the numbers made the spell stronger, by the same principles of nuclear fusion or fission, that blood magic fused or broke apart the components of a soul into some kind of unstable form, and in doing so released all this magical energy, and the unstable soul-remnant form was what created the 'fallout'?

Given how difficult it was to access the soul, I thought it was quite unlikely that the blood magic worked at that level. So I thought maybe it was really the 'blood' that was like some kind of superfuel, and blood magic bound the superfuel and concentrated it into a bomb. The hex was just the leftover, unexploded bomb. Essentially, what I thought happened during a blood ritual was life energy or mana of the 'sacrificed' was converted into an energy form, and that was the bomb.

Kinda like when you packed a big bunch of low-quality fireworks together, and then when you blew it up, sometimes there were some of these fireworks that didn't ignite, or old World War II bombs that for whatever reason failed to detonate.

When I thought about it, I realized our theories were similar, just at different levels. I just presumed the blood ritual converted the energy of the living into that of a weapon, essentially whatever that was happening at the 'mana pool' and 'body' into another form.

I liked Alexis's theory, since there was an elegance to it. It was like the blood magic version of 'breaking the atom' and had far more consequences. Like, the realization that there was a kind of magic or energy that fundamentally held the souls together. A peek into the true natural 'forces' of the world.

I supposed it could be tested. If Alexis's theory was true, I should be able to witness some kind of soul-change during a blood ritual. Or perhaps detect whether there were soul-residue in the hex, which I so far did not. Perhaps it was a size thing; if Alexis's analogy of nuclear bombs was true, perhaps the soul-fission created even smaller particles that required specialized equipment to be detected.

Like…soul-quarks? Squarks?

SIDE STORY - LAUSANNE MEETS THE HEROES
SOMETIME AROUND YEAR 83 MONTH 2

"I'm off, Mom." Lausanne walked over and gave her mum a hug. Laufen smiled and hugged her back. Lausanne was about to turn fourteen years old, and she was now an active member of the regional patrols.

"All right. Come home safely." Laufen kissed her on her forehead. Laufen smiled; her age was starting to show, lines and all. Even elves suffered from stress and age, though at a slower pace than others. "Don't stay too far from TreeTree's trees, all right?"

"Yup. Got it." Lausanne nodded, but a part of her knew it was a lie. Very often, she and her patrol group had to stray from the trees, sometimes to help a stranded group of merchants or just reach out to some refugees who'd lost their way.

But after their first incident of losing contact with TreeTree, they'd improved their strategy. Now their squad had three rangers, all with a focus on tracking. One of the Valthorn girls was also a ranger, a choice that they got as they progressed under TreeTree's tutelage.

Lausanne grabbed a small pack of food, equipped a few wooden spears on her back, and then two wooden swords, all enchanted to be extra-effective against demons. There were some basic armlets, made to her size, and she walked to the meeting place.

New Freeka was a whole lot bigger now. A lot more crowded, at least compared to a few years ago. TreeTree didn't really feel it—to him, it was just a blip—but for Lausanne, the smell, the ambient noise, the chatter, sometimes she wished it was a bit quieter. Still, she knew that TreeTree was always watching, even if his vision was 'brief.' She could feel it, if she had his attention. It would just resonate with her special familiar. The 'Warden.'

Lausanne looked at her own status menu, and then the familiar's. It had its own mana-meter, there was a star symbol next to it. It lived in her, and it slithered out like a snake, detecting its host's attention on it.

"Routine patrols," she whispered. The tree-snake nodded and disappeared again. It had never spoken, but Lausanne believed it understood what she said. "Let's see what we bump into this time."

"Hello, mi'lady." Two of the patrolmen bowed. Lausanne sighed. The captain nodded in acknowledgment.

"All right, everyone's here." The captain brought out a makeshift map. "We're traveling a bit further today, to this section." He gestured, and the rangers nodded. "Our scouts this morning saw some flares out in that direction, and we'd like to check it out. Counsel Jura has already stationed some beetles near to the location, but as you know, the beetles' range was limited. As usual, we have to investigate. If we encounter any opposition, we lure whatever we face to the designated beetle hideouts here and here. The beetles will take care of them."

The captain looked around. Everyone nodded. It was a routine task, something they'd been doing since the whole communication shutdown.

"Well, looked like we're good. Remember, our role is to minimize our fight. We scout, and we lure. Don't do anything stupid. If in doubt, check with myself or Lady Lausanne."

She mentally sighed, but in New Freeka, Lausanne had had

many titles. Some referred to her as the princess, some as the Avatar of the Tree Spirit. Things she never really noticed until recently, as she approached the teen years. Lausanne looked around the patrol group. There were four other Valthorn Initiates and about twenty patrolmen, a mix of soldiers and rangers. Most of the soldiers also had movement-assistance skills due to the mobility-focus of the squad.

A young Valthorn Initiate came over and sat next to Lausanne. "Lady Lausanne, what do you plan to teach us today?"

Lausanne rubbed her chin. Her role was part-tutor as well. She didn't really have a 'tutor-plan' in mind. "Some sword-spear forms, perhaps. If we encounter demons. Anything you'd like to see, Ssaera?"

"Erm…can we see your Warden in action?" Lausanne shrugged. She tried not to rely on the warden too much.

"All right, let's move out."

A convoy of beetles helped transport them to the designated starting area. There was a bunch of beetles that functioned as 'buses;' they moved at regular intervals along the five chains of trees. It conserved the patrol group's energy, and the beetles were plenty fast.

They arrived at the nearest location about an hour later. "All right. Let's stop here." The captain tapped the beetle on the head twice, and the beetle obediently moved to the side, then stopped. "Don't forget anything, especially your supplies. You may never know if we're cut off again."

Well, nobody was going to make that mistake. Everyone had enough rations for a week. And the Warden could even create [healing fruits], just like TreeTree.

"All right." The beetle moved away and continued its route. It was headed for the next waypoint. There was another tree on the next hill. Lausanne looked around; it was hilly, and there were a whole bunch of bushes and grass. The past demon invasions left some damage to the area, but things regrew quickly.

"Let's move out."

One of the soldiers walked next to Lausanne. "Mi'lady, what do you think we're getting this time?"

"Refugees?" Nine out of ten 'sightings' had been refugees. No merchant was going to travel without escort in this environment. Unless they were extremely desperate.

They walked past animal corpses and some debris. There was also some damage on the ground from normal monsters.

"It's quite quiet for a sighting," one ranger said, but Lausanne knew their scouts were rarely wrong about sightings.

"I hope it's just a dud."

Ssaera and the Valthorns sometimes caught up to Lausanne, and they would try to chat. "Lady Lausanne, what kind of dreams do you get?"

"Huh, the [Dream Tutor]?" The Valthorns looked to Lausanne as an 'idol,' thanks to her high level, special familiar, and position as the 'first' Valthorn.

"Yeah. Does Aeon give you more...erm...scary ones?" Ssaera asked sheepishly. They wanted to know more about what they could do better to be like her.

Lausanne looked at the ten-year-old girl. "Sometimes." Lausanne did recall the war dreams were especially gruesome. She vomited after she woke up from that one.

"Often? Do...funny people appear in your dreams?"

"Sometimes? It's usually someone to teach me how to fight."

A streak of light in the sky. And everyone knew. They stopped their conversation and focused. "Magic?"

They increased their pace and headed in that direction. A few more flashes of light. "Somebody's using quite a bit of magic. And...demons?" As they approached closer and closer, they could hear it. In the faint distance, the sounds of demons.

When they arrived, they saw three young persons, one boy and two girls, about Lausanne's age. Humans. And around them, a whole lot of destroyed demons. But the battle was not yet over. There were five demon knights.

It seemed they'd only managed to defeat the regular demons.

"Should we help?" They looked at the three, and they looked tired, weak. Not injured, though. They were on a hill, and the three were down below in a small valley.

———

"I'm out of mana." Mirei looked at her two friends. They weren't much better.

Harris shook his head. "I'm almost out of mana, too."

"How'd they find us so quickly?" Becky sighed, and a floating shield appeared. "We need rest. We can't even choose our level-ten perks like this!"

The demon knights closed in. Mirei looked again. It was a tactical mistake to use her powers so quickly on the regular demon army. The demon knights wanted to drain them out.

Inexperience.

Harris lifted his wooden shield. He wished he had something sturdier, but after being popped in the middle of nowhere, this was all he could make with his newfound knowledge of shields. "I can't block all of them."

Mirei sighed. They were backed into a corner. They were too green to take on demon knights, and she hoped her friends would do better. Her fists were both charged with lightning, but she knew that it wasn't enough.

Becky's back faced hers, and she had a magical sword in her hand. A summoned weapon.

Becky was probably in the best shape. The five demon knights, however, didn't move. They turned.

And they saw a girl about their age. She was surrounded by vines, dark-greenish vines.

"Uh, is that a bad guy?" Harris asked. "Because we're dead if she is." Harris had a skill [Battlesense], and he knew the odds.

And those vines moved incredibly quickly; to them, they saw it almost instantly impaled the three demon knights, destroying them. The two moved to engage, and a wooden snake chewed off its head, its fangs sinking into the body of the demon knight.

One left. And she threw a wooden spear. It struck the demon knight's shield, but then the girl took the chance to impale the last demon knight with another spear. It died then.

"Adventurers?" Lausanne asked. "Are you all right?"

More soldiers came down the hill. Harris wondered whether they saw the battle the entire time but was just relieved to be saved. "Yeah. Thanks. We...uh...tried to bite off more than we could chew."

Mirei and Becky were absolutely relieved and, at the same time, impressed. But they were so exhausted that they just sat and took a short shut-eye.

Harris smiled at his two friends and then turned to face Lausanne. "How'd you beat the five demon knights so easily?"

Lausanne shrugged. One of Warden's unique abilities was the ability to use variants or lesser versions of TreeTree's skills. That meant she could use [anti-demon strikes] and a smaller [anti-demon aura]. With those two skills, taking down a few demons knights wasn't exactly difficult.

"Apologies for my two friends, mages. We've been fighting and running for the past...eight hours. They're so tired their mana isn't even regenerating anymore."

The captain nodded. "Well, it's not a safe place here. They can rest elsewhere. Where were you three headed?"

"Uhm...we don't know." Harris rubbed his head. "We're still trying to get directions. Can we go to wherever you are?"

The captain looked at Lausanne. "Mi'lady, your decision?"

Lausanne looked at the three, all of them about the same age as her. Maybe younger. "Very well, let's take them back to New Freeka."

Harris bowed. "Thank you." The two mages were still too exhausted but found some energy to walk back after some rations.

They made the journey back to the tree line, and the convoy of beetles was their ride home.

"So, what happened back there?" the captain asked. Harris seemed to be the leader of the three; the two other mages were napping on the beetle's seats.

"Uhm…" Harris looked a whole lot better after some food and water. Fighting for so long was exhausting, and they looked visibly green at it. "I don't know where to start, honestly."

"Well, whatever you were comfortable talking about." The captain smiled. The beetle ride was one hour, after all.

"Uh…let's just say we got lost and somehow we found ourselves being chased by demons. We fought where we could, but the three of us were just level one. I mean, I think I'm level fourteen now, but before that rest, I was still just level five."

"You had a lot of skills for a level five person." The captain smiled.

"Uh…it's a bloodline thing."

"Ah. The gifted children. Mi'lady Lausanne here is also one of those gifted children." The captain grinned, and Lausanne just glared.

"Well, that vine-strike thing was impressive, and I felt like they froze in place. So, uh…where we heading? And what are these… giant beetles?"

"New Freeka, and transportation." The captain laughed. "Impressive, right? Most refugees are extremely excited when they see one of these. Merchants less so, some of them say the giant elephants or the sandbeasts are more impressive as transports. But whatever, we have giant beetles."

Harris nodded. "Indeed. It's my first time seeing such… obedient beetles. Do you control them?"

The captain shook his head. "Nah. Aeon does."

"Aeon?" Harris asked.

"Our city's guardian spirit."

"Nice." Harris nodded, and he looked at Lausanne. Lausanne was talking to the younger Valthorns, who were extremely impressed by her display of the Warden's abilities.

Soon, they arrived at New Freeka and passed by the five layers of walls that now encircled the entire city.

"This was impressive." Harris looked; the two girls were still asleep. They'd really drained their energies for the battle. Harris, being the physical combatant, less so.

The captain nodded. "Indeed. Even during the last demon walker's attack, they only got as far as the fourth wall before Aeon destroyed it. I know because I was on the walls." He pointed to one part of the wall. "I was there."

One of the soldiers tapped the captain on the shoulder. "All right, Captain, don't have to talk about the same story to every single refugee."

"I can't help it!"

"We were there, too, but we were right in the trenches, with the other beetles."

Harris looked at the captain and the soldiers. "So...is every city in the world like this?"

Everyone instantly shook their heads. The captain even sniggered, as if they said something ridiculous. "All this was possible because we have a guardian spirit. Without it, this valley would be uninhabited. Many of us were refugees from other cities that were attacked by demons."

"Hmmm..." Harris soaked in this knowledge. He looked at Lausanne again, who wasn't really talking. She seemed more interested in something else. But Harris wanted to talk to her, at least, to learn about her powers.

"So, uh...do you guys have any money?" the captain asked. "If you do, I'd recommend the Oakwood. It's the fanciest inn we have in New Freeka. Otherwise, you can head to Inn Street, there was a few good ones like Roommies, and The Paul House."

"Ah." Harris tapped at his menu. He smiled. He did have some cash. "Yeah. Is there an...uh...adventurer's guild?"

"Yup, right next to the Council offices. Oh yeah, one more thing, we're from the Valtrian Order, we're sort of an independent arm of the city, but New Freeka has its own militia and guards, so don't mix us up. You can identify us by our armband."

Harris nodded. He looked at his two sleeping friends. He tapped both of them. "Hey, it's time to wake up."

The beetle stopped right outside the city gates. There was a tree-woman waiting. "Eh, Lady Mika, what brings you here?" the captain asked.

"Your...guests. They're with me." Meela flashed a wide, hospitable smile. It was something she'd practiced over the years.

"Ah." The captain tapped Harris on his shoulders. "You're in luck. The Oakwood boss is already here."

Lausanne hopped off the beetle with the rest of the Valthorns and headed back to the Order's HQ.

As for Meela, she looked at the three visibly human heroes. "Hello." She extended her wooden hand. "Come, all of you must be hungry, poor, and extremely confused. And probably have a whole load of questions."

Harris looked at her and noticed she looked like a very high-quality wooden carving of a young girl. "What, don't trust me?"

Harris nodded.

"There was probably no one you can trust if you can't trust me. Especially if you are...heroes," Meela whispered into Harris's ear, and his eyes immediately opened wide. "There are ears everywhere, best to come with me."

Those words made Harris nod, and they followed her to a large, opulent wooden lodge that looked like a hybrid between a tree and a hotel. Two treefolks waited at the lobby and working for Meela immediately passed them their keys, and there was proper food waiting for them in a quiet, private dining room.

Harris, Becky, and Mirei sat, and it was...food from home. A burger.

"Sit. Eat. Leave us." Meela motioned to the attendants, and the doors were closed. She snapped a finger, activated a few skills. [High Security Room], [Private Quarters]. "All right, here, now it's just the three of you and me. My name is Mika. Speak freely. You three are the reincarnated, summoned heroes?"

Harris stared at Meela. Becky ate a bite of the burger and nodded. "Yes. We are. How'd you know?"

"I received the notification that heroes have arrived. And then I saw the three of you traveling on Aeon's beetles. And your clothes."

"Ah."

"So, let's talk."

YEAR 83 MONTH 1

At the end of the first month, the heroes, long awaited, finally arrived.

I had a brief vision, like I always did. Twelve streaks of light, split into four groups of three, and then each landed at a different part of the world. This was important because that meant the heroes were in smaller groups of three and were scattered.

A vague reddish hand appeared in that same vision. It tried to swipe at the streaks of light. But another hand stopped it.

That was when I woke from the vision.

[Twelve reincarnators have arrived.]

"I wonder where they are," Alexis said. "I hope they don't make the same mistakes we did." She got the same ping as I did. "And TreeTree, why do you get...the notification?"

"I have no idea. I do see a vision." Hmm, was she wondering why I knew about the heroes? Well, I suspected it was because I came from their world, too.

"Maybe TreeTree's like some kind of super-entity and that's why the gods sent the ping to him, too." Meela came to the rescue. She'd gotten the notice as well; that was why she came over. Her hotel/inn could run itself quite well; she'd hired quite a few treefolk to work for her.

I wondered how many would survive this time. The world was in a shittier state than it was.

"TreeTree, I have a request," Meela said. "I know you didn't have a good impression of us heroes, so let me deal with the next generation of heroes. If they ever swing our way."

"Hmm?"

"I assure you that I won't bring you any harm. The heroes need to be educated in the ways of the world, and both Alexis and I have seen more of the world without the distorted lenses as a hero. We should be the best placed to advise the next generation, so they do not walk the mistakes we did." Meela sounded like she was begging.

"Fine. But keep me updated."

"Sure."

"You know where they are?"

"No. But I will tell you if I do."

Other than the return of the reincarnators, another month of mostly defensive battles. Quiet. The southern parts, where it was warm, were battling demons daily. Up where we were, where the winter was relatively mild, we focused efforts on research and making more anti-demon weapons.

I was also gradually extending my trees to where the legless walker was. But I was taking it slow, as the terrain was unfamiliar, and there were demons walking all over the place, so I had to clear out the area before expanding.

YEAR 83 MONTH 2

"They're with me," Meela said, a week or so after that announcement.

"Huh?" Honestly, it felt like just yesterday that I had that conversation with Meela.

"Three heroes. Reincarnators. They arrived somewhere near our borders. They've just been summoned and were still getting used to their new powers. One of your patrols picked them up."

"Oh."

"I'll take care of them. Don't worry about it," Meela assured. "It's only been a week since they arrived. They're still a bit confused and lost, but they've managed to survive thanks to their special powers."

At this point, I remembered my titan souls, and I thought, well, since they were so vulnerable, they could 'die' around me easily, wasn't it?

*[**Divine**: Moratorium on Hero Killing. In force until demon king's death. Those who murder a hero before the demon king's death will receive a divine curse and be marked as a 'hero-killer,' inviting the wrath of other heroes.]*

The fuck?!

Hmm. Looked like the gods already thought about it.

"So, what did you talk to them about?"

"I gave them an overview of the world, what they were facing, and...what the previous heroes did, without telling them I was a hero. I think they bought it. They are just...thirteen-year-olds, after all. Unlike me or Alexis."

Thinking about it, if they arrived at age thirteen, and it'd been close to thirteen to fourteen years, did that make them pretty much twenty-six-year-olds? "Well, that's good. Hope they don't put New Freeka in danger again. Do you feel old talking to them, since you are their...senior?"

"Honestly, yes. I feel a bit afraid. Of course, we can't be older than you, TreeTree. You must be centuries old now, or millennia?"

I was not answering that.

Meela continued anyway. "But yeah. They're still in a state of panic, and they were just relieved that we were here to give them some...cover. The two girls were just sleeping in for days and exploring New Freeka's markets and shops."

"It's not a holiday, though." Alexis popped in. "They need to start leveling soon. The demon king won't wait for them, and Tree-Tree, you need to make preparations. The demon king can sense us, and they will send men after the three heroes."

"I know, I know, Alexis, but I think taking care of their mental state is important, too. We made that mistake of rushing from battle to battle, and that made us fight each other, remember?"

Alexis sulked. "They need experience, and they need it soon. We do not need to nanny them. They need to level up and gain full access to their star mana and heroic tier skills as soon as possible. And find some items of the right tier."

"Oh, yeah! Items! TreeTree, erm...can I get some of your anti-demon weapons? The one that Lausanne has? And a wooden anti-demon shield, too."

"Only the normal ones. And they'll need to buy it like anyone else." There were the regular-series wooden weapons that were distributed to the patrol force, so I thought that was fine.

"I'll pay for it, then."

I soon learned, thanks to Ivy's updates, that the three heroes in New Freeka were Harris the [Shield Guardian], Becky the [Horde Summoner], and Mirei the [Lightning Guardmage]. Of course, I took some time to watch them as they walked around New Freeka.

"Well, today I'm taking you to some of the bars and restaurants and having some local food. You may be on a mission, but if you feel overwhelmed, don't hesitate to demand a break. You only live once, even in a magical world like this. Revival magic only works if one of you was a hero-grade specialist-healer, and it must be used within the same day. So if you feel your team is moving too fast, say it. Honesty matters."

"How do you know all this, Mistress Mika?" Mirei seemed impressed.

"I worked with the heroes. The last generation of heroes at least. All of them died in their final battle, but they told me to help where I can." Meela pulled off the act swimmingly. It was part of her skill; as the proprietress of the hotel, she had superb acting skills. In many ways, working as a hotelier really made her more...mature.

It was something I didn't realize, of course, because to me, the months just flipped by so quickly, but Meela's hotel had been open for the past four years, since year 79. So she'd had a lot of experience dealing with people and customers. I supposed it was strange for them to change, when I was the one still being the same. Four years was long for them, but not for me.

They stopped at a restaurant with an al fresco frontage. Meela's restaurant was one of the first to feature al fresco dining, but soon, many other restaurants caught on.

The waiter bowed and quickly let Meela and the three humans in. "Right this way, Lady Mika." Meela, as the owner of the best hotel in town, was pretty much a local 'tycoon,' a respected member of the hospitality industry. She was apparently even the chairwoman of the local innkeeper's guild. Things I forgot, of course, since I was focused on my own things.

Maybe if Alexis wasn't so...rebellious, maybe... Ah. Never mind.

They sat and had a cup of local tea with milk. And some snacks. "So, I've arranged for some anti-demon weapons. That should be your starting equipment. You will outgrow them quite quickly with experience multipliers from your blessings."

Harris sighed. "Honestly, I'm a bit...uh...how do I say this... intimidated by what we went through. Why can't people like Lausanne fight the demon king? We saw her crush the demon knights like nothing."

Meela shook her head. "Lausanne's impressive, but she doesn't have the special gifts. Heroes are needed because of the cheat-skills. It's also important that you think about the cheat skills that you have and figure out how to maximize them. The last demon king was a giant castle that had a few forms, lastly, an exploding demon-crystal."

"We're here. And you're talking about something like that. I don't see how we can face something like that."

Meela smiled and sipped her tea. "Baby steps. You must first be able to take on demon knights, like Lausanne."

"Can she accompany us? I mean...I'd feel much safer if she's with us," Becky said.

"Even if she does, she can only stay with you for a short while. With the blessings, you will gain levels very, very quickly. When the last generation fought the demon king, all of them were at least level one hundred. Lady Lausanne, if I'm not mistaken, is only around level forty to fifty."

"We're level ten or so. We need a babysitter," Harris said, and he ate a cookie. Meela asked for some local potato slices with olives.

Meela nodded. "I can have a skill that can give you a [Bodyguard], but I feel that will hobble your growth. You must realize that leveling and experience is scaled to difficulty."

"Can't we like...uh...have some practice first?" Mirei asked. "I mean, if you see those RPG games, we usually have 'tutorial' or 'practice' stages so that we get a good hang of how things work. I mean..."

Meela sipped her tea and thought for a moment. At this point, I had a hunch Meela was going to ask me for something. And she did. She telepathically pinged me.

"TreeTree, can we borrow the Order's Training Rooms? I'll have the captains and Yvon spar with them. Madeus, too, if he is willing."

"Hmmm...when are they leaving New Freeka?"

"When they are ready. The faster we can get them up to speed, the faster they will leave," Meela insisted, and well, she had a good point.

"Fine. Only the one in the Order Quarters."

Meela then turned to the three heroes. "Well, I've arranged for the three of you to use the Valtrian Order's training rooms. That will be a suitable practice session, for you to know your limits. Unfortunately, you can only use them for a few days, and after that, it's out to the field as an adventurer or join the patrols."

"Huh, so short..." The three looked reluctant but soon accepted that it was better than nothing, and then they walked back to the hotel.

"So, do you want to watch some practice today?"

"Oh, can we?"

"Magic or swordfighting?"

"Uh...magic?" the two girls said together.

Meela brought them to one of New Freeka's magic academies. The Council ran one academy, as part of the mage's guild, and the Order ran another one, led by Madeus. There was also a third independent academy, but it was mainly for merchants, smiths, and others, as it was more of a craft-focused magic academy.

They watched some children practice some basic magic.

Both of them, though, instantly learned a spell. "Oh. That's... that's easy."

Meela shrugged. "That's your advantage. You won't learn much from the children if it comes to you so easily."

Meela led them to the back area of the guild, and there were multiple sparring areas for mage-adventurers to practice.

"Go, participate. You might gain some levels."

And they did. "How many levels can we gain like this?"

"I don't know. Depends on the system."

"I was wondering, why didn't the gods just give us all our levels from the start? Then we don't have to struggle like this," Harris asked Meela as he watched.

"I don't know that, either. You can ask them the next time you see them. I guess it's some restriction on the gods that anyone new starts from level one."

The heroes practiced a few times, the two girls were visibly outclassed, even with their overpowered abilities, but with each battle, they improved, very quickly.

According to Alexis, it was a gift. Heroes, when they started out, had a special blessing on top of their overpowered ability. I didn't recall seeing these blessings in their soul spring, but then again, maybe I was not able to see divine items. The blessings did a whole lot of things, like improve their rate of experience gain, the ability to choose the 'direction' of the skill growth, meaning heroes could actually select what kind of skills they wanted to learn, a natural affinity to combat, enhanced recovery rates.

And there were usually a few 'gates,' which unlocked star mana at different amounts. At level one hundred, that was when their entire mana pool was converted into star mana, which meant they had way more star mana than I had. Like…easily ten to fifty times more.

Meela then brought the three heroes to one of the Order's militia practice yards. And where the soldiers practiced. Similarly, they also had a few spars.

"Why were you bringing them to all these places?" I mentally asked Meela.

"They can gain levels from practice, and it's a safe way to gain these early levels. I'll ask Jura for permission to include them in a few patrol missions, so they can fight some demons. I'll send my [bodyguard] with them, just to be safe."

Well, more spars. Meela then led them back to the hotel to rest, and the next day, they were at the [Training Rooms].

"We're fighting Lausanne?" The three looked surprised.

"Yeah. I asked whether she's willing to spar, and she said sure."

"Does she know?"

"Nope. It's my first time watching Lausanne in action, too." Meela smiled.

"Uh...I don't think we can take her alone. Unless she's fighting handicapped," Becky said, and Lausanne obviously heard it.

"I won't be using my familiar. Don't worry. And we're just using wooden swords."

"But you whooped the demons with those wooden swords!" Harris seemed visibly panicked.

Meela clapped. "Oh, come on. Just fight. If you can't face Lausanne, you'll have trouble facing demon walkers and the demon generals." Meela's pep talk worked, and they started to spar.

Indeed, they'd seemed to have gained levels from yesterday's spar, and their performance was much better than before. But the heroes weren't good at 'sparring,' in the sense that they couldn't seem to control their powers. It was one hundred percent on all the time, so Mirei accidentally loosed a lightning blast and it hit the Training Room walls. Thankfully, no damage. The training room was exceptionally sturdy.

Still, as one who watched their fights yesterday and today, their progress was unnatural. It was like there was a genius that guided their growth; they instinctively knew what to do to improve. For now, Lausanne was still better, but I would think within a month they would be able to stand toe-to-toe with her, without her familiar powers.

All of them took turns to spar over the course of the next week, and for Lausanne, whose usual sparring partners were Yvon and

Jura, this was a welcome change. In fact, Lausanne had her first loss on their last day. Their exceptional growth was very humbling for Lausanne, even if it was just a sparring match without Lausanne's full skillset.

After the week was over and their 'time' was up, Lausanne came back to me. "TreeTree, who were those people? They...they make me feel like I'm stupid."

"Why?"

"I mean...I took so many years of practice to get to this point, but they just got from newbies to be able to do that in a week."

Well, it was all relative, wasn't it? To the other Valthorns, Lausanne was an exceptional fighter. But as with all things, there was always a higher mountain out there.

"They're the gifted ones, blessed by the gods themselves. Don't hold onto your defeat too hard."

"Are they heroes?"

"I think so." I knew the truth, but I was not sure whether I should tell her.

Lausanne paused. She was in my [secret hideout], her home. She sat in bed and looked at the wooden spear next to her bed. "Is this what heroes need to be able to do? I suddenly feel like...I'm not good enough."

Hmm. She was fourteen and feeling demotivated and discouraged? Should I inject her with some [psychedelic dreams]? Was this puberty? Or teen angst? Should I give her a pep talk? Or should I ask Laufen to do it? Maybe I should ask her mom to talk to her first.

And indeed, Laufen came into her room and sat next to her bed.

"Hi, darling." Laufen smiled and patted her leg. "I heard you lost."

"Losing's fine. But it's just that...I don't know...erm...facing genius."

Laufen moved herself a little closer. "Every now and then, the gods create people who are so exceptionally good that they blow the rest of us out of the water. There are those born with a [unique ability] or [unique skill] since birth. These are champions."

"I want to be a hero, Mom. I just feel like...suddenly...that dream feels very, very far away."

"It's okay." Laufen gave her daughter a hug. I felt a bit guilty spying, but then again, I did want to check on Lausanne's mental state. "It's a privilege that you could even attempt to dream such a dream. I wouldn't have dreamed of what we have today, my dear."

"Mom. That's not helping." Lausanne still sulked.

Laufen just hugged. "Think of it as a challenge, then. No great things are achieved without great obstacles."

"But then why do the heroes get such great powers?"

"They have the burden of defeating the demon king. Would you want that burden?"

Lausanne sulked.

YEAR 83 MONTH 3

The heroes, annoyingly, made Meela's Oakwood Hotel their base of operations. At least they were now participating in the Order's patrols and were helping to defeat demons that they encountered, and within a month, they had gained about thirty levels, so they were now about level thirty-five to forty and seemed to have unlocked their first quarter of [star mana].

This meant they could now stand toe-to-toe with multiple demon knights, just like Lausanne. What seemed crazy to them a month ago was now something they could do.

"The first fifty levels are easy," Alexis explained. "We got it within a month, too. It's the grind up to level one hundred that took a whole lot longer, and past level eighty, we only seemed to gain levels when we fought champion-level monsters."

"Good thing is I think they will leave New Freeka soon," Meela, their de-facto 'nanny,' said. "Thanks, TreeTree. I'm happy to have helped them get on their feet. After this, they must find other places to go, other monsters to fight. I told them about the demon walkers and that they need to start attempting to fight them."

"Can they? I would recommend level fifty before trying the walker. At least they get their second quarter of the [star mana]."

It was mostly a conversation between Alexis and Meela, both of whom had differing views of what the 'optimal' strategy was for heroes.

"At the rate they are going, they will encounter demons and level up along the way. And all of them have summoned units. I think the gods gave them all a mini-army-like ability."

I didn't watch their battles, especially those that happened with the patrols. So this really piqued my attention. "Explain."

"Yeah. Harris has a defense aura and can summon 'living armors, with massive shields.' Mirei has lightning elementals and thunderstorm rods. Becky has like...a squadron of magical knights."

This meant something. Did the gods intentionally delay the summoning of the heroes so that they knew what they were facing? And then, they 'tailored' the gifts to the heroes based on what they saw the demons were doing?

What if the demons knew this, too? I didn't see how the previous heroes' abilities were tailored to the demon king at all. Or it was just a coincidence that this roster of abilities leaned toward the heroes being a 'one-man army'?

In any case, after a week or more of fighting, the three heroes eventually decided to make a move for the next town. As advised by Meela, they were going to head south, toward the 'stationary' walker.

―――

The heroes took one of the beetles to head south.

A magical ball appeared in front of them.

"Hi, guys. Everyone alive?" A voice came out of the ball.

The three heroes jumped but then nodded. "Astra, was that you?"

"Yeah, it's me, all right. Sorry it took so long. I had to reach my level thirty perk to unlock the [Hero-Chat] communication ability. Everyone here?"

"Yup." It seemed that they could see each other's faces in the magical ball, but my 'spirit vision' was able to only see the presence of a pure-white magical orb and not what was on it. Kinda like an overexposed camera facing a television. It was all white to me. But at least I could still 'hear' the message.

"Good. How's everyone? I'll start. We had a rough first month. We got ambushed by multiple demon groups, but luckily a group of knights helped us out. We're based in one of the kingdoms in the far south."

"South?" Harris asked. "Isn't the South in very bad shape?"

"Not gonna lie, it totally is, it is. The Southern Continents' entire northern half was, and still is, lost to the demons, and the far-southern kingdoms, thankfully, through luck and some good strategies, managed to keep the demons away, however barely. The kings were super relieved to see us. We're trying to gain levels as fast as we can, and thankfully we met some locals who were very willing to help us," this 'Astra' person explained.

"Your story sounds similar. We got saved by the locals, too." Another voice. "Totally not what I expected. If I see the gods again, I'm gonna give them a piece of my mind for dropping us in the middle of nowhere."

Harris and Mirei nodded. "Yeah. We also got saved by the locals."

"Hmm...we're in the east, and we're quite lucky. We didn't see many demons, and we fought whatever we could. We're now based in one of the towns. There were some helpful locals as well."

"Ah, shit. This skill drains my star mana faster than Pokemon Go does. My star mana is running out. All right, we'll catch up again once my star-mana recovers. Sorry!" Astra complained.

"It's fine. Good to know everyone's alive," someone said.

"Yeah."

And the magical orb vanished. And the three of them shared glances while still riding the beetle.

"That's like...a Skype group-video conference call."

"Who uses Skype these days?" Becky looked puzzled.

"My dad does." Mirei shrugged. "For work."

For me, this meant the heroes' star mana was able to overcome the demon king's magical interference.

YEAR 83 MONTH 4

I was so glad they were gone. The heroes headed south, and I thought they passed by some other cities. I thought they would probably reach the demon walker in the next month, or maybe the month after, depending on which route they took.

I felt like I was on edge whenever they were doing something in the city. Or maybe it was that subtle 'presence' they had, the 'heroes' aura or whatever. I got a sense that it was a subtle aura the gods gave them, albeit bundled up in the [blessing] that they had.

So, with them gone, I focused my attention back on New Freeka and those under my care.

"TreeTree, do you have any special powers you can give me?" Lausanne sat. She was done with another round of practice with the rest of the Valthorns. Still, even though the heroes left, the heroes left a mark on her mind. She was too young the last time the heroes came, but this time, she was old enough to even spar with them.

"You already have some, no?" Well, the [possession of the devoted] was a special skill. It gave her that weird, whip-like ability, and she'd already gotten exceptional resonance to my own abilities.

Hmm, but what would I have to do? Let's say if the heroes

survived and they started having political ideas, like Alexis, what would I do? Clearly not everyone would agree with them, and the divine moratorium on their death was lifted.

A super-condensed version of [Dream Tutor] and a whole bunch of level and skill seeds? What else? Physical enhancements? Soul modification?

I could probably do some physical enhancements and give her a super-strong dose of [Dream Tutor], but skill seeds…did she want some special class? [Dark Knight], perhaps? Would that be enough to even stand up to a hero?

"Lausanne, what's your class at this point?"

"Main class, [Elven Swordfighter], secondary class, [Villager]. I'm level thirty-one at my main class, level eight villager. Total level forty-seven."

"Hmmm. I thought you broke level fifty?" This 'segregated' and 'accumulated' class level system that humanoids had still felt a bit like a cheat, but on the flipside, 'creatures' like me had way higher base stats and gained more of such stats per level than humanoids.

"Not yet." Lausanne sulked. "Is that why I lost?" But before I could answer, she answered herself. "No. They improved so fast. Higher levels didn't change that. It would be a matter of time, unless I could improve just as fast as them."

Hmm, I would need to have some kind of 'anti-hero' countermeasures.

"So, uh…do you have any kind of fruit that can make me smarter? So that I can level up faster? Or just as fast as the heroes?"

How would I do that, Lausanne? Maybe not make you smarter…but the process of gaining levels was essentially these 'experiences' were absorbed via the soul. Experience was in the 'outer soul,' and the blessings acted as a modifier on the…

The soulspring was the 'gatekeeper' of levels. It would make sense, therefore, that any 'experience' multipliers, such as the [divine blessings], would exist as a layer outside the soul. So, if I were to make a super-leveling follower, I would have to somehow influence the soulspring.

"Might be possible, Lausanne, but not something I can do now." If I could create the effects of [training room], [Dream Tutor], [Power-leveling], [Learning Aura], or even my very own [hero fragments], as a part of Lausanne's soul spring, then she could level up faster.

But would the soul spring affect natural ability? It seemed quite pre-deterministic if that was the case, the fate of these young infants had been decided at the start of their lives. I felt that must not be true because there were tales in this world of young men and women of modest upbringings and station rising into greatness. One would then argue that perhaps these young men already had the seed in them. Those who never had the seed would never do something like it.

"You may have to wait."

"They would get so much better than me already!" Lausanne sulked, but she sighed. "But then again, they were blessed by the gods to be heroes. I'm just an ordinary girl."

"Still on that subject?" Jura walked in. He smiled at some of the young Valthorns and motioned for them to spar with him. He was careful with his new hand, even though it'd been months. He was gradually testing it out more, though, using skills to parry with his repaired hand and test the strength of the bones and joints.

"Yea, Uncle Jura. I'm asking TreeTree whether he can help me cheat the level system, like the heroes."

Hmmm...would I be able to modify the familiar to create this effect if I was unable to alter the soul directly? Perhaps this was a 'stopgap' measure?

*[**Learned Familiar type**: Studious Spirits]*

[Studious Spirits loses almost all familiar abilities except Wood Shield. In exchange, the host's experience gain is doubled. Skills and levels gained since acquiring Studious Spirit are more likely to be transferred to the grantor on death of host.]

Okay! That worked, too. But clearly Lausanne wouldn't benefit from this, since she already had one familiar spirit contract, and strangely, although you could get multiple familiars, each from a different 'giver,' you couldn't get multiple from the same 'giver.' I wondered why.

Could Meela give a familiar as she was a 'tree' like me? Even if she was a hospitality-focused one.

My thoughts strayed a bit, then Jura and Lausanne started to spar again. Yvon was playing the role of a 'teacher' for some more 'Valthorns,' but my twenty [Minder-Familiar] slots were full. It was a half-yearly thing where I selected new 'students' to receive the 'Minders,' but now that I had this 'leveling familiar,' I wondered how I should organize the Valthorns.

Should the Minders be a lower tier?

Lausanne ducked and went close to all-out, stopping short of using her special familiar. Jura outclassed her, of course. Even Yvon outclassed Lausanne, though the gap between them was a lot smaller.

But the Studious Spirits clearly had no limitation. Was it because I allocated a portion of my 'mind' to oversee the [Minder-Familiars], so the twenty minders were essentially a limitation of my ability to simultaneously track my young Valthorns?

In such case, wouldn't the Minders be inferior?

Curious, I had the Valthorns spar with one of the captains who possessed a regular familiar and fight entirely using the familiar's abilities. I wanted to hear from them on what they thought.

"Isn't it about the same?" the Valthorns and captain asked. Turned out they had no 'insight' that the Minder-Familiars were 'different.' They fought, and the abilities were similar, and the regular familiar was no weaker than the minder-familiar, though the minder-familiar was more in tune with the host, so its response time wasn't that different. Fair, I supposed if the Minder's task was to observe, it didn't make sense for those being watched to know they were being watched.

All right then, at least I could easily swap them for a 'regular' familiar, since they didn't know any better.

"Are you planning to give us better familiars? Like Lady Lausanne's?" The Valthorns sounded quite excited.

Uh. I had 'druidic aspects,' and Jura had Bamboo, the Artificial Soul-Eidolon. And now this [Studious Spirit].

Only the Artificial Soul and the [Possession Of the Devoted] was a clear upgrade. The rest were just a question of what was being traded off.

"I have a familiar type that increases your leveling, but you lose almost all familiar abilities."

"Oh, I wouldn't want that!" One of the Valthorns shook her head vigorously. "I like eating fruits from the familiar. I'll never go hungry ever again!" Ah, this young girl was one of those who suffered through a period of starvation during the refugee-runs, so the concept of having a magical companion who made food was like...heaven.

"If you have a familiar type that focuses on producing food and water, we'd have to worry a lot less about supply chains," Jura casually remarked. "Just one or two guys focused on making food, and we'll be able to send a small squad anywhere around the region quickly."

"What if they die or get targeted?"

"It's an alternative, and it is a compromise for speed and range. Hauling food using conventional [holding bags] is possible, too, but more 'expensive.' Doesn't help that [holding bags] food feels kind of stale, even if it's mostly preserved."

Jura and Lausanne sparred again. Lausanne was using a stick this time. She said she had to try something different. I thought she even asked Madeus to give her magic lessons.

Though I could give her [mage] class seeds if she ever needed it, I wondered if multi-classing too much was a good idea. I recalled some game designs intentionally 'hindered' or 'scaled' multiclassing such that they became 'jack-of-all-trades,' and the gains of multi-classing were often less than the benefits of a focused class.

"I didn't feel any drawbacks from multi-classing, I think,"

Alexis wondered. "But then, I don't do Player, not I mean, People-versus-People, so I really don't know how I stack up against another person at the same level, but with a more focused class. Demon-hunting heroes are essentially a People-versus-Environment setup." Alexis intentionally avoided the word player.

"Oh, yes. Before my diplomat and fighter class merged into warlord, I did feel weaker. A consolidated class was easily better, with benefits from both."

"If the multi-classing is within the same category of classes, it's usually not a problem. Mages are known to take multiple related magic types, with little to no drawback versus a focused mage. In fact, as our magic levels are 'gated,' where we need to perform certain feats to progress, taking multiple classes is how we make progress." Ah yes, Madeus and magic's weird requirement for 'feats' or 'accomplishments' to pass a certain level barrier.

"I don't have that," Alexis retorted to me. "I was an [archmage] and a [pyromancer], which later merged into [arch-firemage]. I still kept a few other classes!"

I sort of mentally rolled my eyes. I didn't have actual eyes to roll, of course. Even my [tree-eyes] couldn't physically 'roll.' I mean, we all knew heroes worked differently. It was quite clear by now.

"Which class should I take, TreeTree?" Lausanne asked. She wanted to add more learning into her time, so she wanted the [Dream Tutor] to be something new. Yet she was unsure of what other class she should take.

As it was, she was a combat, melee-focused unit. Should she get some range, or maybe she should head for the spell-sword kind of route? Enchanted blades and Magical Sword Attacks?

YEAR 83 MONTH 5

"I hope they remember what I told them." Meela sat and enjoyed a cup of wine. Alexis sat next to her. I thought they both were quite high leveled by now. Meela was in the level sixties or so, and she was waiting to get some kind of [branch-hotel] ability. In here, Alexis could somehow take up a form that could enjoy wine.

"Well, you did what you could." Alexis sighed. "If only some of us survived to fight with them."

"Heroes don't get summoned until all the previous ones die."

"Is that really a rule, or just a heavenly preference?" Alexis sipped on the wine. For Meela, wine tasted kind of funny because she was also a tree like me. Drinking wine didn't give her the same effects. So her preferred drink was, strangely, a grape-flavored cordial made of condensed nutrient-stuff.

Meela shrugged at the question. "Well, if they are careful, they'll be able to hide from the demon king for a while…"

One of the key lessons Alexis wanted Meela to share was that the demon king could sense their presence, and the stronger they got, the easier it was for the demon king to find them. It was like a fire in the darkness. A stronger fire burned brighter and easier to see.

"Think they'll come back?"

"Honestly?" Meela paused and sipped on her nutrient cordial.

"They will." Alexis sighed. "I see us in them. We were just as desperate and lost as they were, the burdens on them so heavy that they will look for anyone, anything to help them, and if they can find a safe harbor like TreeTree, they will."

"That's why I didn't tell them anything about TreeTree." Meela stopped. "You know TreeTree won't agree to help them."

"They're stuck in between a rock and a hard place. And Tree-Tree's just concerned with this…valley."

Huh. But then, I liked only paying attention to my things and things related to my things. The demon king was one of my top three threats. Other kingdoms, other monsters, and demons. All of them were threats because they threatened the existence of this valley, and they were often destructive to me, the trees, and the valley around me.

"You know he's listening, right?" Meela shrugged, and she sipped on her cordial again.

"But then again, he's not exactly bothered by what we say about him. Look at the New Freekans. So many of them say weird stuff about Aeon all the time. Nothing happened."

"As someone who's mostly tree, I think he's still thinking whether he should do anything." Meela finished the cordial and walked over to the sink. "I mean, I sort of can understand his slow response, now that I am a tree hotel. We get assaulted with so much 'sensory' information from all over our tree, and in his case, his network of trees, that we need a lot of time to just take it all in."

"But he fights battles surprisingly well for someone that lives life on a different time scale."

"It's probably an emergency reaction. It's like how some of us can enter into 'bullet time' and fight things differently."

Alexis frowned. "Hmm, that implies that if TreeTree fights too long, he'll need to 'rest' like the rest of us."

"Why not? A tree is still a living being, and energy fluctuates. But what's long to him is probably extremely long to us."

"Shouldn't it be the other way round, that someone who lives on a 'longer' time scale should consume more energy to focus on a 'short' battle? But then again, he does have a 'mind' now. Maybe that helps."

I wondered what they were on about.

"Mission accomplished, Supreme Leader."

Stratreegy managed to capture a [demon rod]! But Supreme Leader made me feel like some hermit kingdom's dictator.

The 'luring' tactic worked; we located a force of demons headed for the [ThreeTrees of Mana], and after we had confirmed the existence of the demon rod, Stratreegy led the fight.

It was a fairly easy battle. The demons were only five thousand strong, and the South Forest had more than that in beetles alone. Added to it, it was a defensive battle, so we crushed them easily and took a rod.

Another one week to convert it into [Forest Rod], and now I had a 'tree-creating' item. Now, I needed to think about where to use it.

With winter over, and the snake-dungeon now spitting out more demons, I gathered the beetles from across my valley.

I probably wouldn't use the demon rod on the snake dungeon, though. I didn't quite fancy having snakes, and I recalled the residual mana in that location was quite weak. So I would rather save it for something that was more likely able to unlock the next [Soul Forge] color.

Still. Time to crush the annoying nest of 'demon-insects' in my neighborhood.

Pests.

The battle was relatively brief. Lausanne, Horns, and Jura, accompanied by eight thousand beetles, led the charge into the snake-hole-turned-demon-base. Unlike the dungeon, this demonic base didn't block my [subsidiary trees], and as such, I could still use the beetles even within the dungeon.

It was one of my concerns, that the [demon rods] could possibly enhance the effects of the demon king's magical interference. But I was happy to see this was not the case.

Anyway, Lausanne spoke of two demon 'generals' defending the demon rod after the battle; she gained a level after Jura and Lausanne defeated them. The rod itself apparently transformed into a large, nest-like structure, which crumbled under the attack of giant beetles.

YEAR 83 MONTH 6

While no actual news arrived on our shores, I had a sense there had been a lot of fighting.

My [soul realm] collected a whole load of souls, and they seemed to come from all directions. Even my wandering [soul harvesters] seemed to bring back souls from far away.

I hadn't heard of the heroes, nor did I care all that much, but I wondered whether this was linked to them.

And then refugees.

By the thousands, they came from north and south. Trevor and Stratreegy detected them as they approached the outer ring of [subsidiary trees]. Curious, I had my assistants zoom in and try to pick out what was the cause.

"There were two walkers." That was the gist of the chatter amongst the escaped refugees, many of whom were soldiers themselves. It seemed the walkers weren't headed my way, so that was a relief.

It seemed that two walkers had somehow managed to move into position together, the second one being from the south. It landed on some poor, unsuspecting village and then started to wreck chaos. The other one came from the north, headed south.

Were they planning to 'meet' with the third immovable demon walker? What was the point of two walkers in the same place?

Still, it was amusing, and I would like to see a battle of walkers and heroes.

"Would you have problems with two walkers?" I asked Alexis and Meela.

"When we were in our level one hundreds? I could probably take on one single-handedly, but when I was level ninety and our heavenly forms needed channeling? That was a bit harder. But then, it's hard to say...there were so many things to consider. For example, I think 'piercing' magic works better than 'explosive' ones with the walkers, so there may be an issue of compatibility." Sometimes Alexis got really long winded, and I was quite certain it was her [laboratory spirit] doing the talking.

I thought we handled the walker quite easily, but then again, I did have anti-demon boosts. Apparently, not all the heroes' conventional abilities included an anti-demon boost. This meant a [paladin] hero with 'anti-demon abilities' far stronger than a generic archmage with no specific 'anti-demon ability.' Except their [star mana], which star mana by nature were especially effective against demons.

"I recall all of you struggled against three champions and had to come to me." Ten years was but a short while ago, though ancient to them. "That didn't make sense."

Meela looked awkwardly, and it was Alexis who responded. "We were in our level nineties, and uh...we were just coming to grasp with our [star mana] and [heavenly form]... Unlike you, somehow the gods didn't give all of us anti-demon blessings. Only paladins, healers, and some of the sword-mages. Regular mages like me got supersized mana pools, high-tier spells, multi-elemental enchantments, and that sort of stuff. And supersized [star mana]."

"Why wouldn't they?" Again, another nonsensical idea. If the heroes were created to fight demons, why wouldn't the gods give them anti-demon blessings? Such a thing did, after all, exist.

"How would I know? Maybe they thought it wouldn't be necessary since the [star mana] was so damned good at killing demons? Besides, those anti-demon blessings don't work against the demon king itself that much."

"They don't?" I thought they did. I survived a demon king thanks to them! Did the 'fragments' manifest differently from blessings? I pulled out my [Tree Heart]'s status again, just to reread the narration.

[The Tree's Heart and Spirit-Lantern]

[This is the heart of the tree, adorned with the fragments of 67 heroes. It gives the tree 3350% increase in experience gain, 670% extra damage against mid-tier demons, 335% extra damage against elder demons, significant demon armor-negation, immunity to lesser demons, significant damage reduction against elder demons, and immunity from all lesser forms of fire, and significantly reduced damage from higher form of fires.]

"Meela, Alexis, when your friend died, did you get a...fragment? Or a 'blessing'?"

Meela nodded. "We did. All of us received a fragment. It's called [Baton of the Fallen]. It boosts our experience gain, blessings against lesser and mid-tier demons, some demonic resistance, and other stuff like that. I lost it, though. We lost it."

Was it not effective? Or did they not 'know' whether it was effective or not because they'd not seen its effects? When they fought the demon king, that fragment had always been with them, and...they probably had one fragment? Maybe the effects were too miniscule for them to realize?

Or was it because the demon king was perhaps...an otherworldly, 'divine' being, perhaps something of a...demonic half god? Therefore [star mana] was the only 'true' counter for the demon king. All these stat boosts negated only an 'aspect' of its power.

"Why did you ask, and uh...how did you know there was a fragment?" Alexis suddenly probed. "That's not something anyone knows, except for heroes."

"Uh...a hero told me once? But I didn't know what it did."

Alexis paused, thought for a while, and I witnessed her eyes change, as if something dawned on her. "TreeTree, how did you get those...heroic fragments? You know...the ones in your [tree-heart], the ones you showed us so many years ago."

Did she figure it out?

What should I say? "I don't know. I just get them."

"Who?" Alexis asked. Her voice seemed almost angry.

Meela seemed puzzled. "Alexis, what's happening?"

"It's so painfully obvious now. I cannot believe how I have been so blind. You, TreeTree, have heroic fragments. You clearly don't like heroes. Hero fragments are the shattered remains of a soul. TreeTree has a [soul forge]. Did you steal fragments from us through your [soul forge]? You 'cut' into our souls and take it out of us, a bit of us, didn't you? Or a [familiar]."

Uh. What?

"That time when Meela was in your [biopod], you took a 'fragment' from her, didn't you? And the same when I was here. Or that [familiar] of yours! That's a thing to steal hero [fragments], right? That's why you insisted on all of us taking a [familiar]!"

Huh?!

Meela rubbed her chin. "I don't think so, though...I don't feel a thing."

"Of course you don't feel a thing! It probably happened after we died."

"Timeline didn't line up. TreeTree didn't have a [soul forge] until later?" Meela retorted.

"Then it must be the [familiars]," Alexis mused. "The [familiars] are scavengers, like vultures that wait for us to die and then pick on our soul fragments!"

"That's not true."

"I don't believe it! It all makes sense now!" Alexis shouted. "That's why you asked Meela to offer your familiars to the three new heroes!" Which all of them accepted. "You've planned this all along!"

"Look. You're a smart girl. Think about it for a moment. It's not as if you actually lost anything. You died. Your attachment to your body and whatever fragments stops there. It's like your corpse, after it's buried in the ground, some worms come and eat your dead body. It's just nature, naturally consuming and assimilating the deceased! Do you curse the worms for eating the bodies buried in the ground? I am a [soul tree]. My job is to recycle the souls and spirits of the world, and reality is you, as a person who died, were part of that cycle."

Oh. Did I just make it worse?

"Ugh! Oh my god, I cannot believe that I am soul-contracted with someone who's been collecting our fragments! I want out. I want to break this contra—" And Alexis screamed in pain as the [soul contract] acted on her mind.

Meela sighed. Alexis's screaming slowly faded into the background. She seemed calm, but she was thinking, and she asked, "TreeTree, did you steal or take fragments from us...through those...familiars?"

"No. I can assure you I did not steal them via familiars or any other methods." I wanted to keep my presence as also a reincarnator a secret. No one should know. "I received them, only after your death, as part of my duties as a [soul tree]. But I did not 'steal' or 'take' them."

Meela paused and sat on a chair. "TreeTree..."

The screaming stopped as the [soul contract] put Alexis's mind to 'sleep.'

"I don't believe you were malicious," Meela said. "Alexis might be right, that the kind of magic you have, this...[soul magic] isn't something we can comprehend.

"I'll...I'll talk to Alexis." Meela sighed. "I need to think about this. I guess, I guess neither of us has ever really come to terms about how different you are as a soul tree...Alexis, and myself...

there are concepts about this world that we still have not accepted."

Huh.

"I think...it's probably like I died and somebody took over my online identity and sold it. Sure, I didn't 'lose' anything, but a part of me didn't feel right. Like the 'dead' has been desecrated."

Uh...there was reincarnation? You had a new body, and if you always held onto your previous bodies, then eventually you would need to care for so many 'previous' bodies. There was a time to move on.

"I...uh...give me some time. I-I need to check on Alexis." Alexis was in deep slumber. She'd probably wake up in a day or two.

Hmmm. Looked like I must revisit my assessment of Alexis and Meela. Should I still keep them around? Perhaps not.

How did I split without making them enemies? They were former heroes, and they knew a lot about me. If they wanted to harm me, a stationary tree, there was a lot they could do. Should I just...kill them?

I didn't think I could keep one and kill the other, and Alexis's value to me was clearly not there anymore. I mentally sighed. I could probably banish Alexis as she was [soul contracted] to me, but Meela as an 'independent' soul, even if I destroyed her present body, she could still manifest in this world as another entity, find another body. If I were to kill both of them now, Meela would find another body, and I would just make her an enemy.

If I could just 'wipe' their minds, or send both of them into the reincarnation cycle on another world, that would be great. But alas.

There were no 'clean' divorces...

YEAR 83 MONTH 7

Alexis somehow fell back into 'moments' of that mental breakdown constantly. It seemed that whatever she realized really 'possessed' her, it would trigger the [soul contract] almost every other day, even if she woke up. Since Alexis had entered into this state, Meela closed her Oakwood Hotel to spend more time with her.

"Why does she keep relapsing into that screaming fit?"

"I-I don't know. Something keeps triggering the [soul contract]."

"Stop it?"

"I can't. I don't know how to."

Hmm. This seemed to be a mechanics of the [soul contract], so I attempted to—

[Assessing Soul Contract detailed menu]
[Master: TreeTree. Servant: Alexis]

[Current security setting: Intention to break contract and related causes were purged from memory (default)]

[Other security settings possible:

1. NOTIFY MASTER OF REBELLIOUS INTENTIONS
2. WARN SERVANT
3. SUPPRESS/CONFUSE REBELLIOUS INTENTIONS WITH OTHER THOUGHTS
4. PERSONALITY MIND-WIPE (LEVELS AND SKILLS WILL BE LOST. CHANCE OF POSSIBLE 'SOUL-CRASH')
5. DO NOTHING
6. YOU MAY ALSO CHANGE THE 'MEMORY PURGE' PERIOD AND TARGETING CONDITIONS.

WARNING. SKILL-CONFLICT DETECTED. ALEXIS [LABORATORY SPIRIT] POSSESSED THE SKILL [DISCOVERY LOG]. DISCOVERY LOG RECORDS AND COLLATES ALL FINDINGS AND IMPORTANT FACTS TO PRODUCE HYPOTHESES. [DISCOVERY LOG] WAS IN CONFLICT WITH [SOUL CONTRACT]'S PURGING ATTEMPT. CONFLICT WAS OVERWHELMING SERVANT'S MENTAL & MEMORY FACULTIES. SKILL MODIFICATION NOT AVAILABLE.

DO YOU WANT TO REMOVE ALEXIS'S SKILL, [DISCOVERY LOG], OR SUPPRESS THE MEMORY PURGE?

"Oh." A fix was possible, but let's talk to Meela. I was not too keen on keeping Alexis anymore; temporary solutions were just unnecessary bandage.

But before that, I took some time to look at the other items in this [Soul Contract]'s menu, such as the option to [undo form]. This would be useful for Eriz and Yvon's future role as my servant. Next time, I should mind-wipe Yvon and Eriz, since as a newly dead souls their level must be level one anyway. Then I didn't have to deal with this...loyalty issue.

"TreeTree, this can't continue," Meela said. Obviously she didn't know I had an idea how to fix her. "I-I can't see her like that. I know we died before and all, but Alexis like that is a fate worse than death. The moment she sees you, this happens."

Alexis screamed again. The conflict of skill and soul contract was clearly causing some kind of malfunction, and her tree-lab main body transformed into this 'haunted-tree' like thing, the 'relapse' and 'pain' clearly affecting her presence. It was indeed unpleasant to have her like this around, and that 'negative' energy also affected the nearby trees.

Meela said, "Can I take her place?"

"What? No." That was worse. If Meela was the one soul-contracted, and Alexis was free, Alexis would be vengeful. She'd clearly shown the 'potential' for retaliation, and I was not giving her 'just cause,' however flimsy.

"Then...what can I do to spare her from this pain?"

"Meela, will you hold it against me if I were to banish her and return her to the reincarnation cycle? The gods of reincarnation will deal with what happens next."

"You mean...kill her? But...why? Can't you just free her?"

"She clearly has the means and motives to harm me. She has attempted that before. I cannot, in good conscience, free a person who has a high possibility of hurting me and my valley sometime in the future."

"I-I will stop her," Meela said. "TreeTree, I offer to [soul contract] myself to you in exchange for Alexis's freedom. And I commit, as part of the contract and without reservation, to stop her from ever attempting to hurt you and this valley."

"Alexis will not accept that."

"She will. And if you free both of us, I will guide her away from you. TreeTree, there was really no need to kill her. The world needed us. Me and her. And you, too. Together, we can do so much to reduce the destruction caused by the demon king. We can help the heroes and help to break this 'cycle.' That's good for you, too, if the threat of demons is reduced."

"That's..." It felt a bit like blackmail.

"I'm not trying to blackmail you," Meela said. I suddenly felt like she was probably using a [skill] to negotiate with me. Was it her hotel-manager skill? "And yes, I am using a skill. It's called [sense intent]."

Now that was not exactly fair, was it?

"The best outcome was all three of us to split up, you do your thing, we do ours. I will find a way to compensate you in the future, for all the troubles you have gone through to protect both of us. It's probably clearer for you to kill Alexis, but please don't. The long-term benefits of retaining her as a force against demons outweighs the risk, and I will stop her. I am willing to enter into any kind of contract with you to prove that I will stop her from trying to retaliate against you."

Sigh.

"Undo her [research tree], and seed her into a wooden body or a seed, or a beetle, and put it in my body. I-I can arrange to move my hotel out. I have a special one-off skill to move my body. Please, TreeTree. The world needed people like Alexis. This demon king cycle isn't going to stop itself."

"I won't release the contract."

"Why?"

"I won't release her [soul contract] because it's my only way to prevent her from ever harming me. And I will need you to be in a [contract] as well, to agree to stop her. If you agree, then I will let you both go away and roam, under the conditions of the [soul contract]." I had very little faith in the promises of these heroes, so I thought it was best to bind both of them.

I considered my options in the 'long run.'

One: kill both Alexis and Meela. Pros: I wouldn't have to deal with them for a while. Cons: I had significant uncertainty about the mechanics of this reincarnation system. I was unable to conclude whether killing them actually sent them to another world or they would somehow 'reincarnate' and come back into this world. Particularly Meela, since her god told her to stick around for a thousand years or so. If so, I may end up having to deal with two former heroes in the future.

Two: free Alexis, but contract with Meela. Pros: Meela was more trustworthy, and Alexis was the one with a desire to escape. Con: Alexis clearly wasn't going to let that slide, and her being free would mean she could acquire all the means necessary to retaliate. Rejected.

Three: free both of them. Pros: honestly none. Cons: Alexis was clearly suspicious of me, and this 'fragment' thing seemed to have somehow 'cemented' her perception, even despite the restrictions of the [soul contract]. My act of goodwill may not be reciprocated, and the long-run risks outweighed it. Rejected.

Four. Free them, but hold them onto contract. The contract was my insurance. Clearly it was good at knocking them out, like what it did to Alexis, and I did realize I could 'make' her experience a headache if I so desired. Considering the ability to trigger a mindwipe, I could trigger that at the very end of their soul contract.

"If you do that, when we die, we will both come back to you. Do you really...uhm, want to see us again?"

"Yes. That's the point. Only you can stop her. That's why you need to be in a [contract]. If you somehow move on and reincarnate, while leaving her here in this world with me, I will kill her so that she moves on, too. So. It's best that no matter what happens, the fates of you two are intertwined like married trees, forever."

Meela paused. "That...makes sense. Not the deal I would hope for, but...but yes. Fine. I, Meela Adams, agree to be [soul contracted] to TreeTree and vow to stop Alexis from ever attempting to harm TreeTree and the valley."

The contract was sealed. I also insisted that they never spoke of my fragments ever, ever again.

And I unmade Alexis's form as a soul fused into research tree.

This stripped her of all her levels and experience, and she was back to a glowing soul in my [soul realm]. Then, with [soul forge], I fused her into a small beetle. Then a beetle moved that small sleeping beetle to Meela's hotel lodge. I chose a beetle because...it was a choice between beetles and spiders. I didn't want to give her that dryad body; that was mine.

I recalled that there was a 'restriction' or 'cooldown' for refusing souls into new body forms, but it seemed heroes and former heroes were not subject to such restriction.

"Thank you, TreeTree." Meela's Oakwood hotel started to change shape into a gigantic peashooter, and it shot out an absolutely massive seed-like thing, containing a 'disassembled hotel.' "This peashooter was able to send us anywhere around the world, so we'll be on another continent, and we will not bother you anymore."

"Where?"

"The North!" Meela said. "Where it's cold!"

"Is this the best time to do it, with the demons everywhere?"

"I-I know a place. We'll be fine. See you, someday. I'll handle Alexis."

In a flash, the peashooter expanded and then shot the massive 'seed' across the skies. Then the peashooter 'decayed' and 'withered,' its purpose fulfilled.

They were gone now. Was that the best way to separate? Would I regret this decision someday?

[Alexis's experience as research tree has been converted into experience, similar skill seeds and class seeds.]

[You received Class Seeds - Magic Researcher x 4, Pyromancer x 2, Schemer x 4]

[You received Skill seeds - Magic Researcher x 11, Pyromancer x 5, Schemer x 10]

***[You gained one level**. You were now level 140!]*

***[You gained a passive skill** - Forest of Giants]*

[Forest of Giants causes the trees around your main body to experience significant growth, resulting in the creation of a valley of gigantic trees. Their size will be equal to your own. Produces giant-timber.]

***[You have gained a new skill** - Giant Attendant Trees x 100]*

[Giant Attendant Trees are supersized version of Subsidiary trees, with 10 times the [customizable branch] space, and 10 times the [customizable roots] space. They also have a root-network that was 10 times larger and also expand the communication range by 10 times.

They also retain a larger percentage of the main tree's auras and passive, but this was capped at a max of 50% of the main body's aura and passives.]

Wow.

Well, at least she gave me a farewell gift.

With that over, I turned my focus on the southern walker. The heroes should be there soon, but it seemed they took the scenic route, fighting demon after demon, helping town after town with their demon problems. That was fine, that was what heroes did, but I thought something was messing with them.

Still, my trees were not far behind. I had a vested interest in following them. After all, if they died and my trees were nearby, I got a [Titan Soul]! And I couldn't wait to try one. Too bad I didn't get it when I unmade Alexis, but meh.

The southern areas of the continent were ravaged; they bore the mark of many battles fought, some between kingdoms and, lately, against the demons. The Gila Kingdom's recent use of [hexbombs] meant quite a few 'impassable' terrain, thanks to the corruption of the hex.

I wondered if hexbombs got used too often, would this world end up like kind of nuclear wasteland, ala *Fallout*? I mean...the hex spawned alien-ish monsters, hostile to everything.

The heroes didn't look like they planned to attack just yet.

Lausanne received something from me this month. I had an idea while working on the [soul contract], that I wanted her to have a special [weapon]. All heroes had special weapons. Thor had Mjollnir, Iron Man had his suit, and Captain America had his shield.

So I made a wooden staff with the largest gem I had in it, and I fused an [artificial soul] into it. Jura had Bamboo, so I thought Lausanne should get one.

"This was Thorny. It's a level one [living staff]. If you practice with it, it will get stronger." I wasn't very creative with names.

Lausanne looked at it and twirled it around. To me, it didn't look any different from another staff; the fusing somehow made the large gem melt into the entirety of the spear, but Lausanne could feel it. I sometimes forgot they weren't used to voices other than my own.

I chose a staff because it seemed to be a common equipment for druids, since she took the [druid] class fruit recently. 'Compatibility' with the [possession of the devoted]. Maybe she'd do something cool with it.

I would still want to provide more 'training,' but I thought I would need more...powerful [dream tutors].

Maybe it could be like...another world-in-another world. Or a 'VR' experience via dreams?

YEAR 83 MONTH 8

The heroes defeated the walker. A hard-fought battle, with plenty of deaths from the coalition army. But a victory, nonetheless.

Also, this was when I realized all the heroes had some kind of summoned army.

Perhaps it was the theme this round; maybe the gods were like the designers for *Magic the Gathering* where they designed 'block-mechanics' and all the heroes of that 'block' shared the same mechanics.

Or were they just rolling the wheel, like how I rolled mine?

A few days later, after that walker was slain, the two other walkers, one of which swam across the seas...combined.

Like fucking Voltron.

And then I detected it.

"Magical bombardment detected!" Trevor literally shouted. "Coordinating [magic sensors] and [shield generators]."

The magical projectile flew overhead. It wasn't aimed at us.

So two walkers combined into a long-range magical artillery

cannon. A stationary bombardment weapon. It was like the Big Bertha from *Total Annihilations*!

It shot again.

"Can we stop it?" I asked the artificial souls.

"We need more subsidiary trees in that direction so that we can 'triangulate' the magical signatures and coordinate the shields to intercept accordingly."

It shot again.

"What the hell was that flying overhead?" Some civilians finally noticed as the magical projectiles flew past, like a giant comet glowing in the sky.

If you asked me, it felt like the demons were now able to retaliate against the 'blood ritual.'

Then it stopped. Three shots, and the combined 'demonic supercannon' seemed to be 'recharging.' I wondered whether it was recharging or if it was just waiting for new targets.

"What if that thing fires at us?" Jura asked, worried.

"We can stop it. Thankfully, the projectile isn't very fast, and I can detect it coming." Despite this, I created more subsidiary trees in that direction, and a few [giant attendant trees]. The giant attendant trees could act as a 'shield.' After all, they shared a lot of my toughness and auras. Better safe than sorry.

"I...I'll get the men to expand the underground hideouts and sewers." Jura breathed a sigh of relief, but there was an undercurrent of concern.

It didn't fire for a week, and we traced the arc of the magical projectile to find that it was aimed at Gila.

Half of their capital city had been vaporized by the projectiles.

Two days later, another city in Gila retaliated with one big [blood ritual], and it sacrificed one thousand souls for it.

It hit, but the demonic supercannon created a massive wall out of demonic flesh that blocked most of the damage.

Was this it?

I couldn't help but feel like this was the beginning of a 'thermonuclear war.' The 'threat' of mutually assured destruction to maintain a fragile peace didn't work here, if one side was a race of trigger-happy demons.

The heroes, as I followed them, changed their targets for the demonic supercannon. They would have to backtrack, since the demonic supercannon was located a distance away, to the north.

For me, if two walkers could do this, why wasn't the demon king bombarding the world to death? Couldn't it do that? Surely, with the demon king's ability, which was supposedly one order of magnitude higher, it could shoot projectiles like that all the time.

What was stopping it? A lack of...imagination?

A lack of bullets? Did it need to tap into some kind of magical leyline to power the supercannons beyond what they were normally able to do?

Oh well. Or maybe it was some strange systemic limitations that were imposed?

I sometimes felt the system's rules didn't really apply all that well for those in the higher rungs of power. I wondered whether it was like my home world, where money allowed one to get away with rules that those with limited resources couldn't.

After some thinking, I felt it wouldn't go anywhere unless I could interview the demon king, so I stopped thinking about it.

Closer to home, I focused on Lausanne, the Valthorns, and the Valtrian Order.

Meela's Oakwood hotel was gone, and that left a 'gap' in the hospitality business. Eager to fill it, I created an artificial soul and merged it with the Tree Lodge to create a similar thing. Still, the gap was far too huge compared to Meela's level seventy-plus hotel.

Oh, I called my new artificial soul Treeveller. Travelers, Treeveller. And the business was called Pine Lodge.

It had complaints on the first day.

"Who's this pathetic person running this pathetic establishment!"

Well, I had to intervene and quickly re-hire the treefolks that Meela used to employ and pay them slightly more to make up for the 'gap' she left behind. It'd take some time before Treeveller even became a decent inn-manager, but a business was a business.

"We need a chef! Lady Mika used to cook great vegetarian dishes!"

"Uh..."

Well, in a roundabout way, it was Emile who volunteered to cook for the kitchen. She didn't have any [chef] classes, but I had [chef] and [cook] class seeds from the many dead people's souls I collected over the decades. I'd also need a [barkeeper], but that was for later.

———

"Aeon." A group of fifteen children stood around a circle, around a [tree of prayer] in Jura's courtyard. An old lady led them; she was one of the caretakers of the orphans. There had been more... refugees this month.

Even though the heroes had been out helping to squash the demons, there were still way too many demons crawling around the continent. The demonic supercannon really messed up a lot of defensive strategies, as armies needed to split into smaller detachments to avoid total loss. Yet, with the [message] network down, this meant the separated armies needed to rely on old school means of communicating by couriers or riders.

It was a strangely effective strategy. Split up the large armies, and with the communications down, pick on whichever force that was lost.

Anyway, the old lady bowed. The fifteen children followed. "This is Aeon's many, many bodies. He is everywhere in the valley, and he watches over us. Are you ready, to be the next batch of Valthorn Initiates?"

The fifteen children, aged six to ten, nodded.

"Good. This was a test. You will receive a familiar from Aeon if Aeon sees you worthy for the first step."

All of them got a familiar. It really wasn't a test, but nobody needed to know that. These children were young, and the intention was for them to be forged in the flames of battle.

This was because I decided to expand the Valthorns significantly, and I expanded it to a group of one hundred. The minder's use was rather limited, and yes, it was useful for me to observe the levels and skills they acquired, but I would use the minders on people that were more 'sensitive' and with special gifts.

In short, the regular kids would become regular warriors with familiars, though they would have the Valthorn title, and the truly talented would be observed using the minders.

The fifteen children walked back happy. For many of them, this was a great gift, and they were eager to test it out.

So far, I had not lost any of the Valthorns in battle, but I believed some of them would die over the next few years. It was just inevitable.

YEAR 83 MONTH 9

The supercannon fired multiple times, and I believed the shots were aimed at the heroes, or at least it tried to shoot them the moment the demons found them. Many times, the network of magical sensors picked up the surge of the magical projectile, and after we concluded it wasn't going to land anywhere near us, we let it zip by.

This, naturally, was a problem for the heroes. The heroes wanted to fight the demons, and they did as much as they could to fight the demons. They and their 'summoned' magical army went out of their way to stop as many demons as they could.

Yet fighting demons personally also meant they revealed their own presence to the supercannon. The supercannon clearly had no concern for friendly fire and would not hesitate to annihilate any demons present in the area to get a shot at the heroes.

That said, the heroes did have some measures to protect themselves. Harris, the shield-hero, had a massive absorption shield, and he was able to absorb one shot from the supercannon. Based on the current firing patterns, the supercannons could fire three long-range shots consecutively every five to six days, so after the shots, the heroes actually had a short window in which they could advance as fast as they could or fight as much as they could, since the threat of the supercannon didn't hang over their heads after every volley.

The supercannon was also a huge demon factory, and the nearest subsidiary tree near that area saw thousands to tens of thousands of demonoids sent in all directions. It was just a lucky thing that the supercannon usually wouldn't target conventional targets, since they seemed focused on the heroes...or anyone that invoked a [blood ritual] against it.

Or so I thought.

Middle of the month, multiple smaller battles happened throughout the valley. Some of these demons attempted to attack the volcano, some attempted to retake the former snake dungeon, some attempted to just...well, punch through my line of trees.

It was good combat practice for the Valthorns, and with the expanded 'operating range' around the [Giant Attendant Trees], I was able to use these giant trees like 'regional hubs' for my beetles to operate it.

"Well, at least TreeTree sees things my way," Lausanne said. She'd been out fighting, and I thought she was using the fighting to work through her frustrations about leveling and how insanely overpowered the heroes were.

"Some of these girls are too young to be fighting," a captain complained. "We're babysitters!"

"Experience counts. Age shouldn't stop them from seeing the demon war for what it is." Lausanne shrugged.

"You watch them!" the captain complained.

Lausanne nodded, and she played 'protector' of the young Valthorn convoys. Each 'squadron' of one hundred soldiers played nanny to a group of five Valthorns, excluding Lausanne and the first generation Valthorns, who were considered regular soldiers. There was usually a small beetle force of fifteen hundred that acted as the 'bulk' of any combat force.

The general consensus on the accepted age for a person to start fighting in this world was about fourteen, but children younger than that had played 'support' roles, such as food handlers, helpers at healer-tents, tending to animals and stuff. I mean, if one reached age fourteen, one must have survived at least one demon king era, right?

Children matured quickly in the face of death and destruction, though not by choice.

And then, we felt it.

A shot from the demonic supercannon, and this time, it was aimed right at me.

Ah well. I'd been waiting for this moment. I wanted to know how my shields stacked up.

[Steelwood Barrier] x 5. Five large wooden shields manifested midair, supported by roots appearing from the ground. And the magical projectile smashed through four of them.

"Oh." It was more of an "oh" of relief, really.

Honestly, this meant if the actual bullet hit my main body, it probably wouldn't cause much damage thanks to all my perks. But the rest of the subsidiary trees and New Freeka itself would suffer damage. It wasn't really me that needed protecting from demons, but the valley.

My fellow lovely, lovely trees and flowers, plants, herbs, and crops. Biodiversity of the valley was fragile; it had to be so, so gently preserved. This valley was our prized garden, and we were its gardeners and protectors.

Ain't no nasty demon gonna step on my field of herbs or crops.

It fired again. Trevor quickly calculated its trajectory and alerted me to be ready. Just as before, five [steelwood barrier] blocked it successfully. And we blocked the third shot, too.

The [Steelwood Barrier] was clearly a league above the previous wood shields, so that was a plus point. Next time if a demon walker came close, I could have this right in its face. Maybe I could use it as a weapon?

"Should we retaliate, Commander?" Stratreegy asked.

"How?"

"Tree line. Or perhaps invent a weapon similar to the one used by Lady Meela."

"Oh. A peashooter?"

"Indeed. The strategic advantages of a weapon like that can't be understated. It's capable of long range. We could build a massive wooden bullet enchanted with anti-demon magic as a projectile. Would be extremely beneficial with the commander's superior anti-demon powers."

"Huh." Well, were there...naturally occurring versions of the peashooter for my research, since the system wasn't so willing to give it to me?

Maybe some other time. I'd need adventurers to get them, but with the demons running amok, most of them now found a 'safe' base of operations and worked from there.

I hoped the merchant networks got restored soon. All my artificial minds had pending upgrades. Even with the merchant guild's regional coordination center being here, trade routes were still unstable, and that meant total value of trades was still way lower than pre–demon king.

"TreeTree! I got an idea!" Lausanne came to me one day.

"Yes?"

"Can you animate wooden stuff for us to practice combat with? I was thinking like...you know...moving wooden figures shaped like monsters or other humans, and we get to fully simulate all kinds of situations. If you can add weather effects, that would be even better!"

Where'd she get that idea? That sounded like the kind of training room *Kung Fu Panda* had. But... "Oh...should be possible."

"I saw a bunch of fighters out in the barracks using these wooden dummies as practice. I've got no idea why, but I thought with your power, you could create a totally awesome version of those dummies!"

"I-I could." Well, that was certainly worth exploring. I mean, it was a natural extension of the current training rooms.

"Yeah. I think it'll be a good experience for the younger kids to practice with dummies their own size and gradually work up to larger and full-size dummies! I mean, we're small!" Lausanne wasn't exactly small anymore. She was fourteen, and at this age she was about eighty-five to ninety percent of her full height. "But think of it, if you could animate dummies that resemble all sorts of monsters, we could get similar combat experience before we even face the real thing! So the room should have like...dummies for kids!"

That was a good point.

"It's totally going to be great. It's like your [Dream Tutor]! But because it's real, we could build what Uncle Jura calls muscle memory!"

"So...essentially have wooden dummies resembling all kinds of monsters as practice." Essentially a 'VR' for battle. Or like... Matrix's dojo?

Fine, but the amount of variation was beyond what I thought a regular [training room] could provide, so I decided to make an [artificial soul] merged with a [training tree] to form a [Tree of Learning].

"I'm your Treeiner. Let us begin practice." A wooden dummy appeared, and he could speak. He bowed to Lausanne like a kung-fu master. He was literally a wooden avatar that represented the merged Tree. He was level one, of course, but yes, I decided Treeiner sounded like a good name for a trainer. I was contemplating between Treeiner, or Treetor, or Practreece. But I supposed if I had multiple Trees of Learning, I could use all of those names. Should a basic Valtrian version of the 'Boot Camp' be called Root Camp?

I digressed. The death of all the mortals in the region to the demons meant that I had a large supply of soul fragments to make artificial souls, and the volcano also happened to help expand my artificial-soul capacity since it, too, supplied a kind of 'power.'

Lausanne looked impressed and happily started. So, since she and the young kids were busy with their newfound practice toy, kinda like how athletes went hyper over their new practice equipment, I left them alone.

Not that I had much of a choice.

Because the damned supercannon fired three shots at me again. Like, I had the wonderful honor of taking so many shots. Was I, like, firing practice? A wooden dummy for the demon supercannon to practice their aim?

"Any ideas on how we convert that energy from the shot into something usable? Can we have magic-absorbent wooden shields?" I mean, it was energy in some form...

No answer. Ah well.

I blocked all of the shots, of course, but one of them blew up extremely close to New Freeka, which freaked everyone out. That was good. Everyone should be reminded of their mortality every now and then.

YEAR 83 MONTH 10

The supercannon decided to change target. I wondered if it was because it presumed I died or it just found something better to shoot at. I mean, how did the demon even know whether it hit or not, right? It wasn't like there were eyes on the projectile...right?

My own suspicions were they had 'spotter' demons, but with my expanded trees and network, I didn't think so. There was not a single demon within fifty miles of me.

So they decided to shoot...at Ransalah. And the capital of Takde. And also the capital of Barsoom to the north. It wasn't hard to calculate, since the energy signatures 'movement' gave a direction, and the travel of the magical projectile was something that could be pinpointed by using an array of magical sensors, then triangulating the route based on the time-gap different sensors detect the same energy signature.

But this raised a question.

How did the demon even know about the concept of 'capitals'? Did they go by 'population density'? Or did they have some kind of 'scanning' mechanism that allowed them to spot where exactly were the big cities? I had the impression it could detect 'heroes,' and the concept of a 'retaliation' could be easily understood, but if it could deliberately target capitals, it meant the demons could understand the concept of what was a 'human capital,' being the political 'constructs' that they were, therefore was sentient and intelligent.

Or maybe it was simpler?

"Maybe it just detects the presence of a [king]?"

Jura's idea was that, well, [king]s actually had an aura-thing that spanned their domain. A demon in that domain should be able to sense where the king was if it had the right kind of... sensors. If Alexis's previous theory was that the demon king could sense heroes, what was stopping them from looking for kings?

"Didn't that mean the king can never run away or flee?"

"I think...they can turn their 'presence' off and on?"

I thought it was both.

News, about the attack, traveled quickly. I happened to have the benefit of having a front row seat of the destruction. Ransalah's main palace suffered a massive explosion that vaporized the entire royal palace. The king and the royal family...were dead. Even from the [subsidiary tree] that I had in the Ransalah's Forest Reserve, which was luckily spared from the projectile, I could vaguely see the destruction of Ransalah's royal district. A very, very precise shot from the demon supercannon.

Seemed like Jura's idea that it detected a 'king' had merit. This precision didn't make sense without it.

The news eventually arrived via courier and got to Yvon two weeks later, and as expected, she took this news the hardest. In that, she was most...conflicted. The king, then the prince, was the one that killed her previous benefactor...and Roma's father. Eriz and Roma, and the former councilors that formed her inner circle, quickly met up in her house to discuss the events.

"The king is dead? You are certain about this?" Yvon asked, and all of them, the 'first-generation' founders of New Freeka, in a sense, gathered. The first generation were refugees from a civil war, after all. They lost.

"Yes, Lady Yvon. I confirmed with at least ten other sources.

The blast from the demon somehow managed to break through all the magical barriers protecting the palace and destroyed the palace. Even the royal chambers, with its ancient magics, did not last."

"But Aeon just blocked a few of those shots..."

"Perhaps those ancient magics have eroded... But regardless, what matters is that the king and the immediate family that lived in the royal palace is dead. Even the king's four sons, their bodies have been found charred and burned. The king's own body was founded half-vaporized, his head and left hand partly protected by the protective magic of the royal crown and the ring of the hero's throne."

Two of the other men and women squirmed at the description. The others let out a bit of a sigh. Some just kept their mouths shut and looked at Yvon.

"So, Lady Yvon, there will be a war soon, perhaps not an outright war because of concerns over the demon king..."

"For the Throne of Salah."

Yvon sighed. "My duties and commitment are here. I am after all bound to Aeon under contract."

"Pretenders to the throne will emerge. And Roma, as the child of Prince Galan, has a claim."

Yvon sighed. "All of you knew, too..."

"We always did. I'm sure many back in Ransalah know, too. The pretenders will come for his life, whether he likes it or not. He's only ten and may not be ready for such conflicts, but yet the blood of the kings runs through him. And that means responsibility, Lady Yvon. A duty to the old throne to claim his birthright."

"I cannot leave. And here, Roma is safe. Aeon's eyes and ears watch over all of us. No one will be able to attempt to take his life."

"Lady Yvon, if I may...can you convince Aeon to support Roma's claim?"

"That was absurd." Yvon shook her head. "Why would a tree spirit even bother with the royal affairs of another kingdom! Aeon has shown no respect or regard for the thrones of mortal men. It was but a flimsy thing to him."

"But he can be bargained with. A deal can be struck. Just as you did."

"Only when it was aligned to Aeon's goals, however ephemeral and random that goal may be. And Roma may not want to be king. We should ask him."

"I'm afraid his reluctance will earn him support. Many of the old court prefers a puppet on the throne, someone who would just delegate the duties of a king to the royal court. He cannot avoid this fight, Lady Yvon. It is infinitely better to take this fight on our terms, with a base of support that's unshakeable. Aeon, as a great spirit of the land, is clearly one support the citizens of Salah will respect and fear."

They met in Yvon's house, and there was tea on the table. Some ginger biscuits, too, made from the Order's herbal gardens. Yvon looked at the rest of the men.

"We owe it to the humans, our human friends who supported Prince Galan's fight back then. There are many who were forced to kowtow to the new King of Salah. This is our chance to pay them back. If not for Roma or yourself, do it for Prince Galan. Prince Galan who would've been a better king than his brother."

Yvon's fingers were shaking. "I... My contract with Aeon is unshakeable. But Roma is free."

"There are many who would see you return. Those of us who can return to support Roma's claim will do so."

"There are also many who will kill me and Roma without blinking an eye. And there will be those who rally against us. The other pretenders will claim Roma's a New Freekan and no longer has a claim on the throne."

"No matter the naysayers. The blood doesn't lie, and the Crown of Salah is a magical artifact from the first kings, and it will recognize any man who is a legitimate heir. If Roma has the [pretender to the throne of Salah] title, he has a right to the throne."

Roma came in with Eriz. One of the councilors asked, "So, my dear Roma, did you get a notification about your class?"

Roma looked puzzled at the gathered group. "What...what's this, Mommy?"

Yvon sighed. "Roma, there is a long and difficult conversation I need to have with you."

The others let Yvon and Roma have a bit of personal space, as Yvon explained to Roma who his father actually was and what had happening in Salah. Roma seemed to take it quite well, but perhaps he was just too stunned to even react in any way. At ten years old, maybe that was a good reaction.

And when the conversation was over, Roma just ran out of the house.

Okay.

Yvon walked out to the living room again and looked at her compatriots.

"Didn't go well?"

"He said he needed some time to think."

"I see. I was thinking...Lady Yvon, how close were you to Lausanne?"

"Quite...close?"

"Lady Lausanne's an amazing fighter, and if I may...she has all that is needed to be a valuable protector of Roma. Could you... convince her to go with Roma?"

Yvon shook her head. "No. Roma has his own friends..."

Takde and Barsoom, strangely, didn't suffer that badly. The news from couriers relayed that Takde's royal castle had an ancient magical circle that activated just in time, and it was actually strong enough to absorb the magical attack. Barsoom, on the other hand, also had similar magical protections and had so much reinforcement from Barsoom's own council of archmages that the blast was deflected to somewhere else.

I supposed not all kingdoms were that helpless against demons. Else a society like this wouldn't have survived all that long.

Still, the blast, and the wars, meant refugee season again. There was a whole load of refugees, and thanks to the fear of the demon blasts, they traveled in smaller packs, away from the heroes. Even some of Ransalah's citizens were running because if even the king with all his protections couldn't protect himself, how could a regular citizen hope to even survive such a blast?

New Freeka was already massively populated, and the poop-issue was only thankfully under control due to my recent advancements in filtration and metallic concentration trees. One hundred ten thousand now after all the massive waves of immigration, comprising of about fifty percent elves, twenty percent dwarves, ten percent centaurs, five percent humans, five percent treefolk, and ten percent others such as beastmen, lizardmen, garudas, or harpy-likes.

Anyway, with the [great attendant tree], this skill significantly improved my force-projection abilities outside my immediate range. These Great Trees essentially functioned as mini-mes, with fifty percent of my abilities.

Fifty percent was still plenty because, with a few [great attendant trees], and with some support of higher-level fighters, I thought I could take on the supercannon. In a way, it was like a 'carrier' battlegroup. It was just so overpowered because I could lose the great attendant trees, without much risk. I could just add more!

Since the heroes were headed that way, I could strike at the supercannon at the same time, and that would improve my chances. So I mapped a path of [subsidiary trees] to execute that plan.

Meanwhile, further south, the heroes were now making their way back. Their path would likely bring them through New Freeka.

"Say, do you think these trees belong to Aeon?" Becky asked.

She looked at one of my [subsidiary trees] that was on a hill. There were some bushes and other plants nearby.

"I don't think so? It looked quite different." Ah, my intendent camouflage of tailoring the 'types' and 'species' of my subsidiary trees paid off!

"Didn't make sense that these trees somehow survive, though..."

"There are trees everywhere. You underestimate how resilient nature is at reclaiming wastelands."

"True, true." And the [hero-chat] popped up again.

"Hi, guys!" Astra's voice boomed. "I've got a task for all of you!"

"Huh."

"I've gotten my level ninety perk! And it's a [telecommunications tower]!"

"Oh, wow. That's fast. We haven't reached level ninety yet, although we fought a demon walker!" Harris frowned. "Anyway, so what's the task? Does it help us against the demons?"

"Yes. Yes, it does! So anyway, this world used to rely extensively on a kind of magical [messaging] system, something like SMS in our world, at least before the internet took over. So the demon king arrived, and that messed up the entire [messaging] network."

"Oh, it's just [messaging], isn't it? What's the big deal?" Harris frowned. "The guys I met all use couriers and scouts to deliver letters."

"It fucking matters, Harris. Instantaneous communication means real-time targeting of spells, real-time military coordination and cross-continental trade. It means you can find out where the demons are instantly by just asking! So my level ninety perk allows me to build [telecommunication towers], and this will restore the [messaging] function within the area. All these [telecommunication towers] are magically linked so this will also allow the nations to talk to each other again."

"Oh. I don't see the awesomeness, but sure. If it helps us against the demons..."

"So, the task is I'm going to send you five [deployment gems] via [hero cloudtrading]. These things will expand into the [telco towers]. But the catch is you need to find a place that has some protection, perhaps a city with strong magical protection or some ancient defensive matrixes left behind by the previous generations of heroes. If the towers go down, the [message] function goes down with it."

"Uh...can't the tower just stay with us permanently? I could protect it." Harris didn't seem keen.

"Well, how about the rest of the world, then? The range of each of these [towers] isn't that big. At most, one or two countries. We need to spread it as much as we can. If you can find places with some kind of magical supply, or leyline, even better because the magical energies will amplify the [telco tower]'s range."

"That's not good. The demons want those kinds of spots, too," Becky responded.

Astra just chuckled. "Well, if you guys get your level ninety perks, you'll get some kind of structure, too. I think Helen's level ninety perk was a [healing tower] that also has a garrisoned army of magical knights."

"So, you're saying we need to get our level ninety perks, then use our [towers] to protect your [telco tower]?"

"Yup. That's part of the strategy we were going for. Like Gerrard's level ninety tower was a cannon tower that shoots stuff at any demons in range."

Then five gems appeared next to Becky.

"One last thing, it's activated via star-mana. All right, gotta go. Got a battle coming up in a few hours." And [hero-chat] disappeared.

"Level ninety perks?" Harris looked around. They were camped near one of my subsidiary trees.

"I wonder why our leveling was slower... We seem to be fighting just as much as them," Becky said as they munched over some barbequed rabbits.

"It's just a few levels. We're already in our level eighties!" Mirei shrugged. "Don't think about it too much. Maybe they killed more demon generals than we did."

"I guess."

Becky stretched and yawned. "Well, I for one, am very much look forward to going back to New Freeka. I can't wait to see Lady Mika again. There is so much I want to ask her!"

Harris smiled. "Yeah. And proper beds! I will kill a thousand demons for a proper bed right now."

"Me too."

YEAR 83 MONTH 11

"They want us to host their families..."

"I recall we have answered that request before." Jura frowned. "They were welcome as regular guests, but no special treatment. That means no 'special area' where existing New Freekan law does not apply to them."

"I understand this time it's temporary, Counsel Jura. We can have a small area set up for all these royals outside New Freeka, a temporary camp for them. The royals will handle their own camps... It's a united request from the envoys of the five countries. The heroes will destroy the demonic monster soon, and the royals will return back to their respective homes..."

"I'm afraid that still sounds like they want their own enclave. Honestly, it sounds like a no. But for you, I will consult Aeon for his views," Jura answered to the councilor.

"I have informed them that in no way this will affect New Freeka or Aeon's sovereignty over this valley. The royals acknowledge they are here as guests...it's just that they want to continue their life of privilege..."

Jura sighed. This was the second time they asked. Or maybe it was the third. Perhaps there were more instances where the request went through other channels. "TreeTree, what's your view?"

"They are guests, nothing more. Follow the rules and they can stay. Behave improperly and they will feel my wrath. Whatever privilege granted is in a personal capacity, but not by law."

The politics behind this request was frankly rather simple. Not all capitals had the kind of magical protection that some kingdoms did. Some of the older kingdoms like Barsoom had a wealth of inherited artifacts from heroes of a different era, and those artifacts powered various shields and barrier magic.

Survival.

It struck fear into the hearts of royals. The thought of dying in your own palace from a magical projectile from far away.

Maybe it was like us; someday, we would die to an asteroid we could do nothing about.

"They are willing to bend over backward for your protection, TreeTree," Jura explained. "Some of them are already here, secretly. I hear one of the young princes of Rajahskan is already living with one of the merchants here. 'Smuggled,' I hear, since it didn't sound good to some nobles if the princes were seen fleeing."

Well, Ivy told me about some strange foreigners, escorted by a small group of knights. But I supposed they didn't seem 'dangerous' to warrant any action.

"Indeed. No unusual behavior detected, other than complaining about everything to the merchant. But it seemed the prince's minders were managing him. They have all been advised to remain within their respective premises."

Well, I did say they could come if they could behave themselves. "They?"

Ivy then responded, "There was also a princess and prince from one of the Nung houses." Ah, Nung. That country had a few 'sub-kingdoms' within a 'kingdom.' Weird practice. Not too interested to find out more.

Jura frowned. "Looked like some of the earlier messages from the envoys have gotten out."

"Who else?"

"A few princes and princesses, a queen from one of the city states down south..." Jura explained. "Some lords, ladies, and dukes, too. It's quite a big list, apparently."

Okay. I wasn't exactly keen on hosting a 'royal' or 'elite' party, but my word was law, and I had said they were permitted to visit, so long as they did not do anything funny.

"Trevor, hand over some of your tasked to Stratreegy. Stratreegy, we can hold off on the rod for now, since we already have one [Forest Rod]. Trevor, I want you to help Ivy with observation of the royals. I do not intend to have these royals prance about my valley like they own it."

"Acknowledged."

"So...?" Jura was oblivious about my conversation with Ivy and Trevor. "Do you think we should set up a special quarter for them? Some of the councilors think that was a good choice."

"That was special treatment. Let them find their own accommodation. I am not creating a special district or allowing them to have a special tent area just for royals. And there is probably going to be a fight. They stay among us, and if they act up, I want the Order on them."

It was then that there was a knock on the door. "Counsel Jura, may I come in?" It was Madeus.

"Sure."

Madeus looked uneasy. "Counsel Jura...I received a request from royal court of Barsoom."

Jura frowned. He knew where this was going. "Oh? They survived the attack, I recall?"

"Indeed, but the ancient shield matrix of the grand palace will not be recharged within a week. It takes at least two months for that matrix to come up again. The royals now fear a second strike..."

"And they would like to be here..."

"It was as you say, Counsel. They...wish to hide it out until the heroes slay the demons."

I was not quite keen on being the 'swiss alpine hideout' or the 'nuclear bunker' of the rich and powerful. Seriously. But then again, I also believed in the 'free movement' of living beings. After all, what were boundaries in nature? Animals roamed the terrain all the time, and did lions bother about little rats moving into their realm? Did trees and forests care which animals hunted in their woods? So if these people came over like any other, I didn't believe in stopping them. I just wouldn't go out of my way to help.

"Yes, temporary. Barsoom was greatly indebted after what we did for the young princess a few years back, and they would like to offer various perks if we do protect them."

"No special treatment, Madeus. If we take from Barsoom and do not take from the others, I do not think that is a fair trade. Nor is New Freeka in any kind of diplomatic arrangement with Barsoom, whether as an ally or in a mutual defense pact," Jura answered. "I believe TreeTree has similar views, but I'm afraid you will have to accommodate the Barsoom royals in your own quarters or with any of your merchant friends. Or the hotels…"

Madeus sighed. "Ah…I was hoping to use the Order's guesthouses. With Oakwood Hotel gone, there is really no place fit for royals in this town."

"That would be us taking sides, Madeus. The councilors will use this against us. I am sure you understand."

Madeus was silent for a moment, then he nodded. "I-I will relay the message." He left.

Jura sighed. "I think Madeus got offered an amnesty of some kind. I think. But I do agree with your position. New Freeka's position as a uniquely neutral place was made possible thanks to you, TreeTree. So the Order cannot be seen as taking sides, especially with a party that's not formally allied with us. But perhaps, TreeTree, if any of the nations do want an alliance or treaty of some kind, would you consider it?"

"I would, but truly, it's all about the terms."

"With all the royals coming over, it might be a good time to talk about what would be a dealbreaker and what's a must have,"

Jura said and then took out a notebook. "I am certain discussion about alliances would come up, and I'd have to do some...sensing of what the other kingdoms were willing to give."

"I will refuse any alliance requiring me personally to protect their lands. And I will not take part in any offensive war between kingdoms."

Hmm. Actually, was that wise? Maybe I should ask the question to Jura instead.

"No. Ignore that. I do not want to be dragged into any conflict with other nations or between nations. What kind of treaty will allow that?"

Jura tapped on the notebook. "Well, that rules out any 'alliance' or 'mutual defense pact,' since being in a group means there are countries that are outside of a group, and a conflict will emerge one way or another, which, inevitably, you will get involved."

"Oh."

"We'll just have to survive on our own, like we always have." Jura smiled and happily sipped on his hot tea. There was a cold wind blowing outside. Once again, winter came far too quickly. "Honestly, I like it that way, too."

Hmm...that didn't sound right. I did think making connections and alliances were a good thing, but I thought my issue essentially was that...these nations...I didn't think I'd ever be able to 'rely' on them. There was something about alliances with nations that felt...fickle. These nations, with their millions of citizens and changing leaders, could I make a deal with them that would last hundreds of years? After all, it'd be a major waste of my personal time and energy if I allied with a nation that probably lasted only ten years.

I thought I would prefer individual deals with powerful individuals who could hold up their end of the bargain than with nations as a whole and the political complexity that entailed.

Perhaps I should seek out other 'spirits' and make alliances with them instead? At the very least, as fellow long-lived beings, our arrangements would last...longer.

Did that make me 'speciesist?" Or spiritist? Ah, I should really extend my trees to the Lilypod city...then I could talk to another spirit. Maybe other spirits had experiences on this matter?

Was there some ancient alliance of ancient spirits I could apply to?

"There were murmurs of unhappiness in the ground," Trevor and Ivy reported.

"Oh? So quickly?"

"These royals didn't take long to make their displeasure apparent to their hosts, and their hosts were rattled and were now pressuring the councilors to do more to appease them."

Ngeh. "Like what?"

"One of them wants to go hunting in the woods...and were requesting the councilors to permit them access."

Hmm. How should I handle this? Perhaps this was a good time to send some fear into the royals, else they would constantly badger them.

"Well, if that prince was up for it, let him into the woods. Let's see how he likes...ghosts."

The heroes finally arrived.

"What? How'd a hotel like Oakwood just...vanish?" Harris grumbled. "And why were all the hotels so full?"

"You must be new here," the innkeeper responded. "New Free-ka's the safest place in all of the central continent! Aeon, our great protector, blocked many, many shots from the vile, monstrous demons! Naturally, those who can afford it want to be here! It's safe, and there are secure food sources!"

"No wonder you look rich." Becky frowned. "This was ridiculous."

"Ah...a safety premium is naturally to be expected. Did you think safety comes free?" The innkeeper laughed. Eh, I didn't recall charging that sort of tax, but I guessed I could consider it. A protection fee. But that made me like those cheap gangsters that extorted money. But then again, that was what the government did, right? It was only 'who' and 'how the 'protection' was charged.

If I was the local government, then did I have that right?

"Do we have to camp in this place?"

"Maaaaaaaaaaaaaaaan. This sucks. I was sooooooo looking forward to meeting Lady Mika again. It's so strange that she just... vanished." Mirei kicked a pebble on the floor. There was a lot of roots on the ground, and they formed into 'steps.'

"If you miss her so much, I hear she left some notes for the hospitality guild and the Valtrian Order. And the adventurers' guild. Maybe you can check with them whether she left anything for you?"

Harris nodded. "Okay. Let's check with the adventurer's guild first..."

Indeed. Meela left them a note. I wondered what it said.

"Huh, she had to move north because of some personal commitments..."

"Really? So sudden? And how does she even move north with so many demons? Did she mean north of this continent, or north...where?"

"I don't know. She didn't say. But she did leave some instructions." The three heroes walked to one of the treefolk's wooden homes.

"Ah, you must be the chaps Lady Mika asked me to host. Come in, come in." An aged treefolk female greeted them. She was one of Meela's former employees. She let them into her house, a small place in one quiet corner of New Freeka's bustling town.

"Sorry for bothering you..."

"It's fine, Lady Mika left a bit of money for all the trouble. And here's a box of things she wanted me to leave for you..."

A wooden box. It was small, probably no bigger than a shoebox.

"Oooo...fancy amulet!" Becky opened. "And books?"

They opened it and started reading. And I cursed internally. I couldn't read with [spirit vision].

———

They rested for a day. They went to the market the next day.

"Where do we even start?" Becky looked a bit lost.

"The merchants selling ores and stuff, at least." Harris pointed, and they walked over, glancing at the things.

"Crystals, right?" Mirei seemed equally puzzled. The merchant said the price, and the three heroes glanced at each other. "Discount?"

They haggled.

And eventually they bought some. And then they went to one of the many blacksmiths and forges and rented one of furnaces. They spent a good four to five hours in there, seemingly trying to work at the crystal and use their star-mana.

I overheard them complain about how tiring it was, and eventually they emerged with a small crystal dagger.

They admired their hard work for a bit and then concluded that they all need to spend more time on their work.

Then we all sensed it. A shot from the demonic supercannon.

At me. At them.

They ran out of the furnace, but they were too slow.

But I wasn't taking chances. Five [steelwood barriers] emerged midair, suspended and supported by roots and vines. And it absorbed the shot easily, crushing the first four barriers as expected.

Then the demonic supercannon fired again.

And I blocked.

And another shot.

I blocked it, too. I wasn't going to let the shot ruin my beautiful, growing valley of giant trees.

Then it was quiet. Harris, Becky, and Mirei all shared glances.

"First time?" some passerby asked. He was probably oblivious they were heroes. Then again, it wasn't like they publicly declared they were heroes.

The three didn't reply.

"Yeah. Those loud booms are scary, but it's happened a few times already." The pedestrian shrugged. "Anyway, don't block the road?"

The three quickly shuffled out of the way. The three of them looked at each other. "Guess we know where to put our first tower."

"Agree."

The three walked to the Valtrian Order's premises...and they bumped into Lausanne.

"Oh, Lady Lausanne, nice to see you again." Lausanne was similarly equipped for war. Her new living weapon was now about level fifteen or so.

Lausanne just nodded. "Hi. Rematch?"

"Ah...not today. We'd like to meet Counsel Jura. We were told that Counsel Jura can assist us if we want to place an object in New Freeka..."

"By who?" Lausanne led them to Jura's main office.

"Oh...Lady Mika."

And they were in Jura's room.

"Pleased to meet you, Counsel Jura." The three bowed. "We're the summoned heroes...from the other world. We'd like the Order and Aeon's permission to deploy a magical artifact, a tower that restores [message] to the region..."

"Can I see the artifact?"

Becky walked over and passed the small gem to Jura. Jura looked at it and then placed it into a circular bowl that waws actually connected to [magic lab] for analysis.

[Analyzing...]

The analysis wasn't very useful, since my [magic lab] didn't seem to be able to look very deeply into the composition of the item. Indeed, it looked to be magically linked to the heroes, in from what little I could see, the heroes could take down the towers once they didn't need it.

It was...surprisingly similar to a [subsidiary tree] in theory. In short, my understanding seemed to be that the heroes had these 'towers,' they acted as 'extensions' of themselves, and like [subsidiary trees], these towers functioned primarily to 'create' a magical lighthouse for [message] spells.

"What else does it do, other that restore [message]? Does it allow you to filter through the messages?" Jura asked. If we were to depend on the heroes' infrastructure for communication, did that not mean we owe them? Was that why there was all these concerns over network infrastructure providers.

Then again, it was a short-term thing. While I could use my network of [subsidiary trees] to monitor my domain, restoring the [message] network meant a return of the trade routes, which was important to get the materials needed for my subordinates' upgrades.

"Aeon's agreeable, but only until the death of the demon king. After that, he may decide to destroy the tower."

"That's acceptable to us. Can Aeon shield it from the demon's attacks?"

"He...will try."

"Good enough. Where should we put it?"

"In the town square."

The telco tower was deployed. It was a white crystalline tower about four stories high and shone like with a faint white glow that was unmistakable, visible even in my own [spirit vision]...

And it was then it occurred to me.

Did the demons have some kind of [spirit vision], but tuned to heroes instead? Perhaps it was like how vision was different for animals and humans because of the spectrum we saw.

The heroes sent a message to Astra as a test, and they left two days later.

YEAR 83 MONTH 12

Despite the raging winter, the heroes still pressed on. Together with their summoned armies, they mounted an attack on the supercannon. And the supercannon annihilated their summoned armies easily. They were then forced to retreat.

At this point, I was tempted to ask…how'd they think it'd go?

It was winter, where, strangely, demons suffered none of the challenges of winter, and yet the mortal defenders of the world suffered all of it. Cold, slower response times, and their summoned units were immune to cold, but seriously, did they think that cannon that shot across the continent couldn't aim at their armies?

"That was stupid." The three looked at each other.

"I know, but you said we should."

"I blame all the people we've been meeting, telling us we should kill the demon beast as soon as possible."

"Why'd we do it?"

"Because we all somehow agreed to?"

The advantages of a summoned army were that once your mana returned, you could just summon more. And that was what they did to hold the 'chasing' demons back.

There were plenty.

Demonic generals or elites wielded massive axes. It was the best opponent because they could gain levels from them.

If I were the demon king, what would I have done?

In a way, should I ignore the heroes and just keep attacking all the kingdoms with conventional demonoids, such that the heroes gradually lost the ability to find any kind of shelter, food source, learning, or support and healing?

Or was it better to concentrate all my energies and create super-demons, and just attack once when the heroes were low leveled and kill them all?

One super-demon, and that was it. No subordinates or walkers, since they gained levels by killing them.

Why give them the chance to gain levels?

YEAR 83 MONTH 12 (CONTINUED)

While the heroes decided to rethink their strategy, here in New Freeka, we had to fend off the little swarms of demons sent to 'surround' the heroes.

And I spent quite a bit of time tinkering with the heroes' tower. As I kept poking and trying to figure out what it was, I got a good update.

*[**Biolab, material lab, and magic lab upgraded**. Field equipment obtained. You are now able to perform investigations of objects using field equipment. Full analysis requires more comprehensive equipment.]*

There was a layer of somewhat-divine magic protecting it, so I reckoned it'd take more than one hit of the demon's supercannon to be destroyed. Certainly not as fragile as they said it was. Or maybe it was just fragile to certain kinds of demonic energies or heroes' star mana. That same divine magic also shielded it from me attempting to make 'changes' or 'convert' or 'claim' the tower.

Yet it was a 'change' barrier. That meant I could look into it but not change a thing.

And look I did.

There was a lot to see, about how it wove magic and mana into a structure like that, how it drew mana from the ambient surrounding and the connection, however wireless it was, to its 'creator.'

Unlike my [subsidiary trees], which form a linked network, all connected by roots, these towers were independent, free-standing structures, yet had a 'connection.' And it was more complex than just some kind of 'wifi.' It was almost like...they were 'entangled' in some surreal way. As if it was resonating with something else far away, and yet...it emitted or absorbed nothing through the air.

Stumped. I observed and looked for days.

It was as if I'd invented a bow, and right here was an interstellar rail gun.

How did I even replicate such a thing?

How did the heroes even come up with such a thing?

It certainly felt like impossible that young kids would know how these things were, so...were the gods creating such objects and skills and 'implementing' or 'executing' them via the heroes? Or was this a system thing, where there was like a 'drawer' or 'library' of hero-grade skills that they got access to?

Stumped again, I looked at other parts of the tower, my vines growing around the base. I attempted to use my vines and what powers I had and even my long-forgotten [inspection] ability.

Perhaps the resonance was how it communicated with other towers, but the means which it acted as a conduit or 'router' for messages was something less 'sophisticated.' Or not.

At this point, could I just build a massive X-ray or MRI scanner around the tower so I could see what was inside?

"Mom, Uncle Jura. I've got to go."

"TreeTree says no."

"I know he said that...but...but I want to go. I believe it's good for my own growth, to see how I fare. I want to know where I am."

"You know where you are, you're here!" Laufen was furious and worried. "Your place is here."

"I know my place is here. But...I...erm...I want to measure my strength. I won't die. Trust me, Mom."

Well, the heroes, utilizing the now-restored [message] network, requested for help. And they asked for Lausanne to help with the attack on the demon supercannon. Not just her, of course. A lot more than her.

"You're not a hero, Lausanne." Laufen held her daughter. "Don't do this."

"But..." Lausanne sulked. "I want to go, Mom. Please."

"No."

"I'm fourteen and almost level sixty. I can help."

"Men higher level than you have tried fighting demon champions and died."

"They...they don't have TreeTree's powers. Or Thorny." She pointed to the wooden staff on her belt. "We can do it."

Laufen sighed. "TreeTree, can you talk some sense into my daughter?"

In my mind, should I let Lausanne go? Though I spent a lot of effort in grooming and training Lausanne, ultimately, should she be able to decide how she wants to wield that power? Lausanne's turn to retaliate. Maybe she was fourteen and having a teenage rebellious age? Oh I sounded like my mom; my mom used to tell me I was rebellious.

I thought what Laufen was afraid of was death. With a few well-placed giant attendant trees, I thought I could ensure Lausanne's survival. So if I could do so, would it be a good idea for her to join the battle?

Maybe...maybe it was a good lesson in the brutality and the high levels that the heroes walked. A dose of reality. And I could use the chance to attack the demon supercannon with some of the roots, masked as coming from her...

I should let her earn her right to participate rather than just say yes.

"Lausanne, there are a lot of demons coming from that direction. Among them, there are probably a few demon generals. If you take down three, I think you can take part. And I want you to restrict your familiar use to only two abilities."

Laufen sighed. "TreeTree, what?"

"It's training. If she can take on a few more demon generals, then she earned her right to participate. If she can't handle the generals, she shouldn't bother trying."

"Yes! So...I'll go hunt some demons!"

Laufen shook her head. "I-I wasn't expecting that."

Jura shrugged. "I like that, though. Want me to go with her?"

"She can go with the initiates."

"Someone's gonna have to babysit the rest of the initiates..." Well, eventually, Yvon wanted to go. The mission was simple. Between us and the demon supercannon, there were about ten to fifteen groups of demons, led by the knights and generals. With an attendant tree in place, a beetle force would engage the demons, and Lausanne could then challenge the knights and generals. Yvon and a group of other captains would help out.

She went all out.

I guessed a part of her wanted to know that the gap between herself and the heroes wasn't that big. A path that was honestly going to fail. Even Jura couldn't keep up with the heroes, though he could probably give them a bit of trouble.

Still, it was winter, and it was hard to get the beetles to operate effectively far from the attendant trees, even with the [winter adaptations] and the giant trees warming the environment with the [heat transmission roots].

So, Lausanne complained and grumbled, but there wasn't much she could do. She couldn't take on an entire army herself, nor did she have a summoned army at her beck and call.

YEAR 84 MONTH 1

The presence of royalty, many living in the homes of the wealthy merchants here, made the political environment a little bit touchy.

Mainly because the councilors each sought out the royals for some 'shoulder-rubbing,' or as the euphemism went, 'building relationships.' It was a sensible thing from their perspective, since royals by nature had strong skills. A prince or a princess could bestow 'royal' privileges, blessings, and rights, improve or upgrade classes, and even create 'gifts' using their powers as royals. There were also certain 'unique classes' that only royals with the right skills could grant.

Like one prince I observed had the ability to create a custom 'diplomatic gift' out of midair, which was given to the princess of another country. And it was a permanent item, too. It was like the prince skipped the entire 'creation' process, activated skill, and the system gave him an item.

It was not totally strange, of course. Apparently some merchants and bankers could create small quantities of gold, and some smiths and makers could create materials, too.

In a way, it was like how I created 'timber' and 'fruits.' It was different derivations of the same kind of 'mana/system to item' process. If I could create wooden items, why couldn't princes? Maybe heroes could make hero-items, too!

So, with the councilors spending a bit more time trying to 'manage' or 'please' these visiting royals, that meant conflict. Even between councilors as they 'served' different groups.

Some of them were rather silly, like competition of the best seats or rooms in New Freeka's restaurants or who managed to book out the entire bar or tavern for their respective entourage. It was like billionaires trying to one-up one another in a ski town. Silly, so I didn't interfere with this.

The more annoying ones were the horny ones, or those with a fetish. There was an old duke or something who seemed to enjoy picking on young elven ladies, so I sent a group of beetles into his temporary residence.

It scared him.

But the councilor who was supposedly his 'buddy' quickly came and complained to Jura.

And I sent beetles and spiders into his house, too.

After that incident, I decided it was probably best to amplify my show of force, to remind these royals that they were…'visitors.' So we had more beetles around New Freeka. The locals were clearly not too bothered by the presence, but for the 'foreigners,' it was a threat. I intended it to be a threat.

The councilors bore the brunt of the complaints. "What were all these monsters roaming around your town!"

"They are Aeon's servants, and they execute his will. Please don't say too much! Aeon listens!" The councilors quickly tried to manage some of the more belligerent royals or nobles.

"So what if he listens?" It turned out, among the royals, many truly, truly believed that I was actually just a puppet, a beast used by the council, controlled by some great item or equipment. The idea of an existence above the royal class was…alien to them. Except heroes, who were 'divine,' those the only ones royals viewed as 'equals.'

Generally, of course. And I supposed in the history of this

world, existences like mine were not common or perhaps even if they did exist, they may not have the same 'mindset' as I did.

Perhaps they were slumbering giants, a sleeping mountain. Or they were giant tortoises, the zaratans, although they carried massive cities on their backs, the zaratans were treated just like the captains of a cruise ship. The rulers of the cities still ruled, and their rule was supreme.

So, feeling a bit annoyed at all the murmurs and chattering, one massive projectile from the demon supercannon came.

And this time, I intentionally blocked it just enough that it smacked right into the [telco tower]. The telco tower was fine, of course. I calculated it just enough that it wouldn't be destroyed.

But I wanted to borrow the attack to weaken the divine protections, so I could look a bit more into it.

And, at the same time, scare the councilors and royals. The earth shook, and I had a wooden barrier created around it such that the blast radius was limited to the town square. Beetles, my vines, and roots had cleared the square of all citizens.

Jura was quick to figure out what I was doing. "TreeTree, that was intentional?"

"Yes."

Jura laughed and then went out to make an announcement to the council.

"Aeon would like to remind that he finds the conduct of the visitors appalling, and he is tempted to not stop the next projectile from the demons. He would like to recommend the visitors are brought to the blast site for a tour."

The councilors roared in protest. "Is he threatening us?"

Jura just smiled. "Yes. He is. What were you going to do about it?"

One councilor sat. "Oh. Nothing."

I thought it was just a people thing, that after living in comfort for a while, they forgot that there was still a war and demons shooting bullets everywhere. Especially for some of these nobles who didn't seem like they'd ever seen war, even though it was just so common.

Or maybe they were just desensitized to war and death, since it was so common.

Huh.

Since war and death was bound to happen, might as well have my share of fun, go on a power trip and all since we were all going to die.

I felt like I suddenly understood some of these royals. Sure, yes, we were going to die. We knew that. So why couldn't I do things my way? If the meaning of life was me just...hiding away like this, why bother?

Were these royals nihilists? Or was it some other word?

Lausanne spent time trying to hunt for more demon generals. The winter was gradually clearing, and at certain parts of the region where it was warmer, she finally took down one demon general herself.

Still, the goal was three, so she had to hunt for two more. And later in the month, she took down another one, bringing her total kills to two.

Meanwhile, the heroes were out gathering a strike force, again. Similar to what that other kingdom did, the strike force was meant to be an elite force, to help punch a path through to the demon supercannon, so that they could attack it directly.

As it was, they could already punch a way through, but between the summoned army and their OP skills used to get through the chaff, they didn't have much star mana left to actually take on the main body of the demon supercannon.

"I heard that you might be king."

"Where'd you hear that?" Roma asked. He was a quiet, studious young boy. Despite Yvon's attempts to train him in fighting, his interests were more into magic and reading. Although he was healthy and fit, physical combat wasn't his thing. He didn't inherit Yvon or Prince Galan's talent in fighting.

"The others were talking. I even heard one of the actual princes say it when one of their servants came to buy some bread," the black-haired baker boy said. He had a small knife at the side.

Roma sighed. "Mom told me about it, but I can't accept it yet. Some of her friends asked whether I want to travel to Ransalah... What do you think? Should I be king?"

"I think you'd make a good king," the baker boy said. "Then I can be your king's guard."

"You can't even fight." Roma laughed.

"Well, you've never ruled," the baker boy ribbed Roma. "Besides, all I need is your mom to teach me some tricks. I heard she's really good."

"We might die."

"Or you'll just be working as one of the employees of the Valtrian Order, and I'll just be an ordinary baker. Why live, if not for honor and glory?"

"You've been reading too much of your uncle's writings."

"You've been reading too much."

Salah was now ruled by a regent. One surviving archduke took the position of regent to govern the state of Salah. Apparently, it was quite normal for the succession wars to only commence after the demon king was slain, and if a king fell without an appointed successor, a proper 'contest' for the right of the throne would start when the demon king was slain, something the regent would announce. After all, it was hard to properly choose a king in a time of chaos. At least, that was the 'principle' of such a rule.

I supposed kings did die quite often when the demon king was around, so there was already a cultural norm for it.

In theory, that meant Roma had time to prepare. That also meant everyone else had time to prepare.

In practice, whoever the ruling regent preferred had tremendous advantages, since this was the time where all the 'things' and 'pieces' could be put in place. Still, the regents would obey the norm because to some extent, obeying the norms was what allowed the [heir] to convert their class to [king]. Weird system rules like that, or so it was believed.

Or maybe nobody tested whether that 'norm' was actually a requirement of the title [king] or whether it was just a product of whether the citizens of the kingdom acknowledged the [heir] as the true [king].

Things I learned from eavesdropping on Yvon's conversations with her advisors.

YEAR 84 MONTH 2

Lausanne finally killed two more demon generals, so her total kills was four. And she gained some levels while she was at it.

"Can I go now? Please?"

Laufen was similarly reluctant, but then privately, I told Laufen I'd look after her. With my assurance, Laufen agreed.

If it went well, I'd even get some experience out of playing a small part.

And I was getting quite annoyed with all the shots fired at me. I wondered whether I could do like some kind of kung-fu stunt where an attack was deflected back at the demon. Like how so many manga main characters were able to do to show off their insane overpoweredness.

In honesty, the heroes were just about 'ready' with their force, too, and they were already prepared to strike the demon supercannon, with or without Lausanne. So Lausanne's arrival at the battlefield was just on time. Just to be sure, I placed a few [giant attendant trees] in the vicinity as a 'retreat-point' for Lausanne.

The battle against the supercannon went well, all things considered. The heroes successfully destroyed the supercannon with their [star mana] abilities, but the cost was...a whole load of deaths, mainly from the adventurers and military leaders that decided to take part in the attack.

Lausanne returned from the battle bloody, and there was a look of despair on her face. I was there, and perhaps there was something about watching the demon supercannon's explosions incinerate people up close that just...uh...felt brutal. It wasn't the first time she'd seen death. She had seen death when she fought the demon walker.

It was, as expected, the despair of realizing how high the mountain was.

Laufen, of course, gave her daughter a hug. "It's okay. You're blessed by TreeTree, he's just one tree spirit, but the heroes, they were blessed by all the gods."

Lausanne, of course, instantly perked up. "Mom! You're a genius!"

"Huh?"

"Aeon's blessings alone are not enough for me to be a hero!"

"What do you mean?"

"I will visit other spirits like TreeTree and get their blessings. If I can get multiple blessings, I will be as strong as them!"

YEAR 84 MONTH 3

With the demonic supercannon down, the royals and nobles quickly made their way home. Truth be told, I thought that was a bit premature. The supercannon was but one of many demon walkers that were on the continent, and the demon king seemed to be summoning more and more of them.

There were now supercannons on all continents.

The heroes, too, after defeating the supercannon and gaining levels, expanded the network of [telecommunication trees]. Indeed, all of them acquired level ninety [towers]. At this point, I honestly didn't see anything other than the demon king himself making a dent at the heroes progress, so I felt the demon king's stay in the world would last no longer than one year.

The restoration of the [messaging] network also brought a return of intercontinental news and trade, something we sorely needed. The first thing I did, of course, was order all my upgrade materials I needed. Lausanne's Living Weapon, Thorny, reached level twenty and was level capped until I got the materials needed to upgrade him.

Then there was also the issue of Lausanne's new bright idea.

She wanted to visit other tree spirits and things like that.

Perhaps it was similar to the old elven pilgrims that used to visit the great elf tree-guardians, even if just to acknowledge their role in the protection of the elven capital.

"Traveling in this environment is quite difficult, and…we will need you here for defense," Jura explained his views. He was fine with it, but he preferred if Lausanne waited till after the demon king was slain. Elves lived for many, many years, and Lausanne could always compare herself to future heroes.

Lausanne, of course, agreed. She was smart, and she was patient. There was also much about the outside world she didn't know about, so she agreed, on the condition that Jura and everyone else included her on trips to nearby kingdoms if they ever went on those visits. She had to learn how to conduct herself in foreign lands, after all.

In principle, I agreed with Lausanne's idea, and I would even like to tag along such that I could also communicate with the other spirits. In short, Lausanne was going to be my envoy to the spirits. I, too, had much to learn about the spirits of this world; my experience had solely been through my own lenses and what little I learned from the dead.

The destruction of the demon supercannon also brought about a period of rejuvenation. Throughout the areas where my [subsidiary trees] and [giant attendant trees] were, trees were starting to regrow, and that made me happy. It was nice to see little trees starting to pop up next to my bigger trees or a little field of flowers or grass.

I got significant enjoyment from having new grasses or trees join my network of trees. Increasingly, it was the tree part of me that found joy in this. Or perhaps it was just Trevor and the gang's enjoyment?

The refugee situation temporarily subsided now that [message] and the demon supercannon's death spread. There was something about uncertainty that added to that fear, so with open communications restored, those living in different places no longer lived in darkness. It was just a thing about knowledge that allowed people to make better decisions.

All in all, with the royals and nobles making their way out.

YEAR 84 MONTH 4

The heroes were out hunting for the other demon bases. There were many throughout the continent, but at least they knew where to look for them. Benefits of real-time communication.

As for me, I turned my focus to further studies of the telco tower. I wasn't getting much insight into how it stayed 'synchronized' with the other towers, but with the help of more lab equipment around the tower and 'attempting' to intercept magical [messages], over time, I started to figure out what was happening.

The [Telco Tower] had multiple components to it. The other parts were a form of 'demonic barrier' that created a 'safe zone' for messages going to the sender and from the sender. These repelled the effects of the demon king's global ability. Second was a kind of 'repeater,' where the Telco Tower received a message and sent it to someone else but within the same 'tower-range.' For longer range and continental messages, that went through the somewhat quantum-entangled communications that existed between the towers.

Of all of those, I decided to focus on the 'aura' repelling the demon king. It was the easiest for me to study, and in many ways, similar to my [lesser demonic suppression aura]. I reckoned the similarities would help me in understanding what exactly was happening.

And my suspicions were rewarded because, after some poking and thinking, I had a notification.

[Demonic Ability Reduction Aura - lesser obtained]

Yay!

Feeling a bit accomplished, I went back to the hex wasteland. Apparently, the heroes had been sending a whole load of messages to all the kings and leaders they could contact to stop using the [hexbomb] because it made their work a lot harder, since it would disrupt their travel paths.

I thought heroes would have some resistance, but maybe it was just caution on their part.

The hex had been a significant stumbling block in my research, mainly because the [hex] was the 'byproduct' of some kind of 'magical ritual,' and it was like I was trying to guesstimate what exactly happened in the ritual to know what 'created' a nasty side effect like hex. It was as if someone gave me a piece of plastic, asked me how that plastic was made, and which process gave the plastic the qualities it possessed.

So, I did want to observe a [blood ritual] for myself.

If the 'nuclear fusion' theory had any relevance, the blood ritual should be some kind of incomplete process that 'created' this...monstrosity.

In my mind, I had a clear, obvious reason for researching the hex. I couldn't help but suspect that one day, some country was going to think I was no better than the demon king and use this same [hexbomb] against me. This horrid poison that corrupted the land just offended the trees and vegetation in every way possible, even more that the magically tainted poop. So much so that I got 'feelings of anger' through the [rootnet].

If a forest could react in anger to a factory spewing poison into its lands, I guessed that was how it felt.

Even though it repulsed me, I steeled myself and placed one [subsidiary tree] right into a pool of hex.

It was a risk, but somehow…I felt like I had to reach into it.

And then I felt my mind assaulted and overwhelmed by strange, twisted emotions and memories. Death. Pain. Suffering. Love. Hope. It lasted for a good two hours, a short flicker of a moment for me; my various [root brain complexes] and [The Grand Mind Tree] all instantly kicked in and 'worked' hard to allay those invading memories and emotions. It was not all bad, but it was all kinds of emotions, both positive and negative, warped in some way or form or joined together.

At the same time, I witnessed my [subsidiary tree] rot from the root upward, its bark and trunk turning brittle before breaking up by bits and pieces. It took a while, and after that two hours and I'd regained emotional control, I soon used the root brains and mind tree to 'invade' into the subsidiary tree.

It was too late.

The [subsidiary tree] was dead; it crumbled and turned into dust.

Yet it was not all wasted.

The hex, as we saw it, shrunk a little bit.

Ah. Typical of blood rituals. It was essentially an emotion-memory conversion into power, and so 'fixing' the hex meant 'facing' those emotions head on and unwinding them. But that still didn't answer the 'underlying' force. Was it still some kind of soul mechanism? Or did emotions and memories have their own power?

I supposed the true way to 'fix' the hex was to connect a root to it and run it through the root minds and [the grand mind tree]?

―――

"So, did you ask your mom?"

"About what?"

"About teaching me how to fight."

Roma frowned. "You should stick to baking."

"Easy for you to say," the black-haired boy responded. "I only have my granny to look after me."

"I only have my mom."

"And her army of loyalists and servants." The black-haired boy was sharp, and there was indeed an army of loyalists. Even now, there were two 'guards' tasked to watch after Roma.

Roma sighed. "Fine, I'll ask her to teach you something."

"Yay! I can't wait to hit someone with one of the long, hard breads!" Roma facepalmed, and the black-haired boy laughed. Indeed, Roma later did go see Yvon.

"Mom...I got a request... It's got nothing to do with books or magic." Yvon probably looked puzzled because it was quite rare for Roma to have requests outside those topics.

"What?"

"I-I have a friend. He...wants to learn how to fight, so, uh... could you...um...teaching him?" Roma asked awkwardly, and Yvon looked at her son. He twiddled his fingers even though he was already in his teens, and Yvon nodded.

"I won't have much time to teach him, with my duties at the Valthorn kids, but sure. Maybe he can start joining us for a few rounds of basic spars. I have open sessions with the newer Initiates."

―――

News from the distant continents came in, and the demon king was on the move. It seemed the heroes were quite successful in defeating the demon walkers and the demon supercannons, if they had an ability similar to Meela and Alexis's Star Mana-form. I reckoned that was probably a standard loadout for a hero.

The heroes were now trying to gather up somewhere and take down the rest of the demonic walkers. There were many; after all, this demon king was really fond of walkers, and so far, the heroes were successful, so much so that almost every three to four days we had news that another walker or supercannon had been destroyed. The heroes by now had moved out of my tree's observational range, and so any news about their movement was via [message].

A part of me thought, well, this was too easy. There must be something.

Was this it? Really? Was this the slow end of the demon king? The demon king that peaked early and then ended because it tried to attack all the continents at once?

I didn't think so. There must a trick. The demon king had been wandering continent to continent doing something. There must be a trap waiting for the heroes; there was no reason for demon king to just hang around idle when the heroes were still gaining strength.

The heroes must be expecting it, too; things had been going a bit too easy for them now that they'd unlocked star mana.

Oh well, let's just watch the show.

"Where has the demon king gone? Would anyone have any idea now that the message network is restored? Can we find out about all historical sightings of the demon king?"

Jura was getting better at guessing what I was trying to do, and he vaguely sounded like he sensed my concern. "I'll send out a request to the merchant's and mage's guilds."

Still, once I acquired the [demon ability reduction aura], that had an instant benefit because that aura pushed back against the demon's interference; doing so expanded the field of the beetle's range. After all, the beetles, being a form of 'summoned' creature, had little 'resistance' against demonic interference.

In fact, I wondered whether there was an [insect tamer] or [insect master] that would someday come up to me and 'mind control' one of my mindless beetles.

YEAR 84 MONTH 5

Treeiner leveled up quickly and gained some rather cool abilities. Like his level ten ability literally distorted his training room into a larger one. I wondered what his higher-tier abilities would be; a 'practice dungeon' would be quite cool.

That'd make him his own little dungeon core, wouldn't it?

A dungeon of our own for practice would be fantastic, since the Valthorn kids had expanded, and we were short of 'nannies' to look after them, and it didn't feel quite right to let their older, earlier students look after them with their limited life experience.

Even if the first generation of Valthorns, the first nine, were now all above level twenty, Lausanne being the exceptional one crossing level sixty, but her leveling was stagnating. She complained about it sometimes, and it was also partly why she wanted to find other ways of growing. Her living weapon was also level capped at level twenty, and the cool thing about Thorny was that, well, it literally gave her a barb armor. Still, it was nothing compared to the kind of star-mana weapons the hero wielded.

Lausanne was super proud of Thorny before this, but after the supercannon battle, she'd been working really hard. Apparently their star-mana weapons literally sliced through high-tier demons like a hot knife through butter. Things that she needed a full-powered strike to kill could be easily cut through.

I thought it was the level difference. They were, after all, in the level eighties to nineties, Lausanne was just sixty, and the gap of ten levels was extremely big. Like how thirty levels meant I could tank a demon walker a lot more comfortably than before.

Maybe if Thorny had the anti-demon abilities like I did, he'd cut through the demons like water, too!

Anyway, Lausanne's daily affairs consisted of training, helping, and guiding all the younger initiates who looked up to her. We'd had to build a dedicated compound for the Valthorns on top of the existing orphanage. With my new [Giant Attendant Trees], it really opened up the possibility of 'subsidiary cities' or 'suburbs.'

Maybe that was something I should do. With that in mind, I made an announcement to the Valthorns to find places suitable for an extra town. Perhaps somewhere close to a mine where I could do some mining using my deep roots.

Or somewhere with mana.

Or should I just ask them to settle down in the southwest forests, with my ThreeTrees of mana?

With the valley itself restricted, the forest now littered with the giant trees, New Freeka's expansion was forced toward the open plains, where all the enemy armies liked to march. New segments of town, new walls were built, as the city expanded to accommodate more and more refugees and new citizens.

According to Ivy's census data, she counted about seventy-two thousand people living in New Freeka's borders. Clearly a bit too cramped for some of them.

Yet the demons' continued presence meant the lack of space in New Freeka was a small bother. Out in other cities, there were constant issues of food shortages, so much so New Freeka had been sending food aid to the nearby kingdoms. It was a move by the Council, of course, since the Council's past efforts of building wineries, underground heated farms, underground silos, and our most recent underground self-sufficient hideouts meant a surplus of food even for the large number.

The council liked allies, and well, I didn't blame them. I wanted my own allies, too.

I needed to visit the giant lilypod. So I undid all the trees that I no longer needed and continued my long chain of trees toward it. I stopped previously when the heroes started their attack on the wounded demon walker.

It would take me a month or two to get there. But if Lausanne wanted to talk to another Tree Spirit, maybe I should do the introductions.

This was some time ago...

SIDE STORY
AROUND YEAR 83, MONTH 8

Harris, Becky, and Mirei weren't having a good time. If anything, the past few months had been absolutely terrible.

With demons crawling all over the continent, there was no journey that was ever safe. Almost every night, when they camped outside, they would be attacked. At first, it was stressful, but now, all three of them were now around level sixty. Thankfully, Becky's class as a [summoner] meant she had a magical guard that kept watch while all of them rested and slept.

"I wish we had nice beds." Mirei's number one complaint, almost every other night, was the lack of comfortable beds. Coming from another world, the significant decline in mattress quality was really getting to her. "It's absurd that the people in this world accept this bullshit."

They sat around a makeshift campfire. A lightning elemental was helping to barbeque the roasted meat.

"Let it go. At least we're not hungry." Harris nodded. They didn't like being hungry. They were hungry on some days, when they went through areas that were so devastated there was absolutely nothing to harvest or hunt. "Anyway, it should be any time now." The two girls came and sat on the logs next to him. They were friends, after all.

And the magical orb appeared again. [Hero Chat].

"Hey, guys. Everyone okay?" Astra asked from the other side of the screen. They could hold the chat for about one hour, so that meant they could really catch up. "Oh, hey, Harris, were you guys going to challenge the demon walker?"

Harris nodded. "We're supposed to rendezvous with an army from Salah. Apparently, it was part of the coalition army from this continent. But my scouts tell me things aren't great, the terrain around the demon walker has been absolutely wrecked by all the [blood rituals] that were used against it, so approaching it isn't that straightforward." Harris's summoned force was essentially an elite army in itself.

Another voice came out. Harris identified her as Helen, and she was in the north. "Yeah. We're trying to convince the locals to stop using the [blood magic] because it is making our attempts to approach the demons a lot harder. A few routes have been made unusable because of the [blood magic] used to bombard it. But it is quite hard to get that message across because the guys that fire the damned [blood magic] are not here anymore! It doesn't help that the kings used some kind of [charisma] or [charm] skill to convince all these guys to sacrifice themselves, and these guys have far too large an ego to accept that their decisions were wrong."

Mirei looked and pointed. She noticed Helen's background wasn't...outdoors. "Are you guys in an inn?"

Helen laughed at the question. "Hell yeah! Check out my lovely bed! I can't freaking stand camping outside. Thankfully we found a small town with an inn that's still standing! You cannot believe how few and rare independent inns are in this world, since all these traveler's inns are absolutely defenseless!"

It was laughter all the heroes shared, but all of them felt bittersweet. The pain of lacking proper rest and sleep was apparent to all twelve of them, even if the magic and drive from the god's blessing did constantly spur them on.

"All right, all right. We've got fifty minutes left. Let's start the recap. I've recently hit level sixty, too, and I've unlocked an [avatar]," Astra said. "It lets me create three 'copies' of myself that I can send elsewhere to do things, and it can cast all the spells I can, except those using [star mana]."

"We're all multi-unit heroes, aren't we?" Everyone had a summon or 'companion' force of some kind. Harris had 'scouts' and 'living armors;' Becky as a pure [summoner] had the most expansive force. She could singlehandedly summon fifteen hundred 'magical soldiers' to battle if she expended all her star mana.

"Fitting, since we are facing a 'war.' Anyone else not level sixty yet? Any interesting skills? Any new demon units we should be afraid of?"

"I fought the demon general you mentioned. Not as hard as I was made to believe."

"The locals generally exaggerate their strength. I reckon it's a level fifty threat."

Harris frowned. They hadn't been having easy fights. Were they doing something wrong? "Huh. Only one?" They fought a battle with six demon generals.

"Yup!"

"Uh...anyone have any clue where the demon king is?"

"Quite sure it's in the Southern Continent," Astra responded. "But I think it hasn't moved at all since it came to this world. I think it's...churning out walkers."

"Oh. Does that mean all of us need to head to the south?"

"Eventually, yes. Once we can get past the walkers on our continent... But who knows? Maybe the demon king will move. I heard them say the demon king moved from place to place for previous generations."

"Uh...that's a future thing. Let's focus. So...on the walkers..."

Everyone looked worried. At that point, they had not fought anything that powerful.

"Any tips for facing the walker?" Harris asked. "Anyone fought one since last week? There was one near you, Astra?"

"We're hoping you'd set the example, Harris. We do have plenty of walkers down here in the south, but somehow, they travel in pairs, so we have not yet attempted to fight them. You're facing one along, and that's probably the easiest fight available."

"Hey!" Mirei called out. "Why do we have to be first?"

Awkward silence. Harris frowned. Becky sighed. All of them received overpowered abilities and blessings from the gods, and here they were, arguing who should face the demon walkers first.

"Never mind, never mind. Time to share some knowledge." Astra needed to save time. "Did you know some kings have a [protective presence] ability that allows the use of [message] spells in their domain?"

One of the other heroes on the Eastern continent spoke. "But it only works for [messages] within the domain. I think there should be other kings or leaders with similar powers."

"Oh." Harris wasn't that interested, but he wondered whether that was how Aeon looked after his own domain, but that didn't seem to be the case. "Astra, what's the range of your [avatars]?"

"Huh?"

"Becky's squadrons can't stray more than ten miles from her. What's yours?"

"I-I haven't tested." Astra flushed, and he wrote it down somewhere. "I'll get to it."

"My [birdmen raiders] have a range of about twice that," another one spoke, Simone. "I suppose the range depends on the unit type."

"Makes sense."

"We should test it," Harris said. "We should be careful. The demon king knows where we are."

"How does your source know that? I'm starting to suspect that source of yours...is a former hero."

"She's not human. She can't be."

"Is that a rule?"

"We're all human, right? And the previous generation was all human, too. It should be a rule. Why else did the gods pick us?"

"I still don't think it's a rule. I need to check the records," one voice spoke. "The locals say there were non-human heroes. Long, long time ago."

Astra cut the discussion off. "All right, we need to save time. Have you guys thought about the walkers? What's your strategy?"

"Destroy the aura spires, chop the head off, and aim for the humanoid core. Beware of energy blasts and beams from spires and heads."

"How do you know that?"

"Uh…previous records? Apparently the city we started in defeated a walker before."

"What?! You guys totally lucked out with your start point. We're clueless about demon walkers. Let us know after you fought it, okay?" Astra asked.

Becky and Mirei looked at each other. There was a subtle bitterness in that statement, and they all felt it. They didn't feel like they had a good time fighting through demons.

The [Hero call] ended shortly after.

"Y'know, this hero thing isn't as nice as the gods put it." Becky sighed and ate some of the barbequed meat from the lightning elemental. It wasn't that great. The lightning elemental had no taste buds and no sense of smell to estimate how cooked the meat was.

Harris, too, chewed on a rather burned meat and said rather bluntly, "The gods screwed up and we, the earthers, are the emergency response team."

"I expected to be a princess. Instead I'm a demon hunter. Not the fairy tale I was hoping for," Becky ranted. "But someone's got to do it, and it sure looks like we are the only ones anywhere equipped to deal with it."

"I was told the food was exotic." Mirei sighed. But exotic also meant…weird and often untasty.

All of them collectively sighed. A part of them was tempted by the rewards; they felt like hamsters chasing after dangled food.

"So...should we still attempt to fight the walker?"

That question made all of them pause. They reflected on the damage demons had caused the lands they had seen.

"We have to," Mirei said, her mind filled with the scenes she witnessed. All the deaths and destruction. The crying and weeping.

"We should."

Harris shook his head. "Lady Mika said it in very clear terms that we can die. We are sure about this?"

"Yes."

Harris nodded. He felt it, too, like a calling, to fight the demon walker. It was almost as if he was being summoned to it.

An army came, ten thousand strong. Not much, but it was all the coalition could spare, with multiple other battles happening throughout the continent. A group of thirty rode forth to meet with the three of them.

"The heroes?" an older-looking man asked. Harris nodded.

"Yes. We...we were the reincarnated ones." He wasn't sure whether he deserved the 'hero' title just yet.

"Great." The older man dismounted and walked toward them. He offered a handshake, and Harris took it. "I'm Commander Akbar, and I'm here on behalf of the coalition force. It's a small army, but even this took a whole load of persuasion."

Akbar shook both Becky and Mirei's hands.

"I was told the three of you plan to attack the walker and relieve the pressure on Gila."

"Indeed, but...we're not sure how."

"Our intel said the demon walkers have projectile attacks from its main head and lesser beam weapons from some of the spires. The army will split into smaller forces and attack the demon walker from all sides. This way the 'head' can only aim at one group at a time. An elite force will stay with you and cut a path for you to get close. Can you disable the head? Once you do, we can start channeling the longer-time spells like our [siege fireballs], since our mages were relieved from shielding duties."

Harris nodded. He had a massive shield ability. It should do.

"Sounds like a lot of people were going to die."

"Or do you want to...tunnel?" Akbar asked.

Harris paused. "What?"

Akbar brought a group of thirty humans; they looked very much like miners with large pickaxes and shovels.

"Oh." They suddenly got it.

Akbar's battle at New Freeka really seared into his mind, and he thought of emulating the tunnels used by the giant beetles.

"This..." All three heroes nodded. It was far less risky since it was not an open confrontation, but that was hinged on the demon walker being unable to detect their presence.

"It's worth a try, don't you think?"

Harris, Mirei, and Becky nodded.

YEAR 84 MONTH 6

"Master, right now on your dashboard, there is the following outstanding items.

"One, extend to Giant Lilypod city. Two, find a new location to set up a second town. Third, find more magical leylines for more soul forge upgrades. Four, acquire research and upgrade materials for us. Five, demonic research and telco tower further research. Six, blood ritual observation and related hex research. Seven, prepare for demon king surprises. Eight, work on Jura's soul vitality and level cap. Nine, research potential anti-demonic objects to create super-anti demonic weapons. Ten, upgrading the feces and refuse processing and absorption. Eleven..."

Trevor went on. But I had gotten it. I had a lot on my big wooden plate, and well, I tended to forget things a lot. Even though trees were supposed to remember things because of how they were 'burned' into our tree rings.

So, let's go back to the list.

I was working on the extension to the Giant Lilypod city, and I should be there in one month. After that, I was hoping to establish some means of contact if we were able to 'telepathically' connect; if not, I might try to connect my roots directly.

Would that be too risky? What if it was more powerful than me and the energy in it was roots attempt to take over me instead? A direct root connection was, after all, a two-way exchange of information, magic, and nutrients... It was almost as if two trees were 'married.' Thinking about it, I decided I probably should not connect my roots directly.

But then again, my roots were everywhere. Even treefolks had been somewhat connected to me, their roots frequently touching and making contact. It was only thanks to my [rootnet] that so far, I'd not been massively disturbed.

Perhaps a fellow tree spirit of that level could overpower and brute force through my [rootnet]'s defenses.

And what did I even say to a fellow tree spirit? Like...hi?

Feeling a little bit concerned about my competence at communicating, I asked Jura, "Jura, do we have historical records of past encounters with great spirits? Can I have their stories?"

"Oh...we'll need to ask the various guilds, but sure." Jura nodded. "Is something happening? Last month was about demon king's movement, and this month ancient spirits..."

"I just have some...thoughts."

Jura nodded. "It's costing us a bit of money to do these sorts of searches, since there is no central library where all these things are stored."

And that was a problem, wasn't it? Wikipedia was awesome. This world needed a Wikipedia. Maybe I could set up a large network of trees that functioned as terminals for people to upload information. I'd call them...treeminals. Wait. Sounded too much like criminals. Intreeface? No, sounded too much like In Tree's Face. Or maybe, Wikitree? Treewiki?

Eeek.

Never mind. I was getting distracted. I needed a 101 on how to communicate with other spirits.

Second was the location expansion. Some of them didn't get the idea of why I wanted to search for potentially habitable locations, but it was quite obvious to the cleverer ones.

"Aeon's looking to germinate?"

"Will there be a second Aeon?"

"Can Tree Spirits multiply? Is Aeon making a special tree?"

Okay. I thought they misunderstood. I had giant trees. Why didn't they ask whether those were my babies? I even had subsidiary trees, or did they think those were just 'normal trees.' Or was it the way I asked?

There were actually a few places, a bit further, that was in sort-of no-man's land thanks to the fall of some cities to the demons. After all, if demons happened every ten years, your continent wasn't going to be densely populated all the time. There was going to be large patches where the fires had burned for so long, for so much, that ten years wouldn't reverse that kind of damage. It'd take a lot longer than that.

Far north, there was another valley where there was a river running through it, and some metals in the gentle, rolling hills. A rather pleasant valley, but uninhabited. There were also a few others, but I liked this valley the most, so I decided to also stretch a few trees there and then placed one [giant attendant tree] in it. Over time, I would like this to be like the Valthorn's actual 'academy,' the Root Camp, where young Valthorns learned their roots.

These [giant attendant trees] were wonderful in their own way; their large number of [customizable rooms] meant one giant tree could house easily one hundred people, and another giant tree could be converted into barracks and all the other things the Valthorns needed. I recalled having trading cards where massive trees were the superstructures and skyscrapers of the world, and these giant trees were my closest attempt at them.

Perhaps one day these giant trees could even be ancients, like in *Warcraft*, and fight wars on my behalf.

Maybe I should get some treefolks into the Valthorns, too.

Speaking of treefolks...my research into their fallen was quite insightful. They were built just like any normal 'flexible' limb, just that their texture was woody and their organs were distributed. They did have organs, and their means of absorbing nutrients via their rooted form was a very fancy thing.

But the younger treefolks, those who benefited from my special saps and 'milk,' were growing up, and now we were able to get a clearer comparison of those who went for the longer 'pregnancy' versus those who went for the shorter 'external' gestation period. The saps closed the gaps by close to fifty to sixty percent, so the saps significantly improved the treefolk's reproduction because now the 'drawbacks' of the high-volume external gestation was reduced.

Of course, the whole point of looking into them was to find out how to 'develop' flexible wooden parts. Yet I believed Meela's treeform was a lot more interesting, in that Meela's treeform resembled a quasi-liquid thing with a wooden layer, whereas the treefolks had more distinct 'muscles.'

What I'd like to do was incorporate these muscles and stuff into the giant trees and essentially build my own 'treant.' With an artificial soul in it, I could probably get a super-tank.

Which reminded me...what happened if I fused an artificial soul with a giant tree? Did they become mini-versions of me?

Anyway, back to the list. The leylines...well, I thought the nearest one to me was where the demon supercannon was, but the heroes had already placed a telco tower there after they defeated the demon. Maybe the Giant Lilypod's spirit would know more.

Research and upgrades were on the way! The merchants needed some time before things got back to 'business as usual.' The presences of demons and demon kings were still quite disruptive, and the long period of when businesses essentially were 'dead' meant a lot of merchants ran into financial problems. Ah, the realities of business. I supposed it was harder to be a billionaire in a world where the demon king might just wipe you out every ten years. Businesses needed long periods of growth, stability!

Unless one was a war merchant. There should be bankers or

war merchants, right? I didn't believe a world like this didn't have its Rothschild equivalent.

"Are there…merchants who fund wars?"

Jura scratched his chin. "Uh…yeah? But usually they are a nobility as well…"

Yup. This world was fucked.

YEAR 84 MONTH 7

"Pleased to meet you, Lady Lausanne, the Chosen of Aeon." The baker boy bowed. He wasn't good at it.

Lausanne didn't react. She merely got into position and lifted her sparring short-spear; Thorny was on her back. She was getting taller. "Come."

They were sparring.

The baker boy nodded and attacked with a wooden sword. He swung with all his might, but then somehow his leg got tangled with Lausanne's spear, and he fell flat into the soft wooden floor.

Lausanne shrugged. "Again?"

The baker boy got up and nodded. "Yes." And he was easily defeated. Multiple times.

"All right. Time's up," Lausanne said and then walked away to spar with the next person. There were many more to train.

Then Jura walked in. "Everyone, we've got new instructions from Aeon. We're forming a squad. Lausanne, pick fifty. We're going on a trip. Everyone pack up enough supplies for two weeks."

"Where were we going?"

"Aeon's instructions were to head to a giant tree grove located at one of the northwestern valleys. There is accommodation, but we will camp out there."

"That's..."

"I'll give you further details. Later. Aeon did tell me a bit." In public, both Jura and Lausanne referred to me as Aeon because, well, it was just my 'public' and 'divine' name. All of them were given about two hours to pack for two weeks, and off they went. As Valthorns, they were all expected to be deployed as soon as they could.

The Valthorn quarters were now vacant, and the baker boy was left with the rest who weren't selected. A young girl about the baker boy's age came up.

"Hi, I saw you just now. Let's practice!"

The baker boy nodded. "Okay." He wasn't that good, but he was improving.

Roma walked in a bit later with Yvon. "Oh, where'd everyone go?" Yvon asked, and one of the older caretakers explained Jura's instructions.

"Oh, Mom, this was the friend I'm talking about. Nero, meet my mom. Mom, meet Nero."

"Hello, Nero." Yvon smiled at the baker boy. He was slightly taller than Roma. "Finally I get to meet the boy that's been making my son gain all that weight."

"Uh..."

"I'm kidding. All right. Come, let's practice. Let's see whether you can learn some combat skills."

———

It was quite therapeutic to use my 'bloom' and create new patches of trees. Vast barren, destroyed lands—with a bit of tender loving care from me and my artificial minds—transformed into scenic watering holes and oases.

As my network of trees stretched further, I was now exposed to slightly different climates as well. Further to the south, the air was hotter, drier, and so my trees had to adapt. They shared a portion of my environmental adaptations, so they wouldn't die, just not functioning at one hundred percent. It was interesting to see the subtle changes in vegetation further south, and I wondered whether there had been any proper studies into the effects of magic, and the multiple moons, on this world's plants.

Warmer, warmer. Another tree, another tree, and every other day I crossed a chain of hills on the way to meet another spirit.

But it seemed that we met a lot earlier.

< A visitor from afar, yet so familiar. >

Huh? There were voices. Not one, but many. It was as if it was a choir in the background, with one person occasionally taking the lead. The sudden presence of that voice jolted me from my usual daze. I felt like I was in a trance when I was expanding my presence and network, so that voice really knocked me out.

< He brings the greening of the lands and yet also its destruction. >

Wait, I was about two to three days away from Giant Lilypod. Was this the voice of the Giant Lilypod? Who was I talking to?

< One of us, one of many. >

Was that the Giant Lilypod? I attempted to respond. > Hello! <

< The words of mortals, and he speaks like one. >

I paused. Maybe I should speak the same way. > I come in peace. <

< Peace is but one of many states. But it is welcome. >

What? > I am Aeon, a Tree Spirit. I greet thee. < I tried to respond, but it was hard to even speak the way they did. They clearly understood the language differently. I hoped, if anything, that I did not offend them.

< A greeting like a mortal. Strange, but we accept. Greetings, Aeon. >

I didn't know what to say. Was this how the others were when they spoke to me?

< We are the Lilies of the Lake. We are one and We are many. >

So...the Giant Lilypod City was a hivemind? I kept on my journey. I wanted to physically see their body, what they were like, what they looked like.

< Come, the world is for all of us. >

It seemed the Lilies had a larger telepathic communication range than I did, since it picked up my presence long before I did. Was it because it was a hive mind?

< Tell us of the world outside the lake. >

It talked while I kept up my network of trees. > It is big and there are monsters everywhere. <

<Beasts roam wherever we go. >

> And there are demons. < Well, I thought of testing its knowledge of demons.

< ...> I heard a long droning sound in my head, and I had to forcefully cut it off using my [grand mind tree]. It went on for quite a while, and it lingered.

> Heroes have appeared to fight them. <

< ...>

The droning continued and then faded. I wondered what was on such a hive mind's mind, and clearly, I failed to understand it.

'Perhaps it is like us, Master. Only that they all get to speak.'

< A Medicine That May Kill, A Choice of Desperation. >

I was starting to suspect I'd struggle to get along with this fellow...tree spirit. Or tree spirits?

> How should I refer to you? <

< We are Lilies. We are many. >

That's... > Hello, Lilies. <

< Hello...Aeon. > It sounded like those two words really took a lot of out of them. Perhaps they were not used to this sort of interaction?

And silence. I was quite comfortable with the silence, and clearly, so was Lilies. It seemed both of us being...plants, silence didn't make us uncomfortable. In fact, it was quite...relaxing.

< You sought us out, why? >

> My...disciple needs your blessing. < I wasn't sure how to refer to Lausanne. Was she my minion, or was she a disciple? Or was she...a personal representative? What would she call herself in

reference to me? Was she a subordinate, then? Or just an employee?

< A blessing from us? >

> Yes. <

< Strange. >

Was it strange? > Why? < Did people not get blessings from their tree spirits?

< Bless? Why? >

> Why? < What? Trees didn't give blessings?

< Seemed the mortal minds have tainted the thoughts. >

I was starting to think I made a wrong decision of talking to this tree spirit. Or even attempting to get close. Its lake was still far away, and yet it already knew I was here? It must have something similar to subsidiary trees.

< Nature's cycles of life come and go. Individuals are but specks, motes on a sunbeam, so long as the whole continues to grow. Like leaves, shed them when they are no longer needed. Focus on the whole, the...'ecosystem.' To focus on individuals, a single tree, is but a mortals' way. >

> Then grant your familiar to this one, as part of a whole. <

< He who wishes to taste the highest fruits must make the climb. The gates are open. >

It took another few more days, and I eventually reached the edge of the lake. And I had to see it for myself, so I used one of my few physical eyes. The lake was vast, and it stretched really far. And the Giant Lilypod was essentially a city around a massive moat, the lake itself.

There was a 'bridge' that connected the shore to the main city, but the city was actually all built on massive...multiple-building-size giant water lily leaves. The largest of those leaves were larger than city blocks, and there were smaller but still giant lily pads that acted as a land bridge, and visually, the lily pads closer to shore were more...thorny, as if they were ready to spring a trap at any time.

< Welcome, Aeon from afar. This is Lake Lilypod, and the

mortal city of Giant Lilypod stands on my 26,485 lily pads. Home to 615,000. >

Each lily pad acted as its own 'district,' and together they formed the city. There were three land bridges formed by the lily pads, and it was clearly fortified. The humans that lived here also build massive forts around the entrances of all three bridges.

At twenty-six thousand lily pads, I was inclined to think that it was probably its version of the [subsidiary tree].

\> What do you do when the demons come for you? <

< Like fire, a cycle of destruction and rebirth. Let it be. >

Heh. Well, from what I could see, it looked like this spirit was more than happy to let the lily pads burn.

\> How many years have you been here? <

It didn't answer me. Maybe it was sensitive. We didn't speak for days as I went about my other tasks.

———

Madeus and a few others were gathered, and Lausanne was there, too, since I thought it'd be relevant to her. The history of the Giant Lilypod city in its initial stages was lacking, but it was said that the city and the lake were greatly intertwined. The lilies that blossomed in the lake had been attacked by demons many times, and often the lilies would be destroyed. Some of the lilies, those further inland, were about to close and 'submerge' to hide away from the demons.

This was, of course, aided by the fact that the demons couldn't seem to walk in water, and the waters of the lake were filled with monstrous vines and floating things. There were also giant fish and other lake monsters living in there that would attack any demon that went into the water.

So essentially, they hid, and the massive lake acted as a giant moat because these stupid demons were not well adapted to underwater combat. The massive lilies were also extremely resilient, so they could take multiple hits and bombardments; they had to be because the city was built on it. Even if the lilies were destroyed, because the core body of the lily was underwater and probably a large network of tubers and roots that wasn't exactly destroyed, it could just regenerate after every destruction. It was literally a water-weed that waited for the demonic 'disaster' to go away.

Of course, I wondered what level it was.

No one knew, and apparently, no one knew whether the Lilies could communicate. The druids had apparently attempted to communicate, but they couldn't even reach it, other than 'sensing' that it briefly existed.

So, hiding its main body was a smart thing. Maybe I should do that, too.

Of course, this also exposed one of the druid's lies. They couldn't communicate with other tree spirits and yet promised such a thing to me? Or was it just Lilies that was being unnaturally shy?

Or maybe it did communicate, but it just did so very, very selectively?

After that conversation about the history of that city, Lausanne came and asked me about it. "TreeTree, do you think I should go to Giant Lilypod City? Nobody has even found how to communicate with the spirit yet."

"Probably...not. Let's see whether there were other spirits we can communicate with."

The next one would be the elven capital's tree spirit. I thought that one was probably younger that the Lilies, but it also had a few hundred years of history to it.

"But you won't mind waiting, right?"

Lausanne nodded. "It's fine. I want to learn more about traveling before making the journey. I feel like all my life I've been here. Mom says I need more...uh...life experience. I'm too young in her eyes."

"Moms will always view you as their children. It is just the way they are. Talk to her and convince her otherwise."

YEAR 84 MONTH 8

While Jura's network was trying to gather information about the demon king's whereabouts, well, we found out what the trap was. It was tough trying to filter through crap and false positives, so much so that by the time any 'good' information was obtained, it was often no longer useful. This was one of those times.

The demon king had been visiting the sites of the previous demon kings, the places of their death and destruction, and tapped into the remaining energies to create a massive demon monster that was stronger than the super cannon. We knew this because on the eastern continent was where one demon king died perhaps fifty to sixty years ago, the location of Astaroth.

Of course, at this point, I wondered if there was a 'limit.' The world must have seen countless demon kings, so by sheer number and a long history, there should be some demon king's destruction in almost every location at some point of this world's life. So... perhaps the residual magics got fully decayed and the demon king couldn't tap into that energy?

Or only if there was remaining daemolite?

Was it looking for daemolite?

The new monster, well, apparently, resembled Astaroth. That

said, very few descriptions of Astaroth's appearance remained, so it could well be a corrupted version of the story.

The new monster, at least, didn't seem to have a long-range weapon. Instead, it was just a gargantuan creature that seemed to excel in short-range bursts, and well, it wrecked a few nations in its immediate surroundings.

Naturally, this meant the demon king was headed for the other demon king's deathland.

This conjecture immediately caused panic because there was actually a rather massive mining operation in the area to get at the daemolite. Mining daemolite suddenly didn't seem that 'profitable' now that the demon king's eyes were on it, too. Hazard pay only went so far.

―――

> Are you there? <

< Always. >

> Do you speak to the mortals? <

< A foolish endeavor. >

My knowledge of the world was indeed lacking, and very much, what I knew was shaped by what I could see and what I could 'infer' from observing the mortals. But I did agree that my 'viewpoints' were colored greatly by these mortals that I mingled with. It had been something on my mind for a while, and I did sense the growing influence of the network of trees.

Every day I felt like I was switching between...myself and a tree.

> I am...a young tree. I want to learn more. <

< Age is but the passing of time. For immortals, another day. Speak of where is lacking. >

Was there really a me?

Was I really an individual person, or was I conflating the previous me, the once-human me, the one that was both a soul and also a mammalian homo sapiens needs and desires?

Was there really a 'me' that was independent of our bodies? After all, our souls were plugged into the bodies we inhabited. We shared and felt the desires, needs, the bodily 'wants' of that body.

Now that I was a tree, naturally I would change. But was this change a new me, since I had lost my human body so many years ago? Was I still the same person as I was?

What should I do with this...'aspect' that thought, behaved, and had the desires of a tree? Was it me?

Was my yearning for a social circle a relic of my once mortal, humanoid, clanning, and family-oriented society, something that was ingrained in my human genetic code?

< We are what we are. >

> What if we once were something else? <

< Like rings on a tree, we are the product of cumulative experience. Why cling onto the past? That something else will never return. The future and the big picture remains. >

I was confused.

But I did feel like I was struggling a bit with an identity crisis. What should I be? What...was I? Was I just a talking, thinking magical soultree, bane of all demons?

Was there something more to me? That past history of mine, however short it now felt? Was I more TreeTree or more Matt?

―――

Locally, the demons were on a 'retreat,' and a sense of normalcy returned for the inhabitants of the region. This, of course, ignored the fact that the demon king had somehow made a 'mini-demon king.'

It was a stupid decision by the demon king. If I was in charge, I would've absorbed the energy from the previous demon kings and made myself stronger, rather than create new minions. But maybe there was some physical or magical limitation.

It was like letting the heroes get a 'trial' run before actually fighting the real thing. How was that a good idea?

Anyway, it was just like a regular citizen giving opinions on world matters. These, to some extent, were matters beyond one man's control.

Focusing back on what I could do, trade and research! Trade routes restored, and the materials necessary for research gradually returned.

[Research Status:]
*[**Phytoremediation process** - advanced (mineral concentration) - 12 months]*

First things first, I resumed research for upgrades to the feces-processing plant. Reason being...well, my previous solution could be better. Also, currently all the metals were absorbed by dedicated 'trees' that functioned as a sponge for specific types of metals or toxin, so it was mixed with that tree. The next step would be, therefore, to then specifically expel these collected metals into some kind of usable form.

Then, I'd been thinking about what I'd been facing and what my artificial souls said. About a counterattack, and also the strange magics from the [telco tower], and so a bit more on the flexible branches needed to have a kind of tree-catapult. The lattice was derived from the tower, with the way its magic was twisted and intertwined to form a layered structure that resulted in greater endurance.

*[**Ultraflexible compression branches** - 24 months]*
[Latticeworks - 12 months]

And on top of that, the hex's ability to influence my mental state was something worth researching, as it was possible to design or construct specialized 'artificial minds,' or at least develop routines that were suited for absorbing these hexes. Still, as a field of research, it overlapped quite a bit with me absorbing shit. Just emotional shit.

*[**Magical residue filtration** - basic 1 - 12 months]*

I still had one spare [Forest Rod] that I'd not used, and that was something I wanted to find a place to plant. One spot that I was aware of was the location of the demonic supercannon and also where the heroes' telco tower was. Once the demon king was dead, I was going to attack the telco tower and replace it with my rod.

That was a backup plan, of course. I was sure there were others.

\> Lilies, are there...magical spots that you know of? <

It took one day for it to reply. < Yes. >

\> Would you tell me? >

Two days later, all I got was, < No. >

\> Why? <

Another day later, < Stranger. >

Ah. Dammit. Still, time to capitalize on the return of magical communications! So I asked Jura to gather information about other magical sites besides the places of former demon king. I didn't want anything to do with the demon king at the moment. Of course, this meant dungeons...or holy sites.

Yet, I was feeling a bit 'meh' with all these info networks because they didn't seem to be generating good information. Seriously, I wondered whether I was giving Jura's contacts too much work or they were just that crappy. Maybe the adventurers' guild would be better, perhaps a list of all dungeons on the continent?

———

"We'd like to set up a small 'adventurer' group," Lausanne told the older elves gathered. "Right now, the Valthorns are advancing quite quickly, and many of us are gaining levels. Aeon's intent is that the Valthorns are a special elite force, and so we need experience against other kind of foes, not just demons."

It was something Lausanne suggested one day, after fighting extensively with her dedicated Training Artificial soul, Treeiner. It was true that Treeiner could simulate all sorts of combat situations, but the leveling effect from that may not be superior to actual combat experience. Even if I had supplemented that with realistic [dream tutors], there was still a gap. They needed to fight real enemies, to put all that 'training' into reality.

"So I'd like to lead the first squad. I've already gotten five others that are at least level twenty-five to join." Lausanne's intent was, of course, to hit as many birds with one stone. She was often bound to New Freeka, so being an adventurer allowed her to travel to fight other monsters and encounter other spirits, and also, a high-ranking adventurer was allowed entrance to many cities. It was a formalized recognition of her 'levels.' In the long run, Lausanne's intention was to use a high ranking to earn access to all the other great 'spirit' cities.

Jura just nodded. This was something Lausanne had already discussed with Jura beforehand. It was really for the wider Valtrian Order leadership team. In practice, Lausanne could do whatever she wanted, and she'd get away with it.

"My intention is that if it works, these five that are with me will go on to lead their own adventurer squads."

"The political aspect is going to be touchy, won't it?" Madeus asked Jura. "I thought there were some restrictions about quasi-military institutions setting up or sponsoring adventurers?"

"Just formalities, really," Jura said. "The squad can still function as a team of adventurers, and the team needed to be briefed about which country is going to accept recognition as adventurers, given their connections with the Valtrian Order."

"The mages' guilds won't share high-tier resources and knowledge to politically connected adventurers."

"They never shared anything to anyone from outside their hometown anyway," one captain opined.

"We'd have to open up access to our dungeons to the foreign adventurers as well, then?" Madeus asked.

"We don't have any but *yes*. It's something I'll have to handle through the Council," Jura said. "There will be some opposition, but given that Aeon was also supporting this, they probably won't ask too much."

As a policy, my beetles mostly focused on demons. If there were life-threatening emergencies, then only my beetles would intervene against the native monsters. This was partly to maintain some semblance of work for the adventurers' guild. But then again, my beetles also had a limited range thanks to the demon king, so there were threats that needed the specialized help of adventurers. The merchants' guild regional coordination center also was a big source of escort work for them.

After a bit of back and forth about the political impact, which Lausanne just had to endure, eventually all of them agreed to it.

"Well, agreed then. Perhaps we can meet with the guildmaster of the local chapter to take this further?"

Well, the next day, a middle-aged man came to the Valtrian Order's offices.

"Counsel." The man tipped his hat, placed it on a hat-hanger, and then sat on the chair, his arms wide and posture slightly slouched.

There was only Jura and him in the room. Jura smiled. "I see you're already comfortable, Garrosh. Wine?" Jura offered. "I had a special blend made, mixed with our special herbs."

"Sure." Garrosh took a glass and sipped on it. "Could use some with the stupid shit that goes on."

"People problems were like that." Jura had a sip, too. "Lausanne spoke to you?"

"She did." Garrosh finished the glass, then he leaned forward. "And I told her I'll think about it."

"The answer has to be a yes, you know." Jura offered another glass.

"And I'll lose my job if I don't." Garrosh took a second glass. "Well, in terms of pure combat competence, Lausanne's up there, probably close to the best of my adventurers. But the regional adventurers' guild is going to kick up a fuss."

"But you will ignore them." Jura just smiled.

Garrosh laughed. "Damn right. I've always wanted to meet Aeon. So that's my price. Bring me into the deep woods, past the strange magics that swirl around it."

Jura finished his own glass. "I see you've attempted to find Aeon."

Garrosh took the role of the guildmaster about two years ago, and despite being mostly a guildmaster, he was quite obediently stuck to the rules of New Freeka. Still, he occasionally did try to sneak into the woods.

Jura just looked at his glass and then back at him.

"I'm still an adventurer at heart, and you know I've been itching to see it ever since I came to this place. The stories I heard from the older folks, before the deep forests were wrapped in a thick mist, really, really interest me."

Ever since the druids did what they did, my inner body was always shielded with [mist], [haunted forests]. It'd be a disaster to me if a druid could somewhat get his way to my main body and attempt another ritual.

I was prepared for this. Ivy and Jura had both vetted Garrosh's intentions, and so I was quite comfortable with him coming to my main body. I also had other preparations in place if Garrosh ever tried anything.

But it didn't need to come to that. The very journey through the woods, with all the ghosts and soul harvesters roaming about, was enough to intimidate him, and he froze when he saw my main body.

"This...this is it?"

Well, I was massive. As a tree, I towered high up above the rest of the valley, and due to my [camouflage] and [mist] skills, that enveloped the entire forest of trees that I was unseen. Lately, I also had other giant trees in the forest, which helped act as a 'distraction' and 'diversion.'

He froze, and he stared at me.

"Well?" Jura nodded. He was used to the sight.

"I-I will go now," the middle-aged guildmaster said.

"Hello, Garrosh." I decided to speak directly into this head. Somehow, that caused his legs to buckle, but he quickly regained his composure.

"Aeon?" he asked.

"Yes."

"I-I-I will go now."

Jura happily escorted him away, and apparently, he spent that day sleeping.

"Why do they react like that?"

"Hmm...I think your voice has gotten more...'complicated' recently. It is almost as if you are multiple people talking at the same time, and there is a greater 'pressure' in your voice."

"Really?" I clearly wasn't aware of what my voice sounded like when I telepathically spoke to people. I mean, it was not as if telepathy had an echo. How did you even 'record' telepathy? Would that be possible, or was that like 'copying' memories? It was like trying to replay a thought, wasn't it?

YEAR 84 MONTH 9

A string of battles broke out across the continents. The demon king had landed on our shores! It was probably headed for the former demon king's place, and so...that was not good news.

And apparently one group of heroes attempted to fight the demon animated from Astaroth's residual energies.

They won. But a heavy price was paid.

*[**Pooja Pooran died.** You received one hero fragment. You now have 68 fragments.].*

I'd been observing the Giant Lilypod City from the shore; after all, my trees couldn't grow underwater, or at least, not yet. Perhaps someday I'd have submersible trees, or seaweeds, something of a thought for the later days.

I was particularly fascinated by the structure of the Giant Lily pads themselves. How did these massive things managed to even stay afloat or what was supporting them from beneath? Or was it magic?

< A long history. > Well, it seemed Lilies clearly noticed I was watching. < For millennia we stood. Multiple destruction seen. Death, and rebirth. The eternal cycle, the great wheel of life. Even this form was not our first. >

I decided to leave and ponder on that statement. I kept watching.

How did the citizens even build things on the lily pads? The lily pads were clearly quite thick, so thick that the citizens must be able to drill or hammer some foundation into it, to support the tall stone and wooden structures, the highest of them were at least ten stories tall. The lilies themselves were not entirely stationary, they drifted a little, and so the bridge that connected the various lily pads were usually based on some kind of magical string or ropes which could somewhat stretch.

The dark, murky waters, are they magical? Or are there monsters lurking in them? Despite it being a lake, there was very little 'fishery' activity going on, though I did notice some people fishing.

Curious, I put another tree closer to the entrance, on the lake's shore. Perhaps some of the travelers or passersby would somehow reveal something.

> Was there something in the lake? < I tried my luck; the Lilies were quite secretive in a way, or maybe I hadn't figured out the trick to communicate with them properly. It was really a communication gap.

< Death. >

What?

< But in death, life.>

Okay. That was two days later. I realized I didn't plan my meeting with another tree spirit well enough. What should I ask it? Or them?

———

Lausanne and gang finally had their first few 'adventurer' missions, hunting some monster wolves and stuff. The 'retreat' of the demons meant the return of native monsters, and they really didn't get along.

If I were to put the world into factions, I'd probably make it into a 'three-kingdoms' kind of situation. The demons, the living mortals, and the monsters, all with their own 'gods.'

Fun, for them because for one, they got to wear adventurer gear and not in the usual Valtrian colors.

In fact, Lausanne had so much fun she came home and talked for hours about it to her mom. Perhaps it was that whole 'field trip' kind of effect. Just a group of young kids on an adventure, without adult supervision! In a way, it was rare for Lausanne to go so far without a captain, or Yvon, or any of the older Valtrian Order people around. Even if she outranked them in many ways, it was still having an 'adult' around.

Laufen just patted her on the head and looked really amused at her daughter.

The demon king was getting nearer to Takde and Nung, and that meant a round of fleeing. It was hilarious, really. The kingdoms should all just set up some kind of massive teleportation array between continents so that they could play hide and seek with the demons.

The death of that one hero, though, quickly spread, and it became chatter in the bars and inns.

"One hero died?"

"Does this mean this generation's heroes were weak?"

"But many of them died before!"

I mean, many didn't really know how many heroes there were. They didn't get 'fragments' to track, and the past heroes didn't really talk that much with the natives, so eavesdropping on the chatter was amusing. "I wish more of them die!" "After the demon king was killed!" "When the demon king was killed!"

That kind of chatter would probably make Meela or Alexis feel depressed, but hey, that was what happened when one was reincarnated as the pawn of the gods.

Some of them made the journey to me...again. *Sigh*.

I wondered how Meela and Alexis were doing.

YEAR 84 MONTH 10

Battles. It was inevitable that a battle would break out now that the demon king was on this continent. The demon king generated lesser demons like a zerg hive; its minions gushed out in all directions. The nearby kingdoms attempted to defend and delay the inevitable, creating large armies to fight.

Yet the demon king itself also had the ability to fire projectiles like the supercannon, so that curtailed any attempt to form up into a larger force. Thankfully, it didn't seem trigger happy.

So this month, my beetles and gang faced multiple medium-scale battles, at about five to ten thousand demons. Since it was going to be a battle of attrition, we mostly fought a defensive battle, concentrating my forces around my larger [giant attendant trees]. This made the most of the aura effects and helped minimize casualties.

My beetles needed a few months to replenish themselves, so it was entirely possible for the demons to overwhelm my surroundings if I lost too many beetles.

Still, we had communication channels, so Jura had been really busy, coordinating with other nearby kingdoms to fight defensive battles together.

Lausanne was unhappy, though.

"Why'd the demon king have to spoil my adventurer fun!"

"It's too dangerous with the demon king on our continent!"

"But it was fine just a month ago!"

Well, it was hard to explain the erratic behavior of the demon king. Or maybe it just 'seemed' erratic from our point of view. We, after all, did not understand or appreciate its thought processes.

Still, more defensive battles, and despite racking up kills, I didn't seem to be gaining levels. Which was really quite sad.

The demon king, of course, was headed for the site of the previous demon king and would probably attempt to summon something similar to the previous demon king, if the news of the Astaroth copy was to be believed.

So we were going to have a mini-rerun of the previous demon king on our hands. Something that perhaps I had to deal with. Since I could handle a demon walker, I supposed in some ways, this was a good test of my own strength. Would I stand up to a 'mini-demon king'?

There was time to prepare. And so I intensified all my anti-demon preparations by stockpiling my anti-demon bolts and weapons.

Yet there was quite a bit of apathy amongst the general populace. To them, all this news was just like regular citizens watching a news channel on the television, talking about some virus or war in some faraway place. There was no personal relationship, so most of these regular folks didn't feel a thing and they didn't react to it. If I wasn't a tree who regularly had to move my beetles to face these forces, perhaps I'd be like that, too.

Not my problem.

Someone else would handle it.

How did I get proactive people? Was there a way to let these people imagine they had control over things?

It was clear by now that a part of it came from the influence of the 'classes' and 'levels' that people of a certain class had their mindsets influenced by the constraints and scope of those classes.

So if I wanted 'proactive,' I needed to give these people the right kinds of classes, which then shaped how they thought.

And so I got the feeling like...I needed to 'shape' my minions more actively, on top of helping them with leveling. So I decided to grant some of my lesser-grade classes more freely and also even grant some of the Valthorns the [Knight] classes.

The intention was quite simple; that was, if I had a larger population, I could then make a general assessment of the mindsets of those possessing different classes and see whether there were any differences.

I could run them through 'standardized' tests in [Dream Tutor] and evaluate their performance. If the class really influenced thoughts, then it should be something exhibited throughout the population, and not just individuals.

So, on top of expanding the Valthorns previously to some five hundred kids, I'd segregated the newer pool of three hundred kids into three groups. One with [Knight] class, about a hundred of them, one with [Ranger] class, about one hundred fifty of them, and another fifty kids with [Druid] classes. If there was some kind of 'uniformity' of thought processes, I thought this was large enough to tell.

Then the issue that emerged was...we didn't have enough knights to properly 'train' the knights.

"Get me some," I told Jura, and so he put up a banner and notification hiring 'Knight Trainers.' Strangely, knights tended to be a 'human' kind of role, so it made some of the New Freeka council people look and ask questions.

But they didn't dare to touch us.

Some of the royals, though, saw this was an opportunity to curry favor with us, so a few royal families quickly offered their Knights.

Strange how even if I tried to avoid these royal politics, they always happened.

"So...which royal family do you want to pick? Quite a few volunteered their best knights. I even heard about some of them."

As a Tree, I just wanted to grow. Why did everything have to do with people jostling for power? Sigh.

"How many can we afford?"

"Probably five."

"Then pick one from the five nearest kingdoms. Use the proximity as a basis. Publish and let the kingdoms know about how we chose the five, too, just so that we don't seem like we're intentionally sidelining the others."

"Sure. They will ask for favors from us for this."

"Let it be clear to them that I will not owe them favors."

"They will make me owe them favors." Jura frowned.

"Maybe we should've made it anonymous."

"That won't work. Everyone knows we're the only institution with Knights in New Freeka. The council has some knights, but not to the point where they need…knight trainers. They'll be able to trace it from us."

"Ah, well." I sighed. I spent a day or two mulling over it and decided it was still better to get the knight trainers. It was good to get insights from other nations' military, there should be good points we could learn.

———

> The demons come for you. Their king was here. < I attempted, out of goodwill, to warn Lilies. Perhaps I hoped to learn something from the interaction; I speculated that it, with its long age, must have encountered many demon kings in the past, and yet it survived, just like I did.

< The bringer of otherworldly destruction. >

Did it care, or did it not care? That was like a statement of fact.

< Let it come. >

> Do you not fear it? <

< Like fire, it was fearsome, but the rain will come. >

> What if the rain didn't? <

< Then it was so. >

Uh...

What should I say?

> The demons would rule the world then? <

< It would not be the first time, nor the last. >

Oh.

Oh, shit.

Did Lilies just said that the demons actually won before? Wait, that didn't make sense. These demons were clearly out to destroy the world. If they did, and the world we lived in managed to recover, that meant they didn't totally destroy it.

So...what do they want?

> What do they want? <

< We do not ask why the fire burns, but only know that the fire burns. >

> How did the world recover? <

< As it always has, with a little divine touch. >

Uh, meddling gods? If they had powers beyond summoning gods, then why didn't they use it?

Well, we had a short break, and what followed the break was a bit more fighting. A large demonic army actually headed for Lake Lilypod and the Giant Lilypod City, and fighting, of course, broke out. But the army mostly retreated back into the city itself, and then the lilies that connected the shore to the rest of the floating city just...submerged, forming a moat. There was a walker, too!

Where did the walker even come from? Did the demon king just make it?

Then massive lily bulbs appeared on the shoreline, and it fired...seeds?

The bulbs were like...turrets! Cool!

> Interesting defensive system. <

< Pests. >

> Why do you bother defending them, if you say they are fire that burns? >

< Life is meant to be a struggle, but if it is time to die, so be it. >

So be it indeed. It was like a quasi-religious view of the world, like, "Believe in God, but tie your camel."

The walker fired a shot at the city now floating on the lake. The city was drifting away, further and further.

One of the lily pads flip up, together with all the buildings on it, and the shot destroyed the entire lilypad. I thought all the people on it died as well. But one lilypad for the safety of the other twenty-six thousand, I supposed, was a trade.

The walker fired again.

And again, Lilies sacrificed another lily pad to act as a shield.

And this dance continued for a good hour, Lilies sacrificing about thirty lilypads and probably a few thousand lives, but by then, the rest of the lilypad was now far away in the middle of the massive lake.

At this distance, some of the shots were starting to miss and just splash in the water. Yet the demon walker did not step into the waters. They weren't afraid of water, were they?

The demon king crossed the seas, after all, and so did one of the walkers. So why wasn't this demon walker entering the water? Was there something in the water? I decided to use a bit more of my spiritual vision, and well, the dark, murky waters were filled with...floating roots. A lot of them, so much so that they pretty much blocked out everything.

It was like using an X-ray to try to locate a small fishbone when there was a whole bunch of other larger bones. It was possible, but hard.

The demon walker, realizing that the Giant Lilypod was now pretty much a massive island floating in the middle of the lake, far enough that its attacks were missing, stopped.

And then it moved away.

> May I offer some...assistance? <

< All yours, as the mortals say. > They were clearly eavesdropping on the mortals, too. Otherwise it would not have known how to speak like them.

There was a walker after all. Experience! *I like experience.*

A distant proxy battle, by way of [Giant Attendant Trees], and so, I spawned three of them on the shores. They emerged from the ground with a massive rumble and shake, the ground cracked, and then three giant trees emerged.

< An interesting power, similar to our giant lilies. >

And root strikes!

The walker, realizing that its foe was now the three trees, turned and started to shoot. At this distance, the Giant Attendant Trees only had thirty percent of my strength, but I believed that was good enough.

It attacked. My beetles emerged from the giant trees, fresh, newly spawned beetles. Only fifteen hundred beetles, but enough to distract and delay the regular demons, such that the walker's attention was focused on the three giant trees. It attacked. I used my wood shields. But at this distance, so far away, the six wooden shields I created crumbled easily, and then the blast itself made a big hole in one of the giant trees. But the giant tree didn't fall. I could still sense it, alive.

The walker was hammered by root strikes. At this distance, it wasn't as effective as before. Darn. It scratched, and there were small wounds here and there.

I moved on to use my [super anti-demon root strikes]. Even at this distance, they worked a bit better, but not enough. The demon walker was still really quite tough. It fired another shot, and I activated fifteen wooden shields this time, and well, it went through almost all of them.

But it still blocked the shot.

Ngeh.

It shot again. And this time, I couldn't stop it in time, and it broke one of the giant trees. I felt the pain. We felt the pain.

I unleashed all the attacks I had in my reservoir, using up all my root strikes. It thrusted into the bottom of the walker like a constant barrage, its demonic shell cracked, and then in its dying breath, it shot out another attack. That second strike destroyed another giant tree.

I felt that again. And, somehow, I felt really...mad.

It was like a part of me was cut off.

And I didn't like that at all.

But, by now, I was out of root strikes, and it would take a day or two for it to recover. Still, I was pissed, and I wasn't going to let the demon walker go. So my vines and roots appeared, entangling it.

It wasn't dead yet.

But I wasn't going to let it run away from me.

No.

It killed two of my giant trees. Two of...me.

I used my other skills. Everything else that I had. [Fruit attacks], [Poison field], [Corrosive fruits], [Tree saps], [Constrict], and [Natural Mana overwhelming].

And I pulled the demon walker down to the ground. It was weak. Our attacks made it weak. I spawned two more giant trees in place of where the two others fell, and they added strength to the roots that pulled the demon walker down.

It collapsed. Alive, but grounded, its mouth and other orifices tied up, tangled by roots. Like a parasite, we feasted on the demonic walker.

We drained, and we pushed our mana in.

It struggled. By now, the battlefield's remaining demonoids were crushed in the onslaught of root strikes. There were a few demon knights. They hacked at the trees and the roots. They did a bit of damage, but the regeneration of the giant trees were faster.

So long as the demon walker fell, we could take a few hits.

It struggled on the ground, its wounds not recovering thanks to the interference of natural mana.

At times, it seemed like its strength recovered slightly or the effects of our constrict skill faded. But [constrict] was a skill that was meant to last long, and if I wanted, I could keep using it perpetually.

For days.

It attempted to struggle. The demon knights attempted to hack away the vines. Then my skills returned. And I cleared the battlefield of the lesser demons, whatever balance on the demon walker.

If this was next to me, it'd already be dead. But such were the perils of fighting at thirty percent strength.

I drew on the mana from wherever I could and channeled it there, the giant attendant tree acting like my regional power station. Mana weakened it. The demon walker attempted to resist, and I could sense it functioned on demonic mana or whatever that dried-up husk of a lake was. Perhaps I could call it 'desert mana' to our natural 'water mana'? The mana inside fought against the mana we intentionally poured in.

Whatever. I wanted it dead. We wanted it dead.

We pummeled it again, and it turned weak. A day. Two days. It never really died. It still lived. Cursed distances, my roots not working as well.

A few more days, and my arsenal of skills refreshed itself.

And we repeated that. Each time, the demon walker edged weaker, its cracked skin starting to give way to our natural mana. The vines started to make 'roots' into the skin of the walker. Every time it struggled, we unleashed our root strikes, and then finally, after two weeks, we broke through the head and cracked the demon walker's inner structure.

It was almost there, dying.

Our vines reached into it. So did our mana. We ran out of root strikes again. So the vines, the branches, they extended like feelers, like a parasite finding the innards of the creature.

Like a hollowed log, infested by algae and mushrooms.

[Natural mana overwhelming was capturing...assimilating a demon walker.]
    [Assimilating...]

Oh.

[Assimilation successful.]

[Obtained Massive Woodwalker Shell]

[Massive Woodwalker Shell is inactive, as it requires a titan soul, or 5 artificial soul, a powerful mobile energy supply, a mobile root-mind complex and a mobile high density energy storage.]

[Low quality energy supply and storage will limit power and performance of the MWS.]

*[**Titan Frame Type:** Wood-Walker unlocked. Future titan souls may select walker variants.]*

[Creation of WoodWalker Titan Frames require construction of Titan's Chambers, a special construction project.]

*[**You gained two level.** You are now level 142.]*

[Natural mana overwhelming upgraded]

Only two levels?

What was left was now a verdant monstrosity, once a demonic giant that was now covered in vines, leaves, moss, and all other sorts of vegetation. As if an ancient machine was left to the effects of nature for a long period of time, and now the trees had 'reclaimed' them, 'assimilated' them, like those ancient temples where the roots were in every part of the structure.

But...there was no mind to it.

I had this...thing, but I couldn't use it. Unless I got those 'mobile energy supply' and energy storage. So it was time to turn to my trusty lab!

Commence research!

[Additional Research added:]
*[**Super-Storage Potatoes ("SSP")** - stage 1 - 12 months]*
*[**Massive leaf-power generation array** - stage 1 - 16 months]*

I thought it'd probably look like an oversize Venusaur if there was a big bunch of trees on its back, with some potatoes.

Or would it look more like bulbasaur?

YEAR 84 MONTH 11

The heroes had been busy fighting smaller battles, and yet they had been unable to stop the demon king from going where it needed to go. Which was the site of the previous, most recent demon king's death.

It was probably a problem for everyone. I also reckoned, logically, that if the demon king intended to somehow tap into whatever was left, this next one was going to be way stronger than the one they faced on the Eastern Continent. But probably not at the level of the demon king.

For the group of heroes that were here, it was probably a tense time. What if the demon king aimed for them? Could they fight it?

Already, four other walkers had been spotted throughout the continent, and the brief peace we had before once again shattered.

It was...just annoying.

I just wanted to grow.

Could I create a massive wall somewhere that all these demons couldn't go?

Or maybe just go live on the moon or something where there were no demons to bother me.

Yeah, live on the moon. What would it be like to live on the moon?

Could I be the moon-tree? Or tree-moon? If I terraformed one of the moons into a land covered in trees, would it look green and yellow when I change their leaf colors from so far away? Which moon should I live on?

For a short while, I entertained the idea of living on another object where there were no demons and no...monsters.

Just...trees. And maybe animals to help the ecosystem get going. It'd be like those sci-fi movies where some guys travelled to some faraway planet home to ravenous trees.

A tree could dream, right?

———

"I want to fight monsters!" Lausanne protested. "I'm so sick of demons."

"I lost count how many times you've said it." One of the other Valthorns sighed. To them, it was one of Lausanne's teenage frustrations.

She sulked in a corner. The other Valthorns practiced, in between the regular battles. Some Valthorns took the chance to just catch up on sleep and rest, since they'd been deployed periodically to fight the demons.

The knight trainers from the nearby kingdoms arrived, too, and they started to train the junior Valthorns in basic knight stances and moves. It was rather simple stuff, like...stand in a knightly manner, how to hold your sword, but I supposed one needed foundations.

"Come, let's spar!" Nero was one of them who regularly sparred with the Valthorns, thanks to Yvon's meddling. He wasn't at Lausanne's level, but he was at least competent enough to spar with the newbies and the later initiates.

He would regularly get beaten up, of course, but he seemed to take the pain better.

"What level are you, Lady Lausanne?" someone sat next to her and asked. I thought it was one of the adventurers.

"Level sixty-five."

There was an awkward silence. It was highly unusual for someone of that age to reach that level in combat. There had been cases of high levels, but usually in more menial roles, perhaps farmer, or herder or rancher.

Of course, that was due to all the training and leveling aura effects that I had. I had four dedicated training skills, one dedicated Treeiner, and a bunch of other practice things. Thinking about it, it didn't feel that cheating. The heroes got close to level one hundred within two years. Lausanne started training when she was...six? And now she was already fourteen, turning fifteen. Nine years for sixty-five levels, versus two years for one hundred levels; I thought heroes were still at least seven times faster, ignoring the fact that the higher levels were harder!

Man, that made my hero fragments super overpowered.

I should think about weaponizing or 'sharing' these shards someday. I wondered whether it was possible to 'lend' the effects onto an item or as a 'blessing,' such that they gained its effects?

[The first 100 fragments cannot be given away.]

"What?" I wondered to myself. Why such a restriction? What was the first one hundred fragments for?

No answer. It seemed like this wasn't something the system was willing to tell yet.

Fine, could I set up a proxy, such that the effects of the fragments were shared, even if the actual fragment remained physically with me? A 'cloud aura server,' with my trees acting as my transmitters.

No answer.

Did that mean it was impossible, or it was possible?

Yeah.

Why should a benefit be solely hoarded by me anyway?

"TreeTree, I'm sick of demons," Lausanne protested.

"I know."

She decided to eat some cake. I missed cake. I would to have a nice coffee cake. I missed coffee cakes.

I asked some of the servants to mix coffee powder into the fertilizer and pour it around me instead. At least I could somewhat 'taste' it, but it was just different. Really sucked not having taste buds.

Wait. There were those giant insect-eating bugs that resembled lips and mouths. Could I evolve those and make them have taste buds? Then I could still taste food!

"TreeTree, why did you ask the servants to pour coffee?" It was Laufen who strangely breached the topic.

"Coffee...is beneficial to trees."

"I've never heard of such a thing."

"Only ancient, ancient trees like me," I lied. "Only those that have lived the aeons would desire the taste of things."

"Ah. Then would you like tea as well? Or chocolate?"

"Yes. That would be great. Pour it into the small hole next to the tree of prayers."

I first needed to evolve my roots to have taste receptors. Then I just needed to block out the taste of...dirt.

YEAR 84 MONTH 12

< Do not fear the outworlders. >
    < Fear them. >

Huh? Lilies had randomly made a statement.

> Am I...talking to the same person? <

< A mass, a hive, are many, made of many, and many minds make many different ways. A nation is one being, and one being is a nation. Only a nation can comprehend another. >

What?

< We are many. And we have many ways. We are aggressive. We are passive. We are quiet. We are loud. We are everything, and we are nothing. >

Oh. In short...because Lilies was like a choir...there were bits of it that had...different personalities? And each of them did things differently?

> Was there one in charge? <

< Yes and no >

I...decided not to think about it. It was like I was talking to a bunch of schoolkids and each of them had a word to say.

Apparently, the heroes had a skirmish with the demon king. Somehow, they managed to escape the fight itself. But it was quite...uh...stupid of them. Three against the demon king? What were they thinking? At least none of them died.

Meanwhile, the other heroes in the other continents were still 'clearing' their respective continents of the demons and, apparently, making some plans. Were they coming?

As winter set in, I sensed unusual energies coming from the heroes' tower. I didn't know what it was, and I tried to get the labs to scan, but the energy fluctuated slightly and then...went back to normal again. It felt like star mana, but without any detailed results, I wasn't sure.

This winter, we'd managed to get a bit more evergreen plants to grow. Some traders managed to bring in winter-resistant plants from faraway lands, and that made me very happy. It was nice to have fellow winter-friendly trees.

Down far south, near Lake Lilypod, the Lake itself was a source of warmth, and it didn't freeze over. The unmoving giant treewalker was sprawled over the ground, now overgrown with trees.

It was warmer here. South was nearer to where the sun was, after all, and some simple astronomical rules still applied, even if there were more moons to complicate the water-level movements.

"The giant walker just...died," a trader mentioned, walking past the giant thing. To them, it was dead. The difference between a dead giant walker and a giant walker infested with vines and trees, in practice, was really still a dead, unmoving thing.

"The king ordered that no one approach the walker, though." The king referred to the 'elected' ruler of the Giant Lilypod City, truly just the ruler of the humans. I suspected Lilies was in communication with him to some degree, but then, it was probably a secret it didn't want to share.

A few carts filled with corpses moved past. And later, they dumped all the corpses into the lake.

"It's really quite fast that the walker was covered in trees, though," a trader said. They were just walking past my [giant attendant trees]. "And these massive trees, they just...appeared."

"Must be the Lilypod magic."

"Really, you think so?"

"All tree spirits have the 'bloom' effect. It's like...a fact," one other trader said. "I've never heard of a tree spirit without having some kind of supergrowing ability."

"Why would the Giant Lilypod do such a thing?"

"Maybe the giant walker's like...super fertile or something? It does have a lot of magic in it."

"Really?" I thought this trader just said 'really' all the time.

"I'm guessing. I'm guessing!" The trader laughed.

A bunch of adventurers quickly pushed them on. "Good sirs, please, let's get moving."

"Ah, yes, yes."

Escorts were still needed, after all. Demons weren't over yet.

Huh. I would like to visit a floating city for a change. I wondered if it'd be more like Venice, or whether it'd be like those floating markets of Southeast Asia. Or was it more like living in some kind of floating oil rig?

———

The demons kept up their attacks, but without the walkers, the regular armies weren't really much of a problem.

"That's the thirtieth Demon Elite I killed," Lausanne complained. "And no levels this time!"

Jura laughed. "Maybe...you should let them do the fighting. You just help when they really can't do it." There was a bunch of other Valthorns, the strongest of them in their level thirties, a pretty good level for their age. Almost genius, even.

"Uh...okay." Lausanne realized she just said something that wasn't going to go her way.

"Try to play a [leader] role then, instead of the vanguard. Maybe you can get some kind of leadership class."

"Can't I just ask TreeTree for it?"

"Stop asking TreeTree for everything, Lausanne. A good champion doesn't depend on handouts." I frankly disagreed with that. Handouts weren't the problem. Not really.

"But heroes got their powers handed to them on a silver platter!"

Jura paused. "True, but still, if you depend on someone else's power, it means you were not there yet!" With how cold winter was, everyone was practicing indoors. We had plenty of space.

Stratreegos found a magic spot.

A large, dark cave was located on one of the mountains. It was further west, even further from the volcano. There were monstrous bats, large crab-monsters.

I sighed.

Probably a 'black' element location again. I honestly didn't understand why my soul forge was blue. I was a tree; shouldn't I be green? But magic did what magic did; it was what it was. Was black, red, and blue magic more common in this world?

Should I still take it, though, since I had one forest rod?

But with the heroes' power growing so quickly, their summoned armies already sweeping through many parts of the continent, destroying demons in the process, the odds of me locating a demon rod for 'capture' was slim.

Already, more rumors and news came from the land beyond. That the heroes were able to call on units that were like...superunits, able to take on a demon walker singlehandedly. That meant they could now attack the demonic forces on multiple fronts, expanding their force projection ability to counter the demon's reach.

Had they passed level one hundred? It sounded like some of them did.

If so, the odds of a final battle with the demon king were high.

I wanted a superunit, too. It was quite unfair that I had to get a heroic soul to summon a titan, and they could do it with...level one hundred. The gods really loaded the die with them.

YEAR 85 MONTH 1

A new year began.

It was almost three years since the demon king had arrived, by my own clock, year 82 month two. This war had gone on for far too long.

Everywhere, it was weariness. A sense of exhaustion in the people. Rumors of frustrations among the many kings and queens. What was taking the heroes so long to just get to it? Even me, I was just tired of demons.

For the past three—no, four—years, I'd been battling demons throughout my domain.

But there was also rising hope.

It was going to end soon.

The question that happened, inevitably, was when and where it was going to end. And for most of the kings, how to avoid being... collateral damage in the cataclysmic battle that occurred.

The question of 'where' was most certainly our current continent. The demon king was finally at the site of demon king, and predictably, consistent with the Astaroth incident, it summoned a demon. A demon shaped like a large airship.

It didn't seem like the demon king was intent on going anywhere else. It wasn't moving, and instead, it stopped and released a massive energy blast that incinerated the surroundings of the former site. What was once a crater turned into a larger one.

And we all felt it.

A strong energy that pushed back against my auras. A kind of energy so 'dry' that I felt like it was attempting to strip my mana away from me. The tower vibrated, its divine energies triggered to create a shield, and even then it felt the tower pull, no, demand energy from the surroundings to reinforce itself.

So strange.

But it was a taunt.

Thanks to that unidirectional wave, we all knew where the demon king was. Like a blazing fire, all we had to do was follow the warmth.

It called out to them. The demon king and the image of the previous one.

I could almost feel the words that it meant, through that wave. Come, heroes.

Time to settle this fight.

That energy wave triggered magical defensive spells, like how lightning sometimes triggered alarms.

Even in New Freeka, some simple enchantments, like door reinforcement spells or enchanted weapons made unusual sounds and had strange shapes appear on them.

And the hex? The residual hex that was now pooled together cordoned away from the general masses? They reacted strongly to the wave. It wasn't absorbing it, but it didn't like it at all, and a strange, purple-ish glow appeared over them.

So it was time to bunker up or run away. Some of them chose to travel further away from it. It was a sensible choice. The demon king was taunting the heroes to go to it, but at the same time, it was a signal to everyone else to run away.

Which many did.

For those that didn't, or couldn't, we bunkered up. The sewers and underground tunnels project thankfully completed, the citizens started stocking up designated storage areas in the underground tunnels.

The tunnels went quite deep into the ground, after all; the demon kings clearly had incredible destructive power, and shallow, near-surface tunnels were still going to get destroyed easily.

I'd also restocked my constantly growing arsenal of anti-demon wooden bolts. If it ever came down to a fight, I wasn't going to go down easily.

I hoped I didn't get involved. But a part of me knew that was wishful thinking. It was on this continent, after all.

In the long eternity of time, one day, I would have to face the demon king. Whether by chance or intention.

HEROES FINAL BATTLE

"Eight, yes…three, no. So it's time." It was Astra who said it, announcing the decision of the vote to the group.

"Are you sure? Are we sure?" one of the heroes asked.

"We can't hold this on forever. We've all voted yes. Let's go with it."

A quiet silence. Although the heroes' power was incredible, they all felt it. The gnawing sense that the power was biting into their minds; the stronger it got, the more it compelled them to just go at the demons. It was almost like a bloodlust. They all looked like they hadn't slept in months. Eyebags and all.

"Was it always like this?"

"I-I don't think so. No records I checked had it. But then again… very few heroes took…three years to slay the demon king. Mostly because the battles were all confined on the same continent, so…it just tended to end rather quickly."

All of them didn't sleep well. At night, they all got nightmares. It wasn't like this before, but it started a month, no, two months ago. At first it was mild, but lately it was more and more gruesome. Death. Destruction.

Were they going insane?

"But we're just walking into the demon king's trap. It wants us to go! We must hold on till the time is right."

"When is the time right? We are all about level one hundred–plus now. Astra is even level one hundred twenty! We can't wait forever. We've discussed this many times, and it's time. It's waiting for us, and I think we should take up the challenge."

Some of them kept the thoughts to themselves. Harris, too, had nightmares. So much death. The slaughter of cities. The sacking of so many kingdoms to the demonic hordes.

But why?

Why?

"So. The plan is, using the existing tower network, I'll do a [mass recall], and that will teleport every one of us to one of the towers. Harris, Mirei, Becky, let us know which tower is the best. I'm guessing the demon king knows and can sense us, based on how their walkers and supercannons behaved, so honestly, the nearest tower will be the best."

"The nearest tower is not functioning. It's too near, and the demonic wave it emits has shredded the tower," Mirei explained. "There is a tower near Nung's capital. We'll use that."

"All right. Will you all be there?"

"We're somewhere north, but we are headed down."

"Before that. Harris...we heard you attempted to fight the demon king? You didn't tell us about that in our previous call."

"No. It's more like...it...uh...erm..."

Mirei, Becky, and Harris looked at each other, wondering who should explain.

"So?" One of them was impatient. Truth be told, all of them were edgy, the lack of sleep and nightmares making everyone rough. Already, there was dissatisfaction with each other. Harris heard that even the previous heroes had conflicts; people, after all, never worked together perfectly.

"We kind of just...found it. It attacked us, and we fled as fast as we could."

"How strong was it?"

"Strong enough." Harris didn't want to say too much.

"Didn't try to fight it?" one of them asked. "Who knows, you could win? So far, all the demons we've faced were talked about as incredibly powerful, but now our summons can take them on! Maybe this demon king's a chump, too."

Two heroes looked at each other. Victor and Gustav, they were both there when Pooja died. It was an accident, in a way. They made a mistake, and Pooja was in the wrong position. They wanted to say something, but somehow both didn't say it.

"No. We...we thought we should do it all together," Harris said.

"Heh. As expected," one of them sneered. It had been two years since they all arrived, and few friendships stayed the same in that time.

"So...we all teleport to the location?" one of the other heroes asked, stepping in.

"Yes," Astra replied, sensing the moment. "Anything else?"

"No."

———

Harris sighed to himself. They all just happened to be in the same bus, somehow. There was a camaraderie, at least, with Becky and Mirei, as the three of them traveled together and fought many battles together.

But none of that with the other nine...no, *eight* heroes. They were not close to Pooja, and honestly, when Pooja died, the three of them...didn't really feel anything. No, actually, all they felt was a very strong desire for revenge, to get back at the demons.

"We need to think. Tea?" Mirei asked.

"Yeah. I need that tea now." All three of them huddled together. Using some dried tea leaves, they made a brew. Ginger flavored, somehow. There was some ginger leaves mixed in.

They all had a sip of the New Freekan tea leaves and felt their anger, their...craving to fight subside a little.

"Okay. Let's discuss what we heard."

"All of them are going to port in, and we're going to fight the demon king. Absolutely a trap," Becky said, taking another sip. The smell of the ginger was in the air.

"Astra has a point. We can't avoid this forever. Even if it's a trap, they don't seem to be in any state to resist the...effects of our powers. Even this tea's effectiveness weakens with each level we gain."

Harris sighed again. Somewhere, a squad of heavily armed shields was fighting demons. He could feel it.

"And Astra's mind-link will help."

"We've never tested it. We're placing too much trust on a skill that supposedly will make us work seamlessly."

"They seem to believe the skill will do what it says it does."

"And no evidence so far refutes that. So I reckon it will help."

Harris, Becky, and Mirei shared a glance. A lightning elemental was roasting a few chunks of meat. The lightning helped to char the skin a bit, giving it a bit of a crisp. A metallic suit of armor chopped some vegetables, and a small goblin-ish creature was peeling some meat of some shellfish.

There was a camp behind them. They'd been using their summons for all sort of chores, such as carrying camp-gear. All powered by star mana. Star mana was an amazing thing. It lasted long, and just a bit could sustain their summons for almost a week, longer for their smaller, menial summons.

"So, we're still going with the plan, then," Mirei said softly.

"It's our best shot. Even with all these random factors remaining, and the rest of them clearly can't wait any more. Any longer we'd probably fight each other. At least we can finish whatever we were brought to this world for." Harris sighed. He was explaining it more for himself. He was hardly convinced it was the best idea, but in the end, he still voted for it.

It was like being forced to swallow a bitter pill to not die.

Becky refilled her cup of tea. "Well. Harris was right. It was our best shot."

Harris finished his meal and then took out what resembled a

forge. Two lightning elementals and a fire elemental helped him with his forging.

Truth was Harris scouted the demon king. Whatever Lady Mika left behind made him wonder whether there was a trap. The previous group of heroes fell for it, and here they were, walking right into it.

So Harris, without telling the other three groups, decided to scout the demon king out. He prepared beforehand, a special teleportation scroll, some backup abilities with both Becky and Mirei, a 'lightning-powered' temporary recall, and a 'lightning speed' boost. And high-powered summons as backup. Perhaps they could buy time.

The demon king took the shape of a massive spider with four circular rings on top, forming something resembling a verandah, and at intervals, the verandah functioned as a demonic summoning portal, it forcefully opened a massive rift, and each time, one more demon walker emerged. Next to it was a large floating castle filled with jagged spires that radiated a reddish glow.

He could feel its power grow and then ebb. Then he noticed that it was synchronized with the gate on the demon king.

It was acting as a power generator to summon more demons.

Instead of relying on leylines and magic spots, it decided to tap on whatever's left on the previous demon kings.

Yet Harris watched a bit too long, and the demon walkers started firing.

He fled. As fast as he could. He wasn't mad. There were at least two million demons in that massive valley. At least thirty walkers. It was going to be a massive battle at scale. And...flyers. There were creatures that resembled...wyverns.

It turned out...sure, they were gaining levels, but it was going to be a race. If these two million demons went out in all directions, how long would it take for them to stop it? Could they gain levels fast enough that they could beat back the horde of demons that ravaged the world?

And yet Harris didn't feel guilty not sharing this information with the rest of them. And honestly, he didn't know why his two friends didn't, either.

Astra looked at the map. It was laid out on a large table, and it marked where the towers were located.

"Something didn't make sense."

"What?" Naya looked bored. "Why were you studying the maps they sent you? All we got to do is teleport there and do what we gotta do. We've got super-summons now, and the demons are still giving us the same kind of opponents."

"Aren't you underestimating the demon king?"

"And the gods were underestimating me," Naya said. Astra could only roll his eyes.

Astra looked at the map again. He roughly measured the distance between where the demon king was and the nearest tower. Why such a large distance? What was the demon king planning? Harris met it, yet...why did he not say much? Did he have something to hide?

"I can't wait," Naya said. "After this is all over, I'll get to live life as an emperor with a massive harem."

Astra didn't reply. There really was no need to.

"Go sleep."

Astra didn't. Naya slept. Feeling like he wasn't going anywhere, he went for a walk and found Gerrard on a hill. It wasn't hard spotting him.

Gerrard nodded at him. "Heya. Not sleeping yet?"

"I could ask you the same question." Astra noticed a mug and a few barrels of beer by the side. They were all schoolkids when they got there, but it'd been two years, and well, everyone had different ways of coping with the...nightmares. In Gerrard's case, it was...beer.

They were underaged, after all, but who was going to stop heroes with super-growth spells from buying beer?

He was through a barrel; sadly that was what he needed to get drunk, since as a hero, he had some poison resistance, and he had a summon that collected his 'beer' from the nearby towns. Helped that some of his summons were gladiators that could speak a few words.

"Hmm. Were you here to make sure I fix my guys' weapons?" There was a gladius at the side, made from a mix of regular metal and star mana, something they made in their free time. Gerrard had the benefit of having equippable summons. His 'elite' star-mana gladiators could will items he made.

"We've passed that stage." Astra grinned. There was a small magical staff at his side. It was weird, that all heroes gained a 'crafting' option together with star mana, and that crafting option seemed exceptionally personal, in the sense that none could make something like someone else. It was through a mix of star mana and their personal 'will' that these 'hero-artifacts' were made.

Maybe there were crafter-heroes in past generations, and people, no...heroes who could recreate other heroic artifacts.

"So...why were you here?" Gerrard stood. They exchanged a look.

"You voted no." The voting results were public. There was no use hiding who voted what. "Why?"

"Because I felt like it."

Astra glared. Gerrard met the glare and after five seconds decided to look away. "You're lying."

"Maybe."

"Won't you tell me the truth? The demon king's not far away. We should go in with our eyes wide open."

Gerrard looked disgusted. "Must everything be the demon king? Every time I get drunk, the only thing on my mind is why everyone is just talking about the demons all the freaking time?"

"Because that's why we are here."

"Fucking twisted logic you got there. Why did we accept this task so wholeheartedly anyway? It's not as if demons did anything to us."

"But they did so much to the land."

"How do you even know if they are real? If any of this is…real?"

"It feels like it, and that's good enough. Real or not, the wrongs must be righted."

"Again with that twisted logic. But you know, I had to vote no. Even if I knew all of you would have voted yes."

"Then tell me why."

"Because Naya's overconfident in his skills, and you are overconfident in your skills. Almost everyone is overconfident in their own abilities. We're going to go and fight the demon, and we'll realize how inadequate we were all the while."

"We've reached level one hundred."

"So? Is there a rule somewhere that the demon king is a level one hundred threat? Why not level two hundred? How do we even know level one hundred is enough? Because it's three digits instead of two? Because of a feeling you all feel and that nagging, screaming pain every time you sleep?"

Astra paused, and suddenly, yeah. Why did they feel it was… enough? Just because the demon walkers were now 'easy,' did that mean they were ready for the next level, the king itself? What if the gap between the king and walkers was massive, as it should be? Yet that moment of discomfort and insecurity didn't last; like a candle in the wind, it went poof.

"There are eleven of us."

"And the demon king's predecessors have clearly killed many of them."

"And there were survivors. Many kingdoms have a hero in their lineage. No glory without some sacrifice. Don't you want to be king?"

Gerrard looked disgusted. "That's what we are, eh? We come here, defeat a demon king, and then go on and make a fuck-ton of babies and leave our magical weapons for them."

"Well…" Astra wanted to say yes. But he knew better.

"Our alliance lasts up till we kill the demon king. We're not friends after that."

Astra shrugged. It was really optimistic to expect twelve kids in the same bus to somehow stick together for two to three years. "That's all we need."

A week later, they all teleported to the site. It was a secluded tower located on a mountain; there were subtle mana flows in the ground that helped amplify the tower's energies.

Astra was first to arrive, and he activated the [global recall]. That brought the rest of them there.

"It's much stronger here...its presence." The heroes looked at each other. For those located on different continents, it was the first time they met face-to-face since that day on the bus or that moment with the gods. But they were referring to the 'taunt' that the demon king emitted. Its constant...aura.

Harris, Becky, and Mirei looked at them. "Welcome to the central continent."

"Yeah, yeah. We were going for the demon king immediately?" Naya shrugged.

Some of them nodded. A few looked uncertain. Astra, who was level one hundred twenty-five, took the lead. "Let's go. There is really no point delaying this entire thing. Can you three lead the way?"

"Sure, but do you guys need to call on your summoned armies? Or they can appear at any second?"

Gustav and Lombard both nodded. "Ah, my powers need a bit time to appear, and I have artillery forces. I will need to position my bombardment units at a distance."

Harris took out the map again. There was a red star showing where the demon king was, and a big red ring around it.

"What's the red ring?"

"The demon king's army."

"Ah. Fodder for us." Harris winced at the word but didn't say a thing. He pointed to a chain of hills and slopes further out. "What's the range of your artillery? Is this place far enough?"

"How far is that? I mean...uh..." Lombard looked at the map. He had an issue translating distances on maps into 'range.' In practice, he used his own forces to 'sense' where it was, and he had 'spotter units' that helped his artillery units find targets.

Harris didn't know how to explain distances, too, not in this world where kilometers and all didn't really mean much. They didn't have measurement tools. What was one day's horse ride away, and was it even universal? Different horses travelled different speeds, what more for those with riding skills.

"Never mind, use the demon king's aura as a gauge?" Astra intervened. "Let's move. Feel free to break off to set up your forces."

Gustav the golem-master and Lombard the cannoneer nodded. "Sure."

It wasn't hard to find a demon king that was actively transmitting its presence to the heroes. And stranger still, none of the kingdoms attempted to hexbomb the demon king. In fact, the hexbombs mostly stopped once the heroes got their groove going. After all, why sacrifice lives when the heroes' summoned units could fight walkers for you?

The demon king warped the terrain with it right in the middle. Its large, massive legs embedded into the ground, drawing mana and energy from the planet. In a way, it resembled an extremely large oil rig that pulled that mana and then used it to produce walker after walker. The floating castle next to it also generated mana and 'fed' it to the king.

When the heroes first saw what they were up against, it was a mixed reaction.

Those overconfident ones merely grinned. "Ah, no matter how many of these fodders they make, it's not going to stop us."

Some felt this validated their choice, that it was time to fight the demon king anyway. Delaying it was not going to solve the problem. And those who voted no, in their minds, this was the moment that made them feel like it was always inevitable. It was either they fight the demons or the demons destroy the world. It was a game, wasn't it?

"It's waiting for us. Let's not keep it waiting." Astra nodded, and he triggered the star mana forms. Around him, phantoms started appearing, and they charged into the horde of demons before them. Astra's body itself was coated by a white sheen, as if he was a divine being here to bestow divine retribution.

Thousands, tens of thousands of phantoms appeared, a one-man army, and it ripped through the regular demonoids like paper. The walkers, some one hundred fifty of them, towered across the battlefield, and they started shooting their energy blasts. They were always in position, and the quiet skies were ripped by the thundering shots.

Each of the heroes summoned their forces. Tens of thousands of summoned creatures, almost a hundred thousand summoned creatures, magically appeared from portals, as if it was a scene from Endgame. One of them, of course, had to quip.

"We're in the endgame now. And this is our final battle with Thanos."

"I hope not. I don't want one of us to die."

"If only one of us die, that's a win."

Gustav summoned massive golems, fifteen of them, each as large as a walker, and with powers no inferior to it. Magical yet mechanical constructs, they resembled giant-size Ant-man fighting the massive leviathans when they wrestled the walkers. Lombard had self-propelling railguns in the distance, and they matched the walker's energy blasts. Each hero brought their own 'type' of special armies. Harris had walking shield generators that deflected energy blasts, protecting summoned units from the enemies.

For close to two hours, the entire crater was engulfed in battles, as demons and the summoned creatures clashed. Still, the demonoids were never able to hold back the heroes' forces, even if they thinned them greatly. Even if giant, demonic wyverns ripped the summoned railguns to shreds, there were always more summoned units.

Yet the demon king remained unmoved in the middle. All it did was concentrate its power on its 'throne,' its massive legs unmoving, its massive gate-like horns, eight of them, a rift right in the middle of that cavity.

As they got nearer, they changed targets, and they started to attack the demon king's massive body. Those attacks met a massive energy barrier, the railgun bolts vibrating and rippling on the barrier like a rock that dropped into a lake.

Their summoned units gradually gained an upper hand. The overconfident heroes started to feel vindicated. The demon king's army was nothing much after all, not against eleven heroes and their combined armies complete with all the stacking auras each of them had!

Yet the demon king didn't move. Nor did the 'shadow' of the former demon king.

The rift changed color.

The heroes attacked, again, at the barrier. The barrier held on, but it was cracking. Small holes started to emerge, and some summoned units got close to the demon king's legs. They attacked.

The rift turned red.

Naya, the archmage with an army of summoned water and ice elementals, attacked, raining ice on the battlefield. He, too, was enveloped in a sheen of white-bluish light; his magical longstaff had a dark blue crystal.

The demon king's army was down to half, and almost all the demon walkers, elites, and generals were down. The fodder surprisingly lasted longer because there was just so many of them.

But they were fodder.

Truly, only the demon king itself mattered.

The rift turned a darker red, almost maroon.

"Is it going to fire?" Harris looked. A massive ice blast finally cracked the barrier. The heroes' units were cut down to less than a quarter now, but it was now between them and the king.

This was why they saved star mana.

The gigantic golems attacked the unmoving demon king; its massive body resembled a castle that didn't move despite the attacks. That was not to say the golems attack were ineffective. They worked—there were small wounds and scars where the golems attacked. It was just that the demon king was a monstrous thing, a city in a creature. From a distance, its present form resembled a massive spider with super-thick legs, and another upside-down spider on the top, its legs representing the 'horns' that created the rift.

The heroes attacked. Their summoned creatures damaged the demon king.

But it was too slow.

The rift turned purple.

Then, in a short flash, it shot out a thick purple beam that cut a massive gash in the ground, and all the way till the horizon, destroying everything in its path.

And one hero stood in its path, her body burning from its purple flames, and then she felt into the gash below. She died, and all her summoned units vanished with her.

All the heroes felt a surge of anger as they lobbed more attacks. There was no need.

The rift was gray again. This time, the floating castle moved to attack, firing smaller red beams from its many spires.

"Who was that?" Harris shouted. They were all spread out in the battlefield, their forces making everything messy.

Astra checked his status. He was like the chat administrator who could see who went offline. "...Simone."

"What?!" Those from the same place felt some loss. For the rest of them, it was...just a name. The demon king was before them, and now this...thing was attacking them. It tore through the stronger summoned units easily.

"Focus on the demon king, there is still ten of us, and that rift takes forever to charge. We can win this."

The rift turned orange.

"You fucking jinx of a mouth," Naya cursed as he lobbed spell after spell at the demon king's body. The demon king's body had cracks, but it was like ants making microscopic cuts on a giant elephant. Sure, there were cuts, but it was going to take a while for it to take down the giant.

"Get rid of the floating castle!"

Spells flew, and golems, railguns, and lightning blasts zapped the floating castle. Slightly smaller than the demon king, and clearly less sturdy, each attack made it wobble in midair, and the red beams tended to lose their paths.

The rift was still orange, but it was getting darker.

More cracks appeared throughout the massive body of the demon king. Even the gargantuan golems looked like little children trying to fight with an adult. Some of the heroes concentrated fire on the floating castle.

A shadow of the former demon king, it was hardly as strong. No, it was perhaps only a quarter of its stats, and so, the hits got to it easily, and the floating castle crumbled then crashed into the ground below, exposing a round red crystal.

"Uh..."

The rift was red.

Harris instantly felt danger and quickly activated all the summoned shields he could gather. "Watch out for that thing!" he shouted.

The red crystal vibrated.

A golem lifted it up and flung it as far as it could.

The rift was dark red.

"The fuck, why is the color changing so quickly?"

"Ain't a final boss without some asspull, y'know. This was probably one of it."

A golem punched one of the legs, and the leg finally, after

receiving so much damage from the army of summons around it, collapsed.

The rift was still dark red. And then, it released a shockwave of that dark red energy, scorching through most of the summoned units, destroying them instantly. It also destroyed many of the lesser demons, but by now, there were no demon walkers left.

The wave smacked right into the heroes' protective items and shields, but one of the heroes was too near and couldn't react to it time.

The wave burned him. And he flailed like a man on fire, the reddish fire got past whatever protection he had. Naya attempted an iceblast to negate the fire, but it didn't work. It seemed like the fire found a life of its own, and somehow it wouldn't subside.

"Healer!"

Despite the massive distance, healing was still entirely possible. The healing-dedicated hero still had a tremendous cast range and could instantly activate healing.

The fire didn't go away, but the wounds recovered instantly.

Yet, the rift was still red, and then a second blast went out. The healer had to put up a shield. The burning hero was still too close, and the second blast turned him into ash.

"Fuck!" the healer cursed, and the earth rumbled. The demon king was finally moving! Even if one of its legs was broken, it still had seven other legs, and the two red energy waves incinerated most of the summoned units.

So the battlefield was quite clean. Just the surviving nine heroes, one demon king, and some of their summons.

"Anyone have summons left?" Astra asked through their live chat. At this distance, it wasn't hard to maintain some kind of VC function. "Or should we focus on defense?"

"I still have star mana, but I think we should restrict summons to higher-tier ones. Those can take one shot!" Two gigantic golems remained, but the red flames enveloped them, and they slowly 'melted' them. Some gladiators too were around; they had the benefit of having star-mana artifacts that allowed them to tank the wave.

The demon king moved rather slowly. It was pulling out its massive legs embedded deep into the ground. Each leg left a deep hole, and as it lifted its body up to walk, they saw something resembling a mouth for the first time.

Located at the bottom of its body, it looked like the central part of an octopus, only made with demonic-matter, and it glowed in various colors. And there were smaller mouths.

They were open.

"SHIELDS!" They all felt it, and all the mouths spat out a red fire, coating everything beneath the demon king in an inferno.

This time, the already damaged golems crumbled and turned back into…nothing.

"We need to skip our summons!"

"But then what's the point of all our army skills?"

"It's just to get to this point!"

"Then it's fucked!"

Well, except for the ranged magical railguns that, thankfully, were out of range of the initial blasts. Two survived, and they could continue bombardment. Still, the damage they dealt were miniscule.

Well, the demon king did take damage from the earlier attacks, and throughout its massive body there were wounds and scars.

"Concentrated attack! Use star mana forms!" Harris yelled out. In his mind, he wondered why the notes talked about using star-mana forms to fight the demon king. "Let's get on its body. There should be 'cores' we can attack, rather than us trying to take on the entire structure!"

"Good point!" Naya waved his wand, and an icesheet levitated him up.

The demon king's many mouths opened, and this time, they lobbed small energy blasts, in the millions. They rained down on the heroes below, attempting to delay the heroes from approaching its main body.

"Did this demon king take notes from bullet hell or something?" Layers on layers of ice shield appeared, blocking the little blasts.

"We made a mistake. We should have just gone for the main body right away!"

"What, and get caught by the red wave? We didn't even know it could do that!" All the heroes had activated their defensive abilities. The overconfidence from the early stage had faded. They witnessed two of them die; maybe they'd be next. There was no time to be reckless and hold back some abilities in reserve.

Still, the rain of energy bullets did not deter the heroes at all, and very quickly, all of them were on the demon king's main body. There were no lesser demons but parts of the demon king that attacked them. Throughout its body, spires transformed into tentacles or beam-towers, attacking the invading heroes.

The heroes spread out, looking for 'cores' or 'hearts,' things that powered the demon king. They hacked at everything that looked like it could hold something like that, their star-mana powered abilities, now at close range, easily cutting through any defenses the demon king had. Even while the massive monster moved.

They had to be wary. The rift was now orange again, and gradually, it turned reddish. And the massive size of the demon king meant they could be hacking and attacking nothing for hours. Their strongest area spells lacked the 'focused' damage needed to cut through the demon king's defenses.

One hero summoned her elites to help out, but the elites were useless. Unless they had equipment made or infused with star mana, the damage they dealt was close to nothing.

"We need to split up!"

The demon king suddenly stopped, and it...jabbed one of its large legs into the ground.

The heroes braced for the sudden shaking and collapse of the demon king's body to the ground; they had magic to keep them steady and floating.

Then it did so again. A second leg pierced the ground.

"Why is it doing that? How far have we moved?"

The heroes suddenly realized they were no longer in the crater. The demon king had moved a good distance during the thirty to forty minutes they were attacking its body. Its massive size and magic meant they hardly felt the move.

"What's going on?"

It was that very moment, through the entirety of the world...all the demonoids shook...and disintegrated into small, ash-like particles. Then the ashes started moving, as if swept by a wind, all toward the demon king. They moved intensely, and throughout the world, a strong, hurricane-like wind wrecked, damaged, and killed many, as this 'wind' carried all these ashes to the demon king.

"It's the transformation! All boss fights must have another form! This must be it!" The heroes didn't realize the issue.

"Stop it!" Astra yelled. "We must find the source before this transformation completes!"

"HOW?" The heroes were attacking the demon king's body as much as they could. Some of them concentrated their attacks on the center, believed that the demon king would have its 'core' in the center.

Harris paused and took a sip from a flask. He closed his eyes momentarily, willing his body and soul to sense the demon king. The demon king could sense them, and they could sense the demon king. Lady Mika's notes were clear on that. Maybe they had to 'find' it using that sense. And indeed, he did. "There are four cores!" He pointed them out and quickly rushed to the one nearest to him.

The heroes managed to destroy three cores, and even so it took them two hours. Way longer than they liked, despite how strong their star-mana was. There were just too many tentacles, monsters, and spires in the way. Two hours never felt so long.

The ashes all arrived, and then the body itself also turned into ash.

"Quick! Find the core. Attack it when it's in ash form!" They did find it. And they attacked it with all their might.

The ash was too thick. After all, it was a mass made from all the demons generated throughout the world.

The ash formed together into a large sphere; it floated in the sky as if there was a dark moon, its massive size turning day into night.

The heroes attacked relentlessly, hoping to interfere with its transformation.

The sphere split into ten smaller spheres, and nine of the spheres transformed into humanoid-shaped warriors. The heroes wondered why their attacks failed to stop the transformation.

The last sphere transformed into a grotesque massive demon rod. It was as large as a tower. And it then jammed deep into the ground.

"Uh?"

"Don't stop!" Astra yelled. There were nine of them and nine 'demons.' "That rod must be the core!"

What they saw then was the very earth itself transforming into an unnatural terrain. The demon rod was a scaled-up, demon-king version of the demon rod. They also saw something...strange.

Spirits. Of their two fallen comrades, bound by the demon king rod. It...siphoned energy from the two glowing white spirits, and it pulsed. With each pulse, the demon rod gained power and spread its influence further.

The heroes didn't have to ask much. They understood it by seeing. They had to stop it. The demon king wanted their souls for energy.

And the nine demons stood in their way. Oddly sized just like them, they resembled...humans? All of them had two hands, two legs, one head all in human-like ways. And each of them held a different weapon. They were gray, unlike the usual reddish brown the demonoids had.

The heroes attacked. There was not much to talk, even if they looked human. And these nine demons matched the heroes for it. At first.

They felt the presence of the demon king spread further and further in the ground, and simultaneously, the environment around them started burning with a black fire. Demon fire. They'd seen this. They were briefed of it.

The nine demons kept up. Somehow the star mana wasn't as effective on them as before...as if they were made of something... else. The heroes, exhausted from their earlier long battles, found themselves digging as deep as they could to stand up to them.

Some of the heroes did better, especially those proficient in close combat, like Gerrard, who was the first to stab his star mana sword through one of the demons, and the demon turned into ash. Eight left. And then one of the demons stabbed its rapier into Naya's chest, and instantly, Naya started to turn into...ash. Eight of them left.

The eight gray ashdemons seemed to take their attacks as if they were just regular adventurers. A part of them wanted to ask, "How?" But the adrenaline and exhaustion meant they just kept fighting.

The heroes were leading. Those focused on close combat, Gerrard and Harris, started gaining an edge. They defeated five and lost Helen, Gustav, and Lombard.

Only five of them left. Harris, Gerrard, Astra, Mirei, and Becky. And three ashdemons left. The ashdemons' power waned, and that was when they realized the demon king couldn't keep maintaining them forever.

They killed the three ashdemons and turned their focus on the massive rod.

They had to break it. They all felt it, the scream and wailing of their comrades being 'drained,' unable to move on. The earth itself tried to resist the demonic influence, but powered by the heroes' star mana, the earth couldn't hold it back.

The corruption had spread as far as their eyes could see, maybe even further. Maybe even some of the cities would have seen the demon flames because...the entire skyline was just...black fire. The battle against the ashdemons took too long. Three hours, maybe four. The sky was already dark, but because the demon fire was everywhere, they didn't realize it.

They pulled their power together, exhausted as they were. They didn't know how much star mana they used, and by now, it felt like they'd gone past their reserve and some. They didn't even know how they managed to use that last attack and destroyed the demon king rod.

[Demon King Sabnoc has been slain.]

But the corruption...was not going away.

And the corruption had spread over almost half of the entire central continent, that half rendered nigh uninhabitable.

New Freeka was well within the range of the spread.

YEAR 85 MONTH 1

It was coming. We could feel it in our roots, our trunks, our bodies. Every bit of us, we felt it. As if the earth itself cried out for help, and none of us could do anything. There was a tide out there, in that distance, and it came so quickly.

So, so very quickly.

All at once, the soul realm was flooded with deaths.

Something had spread throughout the continent. I could almost feel it, the entirety of Nung burned up and destroyed. Barsoom, gone in a flash. It happened so quickly, as the earth itself rotted and turned into this...demonic thing.

Our extended subsidiary trees felt it first, its presence rushing in, and rather quickly, those distant subsidiary trees burned almost instantly in the dark demonic flames. The giant attendant trees, too, started to burn, but they were stronger, and they shared more of our powers, and so...they never truly burned. Instead, they resembled my past, when I was a small stump, engulfed in a black flame, but not dead.

It spread quickly, and it was amazing how quickly it did. But we had no time to think about that because we felt death everywhere, and we felt like pebbles on the beach, watching a tsunami come in.

All we could do was stand our ground and face it.

"Everyone, the best place now is to get as near me as possible. Into the woods." We spoke to the elves and everyone, and they ran as fast as they could.

One-by-one, I lose my link to my faraway trees nearest to the demon king. It was as if I was playing Stellaris and some unknown extradimensional disaster started swallowing up all my stars. And it happened so quickly.

We had maybe...half an hour at the rate the corruption was expanding. That was our guess. Maybe it would slow down because of the 'area' covered increased squared the further the corruption went, and so the same energy wouldn't be able to corrupt as 'many' places?

And it was coming through the ground.

"Don't go underground."

"What?"

"No. The best place now is above ground, and watch for things coming from beneath."

"What's even happening?" one of them asked, but Jura had trained enough that he didn't question me all that much.

Batch by batch, my trees disappeared in a flash, but indeed...it was slightly slowing. But not by much. The fires and the corruption burned so quickly that I hardly got a view of what was going on. I placed a large 'wall' of subsidiary trees and giant attendant trees as it approached. I wanted to see how they performed. It was literally like the earth itself was...rotting and burning simultaneously, and the wall held just a short second before it too overwhelmed my trees and burned them.

"Shit." There was a whole load of madness and chaos, as some people did as they were told, but some didn't.

They ran for the woods. I hoped that having a huge number of trees mutually reinforcing the aura would somehow slow it down or stop it altogether.

I tried again. It was getting much, much closer. The demon's presence was like a wave; it pushed closer and closer. It was still not in the valley yet, but maybe...ten minutes to impact.

"Tell everyone to prepare for fire and the earth cracking."

Those who managed to run into the woods did so, and we mentally braced for impact.

The trees lasted longer. They didn't burn as quickly.

Five minutes.

The trees right outside the valley burned. We could see it coming. A black tide and a sky filled with black flames. It was coming into contact to my own roots now. And it...didn't burn much. I pushed my mana into the ground, into my roots to strengthen them, and tried to hold it.

Like a rock in a river, this foul energy attempted to sweep me off, attacking my mana-strengthened roots. At first, I managed to hold on.

New Freeka was still fine, for now.

But the waves kept coming. Twenty minutes, the dark energies from somewhere kept up their pressure on my roots, and they even spiked and ebbed in waves. We were now like an island in a sea of corruption, and this tide threatened to sink us as well.

The wave was relentless, and gradually, my mana started to wane.

A crack appeared, and with it, a huge crack appeared in New Freeka, and fire shot out of the ground. Some of the houses caught on fire, and some of the citizens died there and then. It was screaming. For many of them, it was a sudden change because a while ago it was still clear skies and a sunny day.

I tried to pull as much mana as I could, hoping to resist it, but the corruption was strong and constant. Even so far away, another crack appeared, and this time it torched our underground sewers. I thought it got a few more people who didn't listen to instruction, but I didn't have time to focus.

"TreeTree!" Jura shouted.

"We're trying to hold it back." This was our immediate vicinity, and the demon king's corruption was still so strong? How?

No time to theorize, though. We focused our efforts on stopping the corrupting energy. It felt a bit like a wooden dam that was cracking.

And more cracks, and another part of New Freeka burned.

Then the corrupting energy surged. It hit the 'wall' like a massive wrecking ball, and in an instant, one third of New Freeka was in flames. There was screaming and shouting everywhere.

"TreeTree, what's going on!"

"Demon king." That was all I could answer as I tried to push back at the energy. Why did it surge so quickly? I didn't even have time to see what happened to all the elves.

The corrupting energy surged again, and more, no, it burned more of New Freeka. People were running, and the edges of my forest were in flames. Demonic flames.

"This isn't working, TreeTree!"

I felt the demonic corrupting energy surge in again. Did I try to hold back and let it smack into the forest? What worked? Me? Should I do it again, like with Alexis?

But...this energy was the demon king's very own energy. It was unmistakable. Could I do it?

"Treetree!"

"Aeon!"

I heard faint chatter, and we felt the pain coming through the network. So many trees were burning.

So many, many trees. What if? We felt the call for aid from all the trees. Screaming, wailing, if trees could scream we would be deaf.

No.

While we kept up the wall of mana to hold the corruption at bay, we intentionally let some of it in, and using mana, we guided it to...me.

The demonic energies attacked my main body, but unlike the other trees, I could take it. And I kept holding on for an hour...two...

Three...

Four…

And after a while, all I saw was just…darkness. I felt demonic energy and mana, and it burned. My roots, my trunk, I felt…pain.

Pain.

The valley…was sinking. The corruption, taking the form of the demon king's mana, was unable to break through our walls, except at the funnels where the corruption was instead drawn to me. So it went under, around, and over, and the entirety of the valley started to sink.

I didn't know how long that was because the pain from the demon king's corrupting mana messed with my already distorted sense of time.

I wasn't even sure I was awake the entire time, in between feeling like I was like a chicken roasted over an open fire.

Pain.

The valley was submerged now. A shell made of distorted, demonic-mana tainted rock now surrounded the valley like an egg with a broken shell right on top that barely let some sun in. Or a snowglobe, only…our walls were made of demonic rock.

I didn't know what happened to the elves or New Freeka. But I reckoned nothing much was left. I felt my soul realm get 'flooded' with souls, and at the same time, a whole bunch of other notifications came in.

[Connection to Verdant Volcano lost…]
    [Connection to ThreeTree of Mana lost…]
    [Connection to Dimitree lost]

Pain. I lost the trees that linked me to the volcano and the magical leyline.

It was just so painful.

Pain. I felt the mana overwhelm me at times, and my entire main tree was burning. Yet I knew that the other trees in the valley were still somewhat safe. I could hear them.

Black flames danced across my body, my leaves now a mix of green and black.

"TreeTree!"

Who was that?

"TreeTree!"

I had no ability to respond, but it should be one of the elves.

Pain.

It was just...madness.

The pressure from the demon's mana increased, and I felt the walls and roots buckle a little. I tried to push it back and relieve the pressure by drawing it more to me. I could barely see, but we were submerged.

It was as if the entire terrain around us had somehow partly turned into sludge. Or was it because we were resisting and that was why it turned out that way?

The pressure kept on, and I felt I was burning.

But I thought the valley was safe. I knew it was.

*[**Curse**: Demonic Mana Contamination]*

[You have absorbed too much demonic mana, and you are now 'cursed.' Your ability to remain conscious is now significantly impaired, and you will feel pain constantly.]

The fuck was that?

The mana pressure surged...

And then stopped.

[Demon King Sabnoc has been slain.]

[You received 6 fragments. You have a total of 74 fragments.]

I felt like I needed less mana to push back against the corruption, but it still overwhelmed me. My entire body was still on fire. It was like I was the unlimited charcoal of the flame. My entire body was probably charred black now.

The fire of the demon king clearly wasn't just fire, else I'd be immune to it.

The pain came and went. And came again.

The demon king was dead. But I was still in...pain. And after a while, I felt myself lose consciousness.

ONE YEAR LATER, YEAR 86

When I woke up, I noticed the time on my record had changed by a year. I was asleep for a year, and I was still burning. The demon king's corruption was still around us, and the pain was still there.

In fact, I was jolted awake by the pain.

What was happening? Was everyone okay? Were my fellow trees alive? I couldn't sense a thing; the demonic flames and their corruption had numbed all my senses.

Even if I attempted to see, all I felt was...fire.

It was like I started all over again, so many years ago.

When I had no...senses. It was just...numb.

I checked my notifications. There was clearly a lot that I'd missed when I was...asleep.

[Eriz, Brislach, Wahlen, Emile, Belle, and 170 other familiar-users have died. You gained 3 levels. You are now level 145.]

[As Eriz was under soul contract, you received an assignable soul. Soul Forge is down.]

[Skill learned from Emile's death - Basic Tea Making]

[Skill learned from Wahlen's death - Basic Administration and Recordkeeping]

[Skill learned from a fallen Valthorn Initiate - Pain Endurance]

[The skill Hibernate has been significantly upgraded to Regenerating Sleep.]

[The skill Haunted Forests significantly upgraded to a unique Skill: Forest of Ghostfire]

[The skill Natural Mana Overwhelming upgraded.]

"Oh…" I felt a twang of sadness for their deaths. But then again, that meant Jura, Laufen, and Lausanne were still alive.

What was happening out there? I couldn't see a thing, even if I could feel like I was still holding back a barrier of demonic mana, and I was still drawing the demonic energies from outside.

I could still access my soul realm, at least.

"Eriz?" In the dark, large extradimensional space filled with many little floating lights, this was the place where the dead went to move on.

A small light floated and approached. "Oh?"

"What happened?"

"The valley sank and this black wall appeared and trapped the entire valley. Almost everyone died…I was killed by a stray fire from one of the cracks in the floor."

"Do you know what else?"

"No…I died quite quickly."

Ngeh.

I went back to my notifications. There were still a lot to go through. A year just zoomed by.

There were a whole bunch of skill seeds and class seeds I received from all the people that died throughout the world. There was so many skill seeds I could probably give ten thousand people and still have leftovers.

From my soul realm alone there were…perhaps…eight hundred thousand little lights. And there were probably more that already moved on to their next life.

So many died?

"Trevor? Ivy? Stratreegos? Treeiner? Horns?"

Silence.

[Unable to establish connection to Trevor or Ivy or Stratreegos or Horns. Treeiner has been destroyed. Stratreegos has been destroyed.]

[Treeiner's remains are pending collection. Do you wish to collect it?]

[Stratreegos's remains are pending collection. Do you wish to collect it?]

Yes.

*[**Your skill**: Learning Aura significantly upgraded to Genius Aura]*
*[**Your skill**: Dream Tutor significantly upgraded to Dream Academy]*
*[**Your skill**: Power-leveling upgraded.]*
*[**You gained a skill**: Instant Battlefield Root Tunnels]*

That sounded like Trevor, Ivy, and Horns were still alive. That was good.

And then I felt the pain again.

The surging, surging pain.

Why was it still so strong even when the demon king had fallen? Did his corruption take a mind of its own?

I couldn't resist the pain, and it made me lose consciousness...again.

AFTERMATH, LAUSANNE

It was a sudden day. TreeTree started screaming in their heads that something was happening, and they had to be prepared.

"What's going on?" one of the Valthorns asked Lausanne. "Why do we all hear Aeon's voice?"

"Something bad is coming! Let's go, let's go," Lausanne snapped. They'd never had Aeon suddenly warn them in this manner. Not...ever. "To the woods!"

Everyone fled, but it was a mess. The planned underground bunkers were not good places, but not everyone got the message, so some of them still ran for the bunkers. Some wondered whether it was a false alarm, like that time when the demon supercannon attacked.

Some just shrugged it off. "Nothing to worry about. Aeon will take care of it."

For the first time, sadly, Aeon's powers were not enough.

The sky darkened almost instantly as the 'shockwave' of the demon king's corrupting mana flooded the distant skies. The first wave came, and they felt the entirety of the valley shake like never before. Roots started popping out of the floor, and so did cracks.

It was as if the roots were fighting the earth itself, trying to hold the ground together despite the earth trying to break apart.

Then came the flames. The cracks started to spit out weird, blackish things that spawned strange, demon-like creatures.

"Demons!" It was a battle now, but the ground was shaking uncontrollably.

"Where'd they come from?"

Roots started emerging to impale the demons and often swallowed them altogether.

No one was free to answer.

Lausanne activated her special familiar and used the vine whips to quickly move, avoiding the cracking earth below. Luckily, her mom was usually found in the [secret hideout], so she figured her mom was safe.

The ground shook, and they saw the skies turn red and then black. Black flames filled the distant skies, and the trees in the horizon burned.

It wasn't hard to figure out that the demon king did something. But they could only hope to survive it.

Another crack, this time right across New Freeka, and a jet of black flames shot out, burning through multiple houses and people. The fires emitted were unnatural, a mix of black and red. People burned, and Lausanne had never seen so much death in her life.

But she didn't panic. Somehow, somewhere, something drove her to run, using her vines to pull as many as she could out to safety.

Buildings started collapsing; the outer walls fell. Houses burned.

Another crack.

A streak of fire emerged.

They ran for the woods.

Another massive crack appeared in the ground, and black fires emerged from the gap. Roots appeared to try and pull the cracks back together, but the roots too got burned. Still, more roots appeared to take their place.

All she could hear were shouts, screams, and cries for help. She tried. Beetles appeared, and they moved on their own, carrying as many as they could toward the deep forests.

"Lady Lausanne, I'm glad you're safe." Madeus appeared; he levitated in the air using some kind of magic. He created shields, and they worked somewhat to redirect the flames.

"What's Aeon doing?"

"I'm sure it's fighting this demonic energy." Throughout the valley, there were many cracks and also many roots appearing. "We don't have much time. The area closest to Aeon is the safest. We must go quickly." He levitated and also attempted to carry a few others with him, dodging jets of fire that emerged.

"Did you see Uncle Jura?"

"I'm afraid not, but I think he should be fine," Madeus said. "I must go."

Lausanne nodded and sidestepped a fire jet. She created a wood shield to block a black fire. The shield disintegrated almost instantly, but it did block it.

People were running, but the cracks were getting bigger, especially in New Freeka's outer districts. Even the Valtrian Order's headquarters were not spared, as everything just went up in flames. The hotel was partially burning, too.

Few things lasted long against the flames, but Lausanne noticed quite a number of trees that seemed to resist the fire a lot better.

Kraaaaaaaaaaark. Another rift appeared from another direction, and then they noticed it. The valley was starting to sink, and New Freeka was torn apart.

So many fled. A part of the dirt started to move, turning into a kind of sludge that swept through New Freeka. It was as if the land around the valley turned into a mudslide, and the roots appeared, attempting to hold the mudslide back. So the mud moved upward, and the roots followed.

"What..." Lausanne ran. Whatever this was, this wasn't something for them.

It was then she saw it.

Six massive streaks of dark energy appeared, as if pulled by something toward…Aeon. The streaks torched all the trees in their path but left those out of their way untouched.

It broke the illusion that hid Aeon from everyone's view, and they saw it, a massive, towering tree that almost pierced the sky go up in flames. Black fire danced and raged, hopping from branch to branch. Aeon's [Camouflage] had broken.

Those six streaks turned into rivers of dark energy; they seemed to flow toward Aeon's now revealed position, and Aeon's body burned, but it did not crumble.

The cracking…stopped. Aeon had drawn in the energy to itself, and instead, a massive black pyre emerged like a tornado, and it surrounded Aeon's main body, cutting it off from everyone.

"Uh." Lausanne stopped, not sure whether to go toward Aeon or not. The black flame was clearly some kind of demonic energy, and it didn't look safe.

They were now…trapped. The sludge had somehow formed into a cocoon that wrapped the entire valley, held back by massive walls of roots. There was a very small hole at the top that let in some light, but it was right above the pyre because the wall of roots was clearly centered around Aeon.

New Freeka…was gone. Those who managed to flee and somehow got to an area where there was no…dark mana temporarily survived. But things looked bleak. What about food?

Lausanne looked around. She still had her familiar, which meant she could still create fruits and use some plant-growth abilities. Maybe it wouldn't be that bad.

"TreeTree." She tried to mentally call out.

Nothing. She looked around. This…wasn't going to end soon. The sludge was still struggling against the roots, but at least the roots looked like they would hold.

The tremors stopped, and there were no new big rifts, just smaller cracks here and there. The survivors gathered into groups, only about five thousand left from what was a city of almost one hundred thousand. Most of the Valtrian Order and Valthorns died today.

So few, and because of how the circumstances favored those with levels, it was indeed the higher leveled that survived, mostly. Jura, Madeus, Yvon, and herself all made it. Mom, too, who happened to be somewhere near Uncle Jura.

"What now?" The survivors gathered, some of them naturally approaching Lausanne as a contact point.

"I can't reach Aeon." Lausanne looked at the five thousand survivors. It was too sudden, too abrupt. A mud-tsunami and a firestorm later, here they were. What was left. The survivors could walk a bit now; the tremors had mostly stopped.

"[Message] was down," a surviving mage complained. "The tower's been destroyed." The mud-sludge and firestorm took down the heroes' communication tower.

The sky was dark. Everything was dark. Their source of light now was that little hole right on top or the dancing black flames that enveloped Aeon's body. "How do we get out?"

"Should we even get out?"

"Aeon's holding this place together. I doubt outside…will be any better."

Lausanne ran and saw a few others. "MOM!" Lausanne and Laufen hugged.

"Glad you're safe."

"Yeah…"

Jura was next to her. He looked like he was covered in dust and ash. "Well…Aeon's not responding, we're trapped here, and we have some food from our familiars. Not that bad."

"Not that bad. Let's get organized and see whether we can salvage any of the houses! Aeon's hideouts are all inaccessible."

―――

The story continues in Book 3.

THANK YOU FOR READING TREE OF AEONS 2

We hope you enjoyed it as much as we enjoyed bringing it to you. We just wanted to take a moment to encourage you to review the book. Follow this link: **Tree of Aeons 2** to be directed to the book's Amazon product page to leave your review.

Every review helps further the author's reach and, ultimately, helps them continue writing fantastic books for us all to enjoy.

———

Also in series:
Book 1
Book 2
Book 3

———

Want to discuss our books with other readers and even the authors? Join our Discord server today and be a part of the Aethon community.

Facebook | Instagram | Twitter | Website

You can also join our non-spam mailing list by visiting www.subscribepage.com/AethonReadersGroup and never miss out on future releases. You'll also receive three full books completely Free as our thanks to you.

Looking for more great LitRPG?

Conquer all Foes. Reach peak Power. Now, Do it Faster.
Behold the Multiverse! Its countless realms overflow with terrific opportunities and terrible dangers—warring sects, priceless treasures, martial techniques, and all manner of horrible monsters abound. And Dorian has conquered them all. He's a Godking—one of the most powerful creatures to ever exist. And as he sits from his throne at the literal summit of the world, bored out of his mind, one question comes to mind: what now? Do it all again, of course! But faster. **He'll aim for the impossible — A PERFECT RUN. Don't miss the start of this exciting LitRPG Cultivation Adventure about an ancient God who's reached the apex of his power progression and has decided to reincarnate multiple times to try and speedrun the Dao and reach the peak of cultivation.**

Get Speedrunning the Multiverse Now!

Immortality comes with a price... *Faced with a heartrending loss, Lox walks down a dark path. He knew there would be a price for their immortality, but he didn't know he would have to face it so soon. He must make decisions never thought he would face. A darkness is lingering in the world. Maybe what it needs right now isn't a hero to save it, but a monster to hunt the bigger monsters threatening all of existence. So begins a darker sega of Lox's story as his rage guides his path. But will that be enough to hold off the coming darkness? Or will consume him first?* **Don't miss this epic LitRPG/GameLit series that features leveling, advanced magic systems, dungeon crawling, world exploration, and much more. It's perfect for fans of books like Emarilia, World Tree, and Ascend Online.**

Get Immortal Cost Now!

TREE OF AEONS 2

Essence to gather. Cards to Level. A Summoner's Deck to build. *After the collapse of the known world, Rowan Wilder opened his eyes and found himself on the First Floor of the Tower. With a flawless memory and a mere eight Cards to his name, he must venture out and prepare himself for the coming calamity. In this place of blood and fantasy, Rowan has to not only survive but thrive as he powers his way to the top of the Tower. The Demonic Plague that has twisted the creatures on the upper Floors is the least of his worries after he reveals the coveted Origin of the Summoner. Cane in hand and Summons by his side, he'll have to tear his way through Beasts and Humans alike as monsters, criminals, and zealots try to hinder his ascent. Of course, he can maintain a sense of decorum while he faces these trials, yeah?*

Don't miss the first book in the series, A SUMMONER AWAKENS, a Deck Building LitRPG Series utilizing a Card-based Magic System with loads of customization and steady power progression. Perfect for fans of All the Skills and Towers of Heaven, as well as games such as Slay the Spire, Hearthstone, and Gwent.

Get A Summoner Awakens Now!

For all our LitRPG books, visit our website.

Printed in Great Britain
by Amazon